"Christ, he didn't ravish you, did he?"

"Of course not," Elizabeth Ashburton replied quickly. "Don't you think my father taught me how to defend my virtue? I know where a man's vulnerable parts are."

The corners of Mr. Manning's mouth were trembling, and Elizabeth very much feared it was with laughter. "I won't forgive you if you laugh at me right now."

A wicked smile curved his lips but not a sound escaped. "So . . . what sort of hold does he have on you, Elizabeth?"

"I've told you everything of importance," she insisted. "Now, let go of me."

"Or what?" he murmured. "About to breach my vulnerable parts are you?"

"No. Yours are not in the usual place."

"Really? And just where are they?"

Elizabeth looked at the hardened planes of Rowland Manning's lean face. Here stood a human island buffeted by the winds of his ruinous past. And she took a chance.

All at once she oh-so-gently brushed her lips against his firm mouth. "Here," she whispered.

He exhaled roughly with a hiss.

Romances by **Sophia Nash**

SECRETS OF A SCANDALOUS BRIDE
LOVE WITH THE PERFECT SCOUNDREL
THE KISS
A DANGEROUS BEAUTY

Secrets of a Scandalous Bride

Sophia Nash

AVON

An Imprint of HarperCollinsPublishers

This is a work of fiction. Names, characters, places, and incidents are products of the author's imagination or are used fictitiously and are not to be construed as real. Any resemblance to actual events, locales, organizations, or persons, living or dead, is entirely coincidental.

AVON BOOKS
An Imprint of HarperCollins*Publishers*
10 East 53rd Street
New York, New York 10022-5299

Copyright © 2010 by Sophia Nash
ISBN 978-0-06-149330-0
www.avonromance.com

First Avon Books paperback printing: March 2010

Avon Trademark Reg. U.S. Pat. Off. and in Other Countries, Marca Registrada, Hecho en U.S.A.
HarperCollins® is a registered trademark of HarperCollins Publishers.

Printed in the U.S.A.

10 9 8 7 6 5 4 3 2 1

To

Lyssa Keusch

I will always be grateful to you for leading me

through the publication process with such skill

and tact, and for shepherding each book with

such care.

Acknowledgments

Thank you to Helen Breitwieser for not only being an extraordinary literary agent, but for also being an extraordinary person.

I am especially grateful to all the people at Avon for their support: Lyssa Keusch, Liate Stehlik, Carrie Feron, Pam Spengler-Jaffee, Wendy Lee, Wendy Ho, Tom Egner, Mike Spradlin, and so many more. And to industry professionals who have always been so encouraging: Susan Grimshaw, John Charles, Shelley Mosely, Michelle Buonfiglio, and to all the librarians and booksellers.

And thank you to my husband for showing me what a lifetime of love is all about, and for being the only man who can still make me laugh until I cry. And much gratitude to my mother for nurturing an early love of storytelling, and to the two imps who call me Mommy, yes, you're the reason for everything.

Endless thanks to my circle of girlfriends—Jean, Fairleigh, Anne, Amy, Lisa, Susan, Laurie, Jeanne, Kathy, Judi, Annie, Karen, Maria, Cybil, Louise,

Christina, Carla, Mary Noble and Sally for providing the fellowship and the laughter that sustained me through the creation of this series.

And finally, to Robbie Gordon, a young boy who touches my heart with his joyous, boundless goodness.

Secrets of a Scandalous Bride

The Widows Club

Rosamunde Langdon
m. 1
Alfred Hubert Baird
m. 2
Luc St. Aubyn
*The 8th Duke
of Helston*

A Dangerous Beauty
BOOK 1

Henry   Caroline

Grace Roijen Atholl
m. 1
John Sheffey
The Earl of Sheffield
m. 2
Michael Ranier de Peyster
The Earl of Wallace

*Love With the Perfect
Scoundrel*
BOOK 3

Lara   James

Georgiana Wilde
m. 1
Anthony Fortesque
*The 12th Marquis of
Ellesmere*
m. 2
Quinn Fortesque
*The 13th Marquis of
Ellesmere*
m. 1
Cynthia Crowley

The Kiss
BOOK 2

Fairleigh   ?

Elizabeth Ashburton
m. 1
?

*Secrets of a
Scandalous Bride*
BOOK 4

featuring
Mr. Rowland Manning

Merceditas "Ata"
Candamos
m. 1
Lucifer St. Aubyn
*The 6th Duke of
Helston* (d)

featuring
Mr. John Brown

Victoria Givan
m.
John Varick
The Duke of Beaufort

Novella:

*"Catch of the Century"
in

Four Dukes and a
Devil*

Sarah Lyman
m. 1
Lt. Col.
Pierce Winters

Prologue

In every great life there is invariably a tipping point. A few half moments in time during which a crucial decision hangs in the balance. Many retreat, an excellent excuse on their lips, and a complete disregard for the tarnish to their dignity. But sometimes, indeed only rarely, a man pries loose extraordinary courage and chooses the door so little employed that it creaks open with effort. Invariably it changes forevermore the set pattern of any number of lives, including his own.

Ofttimes it leads to naught but unqualified disaster, for destiny is, undeniably, a fickle friend.

But, then again, in some instances, capricious fate swoops down through the whispering trees, laughs at the impossible, and blows the candles of ill fortune in the opposing, yet proper direction. Some call it haphazard chance. At the end of the long, hot summer of 1814, Rowland Manning—a heretofore unchivalrous blackguard of the first order—called it a *bloody gawddamned devil of a miracle* . . . which more than made up for all that had gone before in his godforsaken miserable life.

My dove,

Where are you? I search for you ceaselessly and yet . . . I cannot discover where you've hidden yourself. Fear not, my love, I shall never give up. Memories of you sustain me in my darkest hours. And when I find you—when this note finds you—we shall never be parted forevermore.

P.

Chapter 1

Beribboned ladies and bespectacled lords were squashed tooth and jowl in St. George's, all strained in readiness for the much-anticipated wedding of one of their own. The beautiful bride entered on pearl-encrusted slippers, a tall stranger beside her.

Chests puffed in outrage. Fans fell from fingers. The archbishop raised a brow. *The audacity.* The unmitigated gall.

How dared Rowland Manning, the most ruthless, enigmatic man in all of England, tread these holy pavers of righteousness? Why, he was the heartless bastard from whom gentlemen shielded their daughters, warned their sons, and prayed their wives never met. Yet here, flaunting before the best and brightest jewels of English aristocracy, the big bad wolf escorted an innocent lamb—with the merest glint of large white teeth showing.

There was but one person not focused on the audacious spectacle. She was far too busy praying.

Numb and exposed in front of the paneled high pew boxes trimmed with every last white flower to be had in London, Elizabeth Ashburton begged for deliverance.

Her feet answered.

"And just where do you think you're going?" The shrewd, wizened visage of the kindhearted Dowager Duchess of Helston peered over the top of a bouquet far too large for her petite form.

"To, um, see to Grace's cloak in the vestry, Ata. I think I forgot to hang it." Elizabeth held the dowager's suspicious gaze like the seasoned campaigner in the art of lying that she was.

"Hmmm. How very thoughtful," Ata murmured, "if not doubtful. Oh botheration, Elizabeth. You've overseen the preparation of the breakfast, and helped with the flowers. You've done enough."

Elizabeth's best friend, Sarah Winters, who stood on the other side of the dowager, sent her a speaking glance, as Ata continued. "Honestly, Eliza, I don't know what's become of the sociable lady I knew in Cornwall." A pert smile erased the wrinkles and doubt lurking in her alert, dark eyes. "Oh, do look at Grace. Have you ever seen a happier, more eager bride?"

The tightness in Elizabeth's chest made it hard to breathe. The swell of trumpet and organ signaled the official beginning of the wedding. No one would miss one stray bridesmaid. She shifted one blue satin toe closer toward the—

"Take my arm, Elizabeth," Ata murmured, a step ahead of her in thought and action. "I need your support. Oh, and Sarah . . . you too, my dear."

Elizabeth's heart redoubled its beat. She opened her mouth but Ata continued, "That Mr. Manning cut it far too close, don't you think? Highly irregular even for a devil of his ilk to arrive three minutes before the ceremony." Ata raised her chin, showing all four feet eleven inches of *hauteur* to advantage.

Elizabeth Ashburton gripped a tiny bouquet of violets as Grace and her unlikely escort walked ever closer. The attention of hundreds of the most influential and most notorious gossipmongers of the peerage drifted toward all of them at the front. They were the sort who would recount for generations the exact number of Belgium-lace flounces on the bride's gown, as well as the number of dukes, marquises, earls, viscounts, barons, and lesser titles who grumbled and forwent a far more entertaining morning at White's Club to offer escort to their wives, mothers, and sisters. Elizabeth was of a mind with the gentlemen. Indeed, she would have rather faced the Light Division's flogging post than risk this sort of exposure. A gentleman's voice filled her mind unbidden . . .

We were predestined, my angel. Surely you cannot doubt it. You were meant for me, and I shall take care of you—protect you, in return. You will soon forget your sadness.

She shivered. The memory always arrived paired with the vivid recollection of his hand resting on her bare arm. His white glove had been pristine save for one tiny drop of blood near his thumb.

She forced the picture from her mind. She wanted so badly to be free of the past. She had been lulled into thinking it was a possibility during the last eighteen carefree months with Ata and the rest of the ladies in the dowager's circle of friends.

Elizabeth pushed back her shoulders, glanced at Sarah on the other side of the petite dowager duchess, and resigned herself to fate. She *would* enjoy this. Danger be damned.

Elizabeth's breath caught at the site of the groom's handsome face, which held such private love and poignant happiness that it was almost too painfully intimate to observe as Grace walked the last few steps to stand before the archbishop. Never had London witnessed such a glorious love match, and even the peerage, as fashionably jaded as they tried mightily to appear, could not muster a single snipe for the perfection they embodied.

Elizabeth's eyes moved to the man who stood between Grace and the Earl of Wallace. His was a bemused, cynical face, devoid of all sensibilities. Indeed, upon close scrutiny it was bankrupt of any sort of integrity at all. The hardened planes of Rowland Manning's face were framed by thick black hair shot through with several silver streaks. She had the odd thought that his eyes should be blacker than the dead of night instead of the luminous pale green she spied.

Elizabeth knew why the earl had allowed the infamous man to walk Grace past the six stately Corinthian columns, down the center of St. George's. He was his half brother after all.

The *bastard* son of the former Earl of Wallace.

Elizabeth shivered at the thought of the two men, one so good, the other quite the opposite, and both so startlingly tall. But only one was capable of laughing and spitting in the eye of God one moment and the devil the next.

Why, Mr. Manning had had the audacity to attempt to take Grace's fortune in exchange for his half brother's life only a few months ago. And studying him now, he appeared as if he hadn't lost a wink of sleep over the entire botched, hushed-up affair.

Elizabeth never fully understood why Grace and Michael forgave the terrible man, but forgive him they did. Love had a way of leading to forgiveness, she supposed. It was simply ironic that it was so obvious that love did not flow in the opposite direction.

As Elizabeth watched Grace float the last few feet to the front, tears pricked the backs of her eyes. Dressed in the blush of pink lamé netting over silver tissue, she appeared like the veriest angel from paradise. Orange blossoms and sparkling brilliants threaded her artfully arranged fair hair. Her signature pearls graced her décolleté. But in her gloved hands, the countess carried the oddest thing . . . a horseshoe studded with tiny rosebuds. Michael Ranier de Peyster, the newest Earl of Wallace, broke into a wide grin and reached for his bride's hand.

"You can't have her," Rowland Manning murmured with a growl of a voice that sounded as if he ate gravel for breakfast and washed it down with sawdust. His eyes half closed in dark bemusement. "Patience, little brother. The bloke with the silver hat will let you know when it's your turn."

A choke of laughter escaped Ata before she regained her composure. "Oh, I do wish Mr. Brown was here." The tiny wizened dowager duchess stood on her tiptoes, and her gnarled hand nudged Eliza. "I still cannot imagine why he insists on brooding in Scotland."

Elizabeth looked into the elderly lady's sad expression, and whispered, "Have faith. Surely he'll come for Victoria and the duke's wedding."

"No." The dowager's dark eyes brewed with melancholy. "I fear he has, indeed, given up, just when—"

The rector interrupted Ata by clearing his throat and commencing the solemnization. "Dearly beloved, we are gathered together here in the sight of . . ."

His sonorous voice faded from her consciousness as Elizabeth darted another glance past the heavy canopy over the pulpit toward the eagle-eyed, starched, and boxed crowd. Perhaps she would be lucky after all. Really, there was no reason to think *he* would put in an appearance.

Surely, a celebrated hero had more important things to do than attending a ton wedding. Her only confidant must have read her thoughts, for Sarah reached behind the dowager and gave her hand an encouraging squeeze.

The archbishop droned on, ". . . marriage was ordained for a remedy against sin, and to avoid fornication; that such persons as have not the gift of continency might marry, and keep themselves *undefiled* members of . . ."

Elizabeth's glance caught on the *defiling* eyes of Rowland Manning as he perused her form. It was obvious he had never sought a remedy against sin and most likely latched on to *every* chance at fornication. When he raised his eyes to her own, the barest hint of a curl at the edge of his mouth betrayed his amusement at her censure.

"Wilt thou love her, honor, and keep her in sickness and in health; and forsaking all others, keep thee only unto her, so long as ye both shall live?" The archbishop, dressed in formal vestments, gazed expectantly at the Earl of Wallace, whose attention was fully absorbed by his beloved.

After a beat the black-hearted brother ground out, "Well, any bloody fool can see he's mutton-headed over the chit."

The earl grinned and finally recited his vows.

Ata murmured for Elizabeth's ears only, "He looks like Judas in that painting, don't you think?" She nodded toward the reredos of the Last Supper. The notorious black-haired betrayer crept along the edge. "One has to wonder. It's always the ones like that . . . Well, I would wager Mr. Manning's kisses bring most ladies to their knees."

"Ata!" The tiny dowager's outrageous comments never failed to shock.

"Pish, I'm certain of it. Why, if he weren't so appallingly corrupt and unsuitable . . ." The all-too-familiar appraising gaze of Ata focused on Elizabeth.

The awful naked sensation of being an object under scrutiny made Elizabeth restlessly scan the pews once more until her eyes came to rest across from her. Oh, for goodness sakes. The pale green eyes of Rowland Manning were inspecting her *again*. Perhaps he'd overheard Ata. His darkly bronzed face was in stark relief against the whiteness of his teeth, now revealed in a mocking smile.

She stiffened. The man appeared to be undressing her in the corners of his wicked mind while standing in the house of the Lord.

And then he laughed softly.

A wave of movement caught Elizabeth's attention,

and she half turned, only to see the very person she and Sarah had managed to evade for the last two years entering the church. A retinue of six scarlet-coated officers flanked him as he stopped at the entrance to the sanctuary. Now the attention of the crowd was caught between the two spectacles—one in the front of the church, and one in the rear.

She darted a glance at Sarah and they both hunched forward to hide their faces. Elizabeth would never forgive herself for her past misjudgments, which had led to their present circumstances.

Ata whispered, "Such an honor. Who would have thought he would actually come . . ."

The last few words of the ceremony were lost on Eliza as she tamped down the urge to run. Only her long years spent following the drum saved her. She would not forget the lessons taught to her by the man she had loved more than anyone else on earth.

The smallest muffled sniff of happiness escaped the dowager duchess as the Earl of Wallace clasped Grace, now a countess twice over, in a scandalously improper kiss as the crowd swelled with a combination of outrage from the older matrons and delighted amusement by the rest.

Flashes of red snagged Elizabeth's attention, and then she knew. He'd spotted her and was now sending his dogs to circle. Her heart pounding, cool reason fled. She dared to look directly at him in the rear of the sanctuary. His blond hair gleamed like a halo beneath one of the silver candelabra while a look of assurance decorated a face Eliza had learned to dread.

Arm in arm, Grace and Michael retreated down

the center aisle, Ata and the rest of the couple's friends following close behind. At that moment, Eliza clutched Sarah's hand. "We'll have a better chance if you go to the back, and I go out the side."

"Eliza, no. You should take the safer—"

"Absolutely not, Sarah. Now go . . ."

She had already darted behind the double-decked reading desk, and skirted the half wall of Corinthian columns in front of the altar to find the panel door feeding into the rector's passage on the side. Now running as if the hounds of hell nipped her heels, Elizabeth negotiated the complicated maze before she found the exit, which fed into Mill Street, at the rear of the church. Ripping the wreath of flowers from her hair, she quickly debated her options in the brilliant May sunshine.

Suddenly spying an enormous, wilting funereal arrangement outside the door, she dropped the violets and grabbed it. Holding it in front of her, she forced herself to slow to a normal pace as she rounded the corner to Mill Street. Through the flower stalks, she saw a scarlet coat and her knees nearly buckled. Sarah was nowhere in sight.

Without a second thought, she grasped the door handle of the nearest carriage, shoved the flowers into the hands of the startled coachman standing nearby, and leapt inside. Before tugging the door closed, she begged the older man, "Just a few minutes, please. A guinea if you say not a word."

The scrawny man smiled, winked above the flowers and bobbed his accord while he began whistling a tune as if nothing had occurred. Eliza released the curtains to fall fully across the windows, and backed into the near crook of the carriage, her ear to the wall. The deep clang from the bell tower pealed the joyful news of another happily ever after.

A cornered mouse . . . yes, that was how she felt. She released the tension in her chest, only to take in the masculine bouquet of scents swirling inside the elegant carriage—glycerin leather soap, tobacco, and that indefinable element of excessive *richesse*. A crystal decanter half filled with amber spirits stood in a casing in the polished rosewood interior.

And then suddenly . . .

Lord, she could hear the driver telling someone, "Ain't seen nobody loikes that, Cap'n."

Blood pumping fast and furiously in her ears blocked out the low, insistent words from the soldier.

"No, that be me master's lady bird . . . No mate, you doesn't go in wivout 'is leave and 'e be—"

A deeper new voice interrupted, "Lefroy, what's the bloody problem? Don't say your past has finally caught up with you. Well, we've no time for this, man." Oh, it was that blackguard Manning's voice, she was certain. "And what in hell are you doing with that moldy thing? Taken to selling posies on the side, have you?"

Now it was the officer's voice, rising in intensity, "Sir, this has nothing to do with your driver. We're searching for—"

"Don't care. Don't want to know."

"But I'm certain I saw a woman entering this—"

"Lefroy, I'll dock your pay if you don't get us out of this bog of humanity in time. Auction's in twenty bloody minutes."

When Elizabeth heard the loud creak of the door handle, she knew her goose was cooked. People said it had to rain on wedding days for good luck. Today, there was nary a cloud in the vast, pale blue sky. And of course she had had the bad fortune to enter the carriage of the last man on earth willing to help her.

She sucked in her breath as the light from the sunny day filled the doorway for the briefest moment before it was blocked by the broad shoulders of the powerful man. He was uttering a foul obscenity over his shoulder as he lunged inside, and so he did not see her.

With irritation, Rowland Manning flipped aside the charcoal-gray tails of his coat within the dark confines of his carriage and turned to plunk his frame down onto the seat. He landed on something far too soft and he sprang up like a scalded dog. "What the devil?"

"I'm so sorry, Mr. Manning. Um . . . I require your assistance." She exhaled. "*Please*."

Ah . . . the juicy widowed morsel from the church— the one with the bountiful hair and the magnificent glittering emerald eyes. He narrowed his gaze. "Really? And what's in it for me?"

She was doing a fairly good job of hiding her panic. Only her uneven breathing gave her away. "Everything I have if you will not betray me to those soldiers."

"Everything? Hmmm, my favorite word."

Someone knocked insistently on the carriage door. "Yes, yes. *Anything*."

"All right. But one word and I'll throw you to the wolves myself," he muttered. In a smattering of moments he wrapped her damned lace fichu around his neck, transferred his hat to *her* head, and flipped up her skirts, ignoring her shocked intake of breath. He abruptly hooked an arm under one of her knees and fit himself snugly between her slender thighs. Surprisingly, she had the good sense to keep her lips from flapping and hid her face against his neck cloth. At the last second, he lowered his breeches, and reached for his crop between the roof's hat straps.

The carriage door wrenched open, and the sound of gruff coughing mixed with coarse guffaws soon echoed behind him. Rowland worked the trunk of his body against hers in a slow, provocative manner, not allowing her to retreat an inch as he tickled her calf with his crop.

He turned his head slightly and addressed the onlookers, "Gawk if you like, you buggers. *Lizzie* likes it, don't you, dearie? But there's a price. Lefroy? Make 'em pay up or be gone." He reached over and yanked the door closed.

He looked down into her wild eyes, which held the same mesmerizing sparkle as a sunset's rays as they bounced off the River Thames. She made a few inarticulate noises, pushed against his chest and budged him not.

"Oh no. We've gone this far, madam. I'll not face the magistrate now. Wrap your legs around me, you fool. If there's a second act, you could put more effort into it. A few moans wouldn't hurt," he growled into her pretty ear.

She was glorious with that dazzling beck of honey-colored hair flowing from beneath his brushed beaver hat, her vibrant eyes spearing him with defiance.

"Give me *that*." She took a swipe at the plaited leather whip he tickled her with, but missed as he raised it above his head.

There was but the thinnest bit of feminine linen separating him from intimate knowledge of her, and he had to give her credit for displaying such pluck in the face of such offenses.

But then, he didn't know her, did he? Oh, he knew she was one of those widowed harpies trying to claw her way up the slippery slopes of society by way of the Helston clan's coattails. But now it appeared her ladyship had a few sinful secrets tucked away in her blue silk and satin skirts. Didn't they all?

She was, indeed, every bit as much an actor in this farcical quagmire of humanity plaguing the earth as he.

Christ, she was so damn soft beneath him, and she smelled so good. His groin pulsed despite the cacophony of voices outside the door, and he cursed foully.

"Lefroy," he barked over his shoulder toward the closed door. "If there be no takers, haul up the wheel shoe and get your bony *arse* on the driving board." Furious that he had lost his usual iron grip on his body, he grabbed the edge of the seat and prepared to recommence the show if necessary.

With a shout, the conveyance jolted forward, and the sounds of the traces jangled.

He jerked away as if her flesh burned him, and whipped her skirts back into place before swinging into the opposite seat. "You're lucky I prefer beds for ravaging," he lied.

She smoothed imaginary wrinkles from her elegant gown as a blush crested her cheeks.

"I don't know what you did, madam, but whatever it was, I wouldn't wager those blades will stop looking for you. There's a gaggle of Wellington's finest out there with enough gold braid to excite a small village's worth of skirts."

She returned his hat without a word and tried to rearrange her hair without success. "May I have my fichu back?"

He tossed it to her and palmed his finely tooled crop. Crossing the space between them, he tickled her tightly clenched jaw with the end loop. "What, no tears? No explanations? Good. Now give me your nibs and nabs."

"Nibs and nabs?" she finally spoke, expelling her breath in a rush.

"You know, those nasty sharp bits or anything else you might foolishly try to use to *thank me*."

"Mr. Manning, I know you'll be surprised to learn that I don't have any *nibs* or *nabs* on my person," she said with all the primness of a schoolmistress. Not that he had spent a moment in school. But he could imagine.

"No? Perhaps a search is in order then," he said, trying to raise the edge of her gown's hem with his crop.

She swatted it away and looked at him sourly. "Look, I thank you for your quick thinking—your *performance*. Really, I had no idea . . . And to reassure you, I've every intention of properly repaying you." She brushed the corner of the curtain and glimpsed outside again. Oh, they were nearing Lamb's Conduit Fields, where she knew someone who might very well come to her aid. "Would you be so kind as to deposit me at the gates of the foundling home?"

"No," he said, without hesitation.

She jerked her attention back to him. "No? Whatever do you mean?"

He ignored her lip-flapping.

"Surely you trust a lady to repay her debts, sir."

He gave her a lazy half smile. "You're good. You've got that righteous air down pat. And you've fooled those toffs well enough. Helston is doubtlessly duped, as are Ellesmere, Wallace, and all their brides."

"You're absolutely right, sir."

He watched her pleat her hands tightly.

"Hmmm. Well, while I consider the terms of payment for saving your hide, madam, we're for my stable yard. Nobs plump with coin won't wait. We can't have them trotting their fickle hides over to that damned uppity fellow Tattersall's sticks, now can we? The pleasure of attending to you will just have to wait."

Before she could respond, the carriage jerked to a halt, and Rowland leapt out without waiting for the step to be swung into place.

He breathed in the air, which was filled with the sweet, raw fragrance of fresh pine and cut stone, the scent of new construction—*and debt*. It was as far removed from the aromas of his past as it could be.

Three classical structures of pale limestone fronted a sprawling, vast series of smaller buildings and enclosures. Stable hands, dressed in the dark blue and yellow colors of the stables, performed their jobs with workmanlike precision, feeding, watering, washing, working the animals with well-honed precision. But above all, it was the beauty of the animals that stood out. They were the only things that mattered.

"You cannot hold me against my will," the lovely little fraud insisted, moving to his side.

Her words drew him back to the moment. "No?"

"No! Now look, I insist your driver take me to—"

"Lefroy, Mrs. . . ." he looked at her expectantly.

"Ashburton," she answered, exasperated.

"Mrs. Ashburton has a fondness for storerooms," he said with heavy sarcasm. "Show her ours."

"But, Mr. Manning. I must be allowed to send a note to the dowager duchess, and to—"

He turned toward the main massive yard now filling with gleaming silk and beaver hats and equally gleaming horseflesh. "You're boring me, Mrs. Ashburton." He waved his hand languorously in the air.

A hint of a breeze in the warm air carried her next words back to him.

"The feeling is entirely mutual, sir."

He didn't pause, yet he couldn't stop the smallest bit of amusement from tickling his lips. Oh, she would prove an excellent test to his finely honed discipline. It had been a while since he'd jousted with an aristocratic female with morals to let. And he needed the practice, if this damned unflagging peg leg bobbing between his hips was any indication, for *gawdsakes*.

Yes, he had a score to settle with the Upper Ten Thousand. And he was doing it through the deep pockets of the lords who flocked to him for superior mounts, and their fickle wives who came to him for an entirely different sort of ride. The past few years, he had accommodated the latter only out of necessity and only when the blackest of moods was upon him.

This pampered lady was ripe for the plucking. She was everything his small ragtag family had not been—well fed, elegantly dressed, and clearly an inveterate charlatan. The only question was how much blunt he could extract from her and in what fashion.

Yes, the lovely Mrs. Ashburton would rue the day she chose to throw her lot in with him instead of going quietly to face her transgressions. Yet those damned eyes of hers flummoxed him with their false innocence. By God, he would wipe that expression clean by the time he was done with her. She knew nothing of his game.

They never did.

Chapter 2

The storeroom was hot and filled with the most unpleasant scent of decaying cabbage mingled with unplucked fowl. But nothing could induce Elizabeth to descend again into the cooler cellar as the sound of scurrying confirmed even worse accommodations.

Although . . . she did not doubt she would jump into the awful, dank darkness at the first echo of Pymm's officers. Dear Lord. She prayed no one had followed Manning's carriage.

In an effort to stem the cascading thoughts of the morning's events, Elizabeth continued reorganizing the goods lining the rows of cluttered shelves. The pickled vegetables were improperly potted, the spoilage evident. *Ugh.* Why, half of the food here would have to be carted away.

She wondered if and when Mr. Manning would allow *her* to be carted away from this awful place. She leaned her head against a shelf. *God.* She'd never been so mortified in all her life.

His raw actions were forever imprinted in her memory—his large hand gripping her knee wide while his hips flexed against hers. And each time she pressed her nose into the folds of her fichu to escape the dreadful smells of the storeroom, his lingering masculine scent brought her right back to the scene in the carriage. His was the aroma of fresh-cut hay and bayberry shaving soap, along with starch and the indescribable scent of his skin. She shivered in remembrance of his vulgar words and actions.

Oh, she should have been terrified, but for some absurd reason, she had not been. She had not been afraid of him for a moment. It was ridiculous. She had thrown herself on the nonexistent mercy of a famous black-hearted, fire-breathing tyrant. But then again, wasn't that precisely what she had needed against Pymm's well-organized detail of officers?

After a slight rustling sound, the storeroom door swung open, and Eliza gratefully breathed in a great lungful of fresh air. "Oh, Mr. Lefroy, thank goodness you've returned. Mr. Manning has no authority to hold me." She stepped over the threshold. "I shall just be on my way, now, and here is the guinea I owe you, sir." She held out the promised coin.

Flustered, the thin man dipped his head. "I'm sorry, lovey, but the master says you're to stay. 'e wants you to 'elp Cook. Said it were part o' the bargain. The two under cooks left wivout notice yester eve."

Elizabeth gazed past Mr. Lefroy's shoulder, only to finally notice a large matron, wearing a filthy apron, studying her with a bleary eye. "But this is impossible. I must go. I'm certain Mr. Manning doesn't want to incur the displeasure of my friends."

Mr. Lefroy scratched his grisly, thick side-whiskers, which hung low on his cheeks and were shaped like iron clubs. "Don't rightly think the master cares if 'e earns anyone's ire, ma'am. And I beg you not to leave for 'e'll strip a large part of me old 'ide off if'n you up and disappear like. You wouldn't do that to your old friend Lefroy now, would you?" He didn't wait for her answer. "Besides, I'm to lock you bowf in the kitchen."

"Well," Elizabeth huffed.

He leaned in with a whisper, "Have a care, Cook is meaner than a badger wiv a 'ound on 'er shoulder."

"But I must be allowed to get word to my friend Sarah Winters at Helston House at the very least."

Mr. Lefroy studied her for a moment.

"Of course, I would pay you for your trouble." She held up her last coin.

He scratched his neck, doubt in his old eyes. "I suppose it be only fair. But keep your coin." It appeared the man had a measure of pride to maintain.

As he left, Elizabeth reached her hand to stop him. "Oh, and Mr. Lefroy?"

"Aye?"

"Make certain no one sees you deliver the message to Mrs. Winters, will you?"

He held out his hand. "Now *that'll* cost you, lovey."

An hour later, surrounded by a mountain of half-rotted potatoes, Elizabeth toiled at the task of peeling, under the thunderous gaze of Mrs. Vernon, who hadn't taken kindly to Elizabeth's efforts in the storeroom or elsewhere.

The cook had taken particular exception to her insistence in mopping the filthy tiles of the floor. The last time Elizabeth had seen such dirt, and such fare, was during the long march through Spain during the rainy season. And even then there had been—

Mrs. Vernon's shriek pierced Elizabeth's thoughts and the dull paring knife slipped through her fingers. The cook's bulky form lay sprawled before her.

"Now look wot you've done, you silly girl," Mrs. Vernon spat out in her virulent strain of cockney. "I told you it would be only good for slippin'. Me back is loike broke. Well, you'll be sorry, is wot you'll be. 'Tis you wot will cook for those sorry coves today."

Elizabeth wondered for the hundredth time how the day had fallen into such shambles in such short order. This morning she had risen from a mound of warm, sweet-smelling bedclothes to breakfast with all her friends in the stately rooms of Helston House in the heart of Mayfair, and now a mere five hours later, she was reduced to being a target for a mean spirited cook's barbs. "I'd be delighted to prepare dinner, Mrs. Vernon. How many will be at table?"

The burly cook smiled, revealing teeth going in an astonishing number of alternating directions. "Slops for thirty-eight. And o' course Mr. Manning's fare."

"*Thirty-eight*? What time is dinner served then?"

The cook chortled. "You've got plenty of time, dearie. Two hours."

"Of course." Elizabeth gazed at the woman on the floor and couldn't decide if she pitied or loathed her more. No one with this sort of irritable temperament could be happy. "Perhaps," she suggested softly, "you would like for me to make you a drop of tea?" With just a few more hints of solicitude, Elizabeth stemmed the vile froth of words spewing from the cook.

It cleared away a good third of the remaining edible items in the vast storeroom to produce an acceptable meal.

"Yer makin' too much, I say. You shouldn't have used the molasses. That be for fattening the horses, not the men," the woman whined from the corner. "The master will take it out o' me wages."

"I'm so sorry, Mrs. Vernon. You can blame me." Really, what would a few more damning words to her character mean at this point?

Elizabeth cut the hot gingerbread into steaming, fragrant squares and whipped the cream. It had been the only truly fresh item in the pantry, aside from some very tough beef she had ground into submission.

The fare was simple, yet seasoned and prepared to perfection. Four enormous meat and onion pies rested beside mounds of mashed potatoes topped with a hint of melting cheese. A mountain of grated carrots dressed with oil, vinegar and a hint of mustard and lemon lay nearby. It would have to do.

The older lady moaned in frustration. "He won't like it."

Eliza hoped he would, for there wasn't enough time to prepare something different for him. She didn't want to face the blackguard without putting him in a more amiable mood. Tempting Manning with food was the only option she could think of at the moment. Besides, her pride forbade her to prepare anything but the very best she could muster. And she had learned from her father and the men under his command that there was nothing that could soften a man's disposition more than a good meal. Especially on a battlefield. And if Mr. Manning was not a battlefield in the flesh, then Elizabeth would eat her lace fichu.

Oh, this entire situation had gotten out of hand. She should be planning her escape. She prayed Sarah had evaded Pymm's men as well. Elizabeth had to leave before the soldiers thought to search this place. How much time would pass before someone would think to follow the lead that captain would be sure to offer?

The sharp clang of a bell echoed in the distance. "That be the end of the auction," Mrs. Vernon muttered, refusing to lift a finger. "Best be ready. Footmen will come to haul it all to the men's dining hall."

"And Mr. Manning?"

"Takes 'is supper on a tray. But 'e doesn't fancy eatin' wot the others eat."

"Really?"

The cook enjoyed having all the answers and appeared pleased to quite obviously withhold a few. " 'e dines in his working quarters."

The footmen, eyes round with wonder, disappeared with the vast quantities of food for the stable workers. Elizabeth arranged a tray for Mr. Manning, abundant with the foods she had prepared with such care. The man had to have an enormous appetite given his great height.

A footman reappeared. "Mr. Manning will see you now, ma'am. Let me help you with that. It smells delicious. Thank you for preparing such fare for—" The brawny young man, who appeared to be the sole employee proficient in the King's English, stopped after a glance at the cook got the better of him. He escorted Elizabeth to Mr. Manning.

On the other side of two tall ornate doors, Elizabeth found herself in a stately long room. Bronze figurines of dozens of racehorses graced the tables and shelves separating her from the man sitting in the distance. A long series of equine paintings decorated the dark paneled walls. Rowland Manning was ensconced at the end of the room at a desk devoid of any sort of ornamentation. That one plain bit of furniture appeared out of place given the gilded pieces in every corner.

When Elizabeth approached, Mr. Manning didn't bother to raise his head from a neat pile of paperwork. "Set it here," he said, indicating the side of the desk. "Wait over there." He waved a dictatorial hand toward a bow window and then continued to address his attention to his work.

She did as he bade without a word. After settling herself, she allowed her gaze to wander back to him. He had removed his coat and rolled up the shirt linen of his sleeves. His darkly bronzed and muscled forearms spoke of long hours of physically demanding labor in the sun. They were not covered with the profusion of hair like those of the men she had known in the military. Instead, they were corded with veins and sinew. His hands moved to spread wide over a ledger; his fingers, long and strong—suddenly gripped the ends. She shivered. He would be capable of snapping someone's neck. These were the same hands that had held her firmly in place beneath him in the carriage. The same hands that he would want to use to extract payment for his efforts to hide her. She wrenched her gaze away.

The vast expanse of Manning's yards beckoned to her beyond the three windows. It should be so easy to slip away. A mere fraction of an inch of glass separated her from freedom.

Out of the corner of her eye, she saw him turn a

page. But the same thoughts that plagued her in the storeroom dogged her now. Where would she go? She had no more coin, and she didn't dare return to Helston House. Surely there would be a watch there. Well, she would just have to hope Lefroy was an honest man and would get her note to Sarah.

What on earth was that smell? Rowland switched his attention from the ledger back to the purchase documents in front of him. Without thought, he unwound the fork from the plain napkin and paused to continue reading. *Damn*, Lord Vesington had gotten that filly off of Edelweiss for a song. He shook his head. He had spent far too many hours training this particular horse, who showed so much promise.

A pox on Wellington for his bloody ill-timed moment to end the war. Rowland would be a dead man if the cavalry did not live up to the terms of the contract now that the damned frogs' emperor was penned on Elba. He stabbed blindly in the direction of the plate of food on the side of the desk. How in hell was he to meet the staggering construction costs at this rate?

With a blaze of potency, something hideously delicious registered on his tongue, and a flood of hunger was loosed. He immediately tossed the fork aside with a clatter. "What the devil is this?" He looked toward the beautiful fraud at the bow window.

Wide, startled eyes met his own. "Pardon me? Are you addressing me?"

"And just who in hell else would I be speaking to?" He picked up the small dish containing a dark brown breadlike square with white froth on top. Crossing the expanse of floorboards separating them, he slipped the dish in front of her. "I said, what the devil is this?"

"Why, gingerbread, Mr. Manning. Don't you like it? Most gentlemen do. But you should save it for last."

He hardened his face into a cold smile. "Well, that explains it."

"Explains what?"

"Why I have a disgust of it."

She stiffened before his eyes. "I'm sorry?"

"I think we both know I'm no gentleman, Mrs. Ashburton." He placed the dish on the low table in front of her knees and walked back to his desk. "Return it to Mrs. Vernon when you go. And tell the cook I will sack her if she dares to make anything remotely like this again."

He sat down and resolutely picked up a bill of sale in one hand and his fork in the other. He was annoyed he could sense her eyes on him as he took another unseen bite from the tray. *Oh God . . .* he carefully returned the fork to the tray and pushed the entire affair aside.

"You don't care for the meat pie either, Mr. Manning?"

"No."

"I suppose I should admit that Mrs. Vernon cannot be blamed. If I'd had a bit more time, perhaps I could have prepared something more to your liking. I realize I'm in your debt and I was hoping to thank you properly with this simple meal."

Rowland gave up any hope of finishing his accounts and pushed back slightly to balance on the back legs of his chair. "I should have guessed. And where in hell is Mrs. Vernon?"

"She slipped and hurt her spine."

"Is that so?" He looked at her skeptically. "And just how did that happen?"

"In the kitchen an hour or so ago."

He waited.

"On the floor I had just mopped."

He dropped back to all four legs of his chair. "Mrs. Ashburton?"

"Yes?"

"Stop meddling. You'll not pay off your debt to me in that fashion." He looked at her with vexation. "Although, if you'd like to add to it, you're doing a fine job." It irked him no end that one female could cause such havoc in such a short frame of time.

"Mr. Manning?"

"Yes?"

"Did you not request that I help Cook with dinner?"

"I asked for you to *help*, not *hinder*, the cook," he said dryly.

She appeared as if she was attempting to check her ire. "Do you think we might discuss this in a rational manner? I've had a bit of time to think about all of this and—"

"Go ahead, madam. I'm all ears. Just how do you propose to repay me for baring my *arse and ballocks* to a dozen of Wellington's finest?"

He watched her swallow, before a coughing fit erupted. With a sigh, he stood and walked toward the sideboard. Extracting two glasses, he poured dollops of spirits from the decanter. "And more to the point, how shall we cipher in the danger of assisting a criminal?"

"I haven't committed a crime."

"Really?"

"Absolutely not." The hint of a blush crested her cheeks.

"Mrs. Ashburton, your bravado mars the performance. Now, then. Why were those soldiers looking for you?"

She stared back at him with a mutinous expression, and he was certain he would not extract a single truth from her.

"I've changed my mind, Mrs. Ashburton. Don't bother. I'm something of an expert on the art of lying, having done it every damned day of my life, and I really don't want to hear your trumped-up story. Shall we get back to the matter at hand? As I recall, you said I could have anything I wanted if I helped you."

"I am not going to . . . to . . ."

"To what, madam?" He offered her one of the glasses and she accepted it.

"You know perfectly well what."

"I should like to hear you say it." It would serve as the first volley in this game. There was nothing like a little disinterest to arouse the opposite in delicate female hearts.

She took a gulp of liquid. He was impressed by her ability to govern a cool expression.

"What is this?" she finally asked hoarsely.

"Water of life."

"This is the farthest thing from water."

"Not in Ireland. And you're changing the subject again," he drawled.

"I will not allow you to do what you pretended to do in your carriage."

"Now there's an idea," he growled to good effect. "But I'm not really tempted, madam." That brought the color back to her cheeks. He wondered if she would be an easy mark, and hoped not. Most women succumbed far too quickly for any sort of serious sport.

"Really? And just what sort does tempt you?"

"Good, honest girls who enjoy being bad. Not bad girls pretending to be good and honest. Although . . . you might show promise if you could just dispense with that false mask of innocence." It was fortunate that he was a far better liar than she—or anyone else for that matter.

The sparks darting from her eyes could light a fire at ten paces. "I've always thought it poor form to offer excuses for one's behavior, Mr. Manning. And so I will offer you no explanations. I can only be grateful that neither of us is each other's favored sort." She muttered the last.

He laughed softly. "Come, come, Mrs. Ashburton, if you can't even bring yourself to tell me what you've done to cause soldiers to be sniffing your trail, do you really think it fair to ask me such intimate questions about the sort of female I favor? And here you are a lady, and all. You are a lady, aren't you?"

Her eyes darkened. "If I agree, then you are sure to think the opposite. I choose not to answer."

"And your husband? Who was he?"

"Mr. Ashburton."

He sighed heavily, enjoying the game.

"And your father?"

She paused, and lifted her chin. "A gentleman."

"Really?" At least she did not scare easily or simper like the majority of the primped pusses he encountered in the occasional ballrooms of desperate lords who issued invitations in an effort to curry his favor. He would—

A damned knock interrupted his thoughts.

"Yes? Come." Damn it to hell, was nothing to run on schedule today? He was not to be disturbed for two hours post auction.

A footman stuck his head inside the door. "Mr. Manning? Mr. Lefroy begs a word."

Hat in hand, Lefroy approached.

"This had best be important. Is Gray Lady dropping?"

"No, sir. The men and I wanted to thank you."

"For godsakes, why? I did not authorize any afternoon off until Michaelmas, and that's six bloody months away."

"Nay. For the dinner. For the gingerbread in particular. Most o' the men 'ad never 'ad it afore."

Without looking in her direction, he murmured, "Don't say a word, madam." To Lefroy, he continued, "Tell them they'd best not get used to such fancy fare, because I'll not—"

Lefroy had the audacity to interrupt him. "I thought you'd want to know the men are so grateful they 'ave taken on the work o' erecting the last o' the fence posts and rails to save you the cost of the other crew of men, sir. They said they'd whitewash all the rooms, too."

"That will be all, Lefroy."

The stable master stared at him for a beat and then nodded before turning on his heel. Only the click of Lefroy's boots against the floor and the door opening and closing could be heard. The weight of the silence became nearly unbearable to him until he heard her stand and carefully place the glass on the table. She followed the same path Lefroy had made toward the door.

"And just where do you think you're going?" he asked.

"To make a list."

"Of possible ways to repay me, dare I hope?"

"No. A list of goods needed for the kitchen and storerooms."

He should have seen it coming. Nothing good came of helping a *lady* in need. Nothing good ever came of helping *anyone* in need. "And I suppose you now think this gives you license to sack the cook. Only pampered, lazy dandies require bloody gingerbread, Mrs. Ashburton. And I did not bring you here to take over my kitchens. I have other plans for—"

She stuck her pointed little chin in the air. "I regret to disagree with you. Even a beastly miser can see the benefits of a different sort of fare than Mrs. Vernon's rotting concoctions. Now I shall stay for the next few days to arrange for your pantries to be restocked and also for several cooks to be interviewed. But, I leave it to you to attend to Mrs. Vernon." She pushed back that magnificent mane of hair, lionlike in its wild hues. "And that, Mr. Manning, is how I shall repay you for your efforts this morning."

"Really?" He took care to lower his voice to a growl. "I fear you've underestimated the cost of saving your pretty neck."

"Oh, fear not. I never had any doubt what you would want, Mr. Manning, whether I'm your favored sort or not and whether you admit it or not. But as a *lady*, I never had any intention of repaying you in such a fashion," she said acidly.

This was not how he played the game. He scratched the edge of his jaw. "The ladies I know never let their station hold them back. In fact, I've always found the grander the title, the bolder the wench. Duchesses, in particular, are a frisky, demanding lot," he said with a smile that twisted one side of his mouth.

She collected the tray, not a ruffle out of place despite his outrageous words. "Yes, well, I'm not a duchess, so you have nothing to fear."

He waved her away dismissively. "I've more important things to do than to fritter away the rest of the afternoon talking cock and bull to a widow, a lady, *and* a liar."

He wondered if she had any idea how attractive she was to him. She was not conventionally pretty—in the soft, graceful way of most pampered aristos. Her eyes, farouche in that angular face of hers, showed hints of a brand of stubbornness he was all too familiar with since it stared back at him in his shaving mirror every morning. Any fool could conjure up the sort of woman she would be in bed.

She was trouble. He would do well to send her on her way this very minute. There was something about her that spoke of goodness despite appearances. But then, she was an amazingly guileless liar. If he did not enjoy skating on the thin ice of disaster, he would let her go. But he had glided on dark, melting regions for so long, it was where he felt most at ease.

Without missing a beat, she grabbed at the chance of escape. "In future, what shall I have prepared for you then, since you don't fancy this fare?"

He stared hard at her. "Boiled eggs and bread. Twice a day. An apple or orange, on occasion."

She gaped at him but was smart enough to not let another peep escape her pretty gob. Instead she edged toward the door.

"And by the by, Mrs. Ashburton. Dare you set one foot off my property before you repay me in a way *I* decide, I shall hunt you down myself and put a bow around your neck before delivering you to those officers or directly to General Pymm himself. I'm certain he'll be happy to tell me why his men are searching for you."

The merest hesitation in her step betrayed what her words did not. He didn't doubt she'd bring a pretty penny . . . and God knew he needed more than a few of those. Yes, he had but a mere month or two before creditors might attempt to steal away all he had built—with satisfied smiles, no less. They would take great pleasure crowing to all and sundry that his spectacular fall was expected. Indeed, his entire life he'd been told cunning bastards such as himself shouldn't attempt to reach the sun. No, they should be happy scavenging the tidal flats like the mudlarks they truly were.

Chapter 3

Elizabeth scrambled from the narrow bed in the middle of the night. Her door was ajar, and a large shadow moved with stealth within the small, cramped room she had been provided.

Her heart in her throat, she ran to the tiny window and threw open the sash, ready to grab on to the large limb of the tree just beyond. She would not go with Pymm, she would rather—

"A little dangerous to your health, don't you think?" Rowland Manning's jaded amusement was evident the moment he spoke from the dark corner.

She whirled about and straightened her now much wrinkled wedding finery with as much dignity as she was able to muster given her fright. She hadn't dared sleep in her shift alone. "I haven't the vaguest idea what you mean, Mr. Manning. It's hotter than Hades in this cramped room. Just require a little air—"

"Please tell me this is not how it's going to go, Mrs. Ashburton?" He silenced her lie, his words steeped in doubt.

Elizabeth peered through the darkness of the chamber only to see something white in his hands. "I thought I locked that door, Mr. Manning."

"And I thought I'd find a use for the spare key." He continued. "Now then, am I to expect my beauty sleep to be disturbed every night at four in the morning by Lefroy reeking of guilt and skulking about your door? What exactly did you do to make my stable master hop to your beck and call? Well? What have you to say? Please, dear God, tell me you are not some sort of spy? Hate spy stories . . . all that intrigue, all the invariable martyrdom that comes part and parcel with it. Well? Cat got your tongue?"

She still reeled from her dreams of running from Pymm as she walked toward Mr. Manning. "No." She pushed her tangled locks over one shoulder. "I'm just waiting for you to get all your questions out at once . . . and hoping you'll run out of breath," she added under her breath, "or maybe even die."

He clucked. "Now, now, Mrs. Ashburton. Is that any way to thank the man who saved your—"

"Yes, no, no, nothing, and no to the rest."

"Excuse me?"

"The answers you sought." Thank the Lord she was fully awake now, her wits returned.

"Very good, Mrs. Ashburton. Now would you like me to read this entire overwrought letter Lefroy carried as he tiptoed past my rooms?" He dangled a note in front of her. "Or shall I go straight to the point?"

"You opened a letter to me?" Her fury grew as she tried to snatch the paper from his hands.

He avoided her easily. "It appears your 'dearest friend in the world,' Lord help me, a Sarah W., has duped the Marquis of Ellesmere and his wife to provide their townhouse as a temporary refuge. She has apparently confided all your mortal sins to your mutual friends, including that prying dowager duchess. There is some hint of *another* letter but, frankly, it was such a mishmash of melodrama that I lost interest." His hooded eyes gave nothing away.

"I'm certain Sarah did not mention *mortal sins or prying or duped*." She snatched the note from his hands when he finally lowered it.

"Let's not bother with trivialities, Mrs. Ashburton. Your friend now thinks to join you here as soon as she can. Lefroy will, of course, be dispatched to tell Mrs. Winters this is not a hotel."

"Well, I am not a cook, but—"

"On that point we agree, madam."

"But—"

"And I will thank you to stop seducing my stable master with gingerbread or any other of your bloody concoctions."

"Mr. Lefroy? You must be joking. I'm—"

"I've never seen the man rendered so dull witted in our twenty years of association. You are to stop talking to him too."

"Mr. Manning?"

"Yes?"

"The next time you interrupt me I shall—"

"What?"

"Boil your eggs in arsenic."

"Such a temper. You should watch that. You might want to search your conscience to see if that's what got you into so much sodding trouble in the first place. Oh, and by the by, Mrs. Ashburton . . ."

"Yes?" she asked, with ill-concealed annoyance.

"This latest round of lies and stupidity? Your penance is to scour the linens tomorrow. It appears my washer maid has departed. Seems she didn't particularly like the idea of her mother, my former perfectly adequate cook, being sacked by Lefroy."

She tried to cut in, without success.

"At this rate, I wouldn't be surprised if the last remaining female here, aside from you, decamps by the end of the week. And then where will you be, Mrs. Ashburton? I fear I see a broom and dustbin in your future. And think of the impropriety. We can't have you ruining my reputation, now, can we?"

She knew she should be grateful that he hadn't given away her whereabouts. And for the merest moment she tried to figure out why he had not. He was the most unreadable person she had ever encountered. His eyes held naught but mystery. And yet, while he was as harsh a man as she had known, the end result was that he had not betrayed her. And he had not once touched her since that awful interlude in his carriage—despite his vulgar suggestions, and despite the fact that two short corridors separated their chambers, according to Mr. Lefroy.

He could have unlocked the door earlier and ravished her so easily. There were but five people residing in the main building at night: Mr. Manning, two footmen, one maid-of-all-work next door, and now Elizabeth. She was at his mercy, of that there was little doubt. But for some reason she could not fathom, she almost felt protected. Yes, well, she had thought Pymm a hero, too. At this point, with her former spectacularly erroneous character assessments, she should, indeed, jump out the window.

She smiled to herself as he made his way to the door. "Oh, Mr. Manning? Thank you so much for your gracious hospitality." She glanced about the bare chamber. Only a simple cot resided there. "I'd be *delighted* to do your washing, along with all the cooking. And here I had worried I'd be bored, with so much time on my hands."

He retrieved an old valise from outside the door and dangled it before him. "Well, since you're adequately grateful, I shall offer you a reward. If you employ all your ladylike embroidering skills on my mending too, then, and only then, will I reward you with *this* little item Lefroy brought from your friend as well."

"Give me that, you—you *lout*." She stretched up on her toes to reach for the bag he held aloft. He was so very tall she had not a chance. And suddenly, he was far too close to her and she realized that she shouldn't trust her earlier opinion of him. She could see darkness in his eyes, and she could sense the heat and brutal strength of his immense body.

She was such a fool. He had the expression of a great warrior in the midst of battle. A man who knew naught of right from wrong. Of an animal ruled by pure instinct.

She refused to buckle beneath his harsh, hungry gaze. It was impossible to look away. And yet, it was difficult to understand what he sought. If he wanted to ravish her, he was taking his time about it. And then, she heard the crash of her valise falling from his grip to the floor. His hands were now like twin bands on her arms, and the distance between them was closing fast. And yet, she did not a thing to stop him.

He paused a mere inch from her lips and suddenly, just as she expected him to crush her to him, he pushed away in a rush and stumbled back. Rowland Manning reached for her bag at his feet and hurled it into the corner of the tiny chamber. Shocked by his actions, she couldn't form a word under his hot glare. He tore his gaze from hers and a moment later, he crossed to the door with ground-eating strides, a string of violent curses blooming in the air.

An hour before dawn, Elizabeth woke with a start and jumped from the rumpled bedclothes to make her way to the window of the small bedchamber. Lord, she was exhausted and yet as awake as she had been for more than half the night.

Eliza scanned the darkness beyond the tree branches of the window. "Oh, Sarah . . . find your way to me. Please, God," she whispered. Elizabeth longed for her friend, who, six years her senior and the wife of Elizabeth's father's commander, had always assumed the role of wise older sister more than any true relation ever could have. Sarah's steadiness of character had provided an anchor for Elizabeth, whose rash actions had caused them to be cast adrift in the first place. No matter how often Sarah told Elizabeth that she depended on her for her liveliness of spirit, Elizabeth knew she was the root cause of all their worries. Yet, they were like two sisters, one light and one dark, each needing the other for ease.

It had been this way all night. Little patches of sleep between horrid, heart-pounding nightmares of smoke-choked battlefields and running. Running until her lungs burned. And each time she would awaken with a start, sure Pymm's men were climbing the stairs beyond the door to her room.

Peace was not to be found in the kitchen. At least the loaves of bread had risen properly. Eliza had nicked her fingers raw coaxing nuts from their shells to produce the nut bread the dearest men in her life had favored so much, and then she had tended to the eggs and warm pints of milk the dairy maid had delivered.

The kindhearted, brawny young footman, Joshua Gordon, appeared, eyes wide, smile even wider, especially upon finding Mrs. Vernon gone. "I've never smelled anything like this, ma'am," he said nodding toward the steaming loaves. You are the best thing that has happened here since the day Mr. Manning's mare won the preliminary race to have a go at Ascot. Actually, I'm thinking the men might think you are the better of the two." He grinned and whisked all to the dining hall, while whistling a jaunty tune.

Now that she knew the way, Eliza took Mr. Manning's tray to his cavernous study on her own. With each step she lined up more eloquently the reasons she would give to insist upon Sarah's presence for the short term. She hoped Sarah remembered their old signal of a lone candle placed to the right of a sill. After a mountain of annoyed sighs, Mr. Manning had given her the meager remains of a cheaply made tallow candle yesterday.

It had not taken long to see the way of things at Manning's. To outsiders, to customers with gold lining their pockets, the enterprise appeared the epitome of luxury, elegance, and possessed of the best horse stock in Christendom. But to those who worked there, not a tuppance was wasted—certainly not on superior food, nor on any of the small conveniences of life, and especially not on "gawdamned bloody candles for cooks out to bewitch my men," as he had shouted at her. Eliza dreaded to think of what he would say when Sarah arrived. He'd probably call her "another damned nuisance."

The thing of it was that some sixth sense had always whispered to Eliza that she was responsible for her best friend's future. Her actions were, quite possibly, the root cause of Sarah's husband's death, an event that had devastated her friend.

This same sense had made Elizabeth insist that they walk as far and as fast as possible through the war-ravaged forests and fields of Spain, to the coast, where Sarah and she had spent a few of their meager coins to convince a fisherman, with obvious smuggling intentions, to navigate the strong currents of the Bay of Biscay to deposit them on the opposite coast. And Sarah had followed her without question.

Mr. Manning's office was empty of his person, and Elizabeth noticed with amusement how dull it appeared without him. Remembering the bluster of yesterday's short and to-the-point conversation concerning the stump of the candle, followed by the bizarre encounter in her chamber in the wee hours, Eliza smiled. She then balanced the tray on her hip and cleared a small space on his desk, which held mounds of paper and ledgers.

Small words were carved into the inner edge of the desk. Setting the tray on a stack of papers, she looked closer to read FORGET NOT-WANT NOT.

The sound of the door opening made her turn abruptly and she felt unaccountably like a child caught, candy in hand. "I should have told you, ma'am, that Mr. Manning is not about," Joshua Gordon called to her. "But Mr. Lefroy said to leave Master's breakfast here."

"And where is Mr. Manning?"

"In the stables, but he'll be back soon."

Six hours of organized chaos followed. Ever practical and efficient, Elizabeth oversaw the effort to reorganize the kitchen. A pair of superior barn cats had been pressed into service and had tackled the whiskered enemies of the cold rooms below. Joshua Gordon was sent to the market to purchase fresh foodstuffs, and to an employment agency to search for a worthy cook, while Elizabeth and a stable hand scoured the pantries, before she alone turned to the task of supper. Fragrant plum pudding ended a meal of curried lamb with grapes and artichokes. Mr. Lefroy, along with the delirious stable hands from the hall, had nearly cried with gratitude.

Elizabeth carried the second tray of boiled eggs prepared to the minute and a portion of nut bread to Mr. Manning's study. Her perverse nature made her hope he had caught fragrant wafts of the meal the others had shared in the dining hall.

Good God. His breakfast still lay untouched where she had left it. *Stone cold.*

She wasn't sure what made her so angry. Perhaps it was that a cook's only pleasure was words of thanks and occasional praise, combined with the knowledge that she was nourishing a fellow being in body if not in soul.

Yet, why on earth should she care if he didn't like the food she had so carefully prepared to his exact specifications? Well, almost to his exact specifications.

She had so wanted to hear one meager, grudging word of praise from the horrid, arrogant taskmaster that she'd cheated by making her special nut bread. She noticed the remains of an apple in the waste basket beside the table. Irritation mounted and her cheeks burned with frustration.

She shouldn't care. She had something more important to concern her—her plan to leave London, first and foremost. She should know better than to dally where danger could only be found. These thoughts did not deter her from confronting the enemy. It never had before, had it?

The second tray still in her hands, she crossed to the door and stuck her nose outside for the first time since arriving here.

Beyond the meticulously groomed boxwood garden, an immense central yard yawned before her. A vast expanse of very clean, and very new looking stables and fenced pasture beckoned beyond. What Manning's lacked in comparison to the prime location of famed Tattersall's it more than made up for in sheer size. It rested grandly on the outskirts of London, where wilderness met the sprawl of the city. But it was the gleaming, prime horseflesh one spied in every direction that explained its attraction to the masculine fast set.

Long shadows fell from the structures, revealing the lateness of the day, quickening Elizabeth's steps. Ducking past a dozen gentlemen flocking several pens, she negotiated the maze of stables toward a door where one of the men suggested she might find Mr. Manning.

She turned and knocked once with the heel of her

foot and then wheeled about to enter without waiting for an answer. She refused to notice the colossal amount of paperwork before him.

"I'm sorry to inform that it's time to face the trial of my cooking again, Mr. Manning." She plopped the tray in front of him, obliterating the ledgers and papers from his view.

He had not moved a muscle. Finally, his unusual pale green eyes peered up at her, and for the barest hint of a moment she was certain she spied something so raw and primal in them that she took a step back before she recollected herself and lifted her chin. "Well?" she asked, a little deflated.

"Well what, madam?"

"Look, it's half past five o'clock. Don't play the sullen spoilsport. I've made what you asked. It's your job to eat it."

"The sullen—" He stopped, then glanced at the tray for a long moment before moving it to one side of his desk. "I asked for the meals to be left in my study."

"Mr. Manning," she said impatiently. "You are not going about this properly. Men have only to do three things in life: fight or work, in your case, and then eat, and sleep."

"Really? And what are women to do?" he drawled.

"Well, for most females, we must cook, eat, and sleep."

"You've forgotten one important element, madam."

"Now Mr. Manning, do stop avoiding the task at hand."

"You neglected to add the need to *rut*, Mrs. Ashburton."

She sighed dramatically. "If you think to disarm me with such talk, I should warn you that there is precious little you can say that will surprise me. In fact, I could probably tell you a thing or three after a lifetime spent surrounded by—" She stopped herself abruptly. What on earth was she thinking?

"I'm all ears, Mrs. Ashburton," he said, his voice as lazy as his eyes were not. "Surrounded by men, were you? No wonder those officers appeared to know you."

She recollected her mission. "Botheration. Eat the food I prepared, you stubborn mule."

"Hmmm. All those years surrounded by infantry and cavalry and you've never heard the old proverb about leading a horse to water and trying to make him—"

"Drink?" she interrupted, with impatience.

"No"—he smiled with a devilish grin—"*jump.*"

She stepped to the edge of his desk and grabbed the nut bread, poking it under his nose. "Jump over this. I dare you."

He had to give her credit. She was one of the few—no, the *only* woman—who had the nerve to talk to him thusly . . . Most were afraid of him, or the reverse: interested only in all manner of sexual perversion. He suddenly grinned, unused to the feeling of his mouth stretching into a smile.

At that moment she shoved the intoxicating bread into his mouth. He could not help but to chew convulsively and swallow. It took a hill of determination not to stuff the rest of the blasted, heaven-made delicacy down his gullet. "A little dry, don't you think?" A tinge of hoarseness tickled his voice.

"It's perfect, you oaf."

"Such coarseness, Mrs. Ashburton. And such un-dignified behavior. Careful, you—yes, Tommy?"

A young boy poked his head inside the cramped office. "It's Gray Lady. Mr. Lefroy bade me fetch you. She's a-pacing and not droppin' as fast as he'd like."

"Idiot," he spewed as he knocked back his chair to stand. "I was to be alerted at first sign." He turned and poked her in the chest. "This is your fault. That bloody food of yours is addling my men's brains. And by the by, Mrs. Ashburton, since you're so damned fond of the army, may I remind you that an order is an order? Leave those sodding trays of yours in the study. And find me a new cook before the end of the week, or else my men will eat what *I* prepare." He stalked out and the boy stared at her with huge gray eyes, obviously amazed at her ability to withstand the force of his employer's hurricanelike wrath.

"Ma'am? Don't worry about the master. Mr. Lefroy slips him apples and carrots, he does," the boy whispered.

"Perhaps if he keeps eating such fare, he'll grow a tail and hooves and you can parade him around the yard and sell him to the highest bidder."

The boy grinned. Before darting away, he added, "Can I takes the bread, mum? Might be the last I gets, the way things be a-lookin'."

She was being ridiculous, she knew. Lord knew the man ate. Why, he was the height of one of those legendary Spartan warriors and just as ruthless. Still . . . there were those gaunt cheeks of his, and not a spare ounce of fat on him. Why, his aristocratic half brother appeared much more hale and hearty.

She gave the boy the bread, covered the tray, and departed with it in hand. But, curiosity got the better of her. A small group of men were gathered before a huge stall at the back of the stables. Eliza set the food aside and joined them.

A mare paced within, but halted momentarily at Eliza's approach, and whickered. The mare snuffled the straw strewn about the confines of the enclosure and resumed her pacing.

"Is loikes I tolds you. She be awaiting him, she is," an older stableman said quietly to a younger from the edge of the stall.

Elizabeth peered past the jumble of men, all of whom smiled warmly upon her approach, and saw Mr. Manning in the stall, apparently oblivious to all of them as he intently watched every movement of the small gray mare.

"Shhh, Jimmy," the older man warned. "Watch now."

Mr. Manning eased forward, talking to the mare in some sort of incomprehensible language. The mare stretched out her supple, arched neck and blew softly into his empty outstretched hand. Slowly he traced the muscles of her neck with his hands. Starting at the poll, his wide palms stroked past her strong neck to the valley of her chest. Sweeping past her strong, sloping shoulders, he slowed. His work-scarred, beautiful hands carefully noted the movements of her flanks, and the mare tossed her head once and turned sharply to rest her muzzle on the crook of his arm. "Yes, Lady," he whispered with encouragement. He suddenly turned toward the gawking stable hands as if he had forgotten they were all there. "Clear 'em out of here," he said, his hard eyes telling Lefroy what his voice did not.

Mr. Lefroy gathered the man, "Come on, lads, you know the master's rules. The mares need their privacy." While the men and boys grumbled as they dispersed, the stable master turned to Elizabeth and winked. "You can stay if you're quiet-like."

She edged away to sit on a nearby stool. She could see everything through the cracks of the wooden stall beams.

Caught in the beauty of the moment, Elizabeth watched man and animal lost in the timeless moment of creation. Rowland Manning stroked the protruding flanks of the mare and alternated between calming her and encouraging her. Each appeared to rely on the other, the man's quiet, strong patience rewarded by the mare's trust and desire to please. It would be obvious to anyone who watched them in this *pas de deux* of stalwart guardian, willing to bear the weight of danger, and the creature who depended on him. She would not have guessed him capable of such gentleness.

And then suddenly, with the instinct of an animal used to outrunning prey in the wild, the mare quickly dropped her foal; Mr. Manning taking care to ease the newborn onto the straw bed. What she was witnessing was about as far from the norm as possible. Most horses foaled in the dead of night, in the farthest corner from every other living thing, using the instincts with which they were gifted to avoid predators.

At the basest level, horses fretted with man. And yet, everything in front of her now spoke the opposite.

Sitting motionless so as not to startle either of them, Elizabeth watched as Mr. Manning efficiently tended the mare and foal. He rubbed down the animals and peered at the water bucket, and all the while he calmed in soothing, nearly rhythmic tones.

A ray of late afternoon sun poured onto the edge of Elizabeth's gown, and she looked away for a moment. When she trained her eyes back to the crack between the wooden beams, he was staring at her. Oh no, not another lecture . . . just when she was starting to find him—

"Get fresh water," he ordered quietly without a false "please" or "thank you."

Elizabeth merely nodded and obeyed.

Jimmy, the stable boy, watched her in awe as she filled a bucket from the large water trough outside the stable. "The master never let anyone but hisself and Mr. Lefroy get Gray Lady's food or water."

Well . . . progress, finally. It was just too bad she would not stay long enough to find out when he might take food or water from her hand too.

Little did Elizabeth Ashburton know that the next day would bring progress on that front. With an equal measure of disaster.

Chapter 4

The next afternoon, the broad, red visage of Lieutenant Tremont examined Rowland lazily from across the fat man's neat desk. "It will take a lot longer than a fortnight to reconfigure the cavalry's needs, Mr. Manning. Why are you bothering us about this again?"

He wanted to slam his fist down the lazy man's gullet. "Uh, perhaps because until last month, I was to deliver eight hundred twenty battle-ready mounts, according to this contract." Rowland waived the document out of the other man's reach. You couldn't trust the bloody army with a gawdamned thing.

"Yes, well, until last month, we had a war now, didn't we? You *can* read, man, can't you?" The hint of a sneer slid across the other man's thin lips. "Oh, perhaps not."

Funny how much more polite the lieutenant had been when he was desperate for horses four months ago, at the precise moment Wellington was in danger of getting his arse kicked back to Portugal.

The man must have sensed Rowland's murderous rage, and he straightened in his chair. "Now see here, Manning, it's as I told you. We'll probably take the horses. As soon as Wellington and Pymm finish their work here, they're for Vienna."

"I know where the bloody peace talks are." Rowland withheld adding, "you idiot," by the whisker of patience he still possessed.

"Look, we're still waiting for accurate numbers of troops and stock after that last drive to Bayonne. Then we'll know how many replacements we'll request. General Pymm has indicated he wants at least two divisions as a show of strength in Paris and Vienna."

"Yes, well while Pymm and Wellington kick up their heels and accept their bloody titles and laurels for packing off that short, balding frog to Elba, I'm feeding and housing in the country an extra eight hundred and twenty heavy horses suited to face cannon at dawn, not Hyde Park at the fashionable hour." Rowland shot up from his chair and leaned over the stupid lieutenant's desk to press the point. "You can add another two hundred fifty pounds a day for their upkeep until you take them off my hands. And may I remind you that I was promised full payment four bloody weeks ago."

The man cleared his throat nervously and smoothed his thin moustache, a slight tremble in his hand betraying his fright. "Yes, well, we'll have to see about that, Manning. Now then, you will have to excuse me. I have to—"

Rowland waved his hand. "Yes, let me guess. Being fitted for ballroom frocks? Got an invitation to Prinny's little tea party for Pymm at Carlton House, did you?"

The portly lieutenant called out to his two assistants in the hall, who immediately came to his aid.

"At least I won't have to worry that we'll be rubbing shoulders with the likes of you, Manning. Money and power such as yours can't buy everything. Only Quality have been invited to witness Pymm's elevation to duke." The man's wattle shook in righteous, if not ill-advised anger. "Can't imagine what the Earl of Wallace was thinking when he acknowledged you as his half brother. But you can never erase being born on the wrong side of the blanket now, can you?" He turned to his aides. "Who do you think his mother was, men? Do you wager she was a whore or a dairy maid?"

It took precisely thirty seconds for the lieutenant to regret his folly. In that time Rowland rendered inert both weak-kneed assistants with several well-placed blows. But he had not gained his footing in the world to be thrown in the garrison for murdering a brainless lieutenant. Instead, Rowland leaned over the man's quivering mass of glistening porcine skin and bones still sitting in his chair unharmed. "I'll thank you to remember my gift when I see you next," he whispered.

"Gift?" the man sputtered, spittle flying in nervousness.

"The gift of not drawing and quartering you with eight hundred and twenty unpaid for horses. I shall return in three days, and if you do not have the blunt owed to me at that time? Well, I shall tell Pymm or Wellington the name of the incompetent lieutenant *of Quality* who is refusing to settle the accounts of the person who supplied a bloody cavalcade of horses to them in Spain. *Comprende, amigo?*"

*   *   *

He was doing it on purpose, she was sure of it. Elizabeth looked down at the untouched breakfast tray—the one she had carted to his small office in the stable this morning—despite his instructions to the contrary. She sighed. If she had had fewer morals she might have enjoyed returning the same boiled eggs and bread to Mr. Manning's desk until they turned green with mold.

Tray in hand, she grumbled in irritation and headed across the immaculate yards toward the main buildings. Something itched the side of her wrist and she looked down to see the edge of the letter she had found this morning in the deep pocket of one of the two gowns Sarah had packed in the valise. Her friend had taken care to hide it well, stitching the pocket closed. It had evaded Mr. Manning's prying eyes and fingers.

Oh, she was avoiding it. Looking for every excuse to put off what she should have done the minute she'd found it.

Throughout the day, the letter had burned a hole in her pocket. But like a child unwilling to face unpleasantness, she had used a mountain of tasks to avoid scanning the words, which were sure to scald her mind, and allow even more ill-ease to dog her every waking thought.

But her departure was imminent. She had so little to fear, really. She would interview three cooks tomorrow, and Sarah was sure to come or to send word about a plan to leave London by then. And even if no elaborate plan was hatched, as soon as Sarah arrived, they could simply walk past Mr. Manning's pastures and keep walking until . . . well, until they found a remote village where Elizabeth could find work as a cook or a maid. And the way things had unfolded, she could even take on the job of watering and feeding horses, for goodness sakes.

Alas, she could no longer ignore Pymm's letter. It wasn't like her to be so hen-hearted. In a rush she darted behind an oak, put down the tray, and crushed the blood-red seal.

Her breath caught at the first words.

My dearest, loveliest Elizabeth,

I realize when last we met, you were overcome with grief, a very becoming sensibility on the occasion of your father's death. I grieved for you. I was only sorry that while suffering such obvious shock, you took the foolish decision to leave. My Elizabeth, you cannot guess how I feared for you in the midst of the orgy of violence following the siege. Many women were viciously ravished, some mortally wounded.

Yet I refused to give you up for dead. I knew I should find you. And I knew you would not want to disobey your father's final wishes.

I have in my possession his affairs and Mrs. Winters's husband's as well. There is the matter of uncollected pay and a few precious objects you might treasure, including a miniature of your mother, I presume, and for Mrs. Winters, there is Colonel Winters's wedding ring. You know not how it has pained me to be unable to return these items, for I know how much you both must long for them.

My dear, I do hope you have not mistaken my intentions. You do understand the great honor I have proposed, despite your father's unfortunate past predicament? Any hint of which might well fall very heavily at your door. Do I need to point out that your running off would only fuel speculation? I have held off writing a report—for I cannot bear to imagine society's reactions. You must see I want nothing more than to protect you.

I have not forgotten that it was always your way to tease with your bold attentions and then to retreat. I have no doubt that remembrances of our moments together excite your heart as they do mine. I shall never forget your admiration and the desire shining from your eyes each time I returned victorious from battle and we danced and took such joy as could be found at those small, hastily arranged entertainments.

Indeed, when the Prince Regent asked what drove me to such heroic measures throughout our final push into France, I told him it was for love of my fellow Englishmen and for the love of one particular lady.

I shall entrust this missive to the Dowager Duchess of Helston who I spied clutching your arm in church. I expect an audience soonest to discuss our future. And now that I'm assured of your survival, I've every reason to continue to protect what I've always considered my own.

*But Elizabeth . . . you will not toy with my af-
fections any longer. 'Tis but a childish, foolish
impulse. I grow tired of the sport and I am determined to have you by my side as the duchy is
conferred at Carlton House by my most ardent
supporter, the Prince Regent. You shall make a
fine duchess.*

> *Until we meet, my love,
> I remain yours, as always,*
>
> *P.*

Bile rose in the back of Elizabeth's throat, and
the old panic that had led to her ill-planned escape
through Spain two years ago nearly overwhelmed her.
And then she could not stop it. She rushed around the
rough bark of the old oak tree and allowed the wave
of nausea to convulse through her.

It was worse than she remembered. She fought
against the crippling effect of despair, and forced
herself to stand straight. She tried to remember the
advice of her father. This would pass. Everything
always did with time. A decade from now she would
look back on these years and find black humor in
the horror of it. But her father's worldly wise counsel
failed to soothe her.

She wanted to scream at the unfairness of it. All
her father's acts of valor would be forgotten, and her
reputation would crumble with just one false, sala-
cious word from Pymm, a man all of England now
revered.

But she was not without power. Pymm would not

dare utter a syllable against a lady he hoped to make his duchess while she remained in hiding. It was not his way. Her tormenter would only expose her to censure if he found her, and was unsuccessful in his efforts to overcome her resistance to his proposal. In darker moments she wondered if he would have the audacity to bind her bones and haul her to Scotland if she protested. And if she dared defy him before the eyes of the rest of the world? He would not stop at a simple assassination of character. His was the word of a man second to the Duke of Wellington, versus the word of the daughter of an army captain. She had no proof against him.

Oh, it was all so hopeless. Her empty stomach roiled again. She had prayed time and absence would put an end to Pymm's unnatural obsession. But her refusal and disappearance only appeared to have augmented it. She would never master the ever-changing rules of his ridiculous fixation.

She loathed the idea of buckling under the pressure and marrying him. She didn't think she could do it. And she was older now, and trying desperately to overcome her great defect of character—that of action before a thorough reflection on the matter at hand. But oh, how her feet itched to run again. Far, far away.

Her situation was entirely ironic, for she had no natural talent for clandestine affairs. Her father had always said she was just like her mother, far too open, and incapable of carrying off deceit with any degree of success. She was certain Rowland Manning would heartily agree with him.

Truly, if she were to follow her first inclination,

even before running away again, she'd inform Pymm that she would rather marry his lily-livered bulldog than him.

Yes, she'd very much enjoy telling him that he could jolly well go ahead and brand her father and her traitors to the crown and imprison her in the Tower if he liked. But, well . . . she didn't fancy dying quite yet.

"What's got that fair face lookin' like the end o' the world is at hand?" Mr. Lefroy's kindly face peered around the tree.

She jumped. "Oh, Mr. Lefroy. I'm sorry. It's nothing, really."

The older man studied her for a moment. "You looks like you've gots cobwebs growin' 'tween yer ears, lovey. You wants to join old Lefroy? Does you loikes a little gallop now and again?"

She swallowed against the remembrance of the moments she'd spent in Cornwall racing the downs and vales with the widows in the club who enjoyed a little danger. "More than anything," she avowed.

"Leave the tray. You can retrieve it later." He steered her toward the stables. "Nofin' loikes a good gallop to clear away the dismals. Vespers loikes to run wiv a partner. Let's see if'n you can keep up." He smiled wide, showing the small gap between his teeth.

"Vespers?"

"Eventide Vespers," he clarified with obvious pride. "The master's prize racer. She's to have a go at Ascot."

He mounted her in a sidesaddle despite her grumbling. At least he'd trusted her and let her pick a powerful chestnut gelding with an intelligent eye if not the deep chest of the warhorses she had known.

"She's a beauty," Elizabeth murmured as she looked longingly toward the tall, dark bay mare with the star in the center of her fine head.

"Aye, Vespers is that," Mr. Lefroy said as he adjusted his stirrups. "Unless she sees the whip, o' course."

She looked at him expectantly.

"Beggin' yer pardon, ma'am, but she don't care for the notion of a spankin'."

"She's smart then, too," Elizabeth said, a smile finally curling her lips.

Mr. Lefroy's eyes popped out.

"What?" she asked.

He blushed furiously. "You sure are a pretty thing when's you smile, ma'am. You's got dinkles."

She grinned. "Dinkles?"

"Dents in yer cheeks wots drive menfolk mad. Lucky for you I'm too old for yer."

They rode out past the paddocks and rings, past the stand of trees near the northeastern corner, until they came to a small lake. An irregular racecourse was laid out around the perimeter. She studied the layout for a few moments, noting the graduated rises and falls while the two horses jigged in anticipation.

She turned the full force of a smile on Mr. Lefroy. "Loser peels the dinner potatoes?"

He sputtered, and she was off. Oh, the feel of the wind rushing against her face. How she had missed this. The gelding was a real goer. A few moments later, she dared to glance behind her, only to see Mr. Lefroy holding back the mare. What on earth was he thinking?

Over the course of the next three miles, she understood. Eventide Vespers was the fastest horse Elizabeth had ever seen. Despite the great advantage Mr. Lefroy had allowed, Vespers leapt ahead at the midpoint of the course and never let up the pace. What Elizabeth would not have given for the chance to ride that beautiful, sleek creature.

It was just too bad that no matter how many miles she galloped with Mr. Lefroy, she could not lose the sense of dread and disaster looming ahead. Or the sense that she would never be able to free herself from Pymm's obsession.

As the vestiges of the day began to etch their vibrant colors upon the darkening azure of the sky, Rowland Manning approached the edge of the pasture on his return from the disastrously unproductive encounter with Lieutenant Tremont, a man who would last less than a minute before the heat of the cannon. Perversely, it was men like Tremont who always lived to a hundred and two while serving their country on the other side of a desk. It was enough to make Rowland wish he were a bloody revolutionary-minded Frenchie. Yes, watching a few lordly heads introduced to Madame Guillotine would restore his good humor very well—especially if one tonsured crown belonged to a certain Lieutenant Tremont, second son of a minor baronet.

As he neared the stables, Rowland slowed his young bay gelding to a walk to cool him. This one showed much promise. He wouldn't do as a carriage horse. Too small and slight. But he was a pretty boy, with easy daisy-cutting gaits. Perfect for the flood of young ladies who arrived each season looking to cut a dash in Hyde Park. A vision appeared unbidden . . . of Elizabeth Ashburton mounted on the gelding, trotting along a manicured avenue, her emerald eyes sparkling as she laughed gaily. He ground his teeth and forced the image from his mind.

Now, if he could just train eight hundred plus heavy-boned cavalry horses to be just like this well-mannered gelding . . . *Christ*. How he had counted on that bloody contract. And he'd thought himself so brilliant in hedging his bets by forcing that bribe from his half brother's besotted fiancée all those months ago in exchange for arranging Michael's release from Newgate prison. Perhaps his half brother *had eventually* been able to prove he'd been innocent of the murder charges Rowland had brought forth against him. Yes, Rowland had gone soft, returning every last ha'penny to the countess—albeit grudgingly.

In either case, he would have had enough to see him through the end of the next quarter. Instead, he might very well be taken before the magistrate, his enterprise broken and auctioned to the highest bidder. Indeed, the prospect of the poorhouse loomed or—

All at once he saw in the distance a bit of gray muslin hurrying through the exit of the stables to cross behind the large oak, closest to the main building. *What in hell?* He made his way to the nearest stable boy and tossed the reins to him. "Walk him out, Jimmy."

Quietly, he approached the other side of the wide tree trunk. The thick, unbound, multicolored locks of Mrs. Ashburton's hair fluttered in the late-afternoon breeze. She was extracting something from the billowing skirt of her gown. He spied her profile as he came around the tree.

She turned, and before she could alter her countenance, he saw such bleak desperation lining her face—the same expression worn by every last person of his childhood. It failed to produce a single drop of compassion from him. It had all been milked from him decades ago in the poorest of the filthy maze of London's rookeries.

He nodded to the letter in her hand. "More intrigue, Mrs. Ashburton? Glad to hear it. Life was far too tedious and dull before you arrived. Although I must say your fondness for secret notes is wearing a bit thin."

"I suppose it was too much to hope you would not plague me again today." She quickly refolded the letter.

Color returned to her intriguing face, making him thank God he wouldn't be forced to pretend concern.

"Dare I ask what that letter is about, Mrs. Ashburton? I do hope you're not contemplating an ill-advised escape from our cozy little coterie here?"

"Why ever would you think that?"

"You have that look about you."

"And what look is that, Mr. Manning," she asked stiffly.

"Of a scared rabbit trying to fling herself through a gap in the garden fence to avoid the edge of the farmer's trowel."

"Perhaps it's you I'm trying to avoid—and your clichéd ideas."

A gust of cooling wind rushed through the leaves overhead. "Give that to me," he insisted quietly.

She stuffed the note in her pocket mutinously. "No. It has nothing to do with you and it's private."

He raised an eyebrow. "Everything and everyone on this property concerns me, Mrs. Ashburton."

She picked up the untouched tray and began to walk away from him, and he strode in front of her, forcing her to stop.

"Damn you," he muttered. "What in hell does it say to have you looking like a wretched pickpocket before the noose?"

"You have your secrets, Mr. Manning, and I have mine." The light of something very like mischief stole across her face. "But since you are so curious, shall we make a bargain?"

"I do not make bargains with someone already in my debt."

She sighed with exaggeration. "Mr. Manning, do stop being ridiculous. I've paid off my debt to you with interest. I've fed your men the last several days, organized your pantries and kitchen, and have even narrowed the pool of potential new cooks down to two. Now if you want to strike a bargain with me, I'm more than willing to satisfy your curiosity."

He considered her words, balanced the pros and cons of it. With self-disgust, he ground out, "What are you suggesting?"

"For every meal of mine you consume before I leave, I shall tell you one of my secrets."

He could not help but be slightly amused. With exaggeration he extended his arm toward the main building and bowed. "I accept, Mrs. Ashburton.

Never let it be said I could not accomplish two things at once—eating and enlightenment—all on one plate."

This was not going at all as he expected, he thought a mere quarter of an hour later as the witch placed a plate of ungodly food in front of him. They'd haggled over the fare. He had wanted his eggs, and she'd refused to open her bloody mouth until she'd selected a sampling of the dinner fare she'd prepared for his men.

"I shall want to meet those two cooks as soon as possible," he'd said without trying to hide his irritation.

"Will this afternoon be too soon?" she'd replied with exaggerated sweetness.

A portion of fish bathed in a sea of some sort of red sauce lay in the center of a deep dish of creamed potatoes. Several spears of asparagus framed the elegant food. An exotic combination of scents reached his nostrils, sounding off a thousand alarms in his head.

"Now then, Mr. Manning," she said softly as she seated herself next to him in his heretofore unused dining room. "I do hope you'll like it."

He'd constructed the chamber for formal entertainments in future, when he would have accumulated the blunt to lure more customers to his establishment.

"And what sort of fancy quid did you pay for this bloody exotic fish? You're out to beggar me."

"Pittance. I sent that handsome Joshua Gordon to wheedle the fishmonger's daughter with half the amount your cook would have spent to purchase rotted fare."

"You find him handsome, do you?"

She ignored him. "And this fish is not out of the ordinary. I'm surprised you aren't familiar with cod—why, it's the commonest fish in the world. Then again someone who eats only eggs and bread . . ."

"Hate fish."

"Well then, I shan't tell you what you want to know." She suddenly smiled, and the radiance of her face dazzled his senses. It was the first time he'd seen her truly smile.

"Good God. Don't do that."

"Do what?" she replied with innocence.

"Forget it." He steeled himself against her brilliant smile and those god-awful dimples, which spoke of a sort of happiness he knew nothing about. But then, there was nothing to interfere with the savory scents wafting from the elegant crockery. He exhaled roughly. "The first secret, madam?"

"Not until you eat."

"I feel it my duty to inform that that unattractive, nagging way of yours will hurt your chances of finding a new husband, Mrs. Ashburton. Christ, I don't have time for this. It's ridiculous."

"My sentiments exactly," she murmured.

She leaned forward when he did not move and grasped the fork to gently flake apart a section, revealing that the damned codfish was cooked to delicate perfection. Raising the fragrant morsel, which dripped with sauce, she held it before him.

"Give me that," he said, annoyance lacing his words. "What do you take me for? A wet-behind-the-ears infant? He grabbed the fork from her hands, held his breath and introduced the food into his mouth.

It nearly killed him to chew slowly and not tear into the rest. He had acquired the ability at an early age to ignore food. His mother had taught him, and his siblings, although none had learned so well as he.

They had all known food was the way to madness. It was not to be talked of nor dwelled upon. It was parceled out when it was there and forcibly ignored when it was not. Sloth and gluttony were the besetting sin of the rich and titled, they were told. Hunger had the benefit of sharpening the mind, honing the senses, and it also compelled industrious instincts. One only needed the simplest and smallest amount of food to fuel the body, and it was a complete waste of time to spend more than a few minutes consuming it. He put down the fork.

"Delicious, Mrs. Ashburton. Really. A meal fit for a king. Now, what do you have to tell me?"

"You have to take at least five bites before I'll tell you. Five *full* bites," she said pointedly.

He sighed heavily. "You seem to be under the impression that I do not know how to eat, Mrs. Ashburton."

Those mesmerizing eyes of hers stared back at him and she remained silent.

"Oh, for Christ sakes." He picked up the fork and ate three more bites very carefully, eyeing each bite with disdain. And then . . . well, he just couldn't make himself stop. He proceeded to brutally violate each and every rule he had set since a long ago day he refused to remember.

He ate with a vengeance bordering on gluttony. He ate until there was not a morsel of cod, or potato, or even a drop of sauce left on the plate.

He ate until he was satisfied.

It nearly made him ill.

The fork clattered into the empty dish and he threw the napkin over the lot of it.

He stared at her.

"I am not a widow," she murmured.

Well, well. He inhaled deeply. "And why would this matter to me? You said you would tell me something of importance, madam. Although . . . you will tell me now if I am harboring a runaway wife."

"One meal, one secret."

Warm relaxation filled his body, a sensation unknown. "In exchange for eating that sodding fish sauce, I want a great deal more than your marital station."

"Well, I want a good deal more—"

A soft knock at the door heralded the entrance of a footman. "There is a gentleman who would have a word, Mr. Manning. Shall I—"

"Oh, by all means, show him in. Just in time for the tea service—now that all that oily fish is gone. Fetch the gin. Oh, and Joshua?" He'd always liked the blind obedience of the young man.

"Yes, sir?" Joshua replied with reverence.

"Stay away from the fishmonger's daughter: I'll not have a footman smelling of eel in my employ."

Joshua Gordon grinned and nodded as he turned on his heel.

Elizabeth Ashburton, or whoever the hell this woman was beside him, reached to collect the damn plate and brushed his arm in the process. He yanked his limb away.

"Admit it, you liked it," she murmured.

"I'd as soon lie as you, my dear."

* * *

The door to the chamber opened again before Elizabeth could form a retort. Her breath caught. She hadn't known how much she longed to see one of the familiar faces of her group of friends from Portman Square. With a clatter, she released the crockery she'd just grasped and rushed to Michael, the Earl of Wallace as he strode into the dining chamber. She stopped a foot away from him.

"Oh, my lord."

"What? In a week's time you've forgotten my given name, Elizabeth?"

She swallowed. "I wasn't sure if . . . oh, I'm so happy to see you, Michael."

He opened his arms and she rushed to accept the warmth and comfort they offered.

"Are you all right?" he whispered into her hair. "He hasn't harmed you, has he? I told Lefroy—"

Elizabeth heard the long squeal of a chair drawn back in a deliberate manner. "No, of course not," she replied quietly, looking directly into his concerned gaze.

"Sorry to interrupt this tender little reunion, but I've the matter of a hundred things to attend to," Rowland Manning drawled. "To what do I owe the pleasure, Brother dear?"

Elizabeth studied the Earl of Wallace as he advanced toward his half brother. She had thought the earl taller than Rowland, but she realized she had been wrong. While Michael carried the most brawn, it was Rowland who had the advantage in height. Where Michael was a man in his prime, Rowland was gaunt of frame. His cheekbones and jaw were more prominent, his flesh a deeper bronze from the sun.

Rowland was sinewy, harsh splendor to Michael's rugged brute strength.

"Your welcome never fails to amaze, Rowland," Michael said, with a smile just a hint less than it should have been.

"Already tired of playing the bridegroom, are you? Or perhaps you've come to your elder for advice on how to keep your bride happy?"

"Grace sends her compliments," Michael ground out, ignoring him. "And her thanks for aiding one of the dowager's widows."

Elizabeth endured the cool silence of Rowland Manning, surprised he didn't immediately divulge the secret she had just revealed. "It's all right, Mr. Manning. The earl knows the truth; I suspect he just wasn't sure if you did."

Michael's astute gaze traveled from her to Rowland and back again. "I'm sorry, Elizabeth, for what you have suffered. But we are determined to help you. I was chosen to come to you for there are officers keeping watch at Portman Square, and following all of us. Indeed, there are two outside, but—"

She started.

"No, no. You're not to worry. They assume I'm here to see my brother for a horse, most likely. And in fact, I shall decamp to the yards before I leave."

"So kind of you to pay your respects. Perhaps you could shoe one or two while you're here," Rowland said sourly.

Elizabeth had been as shocked as the rest of her friends to learn that Michael had apprenticed as a smithy for Rowland when he'd been just a boy on the run from his aristocratic, disaster-filled past.

Again, Michael ignored the jibe. There was much animosity between the two men—each jostling the other in the soft underbelly of his pride. "Rowland, you are to take part in helping Miss Ashburton and Mrs. Winters depart London."

Rowland half smiled and cocked a brow. "*Miss* Ashburton? No secret cruel husband, then? Just an imaginary spouse? Hmmm. Too bad. I was so counting on another dose of gothic drama. So if you're not a spy or a runaway bride, my guess is you're just a lady in need of a rich nob to pay your gaming debts. Surprised your cooking skills haven't enticed more candidates."

"I knew you liked the fish." Elizabeth smiled smugly as his cool expression changed to a scowl.

Michael darted a glance at her. "I'm sorry, Elizabeth. "I thought he knew—"

"No. It's all right," she insisted.

"And I take it Ashburton is your real name since Michael is using it?" Rowland pressed.

Her face grew warm. "I'm not as creative as you think, Mr. Manning. Of course Ashburton is my name."

"Well, any fool would have changed their name if they were hiding from someone."

"I'm sorry that my capability for deception does not meet your exacting standards," she retorted archly, but bit back the real reason she had kept her name. When Sarah and she had arrived in London nearly destitute, they'd immediately paid a visit to the only person either of them knew—Sarah's mother's godmother, the Dowager Duchess of Helston. Of course, they'd been forced to use Sarah's true name during the introduction and so it had seemed pointless for Elizabeth to assume a different moniker.

Michael hardened his expression and cut in. "Rowland, you are to provide an unexceptional carriage for Miss Ashburton the day after tomorrow as well as a suitable man—not you of course—to play the part of her husband. And this"—he pulled an elaborately braided black-haired wig from the portfolio he carried and handed it to Elizabeth—"is for you."

She inhaled sharply. "And where am I to—" she began.

"The Duke of Beaufort's wedding to our mutual friend, Victoria Givan," the earl finished.

"But it's the last place I should go. Everyone will be there. They're calling it the wedding of the century!" Her stomach clenched in horror.

"Who or what the devil is she trying to avoid?" Rowland's voice was as cold and demanding as a pick hammering at a block of ice.

A frost of silence shivered the air following his blast. The earl slowly withdrew a pouch from his portfolio and spilled the golden contents onto the gleaming wooden table. "For the carriage . . . among other things."

Chapter 5

It was far too much money. Elizabeth now truly was ill. She would never be able to repay her friends. She had no doubt that her friends in the widows club—Grace, Georgiana, Rosamunde, or Ata herself, had provided the combination bribe and payment. "No," she whispered to the earl, "I cannot possibly let you—"

"Oh, yes, you will, Miss Ashburton. I insist." With the sweep of his hand, Rowland pocketed the guineas. "Oh, and Michael? I'll want a second payment in the same amount if this farce plays out without disaster."

"Your gallantry knows no bounds," Michael ground out. "Now, if you will, I require a word with Miss Ashburton. *Alone.*"

Rowland's false smile did not quite reach his mysterious eyes. He finally stood. "Of course. But you shall not dally with Miss Ashburton any longer than ten minutes. As her *abigail*," he drawled with a slight smile curling his lips, "I really cannot allow it." His cool laughter held something more that just mocking. It almost seemed as if his well-hidden sensibilities were bruised for not being asked to stay.

His gleaming boot heels clicked against the parquet flooring as he cleared the carpeting and crossed to the door. He turned at the last moment. "How's that arm healing, Michael?"

The earl straightened, "About as well as your self-esteem, if I had to hazard a guess. You always were a poor shot. You should've stuck to the whip."

Elizabeth bit her lower lip at the tension in the chamber.

Rowland narrowed his eyes. "Seven minutes." The footman shut the door behind Rowland.

Michael turned toward her and grasped her hands. Urgency was evident in his expression. "There are soldiers at every road or path leading out of London. This is the only way. Our friend the Duke of Beaufort has a grand equipage arranged for his wedding to Victoria and he has agreed to help you. Victoria is staying at Ellesmere House. On the way to the wedding, Sarah will attempt to slip unnoticed into Beaufort's own carriage with Victoria while the others enter a myriad of carriages provided by Helston, Ellesmere, and me."

A thousand images and questions formed in her mind, but she allowed Michael to finish.

"When you arrive at St. George's, you and a disguised footman must meander toward the ducal carriage, where you alone must pop inside to join Sarah. That is the only dangerous moment. It is doubtful Pymm's soldiers will dare to search Beaufort's ducal coach as they leave London by way of the main north road. You and Sarah are to stay at Brynlow, my small manor hidden deep in Yorkshire, for now."

"I—I don't know what to say. I can never—"

"Elizabeth, never forget to whom you are speaking. I was in your position not so very long ago. We will find a way, never fear. Although I must admit that our friends, Helston and Ellesmere in particular, are concerned by your lack of proof."

"They doubt me," she said softly. "I do not blame them, I suppose."

He ran his hand through his disheveled locks of brown hair. "I'm sorry, Elizabeth, but as you know, in the eyes of most Englishmen the general is a candidate for sainthood."

She examined her chapped hands. "I know."

Ill at ease, he changed the subject. "I'm so sorry you've been forced to endure Rowland's unwilling, and probably most ungracious, protection."

"No, that's not really true."

"You're not hiding anything from me now, are you? Has he bothered you? There is at least one other female here, isn't there?"

She nodded.

"Remember, I know him. He cannot be fully trusted."

"No. I assure you, he's done nothing to harm me—other than refusing to eat the meals I prepare." When he looked at her with curiosity, she continued. "It was my way of repaying him for hiding me."

"Elizabeth, take care . . . He was born in a rookery, raised by thieves and, uh, unfortunate females. He has the most unconscionable principles—if any scruples at all—especially if a purpose can be better served by using corrupt means."

She had guessed as much. "But his language . . .

aside from his rude oaths, of course . . . his inflection holds none of the signs of poverty."

Michael stared hard at her. "You must have noticed he's an expert chameleon—adopting, changing, to suit every need. He would be equally at home in a den of panderers or Prinny's court. His talent for deception is unparalleled."

"Would it be too forward to ask why he shot you? Was it when you retrieved Grace's fortune?"

"Yes, but there was more to it. He was out to avenge the death of a relation." The earl appeared vastly discomfited to say any more, and for a moment Elizabeth doubted he'd continue. "Few know his mother was a maid at Wallace Abbey. My father, at the age of fifteen—well before he assumed the title, got Rowland's mother with child when she was but sixteen herself. My grandparents turned Maura Manning out without a penny. I don't know how she survived in London without references, but I understood she had some seamstress work, and most likely had to . . . well—"

"I understand," whispered Elizabeth.

The Earl of Wallace flushed. "Howard Manning was born after Rowland. He was the one I accidentally killed while I was trying to rescue a horse he was beating." Michael's hands squeezed hers. "The Mannings had only one good quality as far as I could see, Elizabeth. It was simple blood loyalty. And the day, a decade later, Rowland was forced to understand that Howard was not a relation deserving his fidelity, I think something died in him."

"But what of the blood you share? Why did he not protect you?"

"He saw me as Howard painted me—as a sniveling

young arsonist responsible for burning down Wallace Abbey. He saw me as a murderer and a coward in hiding."

"I'm so glad you were able to learn it was Howard Manning who was responsible," she murmured.

"Elizabeth, you must never forget that where I gained, Rowland lost. I took from him his only estimable quality . . . his ability to trust anyone. He truly is a man without a shred of a heart or any redeeming features, my dear. You know that, don't you?"

"That's not true. He has many good points."

Michael raised one brow in a disconcerting fashion so similar to his half brother that it was comical. "Take care, Elizabeth. Do not conjure up something that is not there. When I apprenticed for him, there was always a trail of very rich, beautiful females" —he appeared vastly uncomfortable—"clamoring after him. God knows why."

She bit her lips to keep from smiling. The two tall, extraordinarily handsome brothers had not the slightest notion—although, on second thought, Rowland Manning most likely knew exactly what he was about even if his more gentle-hearted, noble half brother did not.

He grasped her hands within his own. "Elizabeth, I may have forgiven him for all those years he persecuted me, but I chose to do so because all that went before led me to Grace. And I would willingly go through it again to find her. But none of that blinds me to the fact that my half brother is a black-hearted devil who cares for naught but himself."

"He cares for his horses."

Michael tilted his head and regarded her with grave doubt dripping from his tight expression. "Perhaps."

"And I'm sure he has some sort of kindhearted bond with Mr. Lefroy, if you look past the bluster."

"Oh, my dear"—he shook his head slowly—"don't make that mistake."

"But—"

"Elizabeth, know this. Despite all, I would protect him if it ever came to the point. He is my brother—my elder half brother—and I have everything that should be his if there was any right in this world. My young father loved Rowland's mother. As a child, I sometimes used to hear my father calling for *Maura* late in the night from beyond his private chambers. I did not know until this past spring that Maura was Rowland's mother's name."

"Oh . . . Michael. It's all so wretched."

"It is," he said softly. "And I would not be surprised if there was more to the story. I've often wondered how Rowland survived in the rookery. The only thing I know is that he would be the last person on earth who would ever breathe a word about it to anyone."

Few things in life piqued Rowland's curiosity. It was to be expected. Curiosity was a luxury reserved for those who had time on their hands and money in their pockets.

And yet, for some inexplicable reason, for the first time ever, he left the running of the afternoon auction in Mr. Lefroy's hands. It nearly killed him to do it. At least it was to be a small auction, as the whole of London seemed more interested in attending that bloody wedding of the Duke of Beaufort, better known as the Catch of the Century.

There was no reason for him to attend the nuptials.
He'd been paid to provide a carriage for Elizabeth
Ashburton. And he'd been paid to provide one ec-
static Joshua Gordon, delighted to be elevated from
footman to dandyish false husband of the bewigged
little liar who had lurked in his kitchen all yesterday
with the newly hired cook. Rowland had avoided all
of them like bearers of a plague.

But while he had sat at his desk, groaning from
the weight of bills and accounts, there had been that
damn wedding invitation resting on the farthest
corner, taunting him. The one the Dowager Duchess
of Helston had sent via her own footman.

And so, when he found himself in front of St.
George's for the second time in ten days, he began to
question if he was, indeed, losing his mind.

When he'd set out after Joshua Gordon and Elizabeth Ashburton, he'd had to restrain himself from
looking for the unexceptional carriage in the mob
surrounding the church. He'd come merely as a formality, he told himself, only to more firmly establish
his ties to the respectable Quality; to lull and lure
the most snobbish of the swells to his establishment
versus that of his bloody rival, old Tatts.

There was not the tiniest part of him that admitted
he might have come for another reason. That would
merely beg for disaster.

Under the six great columns supporting the front
pediment of St. George's, a plethora of officers mingled with the beau monde out to impress one another
with their silk, satin, lace, and feathers. The streets
surrounding the church were clogged with carriages
and people straining for the chance to witness the

wedding even more fashionable than the one of the week prior.

He barked at his driver to stop at the outer circle of the crowd, and then descended to make his way on foot. His great height aided his efforts as he barged through the gawkers and other guests to make his way past the twin statues of the marble wolfhounds flanking the grand entrance. Rowland staked a place beside the Dowager Duchess of Helston, who stood with the wedding party in the front of the church.

"I knew you'd come," the tiny lady whispered, a crazy grin decorating her wrinkled face. Her beady black eyes held a multitude of secrets. Out of all of the people he'd met via his half brother, she was the only one whose motives he could not fully decipher.

"Yes, well," he drawled, "I respond well to money."

"Pish. The guineas were for the carriage and well you know it. You did not have to put in a show here. Don't you dare try to fool me, young man."

He stared at her. No one had ever called him a young man. She really was the most confounding old bag of wind.

"May I introduce you to a friend of our family, Mr. Manning?" Without waiting for his response, she continued. "Sir, this is my dearest friend in the world, Mr. John Brown, lately of Scotland—very lately— almost too late if you were to ask me. Oh, I didn't really mean to insinuate that you are late, John. It's the Countess of Home who is . . . oh, botheration." Ata stumbled to a halt.

Brown shook his head and sighed.

The dowager could not seem to hold her tongue.

"Well, if you had chosen to stay at Helston House instead of being one of the house party at the Countess of Home's ostentatious—"

"I told you I'm here conditionally, Ata," Mr. Brown interrupted stiffly.

Rowland sighed. Would the tedious dramas never end?

"We don't have time for any conditions, John," the dowager whispered, her irritation flaring. "Oh, pish. Now I've muddled the introduction. May I present Mr. Manning to you, or are there conditions attached to that too?"

The short, older man had eyebrows as thick and ill tended as a hedgerow, but under them his searching eyes gleamed with shrewd intelligence. Brown bowed slightly and Rowland followed suit. The last time Rowland had seen the old goat had been the night Michael, Helston, Ellesmere, and old Mr. Brown had broken into his study in search of the Countess of Sheffield's bribe payment. Yes, he had come to know the four gentlemen from Portman Square *very well, indeed*, when Rowland had shot Michael during the wee hours.

Ata raised her chin. "You are both to become the best of friends. I shall insist on it."

Mr. Brown had the good sense to keep his mouth shut; only his overgrown brows expressed what he would have liked to say.

Rowland was not so reserved. "*Enchanted*, Mr. Brown," he drawled.

"Likewise," muttered the old Scot, with false cheer in his eyes and cold murder in his heart.

Ata tugged Rowland's coat sleeve until he was forced to lean down while she whispered to Mr.

Brown, "Mr. Manning is here to save Elizabeth if our brilliant plan fails in any way."

"It's unfortunate your age has muddled your mind, ma'am," Rowland said darkly. "I came because *you* invited me." He wondered if there was any way to deter the mad ravings of the old harridan.

"As I was saying, John, Mr. Manning is here to insure her safety. Not that I think for a moment that my plan could in any possible way fail. You see, I've no small amount of experience in setting up clandestine missions entailing much stealth . . ." The dowager's face drained of color. "Oh dear."

"What is it?" Mr. Brown asked quickly.

"Oh dear, oh dear, *oh dear*. It's Sarah," she whispered with much distress.

Rowland casually turned his head and spied the woman who had stood near Elizabeth Ashburton at the last wedding. Her face pale, her gaze trained on the floor, she walked toward them on the arm of a distinguished gentleman.

Rowland shielded the dowager from view. The old woman had not the faintest idea how to go on in these matters.

"John, something has gone awry. Sarah wasn't to leave Beaufort's carriage. She was to wait for—" she squeaked.

"Hush," Rowland interrupted in a harsh whisper.

Mr. Brown glared at him.

"John, do something," she begged. "Something terrible is about to happen. I feel it."

"Lord Wymith is with her," Brown smoothed over. "Give it a moment, Ata. He's taking her to one of the enclosed pews on the far side."

Rowland looked across the aisle only to encounter the hard stares of Helston and Ellesmere, who stood quietly behind the celebrated groom. Their wives sat in the pew behind them as one of them was obviously with child.

All at once the organ music swelled in celebration, and the massive space reverberated with sound.

With the talent of a youth spent in the shadows, Rowland searched the church for possible escape venues. And then he saw *her*.

The damned black wig was slightly askew—very slightly, but God bless her, Elizabeth Ashburton's chin was high and she negotiated the crowd as confidently as a duchess on her way to the well-padded family pew. Only his damned footman might give them away, what with those rounded eyes of his bouncing around in their sockets.

Rowland slowly dipped toward the dowager duchess. "Delighted to inform your worst fears are confirmed, madam," he purred. "And your dream of a heroic rescue? Soon to be dashed too."

"Coward," Mr. Brown replied softly with a huge false smile for the benefit of anyone watching.

The dowager's eyes blazed with vexation. She abruptly brought her cane down on Rowland's foot. "Don't disappoint me, young man."

In the aftermath, Rowland would blame it all on his fool of a footman, who took one look at the only person he knew in the church, Rowland, and made the mistake of leading Elizabeth to stand beside him. Elizabeth stood as still as a statue, her face resolute.

And then the whole bloody affair unfolded like a tawdry black comedy in Drury Lane.

The auburn-haired bride, drenched to the dregs in lace, appeared at the great doors. Uniformly every last chit sighed in rapture as if a bloody miracle were in the making. Or perhaps they sighed over his sodding half brother Michael, who proffered his arm to the bride for support down the aisle.

As Miss Victoria Givan approached her ducal fiancé, the final notes of the music echoed from the high, arched ceiling. The archbishop, presiding over the regal wedding, began the ceremony, his booming voice casting a spell on the elegant crowd.

Moments later a royal entourage encompassing courtly blokes as well as a dozen soldiers and officers spewed through the rear of the church. They stopped short of advancing farther than the last pews.

Rowland dared to look at Elizabeth again, only to find her profile as beautiful and even as he remembered. Never had he seen a woman's face so full of resignation and unwavering courage. Her expression eschewed pity; instead it embraced some sort of hopeless fortitude. She turned her face slightly to acknowledge him. For one brief instant, her glacial mask slipped out of place, and he unwillingly spied the deep recesses of her soul.

A searing blaze of pain burned through the frost encrusting his heart and he tasted bitter fear.

And yet, there was not a single supplication in her expression. Indeed, where there might have been expectation, there was naught but self-reliance. For some curious reason, it moved a tiny particle near his cold heart.

And then, just like a curious case of déjà vu, a murmur passed through the guests, and Rowland's attention was drawn back to the entrance, where General Pymm stood, just as he had a mere week ago, resplendent in his perpetual formal dress. The general, second only to the newly anointed Duke of Wellington, had a way of standing as if he were posing for a sculptor's benefit. Wellington himself appeared moments later only to open wide the door for the bulky form of the Prince Regent to sally forth.

The archbishop was the only one unimpressed with the newest guests, and he continued on, oblivious to the condescension bestowed on the bridal couple and the fervor of royal servants attending to the imperial party.

Rowland glanced at Elizabeth and noticed a tiny vein near her temple beating erratically. His gut clenched. He had the nearly overwhelming albeit ridiculous desire to do something to ease her tension. He sighed, annoyed almost past the point of tolerance.

But really, what did he have to lose? It was not as if anyone would expect decorum from him. If distraction was called for, he could easily provide it with very little loss to himself. He refused to acknowledge that it could very well harm the tender shoots of the more cultivated image he had sought by coming to this damned wedding.

Christ, *what* had she done?

Well, then. When and if the soldiers attempted to close the gap toward her, he would do something so outrageous that all attention would be drawn to him. Surely a few blasphemes in church would not further mar his already eternally damned soul.

At the last moment, he came to his senses. The Duke of Beaufort leaned forward at the conclusion of the vows and swept his new bride into a romantic embrace. But none of the Helston clan watched the couple as they were all staring at him. Expecting him to . . . What on earth?

He wanted no part of this disaster-in-the-making. He didn't even belong here. And he certainly didn't have one bloody reason to save a lying wench with a face capable of slaying thousands. He had problems of his own to solve. Why, he should bundle her under his arm, deliver her to the retinue of officers himself, and demand a reward.

The bridal couple turned to face the congregation. Upon seeing their royal entourage in the rear, the duke and his new duchess bowed and curtsied deeply.

Rowland registered the expression on Pymm's face. The blond general's smile was tight, and his eyes a washed-out blue. The face of London's favorite hero glowed with an ill-concealed, odd excitement.

And then three things happened all at once.

The Duke and new Duchess of Beaufort advanced one step down the aisle. General Pymm advanced one step forward. And finally . . . Elizabeth yanked Rowland's arm so abruptly he involuntarily stumbled into the center of the aisle between the bridal couple and the royal guests.

What the devil? When he stared into her glittering eyes, for the merest half moment, he had the most absurd notion that she was about to jump into his arms.

He was to learn that he had entirely underestimated her.

Chapter 6

This woman, the one who had invaded his dreams from the first day he had found her in his carriage, grasped his neck with both her hands and brazenly, wantonly, and very scandalously pulled him down to meet the softest, sweetest lips he had ever known.

His arms responded despite an orchestra of bells jangling a discordant alarm. Ignoring all, he wrapped himself about her, clasping her tightly to his chest, and kissed her back in the most outrageous, ostentatious fashion imaginable.

If he was going to be involuntarily engaged in this farce, he might as well do it properly. He was nothing if not thorough—and there was something within him that refused to appear the slightest bit unwilling. After all, this was for show, and very easy to enact for there was not an inch of emotions at play—other than the obvious fear her lips betrayed as they trembled against his own.

It was a curious sensation. Long ago he'd made it a rule to avoid kissing. Rutting was altogether another matter when he chose it. As the years had rolled by, it became something he did not choose unless he could not help it. And it irritated the hell out of him. There were days, nay weeks, he felt apart from the rest of the world—almost soulless.

In some distant chamber of his mind, the scornful roar of shocked whispers finally registered.

She finally broke off the kiss, turning her face to his lapel. Yet she did not loosen her tight grip on his neck. It was as if she couldn't yet face the magnitude of what she had done.

"Dare I mention that we are not alone?" he whispered with a tinge of dry humor. "Not that I'm complaining, you understand."

Her hot breath fanned over his cheek.

"Manning? Oh, Mr. Manning, my dear fellow," the amused voice of the Prince Regent called out. "Do take your, ahem, lady bird and yourself off now. You've made it abundantly clear you're not yet well enough trained to be let loose on polite society. Wellington, do fetch my snuffbox. And Pymm, I need you."

The Duke of Wellington, obviously annoyed at playing the lapdog, immediately acceded to the royal order, and Pymm's obsequious bow played to Prinny's vanity while his tight smile proved his fury.

Helston and Ellesmere advanced behind Rowland as the rest of the church guests held their breath, hoping and praying there would be more to this rich scene; the retelling of which would enliven their entertainments for years to come.

"Be a good fellow, Manning," Helston insisted quietly, "and do as His Majesty commands. Here now, Ellesmere and I shall escort you."

Rowland heard little for Elizabeth had finally raised

her stark eyes to meet his, and in a rush he gathered her arm and placed it on top of his forearm. "Make yourself scarce," he muttered to Joshua Gordon, the most feckless footman in all of creation.

He escorted Elizabeth down the center aisle toward the exit, not waiting for the two blasted lords to help him. He could feel her desire to go the other direction as they neared the royal trio, but he would not allow it. They halted in front of the Prince Regent and made a courtly bow and curtsy before easing away.

The prince's voice stopped them. "Oh, Manning? Do tell me, since you're so conveniently here anyway, who shall win the Royal Ascot Gold Cup? I shall forgive you your vulgar display if you tell me true."

"Eventide Vespers, Your Majesty. *My* horse, of course."

"And who is your saucy minx?" the Prince Regent fixed his watery gaze on Elizabeth.

"You cannot possibly expect me to divulge the name of *both* my prized mares, can you, Your Majesty?"

Prinny laughed at the outrageously fatuous remark and then languidly waved a hand in the air. "Off with you, and your raven-haired baggage, too. But I would have a word with you next week."

Her hand was clawing his arm like a cat on a high perch above a howling dog.

As they passed Pymm, the general stepped away and spoke quietly in Elizabeth's direction, "I shall wait on Mrs. Winters this afternoon, *wherever* she may be residing. I would be *delighted* if you make up our party."

Elizabeth's gaze swiveled toward her friend, who stood a mere two pews from them. Sarah's face was resigned and held not a hint of fear. But then, Sarah had never fully believed Pymm capable of performing the cruelties Elizabeth suggested. Sarah had only insisted on standing by her, and following her when she was determined to run away and return to England.

Elizabeth indicated her assent to Pymm with the smallest bob of her head. And then they were outside, and Rowland Manning was pushing past the crowds on the steps of St. George's, past the morass of carriages, until she could finally breathe again.

He stopped before the simple conveyance that had brought her here. Just two words crossed his lips as he opened the door. "Get in."

Elizabeth Ashburton did as he bade, without comment. He closed the door, leaving her alone in the darkness of the curtained interior. The bark of an order met her ears.

"Give me the ribbons, Jonesy. I'm driving."

The carriage glided forward without the usual jolt.

God . . . Elizabeth felt the hot burn of tears threaten to spill over her lashes and used her father's old trick. She pressed her tongue to the top of her palate as firmly as she could until she stopped trembling.

Her heart was pounding so furiously she was certain she would see it if she looked. She felt as wretched as the day she had learned her father was dead.

So was it all for naught? The long journey from Spain to England, the hiding for two years, the endless secrecy? She fell against the leather squabs of the carriage and twisted the small handkerchief she'd found in her pocket. God, she hated the powerlessness of being a woman.

Elizabeth gave herself up to the cyclone of thoughts she had so assiduously held at bay for all these many months, and failed to take notice of the direction they took. It was not until the carriage halted as smoothly as it had started that she wondered where he had taken her.

The door opened and sunlight spilled into the darkness. Elizabeth stared at the hand waiting for hers.

She grasped it finally, and he helped her from the carriage before nodding to the driver. "Return in half an hour, Jonesy."

"Sir." The ginger-haired man nodded respectfully and snapped the ribbons above the twin bays, which instantly set off.

Elizabeth glanced about to find that they were at the edge of a large stand of trees near a river—the River Thames, it appeared. "Where are we?" she murmured.

"Who are you?" he spoke quietly, so unlike his usual harsh demands.

"You already know who I am."

"No. *Who are you?*"

She held her gaze steady on his face. "Just a girl—like a thousand others." She paused, but then felt compelled to continue when she realized he would not speak again. He was waiting and with such a look on his face that she did not doubt he would wait for all of eternity until she answered to his satisfaction. "Just a girl whose father loved her very much. A girl who was not worthy of his affection . . . Just an undeserving girl who cannot make up her mind what to do."

"You," he said, shaking his head, "can't make up your mind? Why, you are the single most obstinate, capable female I've ever had the displeasure to know. Now, we will start again. Who are you?"

She sighed. "Miss Elizabeth Ashburton."

His eyebrows rose a notch. "And your parents?"

"My mother died giving birth to me," she began.

"And who was your father?"

"George Richard Ashburton, captain of a company within a Light Division that served in the Peninsula."

"I knew you were a spy."

"Have you always had this odd fixation regarding spies?" She shook her head. "Don't be ridiculous."

He ignored her. "Well, what in bloody hell are you, then? Why is Pymm sniffing after you like a beggar before a bakery? And what did you mean to gain by that lunatic scene?"

She stiffened. But really, at this point, she had so little to lose by telling him a portion of her past. A small portion. "He insists we're betrothed." The words tasted bitter on her tongue. "And I want nothing of him. I'm sorry, but the temptation for a reprieve proved too great. I guessed Pymm's pride would forbid him to say a word in my direction after I—I kissed you so publicly."

For the first time in their short acquaintance, Rowland Manning was caught speechless. He finally recollected himself. "You stole the peacock's bloody pocket watch, didn't you?"

She looked away, incapable of playing along with any sort of humor. "Look, I realize how ridiculous it must appear to you. Obviously I've no dowry, nothing in particular to recommend. And he's so very rich, and soon to be a duke. But, well, there you have it."

"Uh, I think you are forgetting the part about how he is a goddamn, bloody, sodding *national hero*." His voice rose with each word. "Or did you not know he delivered Boney's hat to the crown, along with a pair of golden French eagles?"

She said not a word.

"All right. I see I shall have to take your word that old sober sides offered for you. Now you will tell me why, God bless it, you haven't seized the opportunity of a lifetime. You'd be a bloody duchess in less than a month's time. Set up forever like a queen. Rings on your fingers, bells on your toes, dining with kings, embroidering cushions for fat fannies or doing whatever the hell ladies do at court—"

"If you see all the advantages, then why don't you marry him?" The last she nearly hissed.

He laughed heartily. "I would if I bloody could. Come now, what is this really about? Because if you think to suggest you'd prefer peeling rotted vegetables in my bloody kitchen to sorting jewels as Pymm's duchess, well—"

"Has anyone ever told you that you blaspheme far too much? It ruins the effect. You might try to limit your oaths to one every other phrase instead of *every* phrase, Mr. Manning."

He stared hard at her. "Why the devil won't you marry him?"

She should have known that trying to converse with him about this would be next to impossible.

"Perhaps I do not think he could make me happy or I, him."

He rocked on his heels and made an exasperated sound as he removed his hat and dragged his hand through his hair—and for a moment she was reminded of his half brother.

"And what does *happiness* have to do with it?" He spoke the word with exaggerated disdain. "Dear God, don't tell me you're a romantic? I would think life following the militia would have cured you of such nonsense."

"I've never been a romantic."

"Well, since you've no one to explain it to you, allow me to enlighten you on how marriage works. You must think of it like breeding horses. The mares are kept strictly away from the stallions during courtship. The owners, or parents if you will, carefully consider the bloodlines, the value of the potential mates, the robustness and likelihood of offspring. Only then is it decided if it will be a good coupling. Unless of course, as in your case, you have a winner of a horse who is full of himself and has broken down his stall to get to a mare's scent that's driving him mad. But what is not part of the consideration is *goddamned, bloody happiness*. For those who desire such fleeting illusions, my dear, that is sought in a completely different paddock." He paused. "After the heir is got."

"You appear to know all about it," Elizabeth replied.

"Of course I do. Into whose paddocks do you think those titled, well-used mares jump?"

While it was obvious he tried to give an appearance

of wickedness in his smile, Elizabeth saw something darker—harder.

He exhaled with annoyance. "You're missing the point. For Pymm's astounding fortune, surely you can overlook a few tiny irritations such as his grandiose ideas of his own importance, his boorish, lecturing tendencies, and his, uh, less than polished wit. But, really, you should endure him even if he whinnies through his nose."

"I cannot." She closed her eyes briefly and then stared past him toward the fast-moving river.

"Why?"

And with that gently spoken word, she wavered, and prayed she would not actually be foolish enough to place her trust in him. But she could not stop herself from telling him, for she had a long history of misjudging others. In her indecision, she produced a nonsensical phrase she barely knew she spoke aloud. "I have no proof . . ."

"Of what?"

"You won't believe me."

"Try me."

"No."

He grasped her arms and forced her to encounter his hard gaze. "Enough. Tell me."

"No."

"Why not?"

"Because you're a hard-hearted blackguard, without a single shred of trust or compassion in your bullying hide."

He arched a brow. "And that matters why?"

"I don't know," she said brokenly. She knew she was babbling now, forming not a word of sense.

"Where is the girl with the fire in her belly? The one who has men eating out of her hand? The one who makes *me* eat out of her hand?" he asked slyly.

"She's tired." She sank to the ground, the earthy scent of the summer grasses almost comforting. Elizabeth gave in to the enigmatic look on his rigid face above her. "My father refused the general's offer because I asked him to. You see, at first I thought Leland Pymm everything noble and courageous, yet as time passed I thought I saw glimpses of an odd and sometimes cruel man behind the façade. I believe I misjudged him initially." She inhaled sharply, and said disjointedly, "Less than a week after the refusal, my father and Sarah's husband were killed at the siege of Badajoz. I believe Pymm had a hand in it."

He grasped her arms and forced her to stand. "Really?"

"I knew you wouldn't believe it," she said, unable to keep the peevish tone from her voice.

"No. It's just I had no idea old Pymm had it in him—never thought he'd like someone as much as he likes himself. A bit gothic, isn't it?"

"I told you it's something I can never prove."

"I'm sorry, but I fear I've missed something," he said. "Why haven't you just told the sodding goat to go to hell? Tell him you don't want the piles of money he would lavish on you, or his bloody title. This is the nineteenth century, not the Middle Ages, is it not? I'm beginning to think you're the one who is . . . Christ, he didn't ravish you, did he? Ruin you for . . ."

Her heart melted a little. He did not once question her certainty of Pymm's guilt, despite her complete lack of evidence.

It meant everything to her. Even Sarah had had grave reservations, and in her heart, Elizabeth feared her friends were helping her despite their own serious doubts as well. Sarah, and Ata, and all of her friends were loyal to a fault.

"Of course he did not ravish me. Don't you think my father taught me how to defend my virtue? I know where a man's vulnerable parts are."

His lips were trembling, and she very much feared it was with laughter.

"I won't forgive you if you laugh at me right now."

A wicked smile curved his lips but not a sound escaped. "So . . . what sort of hold does he have on you, Elizabeth?"

"I did not give you leave to use my Christian name."

His silent mocking smile was all she was to receive.

"I've told you everything of importance," she insisted quietly. "Now, let go of me."

"Or what?" he murmured. "About to breach my vulnerable parts, are you?"

"No. Yours are not in the usual place."

He gaped at her. "Really? And just where are they?"

She looked up at the hardened planes of his lean face—a face that gave away nothing and wanted nothing. Here stood a human island buffeted by the winds of his ruinous past.

And she took a chance.

All at once she stood on her tiptoes and gently, oh-so-gently, brushed her lips against his firm mouth. "Here," she whispered.

He exhaled roughly with a hiss.

"And here," she continued, pressing her lips against the hollow of his faintly whiskered cheek. She pulled back slightly to examine his reaction.

He stood as expressionless and still as a sentry at St. James Palace. Only his eyes tracked her.

She pressed another kiss on his neck and felt his Adam's apple bob. It was the only sign that she had breached the emotional landscape of a man who had formed private walls more secure than any fortress. She suspected he revealed himself to no one, not even to himself. It was the effect of grave deprivation in his childhood, something that could never be overcome. Yet she offered tenderness in the face of such stark austerity of emotions. Her hands barely touched him as they moved toward his taut belly—the root of his hunger.

He immediately stilled her fingers as they gently brushed the buttons of his gray silk waistcoat.

"Wrong paddock," he whispered softly and put her from him.

Mortified by his incorrect assumption, she took a step back. But he followed her, his eyes hard and fixed on her. Without knowing, she found herself backed against a towering oak. He reached for her face, and she swallowed. Yet it was not a caress he sought to give. With gentleness, he disengaged the long forgotten itchy black wig from her head. "This is a goddamn travesty," he murmured, while he pulled the pins from her hair, which she'd tried to flatten and hide. In silence he worked until he extracted the last pin and then he ran his fingers through her loosened locks to massage her aching scalp. It was all she could do not to moan with gratitude.

"I'm very sorry for involving you in that awful scene at St. George's," she whispered.

"It doesn't matter. You can't say I was surprised," he replied. "Weddings do have the damnedest effect on you."

She wanted to weep for his magnanimous attitude. The gentlemen she knew would have rung a peal for involving them in such a shameful scene.

He stroked her cheeks while he cradled her head, heat gathering in his pale eyes, darkening them. One thumb dropped slightly to caress her slightly parted lips. Her breath caught.

And in the blink of an eye his expression changed— his shuttered expression gave way just the merest bit. He cursed softly and leaned his forehead against hers.

She lowered her gaze only to find his great chest drawing in air repeatedly. He seemed to be fighting some sort of decision.

And then, all at once, he closed the distance and dipped down. She could feel his harsh exhalation on her cheek as his lips found hers, and a feeling of intense awareness of the man holding her rushed through her. He bent his knees and shifted his powerful arms to gather her close—his broad chest pressed against her breasts, causing an ache within her.

He groaned and held her as if to provide shelter from a tempest; as if he would guard her with his life.

Dear God above. He was *kissing* her—not like the show in church, or her tentative gesture of tenderness. This was a transferal of emotion.

His mouth teased hers with unforgettably tender yet masculine thoroughness; tasting her, caressing her lips until she relinquished all control. He nipped at the seam of her lips and instinctively she opened to him—making herself vulnerable to him for the first time. His tongue twined with her own while his hands pulled the small of her back more tightly against his strong body. His hands swept lower to cup her bottom more firmly to him, making her very aware of an immense ridge pressing against her.

She was overwhelmed by the raw passion coursing between them. Never had she felt such white heat. But then again, she had only ever been kissed twice in her life—and never had it involved such raw carnality. This was not a proper kiss. This was everything forbidden to a virtuous female. It was everything she should run from. Her feet refused to move.

He had sworn not to do this. His tightly banked desire and emotions were not ever to run amok. He lived by a simple, rigid code of conduct, and he would not be swayed. And yet . . . this tall glass of femininity was dissolving every single last one of his solid rules. It appalled him how easily she got under his skin; the ache in his ballocks radiated, setting every bloody inch of him on fire for her.

It had been decades since he'd truly tasted a woman's lips. A joining of the essential parts when he chose, yes. But this. This taste of everything delicious was the very thing that could lead to ruination.

Christ, she was so sweet, so innocent, and she unleashed a ravenous hunger for tenderness, for touch, for taste, for something so primal and so necessary. For something he refused to acknowledge.

He crushed her to him, reveling in her clean, warm bouquet of freshly milled soap and the softness of her skin. She was the balm for all the harshness in his life. And the honey-warm taste of her tempted him beyond anything he'd known.

She knew next to nothing of kissing. Her lips and her movements were uncertain, soft as a nymph's wings trailing against a petal, and just as fragile. Christ, he was waxing sentimental like a bloody, sodding poet.

She did not shy away from anything he demanded. She allowed him to guide her slender long arms about his neck. She had made no protest as he touched her and tasted her, giving herself so generously. Tangling himself in her silken charms, he momentarily forgot every last one of his hard-won principles.

And he did it with relish—with joy.

The unmistakable sound of someone clearing his throat rended the air. Breathlessly, they broke away from each other and she swung about to the other side of the thick tree trunk.

"Jonesy?" he rasped. "Your timing is bloody impeccable."

"Just as you taught me, sir."

He edged around the rough bark of the tree and whispered one particularly choice raw curse as he awkwardly rearranged the damned massive evidence of his arousal for her. "Come, Miss Ashburton," he said, disgusted by his momentary loss of wits. He offered his arm, and she placed her hand atop it, allowing him to stiffly lead her to the plain carriage. He handed her in and she waited in expectation of his entering the carriage too. She was to be disappointed.

"Where would you like Mr. Jones to take you, then?"

"I have a choice?"

"We all have choices, Elizabeth."

"Are you not getting into this carriage?"

He eyed her shrewdly. "No. I've my own affairs to see to, as do you."

She paused, a faint blush cresting her pretty cheeks. "So, you are letting me go? I'm no longer in your debt, even after today's debacle?"

He gave a curt nod.

"But my affairs . . ."

"Will be brought to you."

"But the new cook—I promised that I'd help her the first day and . . ."

Perhaps if she had hinted—had said just one word of what had passed between them, he would have hesitated. But merely for a moment. He glanced at Jonesy trying mightily to disregard the pair of them with his breathy whistling. "Take her to Portman Square—the long way around. To Helston House. The lady has an engagement."

He glanced at her out of the corner of his eye. Her face drained of color at the double entendre. He turned away to casually collect her forgotten wig from the ground. He passed it to her, along with the pins, taking care not to touch her hands. He then closed the carriage's door firmly and stepped away.

A small voice inside Elizabeth's mind told her it might very well be the last she ever saw of the most misunderstood man in England. He was as confounding as a sly fox during a hunt. But then, who was she to fully understand him or any man? Had she not already demonstrated that she was the very worst judge of character the world had ever known?

Chapter 7

Rowland Manning stared beyond the whorls of dust left by the departing carriage only to see the mudflats of his childhood in front of him. All thoughts of the beautiful woman who was capable of leveling all his scruples with just one taste of her fled at the scene before him. He squinted against the sun to see them.

The mudlarks. The children and old women, bedraggled, in rags and sackcloth caps, were looked upon as pecking birds, not worthy of even being considered human. He inhaled sharply.

Why in hell had he thought to bring her here? He had sworn never to come back. Without knowing, he walked toward the embankment. The river was at its lowest ebb in the never-ending cycle of the tides, the timetables of his childhood.

Christ. The children looked far smaller and scrawnier than he remembered. But then, he had been that same size, most likely. No. He had always been far larger than the others. Born from superior stock, his mother had always said.

Born of a strong aristocratic sire, unlike Howard or Mary.

He pinched the bridge of his nose as the stench of the oozing muck reached his nostrils. It was said that every evidence of sin and the transience of life could be found at the bottom of the River Thames. Only the lowest wretches eked out an existence by dredging through it in search of lost coal and anything of value.

He looked down at his hands and exhaled. He'd never forget the sensation of the slippery muck. All at once he was dizzy and nauseous and remembered he'd not eaten this morning in his rush to witness the scene at St. George's. His legs carried him away from the riverbank, until he realized he'd walked all the way back to the stables, so far and so fast that he forgot all about his breakfast, if not his wretched past.

Elizabeth touched her kiss-swollen lips with the tip of her finger as the carriage moved ever closer to Helston House. She'd had no idea a kiss could engage such a tumult of emotions in her breast. She'd completely lost her bearings when he'd taken her within the circle of his arms. It was as if, for a few minutes of time, there had been only the two of them in the world—and only a purity of happiness between them. Her breasts ached to feel his hard chest against them. She had been lost in his arms and had completely cut loose the multitude of fears that weighed so heavily on her. She had tasted passion, tasted hope.

All impossibly poignant thoughts flew from her mind at the sight of two scarlet-coated officers just past the carriage window. Elizabeth supposed she had always known it would be only a matter of time before she would have to face the man who had been obsessed with her for so long.

And yet, as the small carriage drew near the magnificent Corinthian-columned frontage of Number Twelve Portman Square, her courage failed nearly as fast as her hastily rearranged coiffure. She repinned a loose lock and smoothed the lovely simple blue silk gown Ata had given her the first fortnight she and Sarah had dared to call on the dowager duchess with the vaguest of connections. And here Elizabeth was again, depending on the dowager and other people who had no reason to help her.

Upon spying her descent from the carriage, one of the pair of mounted soldiers moved toward her. She hurried up the white marble stairs, but stopped midstep.

Just like that, she realized she was through with running and hiding. She turned and had the temerity to wave at the man. Surprised, he halted his horse in front of Helston House and dipped his head. She sedately climbed to the landing, where the door opened before she could even raise the knocker.

As Elizabeth stepped inside, Sarah rushed down the grand curved staircase and flew into her arms. The gentlest, kindest lady—one part best friend to two parts wise older sister—embraced her. Elizabeth pulled back finally to drink in the sight of Sarah's fine gray eyes and sweet smile. Just behind her, Elizabeth spied Mr. John Brown and the handsome gentleman who had escorted Sarah in St. George's, as well as the dowager duchess, carrying her little brown dog, all of whom descended the staircase in a decidedly more sedate fashion.

"Oh, Eliza, I hope you've not come out of misplaced fear for me," Sarah murmured. "But in my heart, I admit . . ."

"Yes?" Elizabeth said, laughing and yet with tears in her eyes.

"I'm so glad you're here. I've longed to make certain you were unharmed. Ah, what a fine kettle of fish we've brought down upon us, dearest."

"Not we. I," Elizabeth returned.

Ata tottered forward, her little dog snugly tucked under her arm. "I assured Sarah you would come and then we would make sense of all of this. I really never liked the idea of running away or hiding. It never solves anything." The dowager eyed Mr. Brown with a curious mixture of embarrassment and annoyance.

"Yes, ma'am." Elizabeth bobbed a polite curtsy before the older woman pulled her sleeve, insisting on a kiss on her wrinkled cheek.

Mr. Brown shook her hand warmly, and whispered loud enough for everyone to hear. "My dear, don't listen to Ata. I assure you that running away is a perfectly acceptable thing to do."

"Well!" Ata appeared ready to say something much stronger, but held her tongue. This was a first. There was something very wrong with the way Ata looked at Mr. Brown, and the way Mr. Brown regarded Ata. It was as if Ata did not know precisely what to do or say.

"Elizabeth," Ata finally continued, "come, I must introduce you to the Earl of Wymith, Beaufort's good friend and neighbor in Derbyshire. Lord Wymith, may I present Mrs., no, *Miss* Elizabeth Ashburton to you? I'm so sorry, Elizabeth, I'm still having a difficult time remembering that you were never married."

"No, I'm so sorry I did not tell you the truth straightaway, when first we met."

The tall gentleman's brown eyes twinkled as he bowed over her hand. "Delighted to meet the lady inclined to set General Leland Pymm on his ear."

"Now, Wymith, we'll have none of that . . . yet," Ata said.

"Where is everyone else?" Elizabeth asked softly.

Sarah grasped her hand as if she was afraid of losing sight of her. "They are at the breakfast celebration for the Duke and new Duchess of Beaufort, to determine if anyone other than Pymm recognized you in that wig. Mr. Brown suggested it."

"No," Ata said, petulantly. "It was my idea. I'm very adept at intrigue and I instinctively knew we should try to infiltrate to learn all we could."

Mr. Brown's long-suffering sigh spoke volumes.

Elizabeth studied the expressions of everyone before her. "And General Pymm?"

"He's waiting for you in the drawing room above stairs, Eliza," Sarah murmured, her face pale and drawn.

Lord Wymith gazed at Sarah with great warmth in his expression, and offered his arm to her. "Mrs. Winters, I beg you to take my arm."

Elizabeth watched Sarah's shy countenance as she accepted the handsome gentleman's support. Ah, so that was the way things stood. In the short span of days she had disappeared, the world had spun on, time constantly shifting the state of affairs for all. Even Sarah, the most constant variable in Elizabeth's life, had found solace in someone new, Lord Wymith.

Ata's one gnarled hand stayed Elizabeth's resolution to face Pymm. "Elizabeth, we have but a moment, my dear. Luc, Quinn and Michael have tasked me with informing—not that I ever needed their permission, you understand—well, you are not to accept the general's suit under any circumstances. That is," she paused, uncertain, "unless you truly desire it. We will of course stand by whatever decision you choose."

Mr. Brown edged closer. "Do what is in your heart, lass."

"Words to live by," Ata muttered darkly.

"Perhaps I should return to the Countess of Home's townhouse," Mr. Brown replied, staring at Ata.

"Do what is in your heart, old man," Ata muttered.

Sarah intruded in her patient way before daggers were drawn. "Elizabeth, you do not have to go to him."

Ata continued, turning her back on Mr. Brown. "Yes. What do we care that the general is a decorated war hero and veteran? Did you hear about the palace he is planning to build next to Wellington's? Everyone's taken to calling it Number *Two*, since Wellington's taken Number One, London. It smells of unoriginality, it does, and no one can like that." The dowager's sympathy was evident in her farfetched attempt to tarnish Pymm.

The thing was, the general appeared as perfect as a summer day such as this one. And the kindly dowager was searching far and wide to cloud his character, to make Elizabeth's actions appear less ridiculous. It was an example of one of the many reasons Elizabeth had come to love Ata. None of the militia's daughters or wives, except Sarah, had ever befriended her. Indeed, she'd been branded an audacious, headstrong girl to be avoided. Those women had banded against her the day she'd donned a pair of breeches to ride astride on a long march instead of enduring the jostling carts with the other women. Elizabeth just could not bear to disappoint the only ladies who had ever accepted her in their circle.

"Honestly," Ata continued, "the general has no idea that he is nothing compared to my dear Wellington. I refuse to allow him to win me over, despite his excellent manners this last week."

"Ata, he is still wholly responsible for the success o' the final drive against the frogs," Mr. Brown said, a hint of his Scottish brogue in evidence. "Never forget that. The rest of our countrymen have not. And they love him because he is notorious for leading divisions into battle, and not sitting on a hill and watching it unfold."

"Yes, well, he probably only got into the thick of it when the odds were overwhelmingly in his favor." Uncertainty washed over Ata's expression, making her all the more argumentative. "And shouldn't generals stand at a distance to watch and redirect little groups of men as needed?"

Mr. Brown stared at the dowager stiffly. "Little groups? It's not like a quilting circle, Ata."

It made Elizabeth sad to see Ata and her Mr. Brown still at odds. Apparently, for five decades they had sparred during a never-resolved dance of denied attraction.

"Your Grace," Lord Wymith said, coming to Mr.

Brown's aid, "even the Prince Regent has suggested Wellington could not have chased Napoleon across the Pyrenees without Pymm." He paused and turned to Elizabeth. "Can this general be as terrible as you've suggested? Did you witness . . ."

"No . . . And I could be entirely wrong. Really, it would be no great surprise if I were." Elizabeth glanced steadily at each of her friends—new and old.

"He said he had his officers looking for you because he felt obligated to return your father's affairs," Ata said, uncertainty in her voice. "He has a very pretty way with words. In fact, this is the second letter delivered to you this week. I'm sorry we took the liberty of opening it, but it arrived without a name . . ."

Elizabeth quickly unfolded the note.

Dearest love,

My God, the sight of you . . . It was all I could do not to fly to you. What I would not give to hold you in my arms again. My darling love, you are lovelier than any of the images I carried with me the last many months without you. Soon, soon we will be together and no one shall ever part us again—not for a minute, for I mean to have you beside me forever and a day.

P.

Elizabeth forced herself to address all the anxious faces surrounding her. "It's all right. I've taken my decision. I think I've known all along what I would do."

They all started, and began talking.

Ata won out. "Whatever you decide, we will follow through. Grand wedding, grand escape."

"I'm tired of hiding, Ata," she murmured, her sadness escalating.

The petite lady heaved a sigh of what appeared to be great relief. "Well, still . . . whatever you decide. I'm very good at planning weddings, you know. We will—"

"Hello, Elizabeth." The voice echoed from above them and they all glanced up. Pymm stood at the gilt railing in all his magnificent regalia, his scarlet coat encrusted with such medals, ribbons and gold braid signifying a great warrior in his prime, enjoying success at his leisure. Sunlight from a round window above scattered across him, leaving him bathed in golden light, his blond hair dazzling.

"I require your presence now, if you please." His voice commanded in the same odd fashion as always, cracking to a different pitch on the occasional syllable, as if he were regressing to the higher voice of his boyhood. It caused a shiver to wend its way down her spine.

Ata's mouth clamped shut. It was the first time Elizabeth had witnessed the dowager effectively silenced. As the group began to move to the stair, one last word floated down.

"I would beg a private interview."

They all paused, discomfited by his request.

"I beg your pardon," the general chuckled, a smile carved from his thin lips. "I, of course, do not mean to imply that one of her friends should not accompany her. Propriety must be ensured, especially for a future duchess. Mrs. Winters?"

"Of course, sir," Sarah replied, her voice clear.

Elizabeth and Sarah ascended slowly, Ata's whispered words following them, "A tea tray shall be ordered, and . . ." Eliza heard no more.

The touch of Leland Pymm's very white gloved fingers unnerved Elizabeth as he bent over her hand before leading her beyond the frescoed gallery into the most formal drawing room of the famous residence. The Duke of Helston's spirit emanated from every last detail in the ancient yet elegant Graeco-Roman–inspired room.

Pymm indicated a high-backed chaise with gilt serpents supporting dark chocolate cushions. Eliza sank into the corner as the general's determined eyes and languid hand motioned Sarah toward the front-facing windows at the other end of the long room filled with antiquities of generations of Helstons. Sarah's eyes offered a silent apology to her friend.

He arranged himself and the plumage of his regimentals on the same chaise, far too close for comfort.

He began quietly. He always did. "My dearest Elizabeth," he said, his upper lip pursed in a weak fashion. "I am impressed by your efforts, my dear. You have no idea how much I delight in a good chase."

"So happy I could oblige," she said, her voice strained. She forced herself to look him full in the face. Had she ever thought him remotely handsome? Oh, he was well-enough formed. Indeed, many women following Pymm's divisions had been attracted to the gleam of his blond hair and his blue eyes. Yes, appearance was such a deceptive quality.

As she examined him now, she wondered what was beyond the smirk of his half smile.

"What? No conversation? No more outrageous games? Hmmm. But you know how much I always liked your fire. Although I would insist that you not incense me by kissing the scum of the earth ever again." He laughed awkwardly. "But I suspect I shall miss that playful nature of yours when we are wed."

"You are too fast, sir," she whispered. "I've not yet given you my consent."

"No? I rather thought you did when you walked into this house."

She knew it would go better if she did not incense the beast straightaway. And so she bit her lip to keep from blurting out that the only reason she was here was that it had been obvious that he would follow and keep Sarah under his watch until Elizabeth appeared.

She looked beyond his shoulder to see Sarah suddenly smile; her face lit by the sun streaming through a far window. Sarah drew closer to the sill, her hand resting on the deep brown velvet drapery trimmed with a Greek key pattern.

Elizabeth fended off Leland Pymm by playing to his vanity, for his success was his favorite topic. "You are to be congratulated, sir. I understand the Prince Regent is giving an event in your honor at Carlton House, where the duchy will be conferred."

Pymm lifted his square jaw, and lowered his heavy eyelids slightly. "You heard correctly. And you shall have an excellent view of the proceedings for you shall be by my side, my dear. As my beautiful new—"

The door to the drawing room opened without the preamble of a discreet knock. The man who was determined to confuse her until the end of time entered, carrying the largest tea service she had ever seen. Elizabeth half rose before she saw Leland Pymm's hand, reaching to stop her. She dodged his touch and quickly sat back down.

"Ah, what have we here?" Pymm asked with ill humor. "A *bastard* come to serve us? The same spawn who had the audacity to kiss a lady in church?"

Rowland Manning, a white damask napkin decorating his arm, set the enormous silver tray down on the low table with expert flare and the merest bit of sloshing of the milk. Only one biscuit tumbled from the highest plate of the tiered silver stand.

"Actually, *she* kissed me," Rowland said, without even a sliver of a gentlemanly attempt to defend her behavior. "I had very little to do with it."

Pymm's voice rose. "Can't Helston do any better in the hiring of servants?"

Rowland silently strode to the fire grate and picked up a massive winged chair as if it weighed but a feather and carried it over his head to plunk it down right beside her. He perched on the end of it like a delicate debutante.

"Helston can, and he does," Rowland said. "But you see, he has the damnedest old hatchet-faced crone for a grandmother, and well . . . who am I to say, but she seems to scare off the help in droves. Droves, I tell you." He splashed a dollop of tea into a dish, and looked at Pymm with an innocent expression.

An irritated shuffling noise came from beyond

the door, and Elizabeth bit her lip to keep from laughing—or perhaps it was to keep from crying. Her nerves shredded, she pressed her palms together.

Pymm cleared his throat. "I would ask you to leave us, Manning. I have something very particular I want to discuss with Miss Ashburton."

"Really? Let's hear it."

"Confound it, man. Go away. You're not wanted here."

Rowland ignored him. "Sugar, Miss Ashburton? Or let's see. We also have honey—an unusual choice. Milk?"

"Leave off, Manning," Pymm warned quietly.

"Impatient, General? Have no fear, you're next. You can use the time by considering whether or not you would like a plain biscuit or one of these"—he sniffed the tray with disdain dripping from him—"chocolate affairs."

"I don't want any blasted tea," the general retorted.

"Suit yourself," Rowland replied. He then turned to look at her expectantly, the small silver milk pitcher in midair.

"Milk, please," she said. "No sugar."

"Really? No, I think you should have sugar, Miss Ashburton. I've not forgotten your fondness for sweets such as *gingerbread*, you see." She watched his full lips form the smallest smile as he placed enough spoonfuls in her tea to make a West Indies sugar-cane plantation owner happy for a decade. He handed it to her with a gesture that was extraordinarily feminine.

She had the hysterical urge to laugh in the face of

the tension in the horrid room. The Earl of Wallace had the right of it. Rowland Manning was the greatest chameleon, mimicking the actions of a grand hostess. And yet, his eyes were like a black panther's—in a roomful of rabbits.

"Oh, Mrs. Winters, do join us, won't you?" Rowland curled his little finger as he poured another cup. "My dear, I simply must insist. Come, I think I can guess exactly how you take your—"

"Enough!" Pymm roared.

Rowland stopped pouring. "Oh . . . perhaps you're right. That is a bit too much tea in the cup. Come, Mrs. Winters."

Sarah moved forward and accepted the tea, amusement showing in her face.

"Oh, do let me get a chair for you." Again Rowland crossed to the grate, only this time he paused before returning with a delicate rocking chair. "Hmmm. This will not do. General, you are going to have to sit over here since you refused tea. Mrs. Winters cannot possibly drink while seated in this sort of chair. Far too messy a business."

Leland Pymm's face became contorted with a sea of fury. Waves of anger clashed with unrestrained annoyance. Yes, this was how Elizabeth remembered his face the time she had secretly spied him berating a young drummer boy who had lost his brother in an earlier battle. It was the incident that had solidified all her growing fears about the general.

Sarah stood patiently before Leland Pymm, until with extreme exasperation, the general gave up his place on Elizabeth's chaise.

But while Pymm was humorless and narcissistic,

he was not without tactics. He eased the anger back behind a mask, and waited until Rowland had worn himself out playing the hostess. Finally he asked, "What are you doing here, Manning? Did you not already cause enough trouble? I shall just warn you this one time, you are not to ever get within ten feet of my fiancée again or you shall answer to this." He caressed the large ruby on the end of the hilt of his sheathed silver-and-gold dress sword.

Rowland raised his eyebrows. "Oh pish, General. We both know that rusty thing hasn't seen any use in the last century. But may I offer my sincerest congratulations, Mrs. Winters? General? I had no idea you were to be married. Mrs. Winters, may I offer my services as escort as you trot up the aisle toward your future happiness with the general? I've now acquired quite a knack for it. What?"

Sarah's eyes were brimming with laughter. "I'm sorry, Mr. Manning, but General Pymm has not asked *me* to marry him."

"Well, for goodness sakes, General, what are you waiting for? Mrs. Winters appears very willing."

Leland Pymm jumped from the absurdly feminine rocking chair, and seething, nearly tripped over his decorative sword.

Rowland ignored his misstep and casually retrieved a plate from the tiered silver stand. "Biscuit, Miss Ashburton?"

She shook her head, her mouth as dry as straw.

His eyes narrowed. "No? Oh, but I must insist. I saw to the baking myself. You do know that a cook's only pleasure is the joy others take in consuming what they have so painstakingly prepared, don't you?" He transferred five biscuits to a small plate and forced it on her.

He was a mind reader. Had she not had that very same thought as she had tried to force her food on him?

"I would take a biscuit, if you please, Mr. Manning," Sarah said. "My appetite has returned."

He smiled radiantly. "Why, of course, madam. Strawberry, General?"

"Get up, Manning," Pymm insisted, with his usual lack of wit. His voice cracked again. "I shall see to you at the front windows. Now."

"Oh, of course, General. I never refuse an order, as you know. You do remember that about me, don't you?" Rowland rose slowly, dwarfing the tallish Pymm by four inches. "All those horses you ordered from me over the last few years? The ones I delivered promptly and in excellent health and trained for every possible need of your cavalry?"

Pymm's eyes narrowed and he rudely pointed toward the distant bank of windows, which would afford them a degree of privacy.

Elizabeth watched the two men cross the room, and had the oddest thought. She had not failed to notice that throughout the acts of Rowland Manning's play, he had not taken a single sip of tea or one bite of a biscuit.

Rowland stared at the vainglorious man responsible for providing a large portion of the funds necessary through the years for the purchase and erection of the stately buildings that now dwarfed every other stable and equine auction house in England. He had

always known this man was a fool—a bloody powerful fool with an inordinate amount of luck glued
to his aristocratic hide. But then luck, richesse, and
power had a way of riding together through select
lives.

"What are you doing here?" Pymm asked, his fury
barely leashed.

"Trying to have a word concerning payment for
eight hundred twenty horses you ordered, General."

"I beg your pardon?" Pymm steamed.

"Your underling, that corpulent prick, Lieutenant
Tremont? He had the audacity to suggest that this
contract"—he withdrew the wrinkled document from
his coat—"is no longer valid."

"You're here because you want payment for
horses?" Pymm asked, incredulous.

"Yes."

"Really? This has naught to do with my fiancée?"
Doubt and a peck of unheroic uncertainty darted
across his expression.

"Have you ever known me to give a damn about a
female?" Rowland asked.

Leland Pymm barked with a grating sound that
barely resembled human laughter. "Quite right."

Rowland hated the man more than he had at any
point during their dealings.

"Knew it was just one of her flirtatious games. She
excels in boiling a man's blood. It's a good thing I like
her tactics. Well, look. Since we've known each other
for all these many years, and you've been a decent-
enough sort when it comes to providing cattle when
needed, I shall personally see to the payment, under
one condition."

"Dare I guess?" Rowland lifted a brow.

"Bastards should know their place, even if they're rich bastards. I meant what I said about Miss Ashburton before. I don't want your filthy hands touching any part of her—ever again. She is mine."

He swallowed the urge to laugh. "A bit overdone—just a tad, don't you think, General?" He raised a brow. "But then again I suppose—"

"You know, I've allowed you to overstep yourself, Manning, in private on occasion, because you're one of the more reliable tradesmen I know. But take warning, I've no burning need for your horses now. If you want me to take possession of this herd of yours, I will, but only if *my demands* are met."

"All right," Rowland murmured. "Name your requirements."

"The price is small. You shall keep away from Miss Ashburton. I will not have you sully her reputation or mar my wedding plans. Then, and only then, shall I accept those bloody horses I don't need and you shall have your"—he scanned the contract and placed the paper in Manning's outstretched hand—"seventy thousand pounds as agreed."

"Very good of you, General." Rowland played into the man's love of gratitude. "And the cost of boarding such animals for the last three months will be included."

Leland Pymm smiled, his thin lips stretching over his long teeth. "Of course, dear boy, of course. Oh, and by the by"—he winked with a smirk—"if you see fit to lose the Royal Ascot Gold Cup on Ladies Day, I shall make it worth your while. Shall we say a little bonus of several thousand pounds, then?"

Pymm's outrageousness caused not one hair to rise along Rowland's cold body. He was far too inured to the ways of *gentlemen*. Indeed, he almost enjoyed watching Pymm's presumption of victory.

"Who knows what could happen, General?" He paused, causing Pymm to lean forward in anticipation. "But since we're bargaining, I suppose I should mention that the bastards' code of conduct may or may not force me to reveal to all and sundry that your bride has been serving as *my personal cook* until very recently."

Pymm lurched forward a step before Rowland's hand stopped him. "But I am a generous man, General. I shall promise that my thirty-eight stable hands and drivers won't breathe a word of it to all their cohorts in the great houses in town as long as I receive payment for the horses *and* their care for the last few months."

"You are a scoundrel, sir. A disgrace to gentlemen everywhere," Pymm said haughtily.

"What? No invitation to duel?" Rowland said casually, fully aware the general didn't have it in him.

"You're not worth it. You've not the slightest notion of honor."

Rowland smiled. "On that we're agreed, General." Pymm's blustering reaction bored him to the extreme. The gentleman was just so damned predictable. Was there not a man alive who could provide the least bit of entertainment? But then, Rowland was willing to endure anything at this point to get his hands on blunt before the auctioneer appeared on his sprawling property.

He refused to consider Elizabeth Ashburton and her bewitching green eyes, which had lost their spark when confronted by Pymm. He hated the submission he'd seen in her face—so like his sister's expression all those years ago.

Elizabeth had caught but a phrase or two of the conversation across the long room. She knew, without a doubt, that Rowland Manning could not save her. And actually, she didn't really want him to. She was tired of being beholden to people. She wanted nothing more than to save herself, even if the enormity of the task appeared completely beyond the itch of a chance.

She studied Rowland's extraordinarily tall, powerful frame, and felt heat rise to her décolletage as she remembered how it had felt, her body molded against his. Standing there, Rowland Manning served to make Pymm look everything ridiculous, like a boy berating a man. The austere cut of Rowland's blue superfine coat stretched across his massive shoulders, tapering down to his hips. Buff-colored breeches defined his muscled thighs, while black boots gleamed in a superior spit-and-polish high gloss. Rowland's profile bore the marks of an aristocrat; the clean, chiseled jut of his jaw, the blade of his long nose above his full, wide lips. At one point he leaned back and smiled, his white teeth flashing against his sun-bronzed face.

Sarah grasped her hand. "You do not have to make a decision just yet, dearest."

"I know."

"Good." Sarah's visage gained a wistful expression. "Remember how my husband said that it was always bleakest before the dawn?"

"And Father always replied that he had it all wrong—that it was most grim just before a battle."

Sarah smiled. "And Pierce would then remind him that battles typically began before dawn."

Elizabeth was certain she mirrored her friend's pensiveness. "We were lucky, weren't we? So very lucky to have them as long as we did."

Sarah looked down at their joined hands. "Indeed," she murmured.

It was hard to know what to say given the tension of the room. But any conversation was better than the silence and dread of waiting for Pymm to return to claim her. "I'm so happy for you, Sarah. Lord Wymith appears to be everything Ata suggested."

Sarah avoided her gaze. "His good character is without question. He is everything a gentleman should be."

"Yes," Elizabeth said, feeling awkward. "And he obviously has fixed an interest in—"

"No," Sarah interrupted, her eyes tightly closed. "Please do not say it."

"Of course," Elizabeth said. "I do not mean to discomf—"

Sarah interrupted again, so unlike her usual behavior. "I'm sorry, Elizabeth. It's just that I cannot think of another—" She stopped abruptly before continuing in a rush. "Well, to me it seems impossible to link another man's name with my own."

Elizabeth squeezed Sarah's hands. "It's not, dearest. The man I knew, the man who loved you, would not have wanted you to grieve for him forever."

"I could say the same to you, Elizabeth. Your father would not want you to continue on as we've done. He would want to see you settled, happy." Her friend looked at their joined hands. "I fear I'm at fault for this predicament. I misguided you in our shock and misery after Badajoz. Perhaps . . . we were wrong."

"Why do you say that?"

Sarah paused. "Because for the last week, while I was in hiding at Ellesmere House, the general called on Ata and the others. He came every day to Helston House. Our friends relayed that Pymm was everything good and kind. Rosamunde said that she'd never seen a man so distraught with worry for you. That is the reason he gave for all the officers looking for you."

"Oh, Sarah," Elizabeth replied. "He has soldiers posted in Portman Square and at all main roads leading from town. He will not allow me the freedom of a choice. Are those the actions of an honorable man?"

"Perhaps they are the actions of a man consumed by guilt. He told Helston he feels responsible for not following through with the promise he made to your father of ensuring your safety and comfort. Indeed, a man whose love is so constant could quite possibly not be so awful as we thought. He could not have killed . . . Elizabeth, a spot of blood on a man's glove means nothing in battle—you know that. Oh, I fear I was consumed with grief and perhaps in a fugue, not thinking very properly. I should have guided you better."

"Don't, Sarah. You did everything for me. But General Pymm . . ." Uncertainty filled her for the first time. "It was the look on his face when he came to me after the battle and told me the awful news. Oh, I know I am being ridiculous."

Sarah's gray eyes regarded her with love and concern. "No. Never that. But perhaps you should at the very least hear him out. If he did not love you so much, he would have chastised you terribly for that scene in St. George's this morning."

"It is precisely because he did not chastise me that I worry. I'm but a challenge to him. He wants me because I am probably the only person who has ever denied him. It is only too bad I cannot make him tire of me and leave me be."

"No one here will suggest you marry him if you don't want to, Elizabeth," Sarah said softly. "And your happiness is my fondest wish. I long for you to have the sort of bliss I had with Pierce—even if it was too short."

"Oh, Sarah, I loathe Leland Pymm with every fiber of my being."

"Careful, dearest," Sarah warned. "Hate is a powerful emotion often linked or confused with love."

"But not in this case, Sarah. I know I'm quite lacking in an ability to correctly judge others, but I am not confused on this point."

Sarah looked at her with compassion. "And what of Mr. Manning? Do you loathe him too?"

Chapter 8

One week later . . .

GENERAL PYMM ENGAGED!

*In keeping with the romantic, whirlwind number
of weddings in the wake of our recent great victory
over France, our most noble hero General Leland
Pymm revealed his secret long-standing engagement to the mysterious Miss Elizabeth Ashburton, a quiet, innocent young lady who apparently
dislikes all public and private balls and evening
entertainments. Let us hope this will change. Oh,
can anything be more divinely romantic? Our dear
Pymm secretly mourned and feared dead this an-
gelic daughter of a captain during the hellish chaos
of Badajoz. But now, as in all good fairytales, she
will be wed and made a duchess before the clock
strikes twelve.*

FASHIONABLE WORLD, THE MORNING POST

Elizabeth lowered her trembling hand, which held
the folded section of the newspaper, and would
have had a long laugh if she had not been so grossly
horrified. A quiet, innocent young lady who disliked

entertainments? Was it not her devilish love of dancing and the entertainments offered to officers and
their families that had led to her present difficulties
in the first place?

She could at least be thankful she was alone with a
breakfast tray in her old chamber at Helston House.
The previous few weeks' trials paled beside this official announcement.

Would this continually tightening noose ever give
pause? It was quite obvious it did not matter what
Elizabeth said or did. She felt very much like a bit of
flotsam carried along in an unstoppable tidal wave
of events.

Pymm was executing his objective as if on a battlefield anew. Too late, she now saw his plan. While in
private, he had tried to soften her by gently urging her
to accept him; in the public eye, which she had avoided,
he had gone forward with his ultimate plan, spreading
romantic rumors of their purported devotion for many
years. And English people everywhere rejoiced at the
news of their romance, for there had been little to celebrate during so many bitter years of war.

And while Pymm had not dared to hint to her
again of her father's purported crimes against the
crown, there was never any question as to what he
would do if she denied him. In front of her countrymen, he would assassinate her character and that of
her father. Of that there was never any doubt. And
all because of letters from her French mother's relatives; letters her father had refused to show her but
had insisted should be burned if anything happened
to him. *Oh, Papa.*

In her heart she knew he had never done anything

to jeopardize England. He was the bravest man Elizabeth knew. She had always thought he had been in the midst of trying to save her mother's famous Gallic relatives from the chaos of France, where changing governments, leaders, and ideology cut new paths as fast as a guillotine's blade.

But it was perhaps more serious than that if Pymm's words were true. This first doubt of her father's complete innocence felt like the worst sort of betrayal. She shook her head. No. He would not have placed her at such risk.

And she had refused to confide in Sarah or anyone else, for she would not jeopardize their innocence. They must all remain in the dark and therefore blameless.

Indeed, a person's character was the most precious commodity. With a few choice phrases from Pymm, she could be held up as the ultimate example of corruption, betrayal, and dishonor. She hated the idea that her friends would feel honor bound to stand by her, to support her for the rest of her life, for she would be unable to find any sort of husband or reputable work. And that would be in the best of circumstances. The worst, the most likely, was that she would be carted off to Newgate on charges of treason.

She was caught between the devil and the deep blue sea. And yet . . . within the recesses of her heart she knew she could not marry Pymm. At least, she thought she would not—even if it meant risking a complete descent in the world, or worse.

Well, she would just force herself to learn the art of patience. Impatience was the failing that went hand in hand with her poor judgment. She would just have to wait for an opportunity to extricate herself. Long sieges would, in fact, become her speciality, she decided. Her father would have been proud of—

A knock sounded insistently on her door and Ata burst in without waiting. The diminutive lady tugged at her overly long skirt and rushed awkwardly to one of the two windows in the chamber. She struggled with the window's sash. "Oh, Pip! I saw my Pip."

Elizabeth threw back the bedclothes, grappled with her wrapper, and crossed the intricate marquetry of the polished wood floor. "Where?"

"Botheration! Oh, these old windows," Ata moaned.

"Let me help," Elizabeth said and jerked open the sash using all her strength.

Before she could stop her, the dowager leaned half of her body out the window and half turned to face the sky. Elizabeth grabbed her elderly petite frame to stop her from falling.

Mr. Brown rushed inside the chamber and barked, "Ata! Step away this instant."

Ata reached her gnarled hand up. "Oh, I see her! My dear Pip. Oh, Eliza, help me!"

"No bird is worth it, Ata," Luc St. Aubyn murmured from the doorway.

"Make her step away, Luc," Mr. Brown whispered hoarsely.

The so-called Devil of Helston merely raised a brow. "You've never understood her, old man. The day Ata can be brought under control will be the day we lower her into the ground—and that will only be if we have a strong-enough harness in the coffin."

Ata ignored them. "Oh, Pip, come to me darling.

I knew you'd survive all these months if I left enough seed on the sills." She looked back into the room, her wrinkled face smiling. "Oh, John, do climb out here to fetch her."

Long-suffering John Brown crossed to the window but was stopped by the strong arms of the duke at the last moment. "Oh no, you don't," he warned darkly. "I won't let you die in this fashion. A proper obituary would be too difficult to write if it included an attempt to save a damned canary." With his other arm, the duke hauled his grandmother out of the window and tucked her under his arm, her feet paddling the air to no effect. "You should be ashamed of yourself, Grandmamma."

"Put me down, you hard-hearted brute!"

"No. Not until you promise to be a good girl and never lean out of a window like that ever again."

"You are being ridiculous." Ata managed to disengage herself from her grandson. "I was just showing all of you how far one can lean out the window without harm."

"I'll catch the bird, if you like," said the voice that had haunted Elizabeth's dreams. The deep hum of its tones made her heart trip before she even turned to see him in her chamber.

"What in hell are you doing here again, Manning?" the duke growled. "Have all the servants taken leave of their senses and gone on holiday?"

Rowland Manning had glanced at everyone in the room aside from her. She drank in the sight of him. He appeared even more gaunt than usual, his face drawn and pale. He addressed Luc first. "Your main entry was open and I walked right in."

The duke groaned.

"They're probably hanging out of all the other windows, at a guess," Mr. Brown supplied, without a hint of his usual gummy smile.

"Mr. Manning," Ata said shrewdly, "I would thank you for retrieving my canary for me. It appears *you* are the only man brave enough to help me— unlike the others here." She darted a sour glance to John Brown.

"Let's see what we have here," Rowland said and strode to the window. Examining the sill and then giving a quick glance skyward, he continued, "I'd need a few things. Netting—light in weight, twine, suet, seed, three sticks—two short and one long."

"Finally, a purpose for that cane of yours, Grand-mamma," Luc said archly.

"I'll see to the things you require, Mr. Manning," Ata said sweetly, ignoring her longtime suitor and her grandson as she departed without a backward glance.

Elizabeth studied the dejected expression of Mr. Brown, who stood between the two tall men.

"You expect too much, Brownie," Luc said quietly.

"I don't know what you mean," Mr. Brown returned.

Rowland stood by stiffly.

"You cannot expect her to be happy with your continued residence at Home House," Luc said under his breath.

"It's a large house party," Mr. Brown said defensively.

"As we have here."

"I had hoped to have this conversation in private,

Luc, if indeed at all. But perhaps it's better out in the open." Mr. Brown paused. "I returned from Scotland to see if your grandmother had changed, as her letters all promised."

"Changed?" Luc asked with a blank-card face. "Why on earth would you think a woman with so many years in her dish would be capable of change?"

Mr. Brown appeared vastly discomforted. "She asked my forgiveness for all of her earlier high-handed ways."

"Well, you should count your blessings, for that is a first, old man," Luc muttered. "What more could you want?"

Mr. Brown appeared very ill at ease.

"Spit it out, Brownie. This has festered far too long," Luc insisted.

"Your grandmother has a death grip on a grudge formed five decades ago. It colors our every conversation. Don't ask me to explain it to you, Luc, for I won't. I'm waiting for a sign that she intends to follow through with her promises to change her views on the past."

"Really?" Luc's brows arched. "And if she does?"

"Why," he lowered his voice, "I would ask for the honor of her hand in marriage—for the third *and final* time."

Luc's eyes nearly bugged out of his head. "Do you promise? I shall have your word on it, now. And then I shall fetch her back this minute and have her on her knees, an apology and a promise on her lips."

"No, Luc," Mr. Brown said sadly. "She must come to me on her own. And at this rate, I would not hold your breath. I'm for Home House now." When Luc started to speak, Mr. Brown held up his hand. "No. I'm sorry I spoke at all. And you would do well not to speak to Ata of this for I shall know if you do. But I suppose all is for the best for it saves me the trouble of explaining why I shall return to Scotland shortly."

Luc appeared ready to argue further but then glanced at Rowland Manning. Elizabeth had no doubt Luc would see Mr. Brown in private at some future point to do his worst in an effort to keep his old friend from decamping.

Silence reigned with Mr. Brown's departure. Luc finally glanced first at her and then, narrowing his eyes, at Rowland, who crossed his arms over his chest and stood as still as a statue.

"Why are you here really? What do you want?" Annoyance soaked the duke's words.

Elizabeth pursed her lips. It was as if she were watching a black bull paw the earth in front of an ancient, colossal tree. A tree that appeared so weathered that it would topple over with merely one good push.

And still he did not look at her. "I want her to get dressed."

Her eyes bored into Rowland. When had he even noticed her state of dress?

"And?" The duke's voice was deceptively soft.

"I came to offer my congratulations on her impending nuptials."

"Really?" Luc said. "And?"

"And to deliver this." He withdrew a large, heavy vellum note from inside his coat and handed it to the duke.

As Luc moved his attention to the important-looking document, Rowland finally moved his gaze to Elizabeth. She sucked in her breath. He looked at her with such intensity despite the heavy evidence of fatigue surrounding his eyes. He recollected himself and returned his gaze to the duke.

"Well?" Rowland asked. "Will you accept?"

"It isn't as if I have a choice," Luc replied acidly. "One does not ignore a direct invitation from the Prince Regent."

"I shall trust you to inform—"

Luc interrupted. "It doesn't take a bloody nodcock to figure out you're behind this."

"Good to know you're not a bloody nodcock, then," Rowland replied.

"But one has to wonder why you're so quick to throw her"—he nodded in her direction—"into Pymm's path. He is sure to be there too."

"So you don't approve of him?" Rowland asked, leaning casually against the grate's mantel.

"He's a better candidate than"—Luc paused—"*others*."

"Really? I didn't know there were others."

"I'm so sorry to interrupt the wedding planning," Elizabeth inserted, peevishly, "but would you mind very much telling me what this is about?"

"An invitation to stay at Windsor Castle with the royal party for the four days of Ascot races," Luc said with exasperation. "We're to leave tomorrow."

"I would have a word with Elizabeth now."

Luc barked out a laugh. "Not on your life, Manning. I barely can tolerate the idea of you alone with

Ata's damned canary, let alone one of the females residing under my roof."

"She was under my roof not so long ago."

"And if you were a gentleman, you would have forgotten that fact the moment she left your protection."

Rowland shook his head. "How many sodding times do I have to remind everyone that I am not a gentleman? Elizabeth, put on your gown. I have something to discuss with you of importance. In *private*."

Her heart leapt. Perhaps he had an idea of how to extricate her from—

"Discuss it now. *Here*," Luc insisted with an expression that brooked no argument.

Rowland studied the duke. "You know, whatever you've heard about me is true, and actually much worse," he said slowly.

"Have you forgotten that I'm intimately aware of your character, Manning? There was the little matter of your forcing your half brother into hiding for over a decade, and then there was the matter of bribing the countess, not to mention your former desire to relieve me and the others of this thing we call life."

"Yes, well, you were all in my study at three o'clock in the morning, stealing the countess's fortune back, now, weren't you?" He sighed heavily. "Look, if you're so bloody interested in what I have to say to Elizabeth, then you can stay."

"As if I need an invitation to stay in my own house," Luc said dryly, seating himself in the ridiculously feminine slipper chair nearby. "Go on then."

Elizabeth held her breath and noticed that Rowland appeared discomfited. It was the first time she'd seen him like this.

He studied his fingernails. "I require your nut bread recipe."

She started.

"Look, Ascot is looming," he said. "I need incentive for my men."

Luc's brows rose to his hairline.

"Of course." Elizabeth jumped to the escritoire in the chamber and quickly used a quill to scratch out the recipe. "Is the new cook not competent?" She took care to keep her voice low.

"No," he said, his tone glacial.

"Would you like for me to return to help you today, or to look for another cook?"

The two men spoke at the same moment, Luc's bark overshadowing the other man's assent. "Absolutely not!" Luc insisted. "Are you out of your minds? Elizabeth, the whole of London's eyes are upon your every movement."

"I know, but I owe Mr. Manning," she replied.

"She absolutely is at fault," Rowland said with a hint of a smile. "She relieved my cook, who was perfectly adequate until Miss Ashburton invaded my kitchen."

"I did not fire the cook. Lefroy sacked her."

"Enough!" Luc said with irritation. "Elizabeth, you are to do whatever females do in order to depart for Windsor tomorrow. And you, sir, are to find your own damn cook. Oh, and one other thing, Manning." It was Luc's turn to look embarrassed.

"Yes?"

"I would be in your debt if you could possibly see

fit to actually win the Gold Cup." Luc appeared as if he'd rather be boiled in oil than be beholden to the man opposite him.

Rowland smiled like a fox inches from his next meal. "What's in it for you, then?"

Ill at ease, Luc ran his hand through his black hair. "Elizabeth, perhaps you should leave us to—"

"Pardon me, but . . . *not on my life.*" Elizabeth laughed for she had uttered something no guest of a duke should ever dare to say. Living on the edge of disaster appeared to dissolve almost every last shred of her natural decorum.

"Well?" Rowland purred.

"A fiver," Luc muttered.

"That much, eh?" Rowland Manning rubbed his temples as if they ached.

"Oh," Elizabeth breathed. "You did not wager five hundred pounds on a race."

When Luc did not respond, Rowland did. "I would wager the fool did not."

Her lungs relaxed and she could breathe again. "Oh, simply five pounds. All in fun, then."

Luc's eyes darkened, while Rowland's pale green eyes showed a glimmer of their former spark as he replied. "Wrong again."

"*Five thousand?* Not . . . possible," Elizabeth said, nearly mute with disbelief.

"Such surprise," Rowland murmured. "And here I thought you knew the ways of men. No? Well, I shall be happy to educate you. This gentlemanly wager probably has everything to do with precious honor, and a little betting book at White's if I were to hazard a guess. Mind if I ask who got your back up?"

Luc appeared ready to pounce on his opponent. "Delighted," he gritted out. "Pymm. The man anticipates the duchy a touch early. Forced a wager on every last duke in London that your mare would lose to Tatt's gelding."

Elizabeth watched Rowland's face, and could not see a twitch of surprise.

"The price of ducal pride is indeed high, *Your Grace*," Rowland drawled.

What Rowland Manning had neglected to inform the Helston House circle after he failed in his attempt to entrap that bloody canary would become obvious enough a day later.

He was to be at Windsor. Not in the ballroom, of course, but in the gilded stables. Everyone knew Prinny loved Ascot, almost as much as he loved the idea of housing the winner. And the prince was adept at hedging his bets, inviting both Rowland and Tattersall to house their horses in the royal mews.

Rowland wasn't certain how events would play out, but if life had taught him anything, it was that to have a chance at capturing the wily monkey of success, one had to throw all the fruits of disaster out on a limb, and then watch the possibilities ripen.

Money was the thing that occupied his mind every waking moment of every cursed day. His chest ached as alone he staggered in the dead of night from his vast stables to the old desk in the echoing study in the main building. Every last thing he had built to rule was falling apart.

For the first time ever, the stable hands showed hints of doubt, even if they didn't dare voice them.

The hay and straw man in London had warned this would be the last load delivered. His credit was no longer good. *Unless he won the Gold Cup*, the man had hinted.

The construction of the last stable had halted. *Unless his circumstances changed*, the foreman had informed.

None of them had believed him when he argued that he would soon have more funds, whether he won or lost. He ran his hands down his face. He just had to walk the tightrope in Pymm's circus.

Not that he had a shred of conscience over winning or losing. They were all so bloody stupid, supposing him to have scruples. He would precisely measure which road would bring him the greatest advantage, and do whatever was necessary to win or *lose*. It was just . . . he was so bloody tired. For the first time in his life, he didn't have the energy, the desire that had usually burned so brightly.

He focused on the ever-rising stacks of bills in front of him. Unleashing his tightly furled fury, he swept all of it off the desk. The ledgers clattered to the floor, while the sheaves of paper floated in arcs like the leaves of autumn. And under it all, he stared at the words that were carved onto the simple wooden desk—until they blurred. A flood of advice from his childhood washed over him . . .

"You are the strongest. The one who will overcome. The one who has learned how to go without . . ." Rowland tried to stop the memories. *"You must stand alone—neither servant nor noble. Never forget . . . trust no one, love no one—except your own blood. Never give anyone that power over you.*

It is the means to your destruction . . . as it was to mine."

He sprawled his arms and head across the desk. His temples pounded in agony with each beat of his heart. He wasn't sure how much time passed before the hair prickled on the back of his cold, exposed neck. He jerked upright.

And was certain he was in a dream. No. He never dreamt of anything good. Night was for the darkness of the past—of naught but emptiness.

She stood before him. He could not have described what she was wearing for all he could see was the warmth of her perfectly formed face, her emerald eyes, the casual disarray of her loose curls every color from pale blonde to dark honey. The curve of her cheek became more defined as she tilted her head slightly.

Her eyes held questions yet she did not speak. Slowly, she dipped to place some things on his desk she had brought with her. He heard the sound of crockery and silverware, yet he refused to look at it. A bouquet of scents nearly knocked him from his chair.

"You must eat," she said quietly.

"Not hungry," he replied without emotion.

"You've forgotten what hunger is," she whispered. Her expression held no pity, no censure. It was a mere statement of fact.

"You shouldn't be here."

"I know."

"How . . ."

"Never mind that," she said softly as she came around the desk, unfolding a napkin. She draped it in his lap and as she leaned down, he closed his eyes against the warm, simple soap scent of her. A lock of her hair was loose and it brushed his shoulder. He held onto the edge of his desk to stop from touching it.

She pulled the chair across from the desk to sit beside him—just as she had done the last time she had prepared a meal for him. Only now, he couldn't find the strength to fight her. He closed his eyes and listened to something being poured into a glass. Slowly, all the noises died away.

He reopened his eyes and saw that she had arranged the first bite on a fork. "What is it?" he asked slowly.

"Venison with stewed cherries and bread pudding," she replied quietly.

"My men . . ."

"Will have the same tomorrow. Sarah's here too and she's helping Cook finish the last of it now." She urged him by handing him the full fork. "No more talk."

He grappled with temptation. She appeared to be holding her breath. He gave in without another word, proof positive he was losing on all fronts.

His vision tunneled to the food before him, and he forced himself to go slowly this time. She said not a word as he tentatively ate every blasted morsel of heaven in front of him. As he sopped up the last of the fragrant savory sauce using a chunk of the nut bread she had provided, she handed him a glass of wine.

"No," he said, waving it away.

"Water?" she asked.

"Yes."

As he drank, she placed a square of gingerbread in front of him.

"No," he said quietly.

"Yes," she said even softer.

He swallowed against the knot in his throat. He'd had too much. He'd had enough. He picked up the smaller fork and swiftly plowed through the forbidden sweet. The taste made his mind whirl, all his senses engaged in something so divine, it should be served only in paradise.

She broke the silence. "You should have told me."

He stared into her lovely, unguarded eyes.

"Your cook is perfectly adequate. Excellent in fact."

"Really?" He couldn't keep the irony from his voice.

"It's your face. She is scared of you."

"Smart woman."

"She was too afraid to tell you that you've exhausted your credit with every last butcher, shopkeep, even the fishmonger's daughter."

The blood ran cold in his veins.

"The only good I can find in this," she continued, "is that you've told me time and again you've no pride—so what I'm saying shouldn't bother you. You see I do have pride and my debt to you has been weighing heavily on my conscience."

"Your debt?"

"For helping me the day I met you. For hiding me. For allowing me to draw you into scandal in the middle of St. George's soon after. Cook told me the men have been grumbling that there's been a drop-off of customers since that awful day."

"What have you done?" He wanted the truth, not her reasons.

"Nothing very much." She glanced away. "General Pymm returned my father's articles as well as his back pay. I've settled your accounts with the fishmonger, the butcher, and the two shopkeeps. You—"

"Why did you do it?" His voice was nearly gone.

She refused to meet his eyes. Instead she collected the plates and silverware to replace them on the tray. "Because you showed me a kindness when you did not have to."

"A kindness?" He stood up, his chair grating against the floor. He grasped her arms, forcing her to be still and to look at him. "I've never shown a bloody kindness to anyone in my entire godforsaken life, Elizabeth." Christ, she was so damned beautiful, and so damned untainted by everything ugly.

She breached the small space between them with her hand, which she placed over his heart. "You did not hurt me, did not take advantage, when you could have."

"Give it time, my dear."

"No. *You* would never force me to do anything I didn't want to do. You are not killing me with guilt, and with soft hints, and sad looks like the others."

He felt the flicker of a smile cross the edge of his lips. "Ah, but you've already forgotten the forfeit you must pay for insisting I endure one of your meals."

"I beg your pardon?"

"One secret I would have. Now." He rushed on before she could stop him. "What hold does Pymm have over you, Elizabeth?"

Chapter 9

"**I** wish you would stop asking me such things. No one else assumes Pymm is holding something over me." Elizabeth stalled, unsure what course to take.

In the halo cast by the candlelight, his unusual pale eyes glowed as they bore into hers; his arms still gripped her inches from his stark face. "People usually refuse to ask the question when they fear the response. I don't. Now, I will hear your answer."

She had thought she had memorized every line, every inch of the harsh planes of his face. She was wrong. His face was infinitely more beautiful to her than she remembered. And while every person she knew would tell her she was a fool to place her faith in a man such as he, she could not stop herself from entrusting him with her awful secret. "He would ruin my character, and my father's."

"How?"

"By suggesting my father was dishonorable."

"Bloody hell, Elizabeth," he said with irritation. "When did you decide to place such importance on pride? You've been spending too much time with Helston and his family. Why should you care even if

Pymm suggests your father ran all the way back to London with a herd of Frenchies on his tail?"

"No," she whispered. "It's worse. He would . . ."

"Yes?" he encouraged softly, and reached out to stroke a lock of her hair that had come loose. The whorls of his thumbs reached her cheek and she pressed her face into his large palm and closed her eyes.

"It is my fault entirely. Pymm never would have searched my father's affairs if I hadn't danced and laughed with him to begin with." She exhaled. "He has letters he would make public. Letters from my mother's relatives in France, which my father received during the war."

He sighed heavily. "Do not tell me you and your father really and truly are spies."

She did not reply.

"Bloody hell. You could at least deny it."

"And what good would that do? Of course I'm not a spy. I'm just a silly, stupid, impetuous girl—a girl who loved to dance, and laugh, and flirt with handsome officers."

"And what has that to do with these letters Pymm holds?"

"Nothing. But that's not the point."

"Well, what in bloody hell is the point? What does dancing a reel in Portugal have to do with anything?"

"Everything."

"I'm waiting for you to explain it then," he ground out.

"I—well, when I first met the general . . ."

"Yes?"

"I enjoyed the favor he showed me. I looked forward to dancing with him. I—I preened before him. He said . . ."

"What?"

"He insisted later that I was a flirt. That I encouraged his affections. That I accepted his addresses by every look, every word."

"Well, did you?"

"Over the years, I've asked myself that question a thousand times. I don't know. My father and Sarah insisted I did not. I think I treated him much as I treated every other officer. It's just, I enjoyed the entertainments, the dancing . . ."

He blinked and loosened his hold on her. "Now you will listen to me, Elizabeth," he commanded, his eyes darker than ever before. "Females have the prerogative to dance, to flirt, to find whatever enjoyment they can in this bloody thing we call a life. And these things you are ashamed of are some of the only things a woman is allowed in her enslavement."

"Enslavement?" She backed away from him, not really knowing where she was going. He followed her step for step until she felt a wall at her back.

He placed his hands against the wall on either side of her face. "From cradle to grave you are but man's possession," he insisted. "First your fathers own you, and then they sell you to the highest bidder. Then your husbands control you, and impregnate you, until they tire of you—unless they toss you in the grave first." He added with pursed lips, "If you are lucky, the bloody nob dies first."

"But—"

"Don't be a fool. You should not doubt yourself.

If Pymm possessed an inch of sanity, which he obviously does not, he would have taken your refusal and been honorable about it by slinking off to lick his bloody wounds in private. Am I the only sod who sees it? You should not show an inch of compassion for any man who torments you—blackmails you—even if it is with silken promises of becoming a duchess."

Staring into the most mesmerizing eyes she had ever seen, she regained a foot in the mountain of confidence she had once possessed two years ago.

"What do those letters say?" Rowland leaned closer.

"I don't know."

"What?" His eyes flashed. "You've gone along with this blackmail and you don't even know if they contain evidence of treason?"

"It's not so much what they say as much as whom they are from." She lowered her voice, "My uncle wrote them—*General Philippe du Quesne*."

"Of course, you would choose to be related to the bloody commander of the *frog hussars*," he said dryly. And yet not a hint of uncertainty crossed his hawkish features. "So what are *you*"—he pointed at her chest—"going to do to extricate *yourself* from this bloody mess?"

She smiled. At least she could count on one man in her life to behave in an utterly predictable fashion. And, of course, she would prefer this forthright, unchivalrous man instead of a decorated war hero with an unfortunate tendency toward blackmail.

Naturally.

With her luck, the day a true prince stepped into her path, she would mistake him for a toad.

"You know, Elizabeth," he said, his eyes intent yet his tone impossibly casual, "I like you."

"You like me because I never ask you to do anything to help me."

"True." He leaned back a bit, a half smile decorating his gaunt face. "Except at weddings."

"Yes," she said, exasperated. "But then it's not so much an act of chivalry as much as an opportunity for you to extract compensation."

"Precisely," he said, his eyes crinkling at the corners. "Well, because I like you, I shall give you a brilliant piece of advice." He paused for good effect. "For *free*."

"Yes?"

"For righteousness to prevail, you often need a bit of larceny in your heart."

Her pulse quickened. "What are you suggesting?"

"You are an intelligent creature. You'll figure it out when you're with your friends and your fiancé at Windsor." His eyes half closed, and he seemed in pain as he leaned in to brush a kiss on her forehead. His intoxicating scent rushed to meet her. "I'll be there too."

"Oh," she murmured, "I didn't know."

In the awkwardness of the stillness, she watched her finger trace the edge of his dark blue superfine lapel. The knot of his white linen neck cloth was simply yet expertly arranged. She was so close she could see the tremor of his heartbeat. She looked up. Oh, he was staring at her again, indecision radiating from his hard expression.

He exhaled in a rush. "You're determined to make your life as complicated and difficult as possible, aren't you?" Without waiting for an answer, he dropped his head, his lips a whisper from hers. "Bloody hell. I can't seem to keep away from you any more than that bloody Pymm. You would do well to get away from here, Elizabeth."

She rocked forward onto the tips of her toes and brushed her lips against his. A rush of intense desire flooded every inch of her flesh. The passion of it trilled in her veins as he took possession of her, his hands urging hers around his neck and then returning to grip her ribs without a hint of gentleness.

She had relived the kiss under the tree a thousand times each day. It paled in comparison to the reality of the moment in the privacy of this study as he drew his large hands up the sides of her body. Her knees almost buckled when his thumbs came to a rest on the crests of her breasts.

It was as if he possessed a sacred combination of qualities fated to enthrall her. She could barely breathe, as his hands caressed her body through the thin silk and cotton of her gown and chemise. The most wicked sensations of heat emanated from every pore of her. She knew it was improper, and yet . . . she could not have breathed or moved for the life of her.

"Oh Christ," he groaned, his lips surrendering their claim for a moment before returning for more. His fingers loosened the gathered front of her bodice with more practiced ease than a French maid. She couldn't summon the discipline to stop him. Her voice seemed stuck inside of her throat, unwilling to put an end to the most thrilling moment of her life.

And then his warm lips were gently trailing the side of her neck, only the hint of a day's growth of whiskers sanding the delicate skin of her throat. Oh, if she could only stop the minutes as they rushed by. Everything was so clear in her mind. This was everything right, the way it was supposed to be. The way—

With a groan he lifted her easily and pressed her against the wall; his lips found the tip of her breast and that first trickle of desire became an ocean that welled within her.

She shivered, continued trembling feverishly as he tortured the rosy tip with his tongue, and then suckled her, daring to nip as she fought against sensations unknown to her. Her fingers tangled through his hair.

Gazing through the long, dark tunnel that had become her path in life, Elizabeth now refused to look away from this small hint of light. She gave herself up to it and drank in the perfect beauty of these moments with Rowland Manning.

As he lavished attention on her tender flesh, she could barely breathe. Her lungs ached with the tension. The silence was broken only by the sound of his boots shifting, and of silk twisting against linen.

And then all at once the quiet sounds of passion unleashed came to an abrupt halt, as a soft knock on the door reverberated across the long chamber.

He immediately pulled away from her and rasped, "Thank God."

Chastened by his words and her complete loss of any sense of propriety, she struggled with the edge of her bodice. He brushed aside her hands and expertly adjusted the gathered edge.

Sarah's soft voice floated from the other side of the

door. "Elizabeth, we must go. We might be missed if we stay any longer."

The hardness had returned to his eye as he focused on her hair and adjusted a pin in her locks. "As usual, you have a flair for dramatic exits, Elizabeth Ashburton."

She tried to regain her dignity to ridiculous effect. She could not stop trembling. Her voice would not come as she opened her mouth and so she closed it.

Her last view of him was a jaded smile as he bade her *adieu* with a slight bow. "I look forward to watching your efforts at Windsor, my dear. Do remember my advice."

Oh, she had never felt more awkward. She was now angry, although she could not put her finger on the reason. Of course, she had hoped he would be more taken by her—or by the care she had put forth in arranging the food. Instead, he was more remote than ever as she drew away from his tall, stark figure and his glittering eyes.

My darling,
It brings me such wretchedness to be apart from you still. And yet, I force myself to take a page from your reserves of patience, never forgetting that we will be united soon—never to be parted again. Forever.

P.

Elizabeth twisted the latest ridiculous love note from Pymm in her gloved hands as the carriage approached Windsor Castle late the next morning. Each time the Helston footman delivered the notes she felt like screaming at the top of her lungs in frustration. She wanted to be alone with her memories of last evening, and instead she was forced to read this nonsense.

She laced her fingers to keep them still while she stared out the window. The view was like nothing Elizabeth could have envisioned. She had never seen such majestic grounds.

The wide lawn of the drive shimmered green in the sharp sunlight, every blade standing at attention. Beyond, parallel lines of ash trees surveyed with their feathered gray branchlets that swayed in the breeze. And as if on cue, a cloud of jackdaws swooped down from the castle's ancient turrets like miniature archangels meant to guard those within.

It was good to be out of London town, where the heat of summer had turned oppressive. Here, just three hours west, the air was cooler, the clean scents of nature replacing the bitter aromas of humanity.

From inside one of the Portman Square carriages, Elizabeth gawked as the largest castle in the world fully revealed itself beyond the royal gates. For the last seven hundred years, this hallowed place had seen more than its fair share of refined grandeur and bloodshed. The Round Tower rose like an intricate scepter on the hill flanked by wings making up an endless series of royal apartments and staterooms, all buffeting walks, circles, and gates.

As she and the others making up the Helston party were escorted within, she worried about the days ahead. She hung back as Ata and Luc walked forward with Sarah and the Earl of Wymith. Only Michael and his exquisite new countess, Grace, trailed behind, still wrapped in their newly wedded bliss. Rosamunde, the Duchess of Helston, had remained in London to stay with Georgiana during her confinement.

What had Rowland Manning meant when he suggested the need for larceny in her heart? Botheration, he could not have been suggesting she creep about looking for the purported letters, could he? Just because Pymm was here, it was ridiculous to think he would bring the letters wherever he went. This entire affair was out of hand. She sighed. Her entire life was out of hand.

Hours later, as they strolled the manicured walks through the long golden shadows of a summer afternoon, Elizabeth became more and more mute to her party's attempt at conversation. Lord Wymith and Sarah walked slightly ahead of Elizabeth and Ata, while Michael and Grace disappeared in the direction of the rose garden.

"Pymm has been nothing if not romantic this past week, my dear," Ata murmured, her little cocoa-colored dog trotting at the end of a leash. The pea gravel crunched beneath their feet as they crossed toward the formal gardens. "Unlike a certain hard-headed Scot who insists on having very little to do with me. Really, why did he bother to return, I ask you? I can't imagine why he preferred to come here in the Countess of Home's rickety old barouche instead of ours."

"Madam"—the Earl of Wymith turned and waited for the dowager to draw near him—"May I offer you my arm and my ear, madam? Perhaps I can offer a gentleman's perspective?"

Elizabeth stopped Sarah, affording them the privacy of distance as Ata conferred with Lord Wymith. "He is planning something, Sarah. Here."

"Who?"

Abashed, she replied, "General Pymm."

"What do you mean?"

"I don't know. It's just a feeling I have."

Sarah held her tongue.

"I'm sorry," Elizabeth said on an exhale.

"Dearest, I will always stand by you. I only worry you've been living, and hiding, based on your feelings and intuition for quite a while. Are you certain the madness you thought you saw in the general's eyes was not the grief and wildness we sometimes saw in the men after battle?"

"I—I'm not sure. I'll never be sure, but there was a cruelty to him. Did your husband ever say anything to you about it?"

"No," Sarah shook her head. "Pierce never engaged in idle talk and he was as loyal as the day was long. He was not prone to disparaging anyone unless it was imperative." There was a wistful sadness to Sarah's gray eyes.

"Oh Sarah, I'm sorry. I know everyone thinks I'm being foolish—that I should accept Pymm."

Sarah's eyes studied her, searching, always searching. "Not everyone. But I will admit that the general's devoted attachment to you appears very genuine, despite everything. You do not truly believe anymore that he had a hand in our loved ones' deaths, do you?" She paused. "You know I will stand by you if you choose not to marry the general, whatever the reason."

There were some things one could not even confide in one's dearest friend. Elizabeth just could not bear to see the doubt in Sarah's expression if she told her about her father's letters from her French relative. And she didn't want to drag Sarah into deeper water with her. Sarah had done so much for her already. Had always stood by her. And so she remained silent. Sarah could not help her.

Hours later, she held back her true thoughts again when Sarah knocked on her door before negotiating the corridors to the dining hall.

"Oh Sarah, those flowers are so lovely. You've never worn anything so pretty in your hair."

Her friend blushed. It was the first time Elizabeth had seen Sarah do such a thing.

"They are bellflowers from the Earl of Wymith. He asked me to wear them tonight."

Elizabeth's spirits depressed slightly. Oh, she wanted to be happy for Sarah. Truly. She had been her first and only friend for so many years when the other officer's wives had avoided Elizabeth and whispered she was a hoyden or worse. But she didn't want to see the already hazy memory of Sarah's husband fade. He had been her father's commander, and all their lives had been woven so closely together it saddened her to think everything was unraveling. Oh, she was being selfish, and everything ridiculous.

Sarah's fine eyes missed not a thing. "There is nothing to it. I promise you, my love."

"There would not be anything wrong if there was," Elizabeth said quietly. "The earl is a very good man and he will make you very happy. I'm certain of it."

"We've already discussed this, Elizabeth. I know what will make me happiest. And it is"—Sarah looked away—"*impossible*."

Three quarters of an hour ensconced with one hundred guests fluttering about merely increased the tension between Elizabeth's temples. At least there was one less worry. The Prince Regent had chosen to pass the hour before dinner with his mother, the queen, who insisted on closeting herself at Windsor with dear King George, who had grown quite mad through the years.

But Mr. Brown was not helping to ease the Helston party's overall discomfort. Or rather, Mr. Brown and the Countess of Home were not helping matters.

Ata fluttered her fan with such force that the outrageously tall ostrich plumes perched in her iron-gray curls threatened to give up their roost. "How can he attend to her, hanging on her every word?" Ata's face was filled with uncertainty. "He fetches her drinks when there are footmen to bring gallons of wine to every lady in this room. And yet, he will not spare a second to say one word to me. I don't understand."

"Perhaps he is waiting for you to go to him, Grandmamma," Luc replied, ill ease warring with his usual jaded expression.

"Oh, pish, don't be ridiculous, Luc. Oh, how I wish Rosamunde and Georgiana were here with us. Five female heads put together are always better than one illogical man."

"I wish they were here too," Elizabeth murmured. "I worry so for Georgiana."

Ata patted her hand. "You have enough to worry about, Elizabeth. And Rosamunde is an excellent person to nurse Georgiana in her confinement. And to make her laugh."

Elizabeth stood still, her eyes fixed on the doorway, waiting, now always waiting, instead of her former natural inclination to act. She was soon rewarded. Leland Pymm strode forward, expectation of adulation apparent on his narrow face and puffed out chest, full of medals of glory. Elizabeth could not stop the ridiculous thought that it had probably taken his valet half the afternoon to artfully arrange the fringe of curls on his forehead.

He scanned the room and crossed to her. Oh, where was Rowland Manning? He had said he'd be here.

"My dear," Pymm breathed, his chin raised in an imperious manner.

"Good evening, General," she replied, on her guard.

He urged her forward toward a quiet copse. "I would have you use my given name when we are in private, Elizabeth."

"But, we are not in private . . . *sir.*"

"Yet." His smile was languid. "I have a delightful surprise for you tonight, my darling. A little engagement present, if you will."

At the sound of the endearment, she could not suppress the slow shiver that wended its way between her shoulder blades.

"I don't require any more of your gifts. You know there is only one thing I want," she bit out.

He completely ignored her. "I am determined to see your dimples tonight. You will not begrudge me a smile, will you?" Without waiting for her response he continued, "No. I am certain you will like this particular gift and then there will be dancing. You always loved to waltz. Especially with me. I am looking forward to the many balls we will give when Badajoz House is complete."

Bile rose in her throat. "You would name your house the name of the battle where—"

"That was a memorable turning point in the war. On so many fronts."

"But my father *died* there. Have you forgotten?"

"Hmmm. I shall have to think on that."

Paralyzed by a hot ball of fury and frustration banked in the pit of her stomach, she could think of nothing to say that would not bring down this delicate house of cards. There was a limit to what she dared. If she infuriated him too far, he could very well lose his temper, and all would end in disaster.

"Come, my dear. I do believe His Majesty is arrived to lead us to dinner. As I am a guest of honor, you shall sit across from me, beside the Prince Regent."

Oh, she hated being on display as his fiancée. She looked down at her deep-blue-and-white gauze ball gown and remembered the joy she had felt all those many months ago when it had been bestowed on her as a gift. Ata had been intent on giving new ball gowns to each of the ladies in the secret widows club. It seemed a lifetime ago.

The angels and warriors of the frescoes in the Round Tower's grand dining room stared down at the elaborate long table full of guests. Elizabeth could not have picked a more beautiful place to be unhappy.

"My dear Miss Ashburton, I am delighted to finally make your acquaintance." The Prince Regent addressed her as he cut a piece of meat on his gold plate. Dazzling rubies and diamonds squeezed three of his porcine fingers. "You look familiar. Have we met before?"

Elizabeth stopped herself in time from choking on a spring pea. She prayed His Majesty would not remember her notorious display in St. George's when she had made such a spectacle while wearing the black wig. "No, I do not believe so, Your Majesty."

"I never forget a face." He rested one of his hands on his rotund stomach and studied her before continuing his meal. "Pymm, you've chosen wisely. She has a pretty, intelligent eye, does not chatter on, and she appears demure."

Demure? Elizabeth nearly laughed.

Across from her, the general allowed a half smile to appear on his thin lips. "I knew Your Majesty would appreciate my Elizabeth. Her *loyalty*, her devotion to her country—well, I have never seen anything like it."

She clenched her hands beneath the table, her appetite lost long before she had even reached the table. She wanted to scream. Where was Rowland? He would at least be able to make her laugh at the black humor of it all.

The Duke of Helston sat next to her as he was one of the highest ranking guests. She almost jumped when she felt his hand still her leg as she tapped it incessantly under the table. He deflected the attention on her by addressing Pymm. "When do you and Wellington depart for Vienna, General?"

"A day or so after His Majesty confers the duchy, and Elizabeth and I are wed."

She wanted to slide under the table. It felt as if every single one of the hundred guests seated were eavesdropping, despite the murmurs farther down the acre of table.

"Pymm will make a formidable addition to your ducal circle, don't you think, Helston?" The Prince Regent chuckled, and his jowls waggled.

"Without question," the duke ground out, staring at his grandmother.

A gathering thunderstorm threatened on Ata's expression across from him. She appeared not to hear a word of the conversation. She was staring at Mr. Brown and the Countess of Home as they dissolved into laughter over some unheard remark by several other guests nearby.

"You have not a surplusage of words tonight, my darling." Pymm nodded in Elizabeth's direction. "I will wager that will change soon enough."

She'd forgotten the general's annoying habit of employing words that did not quite fit to pretend an intellect he did not quite possess. She had guessed long ago that he collected rarely used words designed to impress.

Only Elizabeth spied the Duke of Helston rolling his eyes. She had never seen the great man tolerate a bore in silence. The Prince Regent's presence was most likely the only thing reining in the duke's infamous temper.

The man who would be king rose to his feet with the help of several footmen dressed in purple and silver royal livery. Everyone at table instantly quieted. His Majesty raised his gold goblet and his guests followed suit. "A toast is in order, my friends. While we gather for Ascot, I've also requested your presence to celebrate the upcoming nuptials of one of the most decorated men from our great war with France, General Leland Pymm. To Pymm and his lovely fiancée, Elizabeth."

"To Pymm and his Elizabeth," echoed one hundred voices.

"It is a testament to General Pymm's generous heart that I hereby grant him the betrothal gift he has requested. And lest anyone make the hasty assumption that he is a greedy man given my recent bequest of prime land in Mayfair, you shall all be relieved on that point," His Majesty chuckled. "Apparently, he has his bride's fondest wish at heart."

Elizabeth could feel blood rushing to her cheeks as a few murmurs broke out. This was sure to be a disaster. She began to slump in her chair when Luc's hand stilled her again. She sat up.

"Miss Ashburton, you are soon to be one of the fashionable leaders of society, my dear. You will want for nothing. But Pymm has told me of your friend, Mrs. Winters, and the relative poverty she finds herself in after her husband's unfortunate demise on the field of honor. I hereby bestow Barton House, in the northern Lake District, and an annuity of four thousand a year to this worthy war widow in light of her husband Colonel Winters's great service to England."

Elizabeth instantly turned to Sarah. Her best friend's grave eyes widened in shock before she crushed her napkin to her face.

The Prince Regent continued despite the avalanche of excited voices and congratulations directed toward

Sarah. "Does this suit you, Miss Ashburton? Did Pymm choose your gift wisely?"

A flood of happy anguish flooded her breast. It was exactly what she would most wish for. From the last person she wished to be given anything.

"Your Majesty," she whispered. "I am overwhelmed by your generosity."

"You had better thank Pymm rather than me."

She swallowed and addressed the general without raising her eyes. "Nothing could make me happier than to see my friend settled in such a comfortable fashion. I am most grateful for the benevolence of your gift, General."

"Your happiness means the world to me, Elizabeth," Pymm said with a smirk.

Sarah's voice pierced the stillness. "It's too much, Your Majesty." Her eyes were huge in her face, and glistening with tears. "I cannot accept such—"

The Prince Regent waved away her words. "I'm delighted to demand your acceptance, Mrs. Winters." And then he waggled an eyebrow. "Besides, the way I understand it, I might very well be killing two birds with one house, so to speak."

What on earth?

"I will wager I shan't have to make a gift to Wymith when he gathers the courage to wed now, will I?" He roared with laughter.

Elizabeth glanced up only to find Pymm winking at her.

Her world was crumbling apart and yet, she must smile. And then her last remaining ally, the Duke of Helston, a man who could be counted on for his cynical outlook on marriage, relaxed the tense expression on his face.

Oh, she understood it. He was relieved. With her marriage and Sarah's settlement, the financial burden of the last two women under his grandmother's protection would soon be removed from his broad shoulders. And now, with this gift, not one of her friends believed Pymm a monster.

As if he could hear her thoughts, Luc looked down at her face beside him. "Allow me to offer my sincerest best wishes for your future happiness, Elizabeth."

"Thank you, Your Grace." A return to formality seemed the best way to begin the future she had hoped to avoid.

She was to be removed from her circle of friends. Indeed, her best friend was to go to the other end of the country. And just as Rowland had said, she would be stored in Pymm's immense house, impregnated and put to pasture when the general tired of her novelty. If she had any luck, she could make him tire of her quickly.

Luc sighed again so heavily Elizabeth swiveled her head to look at him. "Your Grace?"

He spoke so softly she had to duck closer to catch all the words. "I know I'm going to live to regret this." He shook his head. "The Earl of Wallace is in the royal stables. He passed to me the unreasonable request that you personally bring a drop of tea to a sick man there when we remove from table."

She could barely breathe in her tight corset. "Mr. Manning?" she whispered.

"I haven't the faintest." He cleared his throat.

"Don't be a fool, Elizabeth. It would be better if someone else tended to this. You know Pymm won't like cooling his heels, waiting for you in the ballroom."

For the one and only time in her life, Elizabeth prayed she would not have the chance to dance tonight. Except for her toes, which danced a reel under the table. It was perhaps five minutes—an eternity and a day—before the Prince Regent drew back from the table, effectively ending the royal supper and allowing her escape.

Chapter 10

Elizabeth dashed across the walkways, the light of the full moon helping her negotiate her footing. Who was ill? She was certain it was Rowland. Her fingers were numb and in her haste she dropped the napkin on the tray she was carrying. Breathless, she stooped to retrieve it from the pea-gravel path.

The royal mews were awash in lantern light. An army of stable hands, coachmen, hostlers, and young boys ran in every direction, tending to the hordes of horses stabled in splendor there. She found the Earl of Wallace in the rear of the stables, surrounded by a half dozen men Elizabeth recognized from Manning's.

"Ah, Elizabeth," he said, eyeing her with a smile, "you've brought the tea?"

"What is she doing here?" Rowland ground out.

Oh . . . *he* was not ill.

"Asked her to bring something for Lefroy," Michael replied, nonplussed. "Is there a problem?"

Her gaze dropped to the grizzled man lying in a bed of straw, in the middle of the covey of men. "Mr. Lefroy," she whispered. "What has happened to you?"

The small man looked far older than she remembered. "Oh, it's you, lovey. Dids you bring old Lefroy somfing? Don't know if I can manage anyfing rights now," he said weakly. He tried to raise his head and groaned.

"What's wrong with him?" She looked at the haggard, dark expression on Rowland Manning's face.

"Don't know," he muttered.

"He's been casting up his accounts for the last three hours," Michael added.

"Dinner didn't sit well," Lefroy groaned.

She put her hand to Lefroy's forehead. "No fever. Hmmm. Has anyone gone for an apothecary? Perhaps you would care for some tea, Mr. Lefroy?"

The man appeared almost green, a fine sheen of sweat on his face. He nodded and she helped him drink a little.

"There's no possible way he'll be able to ride tomorrow, Rowland," Michael murmured behind her.

She stared at Mr. Lefroy. "Ride?"

"The Gold Cup," Mr. Lefroy whispered.

"I highly doubt you'll be able to do anything of the sort, Mr. Lefroy," she said softly, then turned to Rowland. "Surely someone else can be found."

His face hardened.

She turned to look at the others next to him. A young boy she'd seen in the stables sidled up to her. "Vespers don't loike men, only women. 'Cept for Mr. Lefroy and the master. Temperamental-loike. Tosses other men off."

"So you could ride her," she suggested, finally meeting Rowland's remote gaze.

He laughed harshly.

"What?" she asked.

Michael helped her to her feet. "He's too big a brute. The other horses will be carrying much less weight. The mare doesn't stand a chance of winning with that sort of handicap."

She looked around her. "You're wrong."

"I beg your pardon?" Michael said.

"Mr. Manning might be greater than all of you in stature but he is considerably leaner than most of you, haven't you noticed?"

A cacophony of questions ensued, each person weighing their opinion. She cut through it all. "Does anyone have a better idea? Or do you want to cry off?"

"Rowland's three stone heavier than any other rider, Elizabeth," Michael said. "That's a considerable disadvantage."

"Well, I could ride her, since she doesn't mind ladies," she offered softly.

"*Absolutely not*," Rowland said, menace rising from every word.

"She be an excellent rider, sir," Mr. Lefroy murmured. "I've seen her meself."

"So you rode my horses without even a by-your-leave?" he muttered, annoyed. "I should have guessed you didn't have enough to do."

"It's an idea," Michael said, a smile breaking onto his face. "Sarah once suggested that Elizabeth is a crack rider. I'm not surprised, after riding across most of Portugal and Spain," Michael insisted, in such a casual tone Elizabeth knew something was off.

She looked at the sea of expectant faces, save one. "Is there any rule against a female rider?"

A few hesitant murmurs assured her there was not.

Rowland's arctic blast overshadowed all. "I'd pull Vespers before I'd allow her on the mare's back."

"And why is that?" Michael crossed his arms over his chest. "Elizabeth's your best shot at the prize."

She watched the black thunderclouds roll across Rowland's face. "I'll ride Vespers, for Christ sakes," he bit out.

"I suppose you're right," Michael replied, glancing at his fingernails. "It might be dangerous."

Rowland cursed and said something caustic about brothers, death wishes, and bloody females.

Elizabeth watched the two men; a seed of an idea already rooted in the landscape of her mind. Really, what did she have to lose? He had said she should have a little larceny in her heart for righteousness to win, hadn't he? She refused to admit that he had obviously expected her to try and steal her family's letters from Pymm. While the others conferred about the change for the race tomorrow, she stooped to whisper a few sentences to Lefroy privately.

He glanced at her and then at his master and shook his head.

"Please?" she whispered.

"He'd wring me neck for certain, lovey."

She stared at him.

Mr. Lefroy shook his head weakly. "Come back an hour before dawn and we'll parlay."

She straightened only to hear Rowland answering a question from his half brother.

"Someone tampered with his food," Rowland murmured, then pointed a finger at Mr. Lefroy. "Your pay is docked. I told you not to eat the night before, old man."

"Are you certain?" Elizabeth asked.

"No." He dragged a hand through his dark hair.

Michael rested an arm on the top board of a stall. "I hear Pymm bet a small fortune against Vespers."

If she was going to do this, she had best leave so she'd have time to prepare. "Well, I see I'm not really needed here any longer—so I shall bid you all good evening. I should return to the castle."

"The best idea I've heard yet," Rowland coolly replied. "And you would be wise not to tell anyone where you've been. Your bloody fiancé is probably shouting down the place looking for you."

Rowland disbanded the rest of the stable hands, tasking each with a myriad of details prior to the most important race on the calendar. Even his damned brother was put to good use. He thought the better of it when he was forced to endure his chatter.

"So, what are you going to do about Elizabeth Ashburton?" Michael murmured as he studied Vespers's hoof resting against the scarred leather apron that stretched between his knees.

If Rowland could not find Michael's words amusing, he could at least find humor in his half brother wearing evening finery beneath a blacksmith's apron. He leaned against the wood wall of the shadowed stall and restrained himself from standing over Michael to examine his work. "Careful, she's still got that stone bruise on the frog."

"It's healed. Answer my question."

"What bloody question?" Rowland scanned the large mare's form for the hundredth time in the last few hours. He had bred her himself and overseen every stage of her development. She had more heart and intelligence than any other horse in England as far as he was concerned.

"You know which question. How are you going to help Miss Ashburton?"

"And why in hell would I want to do that? I've got enough to concern me. And that female has more problems than a thief caught in a window sash."

His brother glanced at him, a nail between his teeth. He plucked the nail from his mouth, carefully positioned it on the hoof, and tapped it into place. "You know, we can do this the hard way or the easy way."

"Far be it from me to deny you your pleasure." Rowland tried to casually peer closer. "Reposition the nail next to it, too."

"No, that one's good. I only redid the first to humor you. Everything is fine, as a matter of fact. At least she's in tip-top shape for the race tomorrow." Michael released the horse's hoof and checked the pastern. "The same cannot be said of you."

Rowland made an exasperated sound.

"You look like you're about to topple over, old man." Michael collected his old blacksmithing tools. "How are you going to pull it off tomorrow?"

"Check the other fore hoof."

"'. . . please'?" Michael requested, a slow grin climbing.

"For someone who has blunt riding on the race too, you're mighty unconcerned."

"I don't have a ha'penny on the Gold Cup."

Rowland raised a brow. "Well, why in hell are you out here helping me then? Thought there was a bloody ball to attend, or do you miss your old life as a smithy?"

Michael chuckled and ran his hand along the mare's rump as he crossed to the other side and examined her hoof. "I realize the notion is completely foreign to you, Brother, but there is this thing called fellowship. It's the fabric of life. You should try it one of these days."

Rowland snorted. "I should have guessed happiness would turn you into a sentimental fool."

Michael shrugged off the words. "You should try it with Elizabeth Ashburton before it's too late."

"You know, Michael, if your lectures are the price for tearing you away from Prinny's entertainments, perhaps you should go back now before you ruin this poignant exhibition of brotherly love," he said, jaded cynicism dripping from his words.

"The others might not see what's going on here, but you and I do," Michael said, determined not to be put off. "She shouldn't marry Pymm."

"Really?" Rowland ground out.

His brother released the mare's hoof and stood slowly. "This might very well be your last chance."

"At what?" Rowland gritted out. Christ, he didn't have time for this.

"To reclaim your dignity and rejoin humanity," Michael murmured.

"You are a step away from wearing skirts, Michael. Must be from living among females and their overwrought emotions."

"And you are a step away from complete ruin on every front." Michael waved his arm. "Lefroy told me the sorry state of your financial affairs. And I don't need anyone to tell me about the state of your soul. I endured it firsthand, like everyone else under your employ."

"Hang Lefroy," Rowland seethed. "And why do you give a bloody fig about what happens?"

"I didn't until I put all the pieces together."

"Well, you can leave it well enough alone. If I can't force my gossiping stable master from his cozy sick-bed then I shall ride Vespers to victory and your conscience will be relieved. And if I fail, I shall find an alternate plan."

"Really?" Michael raised a doubting brow. "And what of next month's creditors?"

"I shall find a way. I always do. That's the difference between you and me, Michael. You depended on your wife to save your neck. I've never depended on anyone else in my life."

Michael's eyes bore into his. "It's because you have never trusted another living soul—except your mother and your brother Howard."

And Mary . . . Rowland's hands fisted.

"And then you learned your brother wasn't worthy of your trust, and so now you stand alone—when you don't have to."

"Trust is for weak fools. Look, if you have something more to say, say it. I don't have time to stand here whining about the past."

Michael folded his arms over his chest. "All right, Brother. For a long time I thought you the most vicious, hard-hearted bastard that plagued the earth."

Rowland smiled.

"But then I saw you with Elizabeth at your enterprise and then again at the duke's wedding, when you saved her from exposure. And just now you refused her offer to ride Vespers even when she's your best hope to win. Now, I'm forced to admit you might not be the man I thought you were."

Michael's unwavering gaze was like some sort of inhuman probe. Rowland would not look away first. They stared at each other, only the sound of the mare's low whicker breaking the silence.

Rowland lowered his eyes.

"Why are you letting Pymm have her, man?" Michael whispered.

He refused to answer.

His brother made an annoyed sound.

Fury grew to epic proportions in his veins. "What? You think she'll find a happy future with someone formed from the muck of the Thames? Someone very likely to end up back there, the way things are going, damnation. You want her to share in the illegitimacy of my mother's Irish name, and sleep every night with a bastard who has seen and done nearly every atrocity invented by the bloody humanity you're so fond of, Brother? Is that what you would have for Miss Elizabeth Ashburton, the innocent daughter of a gentleman?" He felt the warm muzzle of his mare searching his palm. "Leave it, Michael. You know nothing of the matter."

"Let me guess. You think she'd be happier living in pampered splendor and so you deny yourself? You have changed." He shook his head. "The one time your selfishness should make an appearance, and instead you insist on being noble."

"Noble," he sneered. "I don't know the meaning of the word, Michael." He refused to add to the misery by revealing the real reason Elizabeth would be forced into marriage. Pymm's murderous blackmail was not a secret that was his to tell. And none of that made a bit of bloody difference.

Michael sighed. "I have one last piece of unsolicited advice for you."

"More?" he replied, incredulous. "God, no. Stop while I let you still stand."

Michael ignored him. "I suggest you picture Pymm on his wedding night as he debauches Elizabeth Ashburton's innocence. She'll be forced to lie under a man she thinks killed her father—whether he did or not."

A tiny sliver of ice cracked loose from Rowland's frozen heart. "Get the hell out of my sight," he growled. He was a whisper away from grabbing his bullwhip and thrashing that knowing look off of Michael's face. Damned idiot.

At least the damned idiot knew when he'd exhausted his welcome.

Rowland spent the rest of the evening plotting out the ride tomorrow. It would be the greatest long shot. Still. When Vespers was on her game . . . He looked up to find his youngest stable hand bearing a small tray.

What in hell?

"From Miss Ashburton, Master. She said to tell you that it was prepared by her own hand. She also said . . ."

"Spill it, Bobby."

". . . that I was to make sure you ate it so you'll have a little strength," he said quietly. "Said she made just what you like."

He stared down at one boiled egg, two pieces of

bread, an apple, and a small pot of tea. *Finally*. She listened after all. He hesitated for a long moment before he ate and drank without a drop of remorse for the first time in his miserable life. He hadn't eaten in over a day and this wouldn't make a difference in his weight tomorrow other than to give him some small amount of strength, something the last meal she had forced down his gullet had done.

After, Rowland put away the drawing of the racecourse and bedded down in the corner of Vespers's stall. He'd be damned before he'd let anyone else watch over her. Bloody Tattersall and his underhanded maneuver. He yawned so widely, his jaw cracked.

The edge of dawn dashed across the evening sky, chasing night away with its gold- and rose-tinted chariots. Elizabeth dressed in haste, grabbing the most important item—the black wig.

This was complete and utter madness. But for the first time in weeks she felt free of all the bindings of her wretched life—and certain she was right. She could do this. She knew she could. Her father would be proud of her. That, in and of itself, was enough.

And really, it was the only way. She had so little to lose. She had tried patience and demure living, and it had gotten her nowhere. It felt so good to act, and it felt even better to help someone.

It was amazing how easy it had been to get Michael and all of Manning's men in the stable to do her bidding. All those hours in the kitchen had stood her well. The men would have dug a pathway to China if she had asked.

And Michael. For some odd reason, he seemed even

more eager than she. After she had escaped Pymm's cloying words and touches throughout the royal ball, Michael had spent an hour with her discussing strategy, the other horses, riders, and above all, when to make the final push. She tried to take comfort in the knowledge that Michael and Mr. Lefroy would not allow this if they didn't think she had an excellent chance of success. Each told her to trust Vespers, the most talented mare they'd ever seen. She was to stay far on the outside, avoid any hint of danger.

She refused to consider for a moment what Rowland would do to them all after the fact. It was too terrifying. And she was depending on success to soften his ire.

Now if she could just count on Sarah to play her part in the charade. It would be the last time she would ask anything of her.

Rowland struggled to grasp onto consciousness. What in hell was wrong with him? He cracked open his peepers and just beyond him, a shaft of sunlight filtered through the stall door, piercing the darkness and illuminating the dust motes hanging in the air.

"Morning, Master." Lefroy's groggy voice filled his brain.

Using all his effort, he turned his head slightly. Something was very wrong. It was too bright, and his head felt like three stone. Lefroy lay sprawled against the other side of the stall.

He had the notion that there was something very important on which he needed to focus. Something vital. His mouth tasted dry and bitter. "What in hell," he grunted.

"Laudanum," Lefroy said, lying back down with a small groan.

And then the truth rushed to his mind like a furious tempest. *Good God*. It was Ladies Day at Royal Ascot—the Gold Cup race. He swung to his feet, swaying terribly. His head swam. "Where the bloody hell is everyone?" he rasped. "What time is it?"

"About eleven—at a guess, sir. They're at the course."

With the vilest curse imaginable he wrenched his body forward. "Old man, you are relieved. Without notice. Hell, where's my bloody whip? I'll thrash you until you regret the day you first saw my face."

"I already do, sir," Lefroy replied with a wan smile. "Most days, that is."

God, his head was as muzzy as a gin addict's, his balance completely off. What had Lefroy said before? *"Laudanum,"* he whispered to himself.

"I think she put it in your tea last night."

His mind was ratcheting back into some semblance of order. Only one person . . . a thousand thoughts cascaded into place. *The bloody little fool*. She'd break her neck.

He staggered to the edge of the stall and called to the nearest hand. His orders were so coarse and his tone so black, the devil himself would have jumped to attention.

It took less than a half hour for Rowland to ride the six miles from Windsor to the course at Ascot. His head traveled a mere quarter mile behind him. It took nearly half as long again to negotiate the crowd of fashionable fribble crowding the royal enclosure. Wasp-waisted gentlemen strolled in formal wear with ladies draped on their arms. The bloody females tried to outdo one another with ridiculous hats and gowns of every hue and shape.

The stands were full to bursting with more than ten score of spectators determined to see who would take home the prestigious prize.

He grabbed a gentleman's arm without preamble. "The Gold Cup," he sputtered, out of breath, "has it gone?"

The gentleman pulled away from him with a dark glare. "I would thank you to not—"

"Bloody, sodding hell. Has it gone?" he shouted.

The female on his arm looked him over with a giggle. "It's about to begin, Mr. Manning. Look . . ." She pointed toward the starting stand, where a dozen or more horses jockeyed for position.

He began to cut through the crowd using all his remaining strength. His eyes scanned the lineup, searching among the riders for the dark blue and gold colors of his livery. He found Vespers first, her form a half a hand taller than the rest of the field.

As he zigzagged past the last stragglers in the throng, he finally allowed himself to see what he had known he would find.

His gut fell to his feet. The most hideous black wig, now cut short, peeked out from under the traditional jockey cap. The imbecile. She was going to be killed.

He shouted but instinctively knew it was too late. The flag dropped. The crush of race horses sprang forward en masse. Cursing a blue streak, he dashed to the starting stand, his eyes never wavering from the woman whose neck he would break if she didn't manage to do it on her own in the next few minutes.

Clenching his fists, he reached the two men he would later torture privately with his own hands.

"Gentlemen," he said in a venomous spew.

The Duke of Helston and the Earl of Wallace turned their heads in unison and had the good sense to take a step away from him.

"You didn't forget that pistol, did you?" the earl said with a hint of fear to his ducal partner in crime.

"I wouldn't waste your time worrying," Helston replied with false assurance. "Manning doesn't have that damned murderous whip in hand."

"I always knew peers were dicked in the nob. But . . . you are both beyond every expectation, allowing her to ride. I—oh, for godsakes, please tell me she isn't carrying a whip." He was paralyzed with fear as he watched her battling in the rear of the pack.

"Of course not," Michael said. "What do you take us for? Lefroy and I told her everything she needed to know."

"What about the part about my locking her in a stall, and feeding her hay and water for the rest of her life?"

He felt a dig in his ribs and half turned to see the Dowager Duchess of Helston. "I can't see anything. Lift me up, Mr. Manning."

"Ata," the duke groaned. "You're supposed to be in the stands distracting General Pymm with Sarah, Wymith, and Grace."

"He refuses to be distracted. And I refuse to be anywhere near John Brown while he sits beside that—that—"

"Now, Ata," the earl said. "He doesn't care a whit about the Countess of Home. I keep telling you that you mustn't let Mr. Brown see an inch of your anger. He's testing you. He's—"

"Oh, bloody hell, shut up," Rowland shouted. "Oh God—"

A thousand people gasped as they watched Vespers stumble, and then right herself, in the famous long, climbing section of the course.

"She's lost a stirrup . . ." he breathed. "She's going to fall. She's going to finish last, *and* dead."

"Look, she's retrieved it," Michael replied. "Stop mother henning. She's closing with the pack."

The tight loop of the track loomed. It was the one place the tall mare had to hang back. The only section she had a prayer of making up ground was in the long, straight stretch at the end. But apparently that witch, Elizabeth Ashburton, had not a clue. His eyes bugging out, he watched her surge toward the dangerous inside. Miraculously, Vespers raised her tail and unleashed her hindquarters, squeezing between the rail and a small chestnut who had begun to flag. Vespers overtook half the field in the maneuver.

A roar of approval echoed from the massive stand. There was less than a mile left.

Rowland tasted the metallic tang of blood in his mouth and could not move. He couldn't hear another bloody thing as he watched. All he could see was a stand of raised whips flaying the air.

He clenched something and realized someone had slipped a small spyglass into his hand. He raised it to his eye, his hand fluttering like a damned flag. And in that moment he spied the terrified expression of the woman he could not live without.

Oh God.

Chapter 11

"**S**he's making headway." His brother's voice was filled with awe.

Ata giggled with glee and jumped up and down like a girl of six and ten.

"I'll say," the Duke of Helston added, without his usual blasé drawl. "And in fine form."

"Except that wig," Michael said with a crazy shout of laughter.

Half a mile. And then he foresaw catastrophe. She was three from the lead now, neck and neck with Tattersall's gray gelding, and easing slightly ahead. In a flash, Tatt's jockey raised his whip and brought it down on Vespers's rump.

The mare kicked out, allowing the gray to surge forward. Worse, Elizabeth's balance was lost. Rowland's eyes nearly peeled out of his head. He was witnessing death.

His own.

Her breath caught, her mouth as dry as the desert and filled with its grit. She held on to Vespers's mane with a death grip and she willed herself to stay on. Her legs felt numb as she clamped them as hard as she could around Vespers's barrel while she tried to regather a proper seat. "Steady," she gasped more to herself than to the mare. Inch by inch she righted herself even though it cost her in speed.

It was almost impossible to see past the flying hooves of the small pack in front of her. Two, maybe three horses stood between her and the final stretch. In the large dip of the course she kept to the outside, knowing she could not chance another encounter with a jockey's whip. If she was to have a chance, she would have to stay clear of others and let Vespers do the work.

At that moment the jockey who'd had the audacity to whip the mare turned and grinned at her.

Elizabeth's fury nearly blinded her. "Come on, girl," she gritted out. The horse responded like an arrow let loose from a bow with the wind behind it.

Her hands rocked with the ground-churning motions of the mare as Vespers bore down on two horses and passed them at the start of the straight stretch.

This was her last chance. Elizabeth's heart was in her dry throat as she urged Vespers forward. As she closed the gap between Vespers and Tattersall's gray in front of her, Rowland's face flashed in her mind. "Do it for him, girl . . . Please." It was as if the mare understood her, and they rocketed forward.

Elizabeth was still urging Vespers on when she discerned that the roar in her ears was not from galloping horses but rather from the crowd's cheers. She dared to glance to the rear and saw the other horses far behind her. The race had ended a full furlong ago.

At least Vespers was smart enough to know it, for Elizabeth was frozen. The mare slowed to a trot, her sides heaving, and then came to a standstill as someone caught her reins.

Elizabeth looked down, nearly blind. *His* gaze met hers. Gone was the usual blank mask he wore. Pure, wild fury overflowed his luminous eyes. As others reached them in the middle of the track, it was his hands that gripped her waist and tried to lift her off.

But she was stuck like a burr in shaggy fur, and couldn't move. "Release your legs," he said an octave lower and harsher than the excited voices circling them.

Legs? She had legs? And then she couldn't stop the trembling.

"Make way," he barked behind him. She felt him disengaging her boot from the stirrup, and then in one awkward, wrenching movement he pried her from the saddle and placed her on the ground. The track rose up to meet her and he grabbed her about the waist again before she fell. Her legs did not seem to be able to support her. They felt boneless, useless.

"I'll get her out of here, Manning," a low voice said, that sounded remarkably like the Duke of Helston.

Elizabeth finally managed a croak of sound. "Did Vespers . . . did we win?"

"Of course you won," Michael shouted, his laughter nearly overcoming him.

A blaze of voices rang with congratulations and awe. But there was only one she wanted to hear. The only one who would not speak to her—Rowland.

Instead, he transferred her body to the Duke of Helston. "Take her away from here. Don't let Pymm find her."

What should have been the greatest moment in her scandal-riddled life was fast becoming one of her bleakest as the Duke of Helston's strong arms carried her far from the grandstand, Michael in front of her, hiding her from the curious onlookers. She struggled to see Rowland leading Vespers toward the winner's green. His back was stiff until the mare nudged her nose under his arm, seeking his praise.

A carriage waited for Elizabeth, and the two lords bundled her inside.

The petite form of the dowager duchess awaited her.

"You're to go to the Horse-Shoe Cloisters just inside Windsor's gates," Michael urged Ata. "The driver knows, and everything's been arranged."

When the door closed the deluge of emotion Elizabeth had held tightly within flooded her eyes, threatening to streak down her dirt-caked face.

They were waiting for him when he reached the winner's green. The corpulent form of the Prince Regent stood slightly in front of General Pymm and the Duke of Wellington. The latter looked like he'd be far more at his ease in a battlefield than milling about this fancy crowd.

"Hear, hear, Manning!" the prince crowed. "Well done, man. Knew you could do it. Although"—and here the prince leaned forward conspiratorially—"I'd cut Pymm a wide berth if I were you. He bet on the wrong man—or woman, if I have the right of it." The prince winked.

The Duke of Wellington shook his hand without a

word, his usual serious expression gracing the hawk-like face.

"Give him the trophy, Pymm. That's it, dear boy. You never were a good loser—thank God, for England."

A small bouquet of flowers was tucked under Vespers's saddle flap and General Pymm drew close to hand Rowland the Gold Cup, inscribed with the previous winners of the most prestigious race in England's history. A false smile plastered Pymm's face, while beads of perspiration lined his brow and ruined the row of blond curls there.

"Good show, Manning," he said loudly. "Congratulations."

There was little surprise as the general closed the gap and lowered his voice. "Sorry to inform I won't require those cavalry horses after all, Manning. Too bad, isn't it? I should have known a bastard like you wouldn't be able to understand such simple terms."

"What's that, Pymm?" The prince stepped forward.

"Just inviting Mr. Manning to my wedding, Your Majesty."

"There, I knew you could be gracious in defeat, Pymm," the prince said with a chuckle. "Now where is that neck-or-nothing little devil of a jockey of yours? Would very much like to meet him—or *her*."

"Mr. Lefroy's feeling under the weather, Your Majesty," Rowland ground out.

The prince's watery eyes studied him as his jowls waggled. "You can't fool me," he murmured loudly enough for Pymm and Wellington to hear. " 'Twas that female you bussed so outrageously at St. George's, wasn't it? Damned talented little thing. And here I thought she was just a little mud dab you keep on the sly. You wouldn't consider sharing, would you?" The prince guffawed as Rowland imagined ten thousand ways to separate Prinny's head from his rotund form. Out of the corner of his eye he saw that Pymm was contemplating the same thing with Rowland's own noggin.

The Duke of Wellington stepped forward and, with far more pomp and circumstance than either the Prince Regent or Pymm, handed Rowland the purse winnings.

Prinny slapped him on the back. "You must join us at table tonight, man. Everyone will want to hear how you plotted the race." He winked again. "And I order you to bring your magnificent little jockey so we can celebrate properly. She can sit beside me, since Pymm's fiancée has so little conversation."

The general's face was mottled purple with rage.

Elizabeth wasn't exactly certain what Ata said to her in the carriage. Her mind was still reeling with images from the race, the roar of the crowd, and Rowland's furious face as he lifted her from the saddle.

"What are you going to do? What would you like us to do? What shall we tell General Pymm if he saw through your disguise?" Ata flung the questions at her like a seasoned barrister. When the dowager realized Elizabeth was incapable of speech, Ata clucked a few times before a haze of silence settled over them both. Elizabeth could only hear the pumping of her heart, still racing and skittering at the remembrance of Rowland's reaction.

She barely glanced at the timber and herringbone brick of the ancient cloister as she was secreted inside. A maid guided Ata and Elizabeth up a tiny winding stair to a small octagonal room where a bath awaited her.

She could feel Ata's eyes studying her and she looked away. The dowager dismissed the maid.

"I will help you, myself, my dear."

She couldn't move.

Ata sighed, and began to unbutton the dark blue and gold jockey's silks. Elizabeth closed her eyes.

Oh, this was not how she had imagined it would go. She had been sure he would be transported with happiness at the win. It would mean five thousand pounds. Enough to stave off his creditors for a long while.

Ata slipped the hat and wig from her head.

"I can do it," Elizabeth finally whispered.

"Oh, thank goodness. I was certain you were in shock," Ata murmured.

"I'm sorry, Ata."

"Why aren't you excited? You won! I was never so in awe, my dear. You are the bravest young lady I've ever known."

Elizabeth stepped into the steaming water of the copper tub. "No. I'm the most scandalous." She sank into the depths, submerging even her head. She wished she could stay in the warm, calming waters. Everything felt like a dream underwater.

Her breath gave up and she rose. Ata applied soap

to her hair and washed away the grime of the race.

"You shouldn't be doing this, Your Grace." Elizabeth bowed her head and Ata poured clean water over her head.

"Your Grace?" Ata said with a sigh. "Since when did I give you leave to address me in that formal fashion?"

"I don't want to pain your hand, Ata."

"Oh pish," the dowager murmured.

Elizabeth quickly finished with her bath and rose to accept the linen toweling and robe before settling in a chaise in front of the tiny fire in the austere grate.

Ata picked up a comb and began the tedious task of pulling the tangles from Elizabeth's huge mass of dripping hair. She stilled the older lady's fingers. "Please let me do this. My hair is impossible." Her eyes dropped to Ata's gnarled hand that was always fisted.

"Botheration," Ata muttered. "It doesn't hurt, you know."

Before she could think, Elizabeth posed the question not one of the ladies in Ata's secret club had ever dared to ask. "What happened to your hand?" She stopped. "I'm so sorry. I don't know what I was thinking. I shouldn't have presumed to—"

"My husband detested music." Ata paused, her aged face drawn. "And I never played very well, you see."

It was so rare for the dowager duchess to admit to any fault in her person. Elizabeth turned fully on the chaise to face Ata.

"I played the pianoforte. But my true love was the harp."

"I remember your mentioning something about that when we were all in Cornwall."

"It's a difficult instrument. Makes the most ungodly sounds when ill played." Ata plucked at her gown awkwardly.

"You don't have to tell me the story," Elizabeth whispered.

"No," Ata said. "I want to tell someone. I never have, you know."

Elizabeth nodded silently.

"My husband, Luc's grandfather, had a devil of a temper like most Helstons. But you see," she said softly, "there was something more behind it. Something in him enjoyed tormenting those weaker than himself. And I never had a complacent nature. I never could back down from a bully. And the duke was that."

Elizabeth covered Ata's gnarled hand with her own.

"After John Brown left me waiting for him over the anvil in Scotland the summer I was sixteen . . . well, I was so furious I agreed, despite many misgivings, to the brilliant match my parents had arranged before we toured the Highlands. It was stupid of me. The duke was well over a foot taller than me and wanted nothing more than the large fortune I brought to the marriage."

"He hurt you," Elizabeth murmured.

"As I said, he had an unparalleled temper." Ata's black-as-night eyes stared into hers.

Every hair on Elizabeth's arms rose.

"He forbade me to ever touch the instrument again after he first heard me play. Soon after, he discovered me practicing in secret." Ata looked down at her twisted hand. "He became enraged and knocked down the harp. My hand—fingers—were caught . . . broken. No surgeon was called. That is why . . ."

"Oh, Ata," Elizabeth whispered. "No . . ."

They both sat in lengthening silence.

"Elizabeth," Ata said quietly. "I have a confession to make."

She looked at the older woman with the crown of gray locks braided into submission under her cap.

"I only suggested you marry General Pymm because I thought I sometimes spied a darkness in Rowland Manning's eyes. The same look my long-dead husband had. Until today, I feared Rowland was a bully—as heartless a blackguard as my husband. And Pymm? Well, while he might be a bit dour, and well pleased with himself, he at least has shown nothing but blind love and devotion to you. But I fear I might be wrong . . . Am I wrong? Are we all wrong?"

"Why do you think you're wrong?" Elizabeth asked gently.

"I watched Rowland Manning while he followed the race. I've never seen such utter terror on a man's face before. As if he would not be able to go on living if something happened to you."

"Ata, I beg your pardon, but it was not anxiety. It was anger."

Ata tightened her lips. "Allow me to assure you that I know the difference. Mr. Manning faltered, almost fainted dead away, when you lost your balance. Luc and Michael had to hold him back from jumping the rail to run after the pack."

She had no reason to doubt Ata, but the memory of

Rowland's face filled with fury countered the dowager's every word.

"Oh, Eliza, I do wish I could counsel you better. It's just . . . well, as of late . . . actually, ever since Mr. Brown returned from Scotland, I have felt very unsure if I render the best advice."

"Ata, that is not true. And honestly, it doesn't seem to matter what anyone suggests to me. I fear I'm incapable of following advice." She looked at the edge of her hem. "At least I can only blame myself when everything falls to pieces, as it always seems to do."

"Well, I can assure you that admitting any possible error does not change anything," Ata said with a small voice. "I have tried it. Even Mr. Brown tried it. And we are proof that it does not work."

Elizabeth searched the older woman's forlorn face. "You spoke to him?"

"In a letter last spring. Begged his pardon for all our old arguments—my past behavior," Ata murmured. "I begged him to return. And now I regret it, for he is here and quite obviously indifferent to me. It appears disaster is to be the cornerstone of my life no matter what I do."

Elizabeth gently squeezed Ata's hand. "How can you call the last two years a disaster? These many months have been the happiest of my life. Ata . . . your friendship means more to me than I will ever be able to properly express."

"Oh, my darling. I did not mean to suggest . . . Ah, I have muddled this too. What I mean to say is that it is I who is grateful to you and the others for your friendship. I shall never forget any of you, as you forge your young lives."

"You make it sound as if we will not see each other in future," Elizabeth said with anxiety.

"That is not so. It is just that time presses on and each of you will have husbands and children to attend to—and all the mysteries of your lives will unfold. I shall eventually retire to Cornwall. But, fear not, I am too curious to go yet. First, I must see who shall win your hand." Ata continued before Elizabeth could respond, "Come . . . let me help you with your hair ribbon."

As she quickly donned the newly pressed blue silk gown laid out for her, and Ata finished dressing her hair with a blue satin ribbon, Elizabeth wished she had a hint of how her life would unfold. She was so tired of mystery—so tired of choosing the wrong course.

Ata was of the same mind.

That very evening, Ata took her decision. She had watched Mr. Brown and the Countess of Home laugh and converse all through the endless formal dinner. And she had endured watching them dance twice, the countess flirting with John each time the intricate steps brought them together. And yet, when he had finally come to claim a set with Ata, he had not uttered more than two sentences. It was the outside of enough.

When the last notes of the music faded away, Ata tugged John Brown behind the nearest potted palm.

"Do you want to marry me or not?" she asked, fuming.

He took far too long to form a reply. "Are you asking?"

"Are you refusing?" She loathed her defensive, tinny tone.

"Lass . . ." His voice was tired.

A cool trickle of hurt filled her. "You *are* refusing." She really was the stupidest woman in all of creation. She had chosen to love a man who was determined to break her heart twice in one lifetime. "I can't believe it."

"You're asking for the wrong reason," he said gently.

"What do reasons have to do with this? Either you want to marry me or you do not. You've had five decades to consider it. I had rather thought you were inclined at one time."

"I was. But I won't marry you just because you are jealous of the Countess of Home."

"Hang the countess and her fawning ways."

He sighed.

Her temper got the better of her. "I should have known you would back down when it came to the point. Nothing has changed. I'm the fool for thinking it could."

His lips were stiff. "I've explained my actions many times. I refused to allow you to throw in your lot with a poor, young man without prospects at the time. I knew your parents would refuse your dowry. You would not have enjoyed living in a crowded house with my parents and all my numerous siblings."

"You're absolutely correct. I vastly preferred living in an enormous glittering castle with one tyrant," she nearly shouted.

"I know you will never forgive me for the choice I made—and I understand why. I'm sorry, lass. I truly am. And your anger is entirely justified. I am sorry for so many things. I don't want to bring you any further pain or heartache. I—"

"Oh, Mr. Brown," purred the Countess of Home, coming around the palm with a knowing smile. "There you are! The quadrille you claimed on my card is next. Shall we? Your Grace, do excuse us."

Paralyzed, Ata stared after John Brown as her nemesis led him away.

She had won their old argument. Finally. Why then, did it feel as if she had lost everything?

For so many years she had blamed John Brown for her misery. In the past, she had never placed herself in his shoes to understand his reasons. But now she saw they were both of them wrong.

Neither one of them was to blame.

And now . . . it felt as if it was very much too late. There was too much history between them—too much to regret, and too much to forget.

And so Merceditas "Ata" St. Aubyn, the Dowager Duchess of Helston, watched the great love of her life dance away from her.

•

Rowland Manning leaned against a pillar of the folly in the formal gardens, beyond the open doors of the royal ballroom. He was behaving like a bloody fool.

In the end he hadn't trusted himself to attend the dinner. A cloud of disgust permeated his conscience. The cool fortitude he had formerly possessed was slipping fast from his fingers.

He could no longer idly stand by as Pymm tried to solidify his hold on her. The next time he saw the general touch any part of her, he would pound the living daylights out of him. And so he thought it better to remain in the darkness. Perhaps she would appear, and he could make a spectacle of himself privately instead.

Occasional voices drifted from the ballroom and from the balcony nearby. They all chattered about the race, and of the mysterious jockey. Some insisted it was a man, others—the more romantic-minded— insisted it was a girl.

"Thank God that Manning fellow didn't accept His Royal Highness's invitation to dine with all of us tonight," a grim voice floated down from the balcony's steps. He could just make out the silhouette of a fat young man taking a pinch from his snuffbox.

Two ladies stood on the step above him. One of them tittered. "Speak for yourself, Ronald."

"Yes, I see how it is. You enjoy the scent of manure."

"Oh, off with you, cousin. Louisa and I have something far more pressing than horses to discuss."

"You and your sister don't fool me, Pamela," the portly man replied, mounting the stairs with a sigh. "You all flutter about like magpies before men like Manning. Well"—he stumbled over the top step and righted himself—"see that you stay far away from a man like that. He's not one of us, and I'm sure your husbands would hate to dirty their hands to protect your honor."

The two ladies giggled and watched him depart. "Oh, Pamela, I heard Mrs. Lockwood *and* Lady Loudan had liaisons with him *at the same time* four years ago."

"And Lady Rothbyrn the year before. It is said they *paid* him."

"Well," the other replied, "I would too, if I had enough pin money."

The two of them dissolved in a gale of titters.

Rowland shook his head in disgust. Where did they learn to make that god-awful sound?

Finally, they departed, and Rowland closed his eyes, grateful for the coolness of the marble pillar at his back. After a long while, he sighed and bent to pick a few stems of lavender beyond the lip of the folly. He raised his eyes to the balcony and froze.

It was a good thing his half brother appeared at his side in the darkness a moment later. It was even better that Michael applied a stranglehold on him that would have held an enraged bull.

Dinner had been agony. The ball worse. Pymm crushed her to his chest at every opportunity in the movement of the waltz. He seemed to steer them toward other couples for the opportunity to grip her more firmly to him. And each time her eyes flew to his, she would see that same smirk on his face, daring her to say a word.

"My darling, you are exquisite tonight," he murmured in her ear.

She shivered involuntarily and he pressed her closer to him.

"But then again," he paused, "you are not nearly as beautiful as you were this morning."

She stared at him, speechless.

"What? Did you think I would not recognize you? Your friends tried to shield me from the truth. The fools. I daresay they thought I would berate you for it. But they know nothing of my admiration for you, darling."

She did not know how to respond.

He pulled her closer again as they edged the ballroom. "It is the very reason I desire you. Your verve. Just think how daring my heir will be off of you. Tell me, how did Manning convince you to do it?"

"It was wholly my idea, General."

He narrowed his eyes. "Well, just remember that while I enjoyed the display, I only could because no one recognized you." His voice possessed a harsh turn to it. "Soon—very soon— you will have to curb such antics and become a proper duchess. A duchess befitting my station."

She dared not part her lips lest she defy his order just as Ata had defied her husband. She had learned long ago that Pymm's moods shifted on terrifyingly trivial whims.

Without realizing his intentions, Elizabeth found herself waltzing beyond the French doors to the open and deserted balcony. He halted in the cool night air, tightened his grip, and in a half second, his thin lips drew closer.

Good God. He was going to kiss her. Heat and sour perspiration mixed with his overly sweet perfume. She stopped breathing and turned her face away. His lips pressed against the corner of her mouth and cheek.

He chuckled. "You're going to have to do better than that in less than a fortnight, Elizabeth. I think you've forgotten how much you enjoyed it the last time."

She clenched her teeth and forgot to bite her tongue. "That was when I thought you an honorable man."

"I beg your pardon? Tsk, tsk. I am nothing if not an honorable man. Haven't you been paying attention? I'm a living monument to British valor."

"You are blackmailing me into marriage," she dared, unable to stop.

With another smirk, he released her. "My dear, how dare you suggest something so distasteful? You are lucky I make allowances for females. Your reasoning is not as fully developed as a man's. You mustn't tax your brain with such things. Darling, I'm merely protecting you from the dishonorable actions of your father."

She stared into Leland Pymm's eyes, and was certain she spied the depths of madness. It was pointless to argue with him. And so, she played to his lunacy. "Of course. I see your point," she agreed through gritted teeth. "General? It's so very hot tonight. Would it be too much to ask for a glass of punch?"

His doubt warred with an obvious desire to please her.

She would do or say anything to free herself from him for the rest of the evening. She batted her eyes. "Please, sir?"

He bowed. "Of course, Elizabeth. But, I shan't be amused if you are not here when I return."

The moment he disappeared into the mass of guests in the ballroom, Elizabeth lifted her skirts and dashed down the steps to return to the tiny, ancient cloisters as she had planned.

Just beyond the garden, she saw Michael step from

the evening shade of the folly and look at her before turning toward the balcony.

And then, the most poignant apparition rounded one of the small structure's columns, his hands clenched, his face twisted.

He was the man she most wanted to see. The man she feared to see. And yet, she did not pause. Within an instant she was in his arms.

His hands were hard on her shoulders, gripping her to him. And then his lips joined hers, as if he knew how much she wanted to erase the memory of Pymm's mouth. She gave in to the luxury of his strong arms coming about her and she felt him tremble against the desire to crush her to him.

"Come, we've got to go away from here," she whispered. "He's going to return in a moment."

"No," he said, his voice strained to breaking. "I have something I must say to—something I must *do* to that sodding, bloody animal."

Despite his great height, she shook him, barely able to make him budge an inch. "Please . . . no. Please, just help me go away from here."

He finally focused on her, his pale green eyes darker in the moonlight, like a feral animal looking for the kill. His lips tightened and it was as if she could feel the indecision in his body. He wrestled for self-control for a long moment before he recollected himself. "I'll take you anywhere you want to go, Elizabeth—somewhere far, far away."

His words stunned her. It was so unlike him. She knew he was furious with her for racing today. And yet, he appeared far more angry with Pymm for simply kissing her cheek.

He offered her his hand and she grasped it to pull him toward the cloisters. Neither said a word as they rushed along the grassy edges of the walkways, avoiding the crunch of the gravel.

Heart pounding, she eased past the heavy arched door and bolted it. She led him up the winding stair to the small octagonal chamber that had probably been reserved for a monk, under an oath of silence, in medieval times. Indeed, it felt like they were cut off from the rest of the world here.

He dropped her hand and stood as still as one of the marble statues flanking the walls of the gothic hallways in the castle. His sun-darkened skin was pale in the moonlight streaming from the two arched windows opposite each other.

"I wanted to rip off his arms," Rowland whispered, his tone hoarse with tension. "I don't want you near him ever again."

"I thought you were angry at me. Angry for this morning." She crossed and held onto her own arms.

"I was." He exhaled. "I still am." He gripped his temples, his dark hair spilling over his trembling hands. "I shall never forgive you for it. What were you thinking?"

"That I wanted one last chance to do something right before I bowed to the inevitable."

He shook his head, and half turned to stare beyond the window to the starless night.

"All along," she whispered, coming to stand behind his broad back, "I've been telling myself I wouldn't marry him. All along I thought I would find a way to avoid it. But I think I always knew I was fooling myself."

He dropped his head. "You are *not* going to marry Pymm, Elizabeth," he said tightly. "Did you not hear what I said?"

Her spine tingled and she dared to wind her hands around his waist and lay her head on his stiff back. "Don't say such impossible things. Please, I don't want to talk about him."

He made an odd sound in his throat as if he wanted to say much more but did not.

She could not get past the lump in her throat. For so long she had hoped for a private glimpse of the man behind the hard façade and now that he was here with her, she didn't know how to proceed.

"You had better stop this, now," he said quietly, more to himself than to her. "You see, I can't stay away from you anymore without your help."

She swallowed. "I don't want you to."

His back rose with his inhalation. "Elizabeth . . ." He grasped one of her hands and pulled her around to face him.

His eyes glittered like hard glass, his brows like two angry slashes across his face. Not one harsh line of his face softened as he studied her. "I'm going to sleep just beyond that door. I promise he won't find you. I'm taking you away from here an hour before dawn tomorrow. But tonight, you must sleep. You look ready to drop."

Her heart raced. "No."

His lips formed a grim line.

"I want you to stay," she whispered, daring to encounter his eyes. "With me. Here." She felt exposed, her emotions raw in the night air.

The striated muscles in his jaw tensed and released, yet he said not a word.

Slowly, she reached for the three hooks in the back of her gown to undo them. The sash gave way as she pulled one end.

"Are you *trying* to drive me to madness?" His eyes were glazed with pain as he laughed harshly. "Isn't it enough that you've brought me past every rational thought?"

The blue gown fell free of her arms and she stood before him. "I want you," she said simply. "This memory of you. Nothing more. And I don't care if it's wrong. If I must say good-bye to you, let it be this way. Let it be something I can hide in my heart and remember every night . . ."

She watched him squeeze his eyes shut as if he were in exquisite pain. And then he lowered his head to kiss the top of her head. "Elizabeth . . . no," he whispered.

Chapter 12

Rowland didn't dare move—only his cheek rested against her warm head.

He felt her gentle fingers working the knot of his neck cloth and he stood stock-still—unable to summon the will to stop her. Her hands began to tremble as they unbuttoned his linen shirt. She appeared to lose her nerve at the first of his vest's buttons.

If he simply backed up five steps, he would be at the door. He could then turn and walk away.

But then his eyes became mesmerized by the sight of her delicate fingers unwinding and loosening her corset lacing. The flesh above her underclothes was so lovely, delicate—shimmering in the moonlight. He forgot to breathe when she lowered her chemise.

Oh God. His iron control cracked like an iceberg sheered from a thousand-year-old glacier.

An unholy sound escaped his lips. His hands latched on to her wrists. Blinded by a level of desire unknown to him, he could not have stopped if a league of devils tried to hold him back from her. In a rush of movement, he grasped the narrow curve of her rib cage and bent his knees to bring himself to the ruched tip of her breast. He sank into her, his lips catching and caressing the tender bud with a sigh of despair over his inability to withstand her.

She was so soft, so sweet. And he could not taste enough of her. In one smooth movement he gathered her to him, one arm under her knees, the other around her slender frame.

Without knowing how, he found the small bed and lowered her to it. Standing there, staring at the woman in front of him, it was like a dream, so terribly perfect and beautiful that he was afraid he would wake and find himself back in the nightmare of his life.

He would never remember how he managed to divest himself of his formal clothes—all except for his breeches—and Elizabeth of her loosened corset, chemise, and stockings, but he would never forget the sight of her lying before him, her honey-gold mass of hair in complete disarray across the bolster; one arm shyly covered her breasts while the other hand rested above her thighs.

"Don't hide yourself from me, Elizabeth," he whispered as he grasped her face between his hands and lowered his lips to her lush mouth. "It's so rare one is allowed a glimpse of flawlessness."

A tiny moan escaped from her as he delved gently beyond her lips. His hands stroked her locks as he lost himself in the softness of her.

He reveled in the smoothness of her flesh and how it melded to the coarseness of his own. He could feel her heart's jangling beat and her uneven breathing as he moved his lips to kiss her again and again.

He never changed the tenor of his giving, never allowed her to do more than press her plush lips against his own. She was like some delicacy to be revered, and savored. And he was but a starving man before everything tempting and delicious.

Elizabeth's flesh felt like it was aflame from the unseen heat beyond his lips. Each place his mouth brushed, each caress from his gentle hands, brought a surge of fever. And yet, each time she tried to touch him, kiss any part of him aside from his lips, he stopped her, intent on touching, tasting her in his own fashion, on his own timetable.

God. She was here with Rowland Manning, painfully aware of the seconds and minutes that were slipping past them. Tears rose in her eyes.

She had not dared to think he would allow this. It had taken her too long to realize he was a man determined to deny himself every pleasure, every happiness in life. She wasn't sure why he felt such a need to torment himself, but there was one thing of which she was absolutely certain.

There was no other man so good in this world, and so determined to think the opposite of himself. And she wanted desperately to share her love for him, and to leave a piece of herself behind, reserved solely for him alone. She wanted to cry for the pleasure he was giving to her, feeding her soul with such happiness.

"Elizabeth . . ." he whispered, a question in his pained voice.

She didn't want to be diverted from the torrent of emotions in this dream. But she forced herself to lift her head. "Yes?"

"I can't do this. Can't bear the idea of ruining you—hurting you." His forehead lowered to her collarbone.

"Hush . . ." Slowly, she eased up onto her elbows for support. "You're doing nothing of the kind." She paused for a long moment. "You told me a long time ago that women have few choices in their lives. This is one I'm allowed. One I *demand*."

"You don't know what you're asking. This will bring you naught but pain, I assure you." He dragged his lips along her collarbone until he reached the notch of her neck. "You have no idea what happens between a man and a woman, do you?" His question drifted.

"Of course I do." She stroked his hair as she whispered the words.

He raised his head. His eyes were inches from her own. The corner of one side of his mouth held the smallest suggestion of amusement. "Really?" He said it with grave doubt.

She swallowed. "Privacy isn't always possible during war. I—I once came upon a soldier rising from a lake—unclothed—before I hurried away. I've seen statues in London, too."

His long fingers stroked the length of her jaw, and became lost in her locks. "Oh, Elizabeth," he said softly with a touch of sadness, "you know nothing of it."

"I know that part of a man joins with a woman. I'm not afraid."

"Of course you're not afraid." A groan rumbled through him. "I'm the only one with enough understanding and sense to be terrified."

"Why would you say such a thing?"

He sighed. "*Mhuirnin*, I've never taken a woman's innocence. I swore I never would. It's a brutal thing."

There was something dark and desperate behind his words and for the first time she heard a glimmer of the cockney behind his usual practiced façade. She refused to give in. "Well, I'm glad you've never done so. But, *you* are taking nothing from me. *I* am giving myself to you—only this is an even exchange, for you will give yourself to me."

He groaned. "This is impossible. And that's not how it works. There's only one doing the giving and the other doing the taking."

She leaned toward his face and pulled his neck toward her once more. "Please . . . just try." She poured every last ounce of hope into the one word.

He sighed and for a long moment, she was certain he would refuse her. But then he untangled the blue ribbon from her hair. "Give me your wrist," he whispered.

"Why?"

"Elizabeth, if we're to do this, it must be my way. In my fashion."

"You're not going to tie me to the bed, are you?"

His half smile appeared in the way that always made her heart ache.

"I should. It would serve you right for all you did today, and now tonight—tempting me like the devil with promises of heaven." He bound one of her wrists to his own with the ribbon. "This is the way of it in Ireland, my mother's homeland."

She didn't try to stop him. A flood of emotion welled deep inside of her. He was going to do as she asked. He would make love to her . . . Oh Lord, he would give this gift to her. It would be the exact opposite of the infamous medieval stories of *droit de seigneur*, when an English lord was said to have the right to take the innocence of the female Celts of the lower classes before their marriage.

And then she could not think about rituals at all. She could only feel the slight rasp of his beard against her shoulder as he kissed her there and then on her ribs and again lower. He was easing the trunk of his body between her thighs, and lowering himself farther. Everything was happening so quickly.

She grabbed his massive shoulders. He stopped moving and lowered his lips to her belly, dusting a thousand and one kisses on the taut flesh. "*Mhuirnin* . . . my Elizabeth," he whispered, mixing Gaelic and English words with reverence. She wished she could understand it all.

While she was paralyzed with uncertainty of what to do, his free hand stroked her arms, her breasts, and the outsides of her leg until his fingers sought a sensitive spot behind her knees. She tried to relax her grip on his hand bound to hers.

And then before she could say a word, in one smooth movement, he opened her knees wide and dipped his dark head.

She exhaled roughly and tried to scoot away. His hand held her in place.

"Wait!" She tried to close her knees together.

He rose up to face her, his eyes dark with mystery. His hand rearranged her legs closed. "Of course," he rasped. "You've come to your senses."

"No," she whispered. "It's just . . . it's just . . ."

He stroked a lock of her hair and curled it behind her ear. "What?"

"You're right. I know nothing about this—or what I should do. Won't you tell me?"

Rowland pondered her words, trying to ignore the mountain of flesh trying to burst free of the falls of his breeches. It was fortunate he had a lifetime of experience with deprivation. Hunger of any sort was second nature to him. With each beat of his heart, he pulsed for her. Perhaps it would frighten her. Perhaps he could scare her enough to think twice.

"All right, Elizabeth," he said evenly as he pulled himself beside her. "But there's very little to be said. You had the right of it." His free hand unhooked the side of his breeches, and his monstrous length of aching flesh sprang free of the fabric. "This is the part of me that would join with you." He watched her eyes, which for a flicker of a moment showed uncertainty. The muscles of her throat constricted and her eyes rose back to his own.

"That's not at all like . . ."

His one hand shook slightly, betraying his need as he began to refasten his breeches. "I told you this was a bad idea, a bad—"

"I'm not afraid." Her hands stopped his while he listened to her lie with conviction.

It nearly broke him. "You should be," he insisted. "I told you it's all about a man—*me*—taking, hurting *you*." He leaned his head back and closed his eyes. He had counted on shocking her. He should have known better. A female courageous enough to race at Ascot would not be afraid of him.

A moment later, his mind registered the soft, cool feel of her small hand caressing his shoulder, elbow, and coming to a rest on his hip.

He exhaled roughly.

She murmured something that did not register in his mind. And then her hand moved to trace the trickle of dark hair in the center of his chest. A moment later, her fingers dipped to the molded hollows of his gut.

Her touch was hesitant and soft and he wanted to shout with the pleasure of it.

She paused. "May I touch . . ."

He didn't bother to misunderstand. "No."

She continued to caress his chest, her hand trembling slightly. "I'm sorry I stopped you before."

He groaned as her hand drifted to one side, her thumb brushing the sensitive flesh above his hipbone.

In a flash of movement, he was on top of her, a growl of pure desire rushing from his throat. His ballocks were on fire, drawn tightly to his body. He squeezed his eyes shut as his arousal instinctively sought the moist notch of her beneath him. He stopped in the midst of a daze of agonizing desire.

She tentatively kissed his hot brow and he managed to regain his footing. He rested their joined hands next to her face and made a small space between them. Attempting gentleness, he traced his fingers down a path past her ribs to the curls that tempted him so.

Her breath quickened and her eyes became dazed

as he touched her, parting, tracing the silken folds. A blush crested her cheeks and she could not seem to look at him. A moan escaped her and he pressed the advantage, dragging a finger past the plush entrance to her and then backsliding to test the edges. Her hips moved to meet his palm.

She was so damned tight—far too small for a brute like him. *God*. What had he agreed to? As he sunk his finger a little deeper inside of her taut depths, his thumb circled the peak nestled in the curls, edging ever closer.

She was making inarticulate sounds, and it was driving him past the point of no return, past a point of madness no mortal man could withstand. It had never been like this. He'd never for a moment in his life ever lost control. But this ache began so deep inside of him. And then an easing coolness pressed against the small of his back, and he could not stop himself.

He was going to hurt her. Impale her. He was going to break her body and break his oath *never* to take advantage of a desperate, innocent woman.

A woman like *Mary* had once been.

No matter how much Elizabeth thought she wanted this, he knew it was wrong. But the black impurity that was ingrained in his wretched makeup would not allow him to stop. He closed the distance to her aching peak with his thumb, the friction causing a wave of desire to cross her beautiful face.

He was frantic to bring her pleasure. He would not stop until her breath caught and she appeared lost to the world. Only then did he reclaim the age-old position above her, his hand arranging her limbs wide to accommodate his monstrous frame.

Her dazed eyes were teary with emotion and it nearly killed him. His breath ragged, he flexed his hips forward until his hot, raging flesh found plush, wet relief.

Courting her body to accept him, he teased her opening just the merest bit until slickness eased the way. Black dots began multiplying in his field of vision, and through them he saw her passion-filled face below him, her lovely hair spread like that of an angel from the heavens.

With an unstoppable surge, the great length of him pierced her, and he was filled with the most pure sensation of both bodily pleasure and emotional pain so deep and yet perfect. At the same moment a terrible sound escaped from her clamped lips. Black horror flooded him—all the nightmares of the past were before him.

Suddenly, he felt her fingers interwoven with his own tenderly squeeze his hand in reassurance. He looked down at her, expecting to see regret and far worse.

"Rowland," she whispered, tears flooding her cheeks, "Love me."

He wanted to shrink away from her, but for the first time in the never-ending battle between his body and his mind, his body and his starving need won out.

He surged again inside of her, all the time knowing he was hurting her, despite her foolish words. He just could not stop himself. He pushed onward, always forward, could not remember to fall back.

He grabbed her knee and pulled it higher and again plowed forward.

He felt her cooler hand on his back again, seeming to urge him. Blind with need, his body undulated again and again. Taking, always taking . . . until his hunger changed.

He felt such a deep desperation to make her happy, and yet he was incapable of such a feat when he was surely only bringing her pain. He stopped at the sound of a soft moan. Her mouth was half open in a silent plea. He slipped his hand under her hips and tilted her to more easily accommodate him.

Her lovely emerald eyes widened, and he plunged further inside of her. Relentlessly, slowly, he thrust, his tempo even and sure. He pulled her ever closer until flesh to flesh, he covered every inch of her, inside and out. She strained against him, and the whisper of a keening sound met his ear. With a groan he surged onward, grimly determined to give her everything he had, every drop of pleasure he could drag from her. With a cry, she slipped over the high edge of pleasure-pain to find a long, pulsing release.

His ballocks nearly numb with the ache of an iron grip on control, he finally let himself go. With astonishing speed, he withdrew and great pulses of pleasure rocked through him, leaving traces on the soft bed linens beside her.

His heavy head rested on her breast, and he gulped large batches of air. He could hear the wild beat of her heart beneath his ear. Without thought or care to any remaining bashfulness she might still harbor, he forced himself to search for confirmation of the carnal violence he had wrought.

His head reeled as he spied the telltale streaks of blood on her slender thighs. Again, spots of black appeared in his vision, making him feel as if he might very well pass out from the hard evidence of the last of the cardinal rules he had broken.

Elizabeth had known the crash back to the muddy ground of real life was inevitable. But still . . . it hurt.

One moment she had been reaching to stroke his hair, and the next, his eyes had grown wide and dark and he had rolled away, leaving her to shiver slightly at the sudden departure of his sheltering warmth.

"Please," she said, trying to keep her voice steady.

He turned his head, unseeing.

"Will you not hold me?" she asked with a sadness she could not conceal. "I need your arms."

Her emotions whirled; a sort of melancholia seeped inside as the cool night air reached her flesh. She wanted more of him. More time with him. And he was now staring at her with such guilt.

"Wait," he said hoarsely. With his one long unbound arm he was able to reach a length of toweling on the washstand next to the bed. He dipped it in the basin of water.

Gazing at the blue ribbon still binding his wrist to hers comforted her. As long as it was there, they would be together.

She flinched as she felt the cool cloth brushing her thighs. She concentrated on the ribbon, unable to watch him minister to her. And yet, she knew he would not be able to rest until he had his way. And so she said not a word.

The flame of the candle flickered and threw a strange shadow on his back and buttocks. He was such a severely beautiful man. All sinew, and muscle, and bone.

He was improbable, like a great tree standing in a barren desert.

She did not know what to say to him now that the intimacy of the moment was past. She wanted to tell him the rapture she had experienced, wanted to assure him that he had not truly hurt her.

Yes, there had been pain, but there had also been such wondrous feelings coursing through her—as if they were one, as if she was forever a part of him now and he a part of her. Even if they were torn apart they would forever remember these moments together.

She studied his back as his breathing became even.

She squinted. There was a small mark on one of his buttocks.

Without thinking, she reached out her finger and traced the mark on his skin.

He flinched. His head turned toward her, his eyes piercing in the candlelight.

"I'm sorry," she murmured.

"It's to warn you," he said, his voice devoid of any emotion. One brow kicked up. "Although I played unfairly, I suppose. You were supposed to notice that earlier. Before we . . ."

"What do you mean? What is it?"

"The mark of a blackguard."

"*What*?"

"You heard rightly. It's a tattoo."

"Why did you . . ."

He laughed, the bitterness inescapable. "Oh, Elizabeth . . . surely, you've endured enough nightmares for one day."

"Who did that to you?"

The question hung in the darkness, like a secret in a worthless, useless boy—a long forgotten mudlark.

Chapter 13

Rowland debated in the privacy of his mind while she babbled about his bloody tattoo. Oh, he knew what he would do. He had known what he would do as he watched the bravest woman he had ever known risk her damned little neck to win five thousand pounds to save his worthless hide.

"Elizabeth . . . enough. I need to tell you what I've arranged for you."

"Not until you tell me how you acquired that mark."

He shook his head. What did it matter? "It's nothing."

"I'm listening."

He toyed with a small lock of her hair on the pillow next to him. "All boys and men brawl, be they gentlemen or commoners. I lost once—the odds were a bit off. The punishment was this crude tattoo."

"Is that someone's initial?"

"No," he spoke his words soft, slow. "Can't you guess?" When her gaze did not falter he finished. "*B* is for bastard, Elizabeth. So I would not forget."

Over his shoulder, he watched her rise slowly and lay her cheek on his back. She rolled forward and kissed the tattoo, like a mother would do to soothe a child's hurt.

He swallowed. "You're going to France. I've arranged for Joshua to take you to the coast at first light."

"France?" she jerked upright.

He felt like the worst sort of lecher for looking at the beauty of her fragile, naked form. "Yes. It's the only way."

"What are you talking about?"

"You'll never be able to return to England, of course. But, isn't that a small price to pay for avoiding Pymm?" He didn't add that it would also have the advantage of allowing her to cut herself off from the insanity of the two of them together.

"But he would then announce the contents of those French letters to all and sundry."

"And the French will bow at your feet—and protect their own. Since your mother was French, you can claim allegiance, renounce your British citizenship."

"But . . . but I would have nothing . . . I barely speak the language. And I would leave behind everyone. I would never see—"

He wouldn't let her continue, couldn't stand the look on her face. "You would have a portion of the winnings from the race to get you settled."

"But you need the money. You probably need much more than that if I have the right of it."

He lied smoothly without hesitation. "No. I've a contract with the cavalry. I only need a thousand pounds or so at the moment."

She looked at him with doubt.

"I'll provide more for you later. If it's needed."

He wasn't sure how he would get it, but he'd sell the last bit of his soul if required. He could always go back to the beds of the duchesses, marchionesses, and countesses who had courted his caresses, and lined his pockets, and provided part of the funds for his stable. The ones he had sworn off forever. "And your French relatives will probably take you in."

She shook her head. "I don't think you understand. They don't know me at all. I don't think I could expect them to . . . and my uncle might be out of favor. His division—"

"Well, you must try," he cut in.

"No. Not yet. I'm not ready to give up. I was at a low point—despairing earlier. There's still a chance I will find a way out of this."

He shook his head. "Every day—every event you attend binds you closer to Pymm. You must go away while you still can." Without thinking, he lifted his hand to touch her cheek.

And as surely as his words warned, the movement caused the blue ribbon to come unbound from his wrist. It fluttered uselessly from hers.

She did not doze more than a dozen minutes during any portion of the night. He kept her cradled in his embrace, touching her, stroking her with a reverence that made her ache for what would not last. She nestled ever closer to him, murmuring his name over and over because it became obvious that he drew such happiness from her words, and her soft kisses.

But as surely as time crawled inexorably forward, dawn broke through the shelter of darkness that had blanketed them.

At the sound of a light knock at the door, Elizabeth came full awake.

Rowland was three steps ahead of her, struggling with his breeches as she wrapped the bedclothes about her.

She recognized the muffled voice of the maid who had served her yesterday. "Miss? Last eve, the dowager duchess asked me to arrange a tray and bathwater for you. Shall I bring it inside?"

"No, Marie." Elizabeth stayed in the bed. "But I'd be most grateful if you'd leave it."

The maid's voice traveled from the other side of the door. "Her Grace said to tell you she will wait on you after she rises."

As the maid's footfalls from the stair faded, Rowland retrieved the food and a number of steaming buckets. "How did she know you were here?"

"Ata's the only one. I told her I wanted to spend the last night here since Pymm . . . occasionally knocks on my door in the castle, and brings little gifts. It's unnerving and I detest it."

He shook his head. "Of course you have a disgust of presents. You are a traitor to your sex."

Elizabeth smiled. She spied her gown and chemise too far away to reach, and so grasped Rowland's large white linen shirt and pulled it over her head as he brought the tray to the narrow bed.

"I like that on you," he murmured.

"When I was a little girl I used to secretly wear one of my father's shirts to bed when he was away on some distant battlefield."

"Where did you live?" He glanced up from arranging the cup and saucer.

"In Portsmouth. I was sent to my aunt, who took great exception to my choice in nightclothes. But then"—she hesitated—"there were many things she took great exception to. Not that I didn't deserve her censure. My best friend was a fisherman's son who longed to join the Royal Navy. We were forever getting into scrapes, and I was forever in disgrace for not befriending more noble children." She sighed.

She could see laughter teasing one corner of his mouth as he poured milk into the porcelain cup, and then tea. It warmed her heart that he remembered exactly how she preferred her tea.

"And so your father one day rescued you from his tyrant sister?"

"No. He held out hope for far too long that I could be formed into a proper young lady. I was fourteen when I was sent to a school in Hertfordshire that took on boarders."

He turned the handle of the cup in her direction. "So this was the place where you learned how to poison a man's tea and ride like a banshee?"

"Partially."

He cocked an eyebrow.

"I befriended the cook, an older woman from France, who taught me everything about preparing food and also sheltered me from the worst of the headmistress's constant harangues and punishments." She brought the steaming tea to her lips and the scent was delicious. It eased the words she had never dared to admit to anyone. "The school was where I learned I was a complete failure as a young lady."

He waited for her to continue.

She rushed to fill the silence. "I could not be taught

to play any musical instrument, or sing, or embroider, or draw, or paint. I was abysmal in mathematics. The only thing I learned was how to dance, aside from reading books about history, which I'd always enjoyed and . . ."

"Yes?"

". . . gothic novels."

"Of course," he said, his lips holding back a smile.

"And so at sixteen I threatened to run away. My father knew me well enough by then to know I would make good on my promise."

"Smart man."

There was something about the way he didn't utter falsities designed to comfort her that made her realize how trifling her trials as a child had been. Here, before her, was a man who had endured terrible hardships and sacrifice.

"Father gave up all attempts to curb my 'impossible exuberance'—as the headmistress called it, and allowed me to join him in London. He put up little resistance when the Peninsular War began and I insisted on going with him."

"How long were you with him?"

"Five years."

"How old are you, Elizabeth?"

"Too old to reveal it willingly." She laughed awkwardly and then picked up a piece of toast and buttered it before smearing a dollop of apricot jam upon it. "If you share this toast with me, perhaps you can wheedle the number from me."

He quickly rose, only to come behind her—flustering her. His unshaven beard abraded the skin on her neck as he nuzzled her. She was too slow to understand his intent.

"I have another method for extracting the number from you," he whispered. His fingers hovered near her ribs, ready to tickle her.

"Rowland," she said, ignoring him, "why do you do this? Why do you deny yourself?" She turned to face him on the bed.

He dropped his hands.

"I won't play this game any longer," she said, her voice low. "Tell me. Does it have something to do with Mary?"

He started. "Who told you anything about Mary?"

"I heard you murmur her name a few times last night. I think you were dreaming. Was she someone you once loved? Or did she love you?" She tried to keep her voice even, despite her heart constricting.

"Yes." It came out with the smallest huff of air. "But I did not deserve her devotion."

Elizabeth waited, the pain of his revelation engulfing her mind.

His voice was so low she barely made out the words. "She was my sister. Two years younger than I."

"*Your sister*? But I thought you only had brothers."

"Elizabeth," he said, "enough."

There was such pain in the depths of his eyes, she couldn't bring herself to force him. "I am eight and twenty," she said. "And you?"

"Far too old for you." His eyes showed the truth of his years.

She had always assumed him to be much older than

she. Surely beyond his fourth decade. "How old?"

"Thirty-bloody-eight."

She smiled. "You're in the prime of your life." She retrieved the forgotten piece of toast and bit into it. With great care she offered it inches from his mouth.

He gave her a pained expression and took a bite.

She knew he did it only to stop her questions. She pressed her advantage and gave him the rest before cracking the tip of the soft-boiled egg and devouring the contents with a spoon. The second one she prepared for him and he took it without comment.

She poured a cup of tea for him and watched him gulp the fragrant brew.

He waved away her offer to pour more, his eyes still hungry. "How much more time before that harridan comes looking for you?"

"She never rises before noon," she whispered.

"Then we have time."

"For what?" she asked breathlessly.

"Your bath." He nodded toward the copper tub in the corner, and the steaming pails of water he had retrieved from the other side of the door earlier.

Her modesty had returned with the daylight and she nearly became as red as a lobster when he insisted on tending to her, soaping her back, her shoulders. She grabbed the cloth from him as he tried to wash her breasts.

When she rose with a rush of water, he quickly took her place, soaping and sluicing water down his tall frame while she made use of the toweling. Before she had time to dress, he was behind her, grasping her to him. "No . . ." he whispered. "Not yet."

She nearly dissolved in his arms. She had hoped, but had been sure he would not.

He disengaged her fingers from the toweling, and let it drop to the floor. "You've forgotten dessert," he whispered in her ear. "You. The one person who always insists on it."

His seductive words made her shiver. "Dessert?"

"Strawberry Fool," he said, and she could feel his smile on her neck.

"Whatever do you mean?" she whispered. "There's no custard. Only a dish of . . ."

Before she could say another word he picked up a plate of strawberries from the tray and was backing her up to the bed, his arm preventing her escape. A moment later she found herself sprawled on the disheveled bedclothes looking up at him. He wore a length of toweling about his waist—his desire for her quite evident beyond it.

She was so very flustered as she looked into his dark and dangerous face. "Let me guess," she said, awkwardly.

He joined her on the bed, his dark, wet hair sleek against his noble head. "Yes?"

"Those are the strawberries, and I'm . . . the fool?"

"You're very quick," he murmured as he began lining the tiny wild strawberries down the center of her body. "And, yes, you are indeed the fool for scaring ten bloody years off of my miserable life yesterday." He perched a small, hulled strawberry at the tip of her breast and immediately covered it with his lips.

She groaned as he nibbled at the fruit and then at her tender flesh, tormenting her with his obvious expertise. His hands trapped her hips as she tried to move. "Oh no," he whispered. "Don't move. My table manners might go begging."

As the minutes ticked by and the berries disappeared one by one between his wicked forays, he swept his head lower and still lower, nibbling, licking, completely absorbed in his task. She could do nothing but feel like the innocent fool that she was, as her hands moved restlessly on the bed linens.

But then, before she could say a word, before she realized his intent, he dared to dip far below the last delectable piece of fruit. He tasted her with his tongue. She froze in shock, a garbled sound in her throat.

"Delicious," he purred as he rearranged her legs and fit himself more snuggly between them. "Mmmm . . ." His was the murmuring of some sort of dark, wild, beautiful animal of the night.

He was so very gentle with her despite the ironlike grip he used to hold her trapped. He seemed to be trying to soothe the raw ache of her by teasing the maddening peak he would not quite touch.

Soon, very soon, her shyness fled. She just didn't care what he did to her. She just wanted more of him. More time with him.

She dared to raise her head only to see his head nestled between her thighs. Passion welled deep within her, pulsing stronger with each movement of his lips, his mouth, his hands. The ache pulled her higher and higher to some great and mysterious place that seemed too lofty to scale. And then he paused and expertly plundered her peak, pushing her forward to the pinnacle. She was suddenly flying . . . and yet it didn't feel like it had the night before, when he had been within her. Now, she was all alone.

And his subsequent refusal to allow her to ease his own obvious desire felt like some sort of penance he was determined to pay, unearned as it was.

He left her with the greatest reluctance. And only after extracting a promise that she would not leave the cloisters. It was still early; only the dairymaids and a battalion of footmen scurried in the secret pathways of the lower classes. If Pymm was like most gentlemen and ladies he knew, he would lie abed until the sun reached the middle of the sky.

He had plenty of time to see to the closed carriage for her and for a last word with Joshua. If she had doubted his intention to see his plans through, Elizabeth Ashburton was about to find out that when his mind was set, not the Prince Regent himself could sway him.

Little did he know that there was one dowager duchess, who, despite an orchestra of grumbling, rose with another lady who had no trouble rising with the chickens. And when three women put their combined minds together, one man stood not a chance of getting his way.

My dearest,

I had hoped you would wait for me outside last night. But no. I can't express how much this event troubled me. And I cannot bear the gossip—or the sight of you with another.

I return to London and shall make further plans. I cannot tolerate the endless minutes which divide me from you. But soon this will be over and I shall be with you, my angel.

                                              P.

Elizabeth wanted to shred into a hundred pieces the newest missive from Pymm she had found waiting for her in the Helston carriage. But since she was not alone, she resisted and simply refolded it, the eyes of Luc, Ata, and Sarah regarding her with curiosity.

"The same?" Sarah's voice was soft.

"Always," Elizabeth replied. "I don't know why Pymm delights in leaving me these sentimental notes."

"Poetic drivel never helps a gentleman's suit. A change of heart, my dear?" Luc enquired, without a hint of surprise.

She twisted her gloved fingers, avoiding everyone's gaze.

"You are not to put her on the spot like that, Luc," Ata said. "You of all people know these sorts of things must be handled delicately."

Her friends had not a notion of how deep and wide the flood of complicating factors truly was. In the heavy silence, Ata rearranged the plumage of her enormous black hat, while Sarah gave Elizabeth's hand a comforting squeeze.

Luc tilted his head to one side in an attempt to peer at Ata's face, half hidden by her hat. "What were you thinking to wear that platter of crow's feathers in the carriage?"

"I'll have you know these are from the rare Australian black cockatoo."

The duke batted at one particularly large offender.

"I'm certain you know very well why I am wearing this," Ata said quietly, very unlike herself. It was obvious to Elizabeth that Ata was still distressed by the cool manner with which Mr. Brown was conducting himself of late.

"Actually, I'm not certain I do. I've been hearing the most outrageous stories. Unlike others, however, I prefer firsthand accounts," Luc ground out.

"What happened?" Elizabeth asked, relieved she did not have to address their questions.

Sarah quickly shook her head in silent warning and Elizabeth wished she had not spoken.

"Yes, do tell us," Luc insisted, iron coating his words.

"Well, I decided I should employ this era's modern ways if I am to find happiness. There was very little to it, I assure you. I've no idea why such a fuss is being made over my posing a simple question to a long-standing acquaintance."

Luc's expression turned thunderous at her words.

"Elizabeth is a prime example of what females should do," Ata continued.

"I beg your pardon?" Elizabeth squirmed under Luc's hot glare.

Ata leaned forward in the carriage and patted her knee. "You do what you want and ignore all the trivial things standing in your way."

"I'm sorry?"

"You kissed Rowland Manning in public," Ata replied.

Luc shook his head. "Yes, but she had the intelligence to do it while wearing a disguise. You, however, cornered Brownie in the middle of a ballroom."

"It was behind a potted palm," Ata insisted.

"You *kissed* Mr. Brown?" The shock of it sent a giggle to Elizabeth's throat.

"Of course I did not!"

"The Lady Home had a great deal to say about your conversation with Mr. Brown behind that potted palm." Luc sighed. "And she is recounting it to everyone who will listen."

"Proving she is the greatest gossip plaguing the earth."

"So, is it true?" the duke asked casually. "Did you, ahem, ask for Brownie's hand in marriage?" By his cool expression it was clear he did not believe it for a moment.

The dowager duchess's usually sallow complexion flushed. "Honestly, Luc, you have no idea how brazen the Countess is. Did you not see her dance with him *three* times? It's as if she is doing this to spite me."

"You think *she* is brazen?" Luc shook his head. "Well, I beg to differ with you. Never saw a man so flustered last evening. Thought Brownie was about to cock his toes. And I see you have not answered."

Ata snapped her fan into place and flapped it erratically. "He refused," she rushed on at the sight of their shocked expressions. "So that is that. And I'm for Cornwall as soon as Elizabeth and Sarah are settled. It's far too hot and unfashionable to be in town during the summer."

"Oh, Ata," Sarah said, sympathy washing over her grave face.

Elizabeth took up the older lady's hand. "I'm so sorry."

Luc looked as if he had been struck on the head, he was so dazed.

Ata waved away their concern. "It doesn't matter. Really. I'm delighted the matter is finally resolved. And Luc? I will thank you, if you truly care about me, to never speak of this again. I should like to change the subject."

The duke, always the most private of gentlemen, stared at his tiny grandmother, and for the first time ever, did exactly as she bade. He pursed his lips and then turned the full force of his personality on Elizabeth. Such graciousness was not usually at the forefront. "You are to be congratulated again for your courage and pluck during the race yesterday. Indeed, I must thank you."

Ah, she remembered. He had not had to forfeit the small fortune to Pymm. She bowed her head and nodded, unused to this man's praise.

"You must invite Mr. Manning to dine with us tomorrow," Ata said, struggling to regain a smile.

"But what of General Pymm?" Sarah frowned. "He was very unhappy last eve when he could not find you, Elizabeth. He is to stay at Windsor with the Prince Regent for several more days. But he said he would pay a call at Helston House the day after he returns—to take a turn about Hyde Park in the afternoon."

She swallowed. "And I shall go."

Luc cleared his throat, discomfort evident in the line of his posture. "And what shall you tell him?"

Yes, that was the question, wasn't it? It was just

too bad that she did not possess an easy answer. *She itched to act*. And so far, waiting for a solution to present itself had only mired her further and deeper until she feared she would be swallowed up by the tide of events.

Elizabeth gazed at the concerned faces of her friends in the carriage and took her decision. She would go to Hyde Park with Pymm when he returned to town and she would finally out and out ask him if he had killed her father. Of course he would lie if it was true, but perhaps she could discern the truth by his mannerisms. Even if it was her undoing, she had to confront him. And then she would go to France just as Rowland suggested.

It was too bad fate had other plans.

Chapter 14

Rowland had never been so furious in his life. With himself. He should know better by now. Since when did Elizabeth do anything a man ever bade her to do? He should have dragged and shackled her to the inside of the carriage bound for the coast.

No, he should have done all of the above and gone with her himself. Why, she would have twirled that lackwit Joshua Gordon around her fingers within three miles of London's outskirts.

As he rode away from Windsor with the myriad of horses and carriages from his enterprise following his lead, he pondered the dilemma of Elizabeth Ashburton, only to be called back to the monumental concerns behind him. Literally.

At the top of the rise, he turned to survey all the men riding and leading his race horses as well as several drivers in his signature blue-and-gold carriages. The weight of this world of his rested on his shoulders alone.

He searched desperately for a solution. These men and so many others faced certain destitution. With the flood of soldiers now returning from the battlefields of France and Spain, positions in great houses were scarce. If his enterprise collapsed, where would they all go?

Oh, he would survive. He was too bloody stubborn to do anything else. Whether it be at a workhouse, the docks, or maybe even on the high seas, he would survive.

He would start all over again.

But before he considered any of it, he would send Elizabeth Ashburton to France. He would do it before the week was out.

She supposed she had always secretly known the reason she preferred campgrounds to London's ballrooms. The former were far less daunting and the latter far too dangerous.

She understood men and their ways. She would never understand the foibles of the fashionable beau monde.

In so many ways, Rowland Manning reminded her of an officer who endured every obstacle in a neverending slog of battlefields—never complaining, only enduring with grim determination.

As she approached the entrance to Manning's, she fidgeted at the memory of him. She had not seen him for two days and an ache had moved to the vicinity of her heart.

Had all of what had passed between them really happened? It seemed a dream now. Had she really screwed up her courage and rode Vespers to victory? And had she had the audacity to share one perfect night with Rowland Manning?

She missed him.

She missed his starkly beautiful face—even the

black scowl he wore nine tenths of the time. If this was not evidence of love, what was?

She had decided to go to him before he came to her. It would go better if she attempted to catch him off guard. She would endure his certain censure for leaving Windsor with the others instead of escaping to France, and then . . . How was she to explain it to him? How could she make him understand that she didn't want to run away just yet—that she had to confront Pymm before she did anything else?

Lefroy's old, wise face was the first one she saw when the carriage halted in front of Manning's stables.

"You've just missed 'im, lovey. But I'd wager 'e'll return quicker than a bug on a frog's tongue."

She nodded and held out a box wrapped in brown paper.

"Wot's this? Dids you bring old Lefroy a present, then?"

"Payment as promised."

Mr. Lefroy's face cracked into a rare smile as he sniffed it. "'Tis us who should be thankin' you for winnin'."

A slew of stable hands gathered around, the pungent, sweet scent drawing them like bees to summer blooms. Within moments the dark brown squares of gingerbread disappeared. The feeling that she was useful—was needed—brought her fulfillment.

She had missed that. For the last two years, gratitude had been her prime sensation—for Sarah's loyalty and for the dowager duchess's extraordinary generosity in providing for them.

The men drifted away save for Mr. Lefroy. She

brushed at a speck of dust on her practical green walking gown while she stood in the shaded center aisle. "Is he very angry?"

One side of Mr. Lefroy's mouth curved. "Aye. Angrier than a baited bear." He scratched his head. "Thought 'e would toss me out on me ear."

She waited.

"He'll not forgive me for letting you ride Vespers— even if'n you did show Tatt wot's wot. Only wish I'd 'a seen it for meself." He shook his head with a smile.

She leaned the empty box against the stable wall and then crossed two stalls away, where she knew she would find Vespers. She caressed the velvety muzzle and the mare nickered softly. Mr. Lefroy joined her.

Her heart thudded in her chest. "Where is he?" There was no need to say his name. They both knew whom she meant.

"Havin' another go with someone at the war office."

The hair rose on the back of her neck. "Who?"

"Some addlepated lieutenant, or a swell wiv more influence, if 'e can manage it." He paused. "It's 'is last chance, lovey," he said under his breath.

She was careful to keep her voice steady, her eyes on Vespers. "His last chance?"

When he didn't answer her right away, she was forced to meet his eyes.

He shook his head. "No reason te keep it from you. 'e canna keep it a secret from anyone much longer."

"I would never tell anyone."

Mr. Lefroy's old eyes appraised her. "The blunt's all gone. Creditors are nippin' and the war office won't take the cavalry horses they asked the master to provide. Horses they won't take now what wiv the frogs hangin' up their swords. And the creatures be not pretty 'nuf for lords and ladies."

Vespers draped her head over Elizabeth's shoulder, in search of a treat, no doubt. "How many?"

"Eight hundred twenty," he replied. "That's seventy thousand quid."

She nearly jumped out of her skin. "So many. *So much.*"

"They's pastured in the countryside. Cheaper there."

Her heart felt like it had dropped into her heels.

"I should not 'ave tolds you, lovey," Mr. Lefroy murmured.

"No. I'm glad you did. And I already promised I would not betray your confidence." She stared at the weathered face of a man who had more honor and character in his little finger than Leland Pymm had in his entire body. "I've got to return to Helston House. Will you tell Mr. Manning that I called? I came to apologize for—well, for so many things."

As the carriage wended its way back to Portman Square, Elizabeth knew with every beat of her heart that the rules, indeed the entire game, had just changed. Now it was only a matter of how much time she had left and how much she could take away from the table.

The topics of the weather, the days at Windsor, and his absolute favorite subject—the upcoming conferral of the duchy—had been exhausted during the drive toward the verdant epicenter of London at five o'clock on a summer afternoon. Her intuition told her it was time to play out her hand.

"My dear Elizabeth," Pymm murmured, drawing the matched pair of dappled grays to a halt in a shady corner past the grand entrance to Hyde Park. "You've been the veriest minx. Not that I can say I'm surprised." He sent his tiger, the boy riding the sloping step above the phaeton's rear wheel, to hold the horses' heads.

Elizabeth gazed at the shafts of light filtering through the branches of the ancient trees above. In the distance, the carefully combed, elegantly presented peerage of England continued the tradition of preening before one another. On horseback, in carriages of every shape and color, on foot with parasols, they circled the park.

And every blasted one of them sedately turned their heads when they passed in order to glance at General Pymm and her.

"Now then," he said, "we have a few last things to discuss, to plan before the—"

"I beg your pardon, but I have something of importance to say." She rushed her quiet words.

Leland Pymm's brows drew together, his irritation evident. "I won't be put off again, Elizabeth. Now, you are to arrange for all of your affairs to be packed and transferred to my rooms at the Pulteney Hotel on Saturday. We will reside there until we leave for Vienna. You shall adore that city. The entertainments are without question opulent and vastly amusing. And when we return, the main portion of our residence will be ready for our occupancy."

She studied a small black ant as it marched along the edge of the carriage.

"Now, then. Several dressmakers will wait on you at Helston House. It's understood they will create with great haste a trousseau befitting a lady of your new station. I do hope you appreciate what I've arranged."

"Thank you," she said, pretending gratitude she could not feel. She looked up to encounter that awful, smug expression he favored. "But I still have something to say."

"One can hope it will make up for your bizarre behavior at Windsor," he replied. "I did not like you disappearing and I will not tolerate you disobeying me in future. And you could have shown a bit more of the old charm and sparkle toward Prinny—"

"Please, Leland." It was the first time she'd allowed the bitter taste of his given name past her lips.

Happiness comically tinged with annoyance crossed his features. "What is it, then?"

She prayed she would be able to say it without losing everything she hoped to gain. "I am begging you to hear me through," she said quietly.

He tilted back his head and laughed. "What do you want? It must be quite extravagant if you are playing the demure, meek damsel now."

"Leland . . ." God, she was risking all. She was risking her life on a wager that Pymm's obsession bordered on such madness that he would agree to anything to have her.

"Yes?" His tone was condescending.

She closed her eyes and spoke quickly. "Before I marry you, you must arrange payment for the large number of horses you requisitioned from Manning's."

He looked at her as if she was speaking some foreign tongue. Finally the light of understanding dawned and he laughed long and loud. "Good God, but you are fearless. As if I would take orders from anyone, when I only answer to the Prince Regent himself!" He shook his head.

"I don't think you understand," she said, attempting a tone halfway between a determined plea and a polite demand. "You see, I will not marry you unless you do."

Fury boiled in his look and posture. "You ask me to believe that you would risk Newgate prison or worse, all for a bastard horse trader?"

"That is for you to decide," she said with quiet conviction.

His expression hardened, his skin tightly drawn against his skull.

She looked at him steadily and flung herself off the ledge with words that could be construed to mean two very different things. She had little doubt Pymm would understand. "Leland, my father died under *your* command."

It was always the smallest things that revealed the truth. In that moment, as her words hung in the air between them, Leland Pymm's eyes shifted under her scrutiny. It took all of her self-control not to show her absolute revulsion.

"I would have thought you well versed in the rules of war, Elizabeth. Good men are lost every day. Sacrifices must be made for victory."

Her throat constricted, and it took every effort to

remain still. "Oh, I know the rules of war very well. You taught them to me. Better even than my father, I daresay. My offer still stands. I will marry you if you carry out the terms of Mr. Manning's contract, or I will not marry you and you will have the choice to accuse me of treason or not."

His cold eyes filled with rage. "Your loyalty is entirely misplaced and your ability to judge character is deplorable. Manning is nothing more than a bastard son of a whore and brother to a whore, as well."

Her heart skipped a beat. While her soul screamed at her to defend Rowland, her mind knew that to achieve her goal, silence was best.

"I see by your expression you know nothing about the man. I had him fully investigated the day after that ridiculous tea party at Helston House."

Her gaze never faltered.

"The bastard you are lowering yourself to champion had a mother who was a common housemaid. After seducing the young heir, she turned to seamstress work and finally prostitution, which obviously came more naturally to her. His sister had the same deficiency in character. Yes, that is the sort of stock he is made of." He spat out the words. "Manning was nothing more than a pickpocket and a mudlarker, a scavenger feeding off his betters, until he was lucky enough to secure a position in a disreputable stable. He can't even shoot straight, according to reports this past spring, when he tried to take money from a countess *and* kill his noble *brother*. Is this a man who deserves any sort of charity?"

She concentrated on keeping her hands relaxed, and her teeth ground together. She stayed her course.

"It is your choice, Leland. Pay the man and have me as your bride, or not."

The evil in his eyes pierced her. "I can promise you one thing, my dearest Elizabeth. If I find you've allowed him to touch you—to take that which is only my right to possess—I shall not only punish you as any husband would, but I shall also deal with him as the rules of honor allow any gentleman."

She knew if she moved an inch from her stiff position, she would break into a million pieces.

"Well? Has he had you, Elizabeth?" he asked in an eerie, quiet voice that did not match the lunacy in his eyes. "Oh, fear not, I will marry you—I will have you—no matter your answer. And I will learn the truth on our wedding night. But"—and here he tucked a curl that had become loose back under her hat—"it will go easier for you if you tell me the truth of it now."

All those times Rowland had told her she was an abysmal liar revolved in her mind, nearly hamstringing her. "I am a lady, Leland, and I would not do anything to bring dishonor to myself." She paused to take a breath. "So what is it to be? Am I to stand up before God, and all the noble families of England to marry you?" She didn't wait for the answer. "If you still desire it, then bring the treasury's gold guineas to Helston House and I shall have them transferred to Mr. Manning."

Oh, he blustered, his face became blotchy with rage, but even the most celebrated general in London could do little under the sharp-eyed gaze of the peerage parading nearby. And so he agreed—reluctantly. Very reluctantly. "I cannot and will not provide gold.

He shall have to be satisfied with a bank draft."

"I'm not a fool, Leland. It will be gold or I shall not go through with it. You see, you hold all the cards except one. But it is your choice, ultimately."

He smiled slowly, his look cunning and greedy. "All right, my dear. It isn't as if the guineas will be coming out of my pockets. But I shall only do it under two stipulations."

"Yes?"

"First, the transfer shall occur at Carlton House, where I will arrange for us to be married *immediately* after the conferral of the duchy—not the morning after. And you shall write to Rowland Manning to clearly state your distaste for him. You shall insist that he is never to disgust you with his presence again. He is not to ever know you had a part in this bargain. Do you understand?" His voice broke into an awkward high pitch on the last word.

He had no idea. He was a complete idiot. Did he really think she would want to torment Rowland Manning by professing her undying love for him while marrying Pymm? "Of course, Leland. For once we are in complete agreement."

"There. I knew you could be obedient if you made an effort. Now give me a kiss to show your gratitude, my sweet. Only three more days and then . . . well, you shall be under my protection forevermore."

Rowland had always suggested how absurdly gothic her turn at life was. She could not have agreed more. The general's face was moist when she forced herself to kiss his cheek. And his scent . . . the sour-smelling sheep's wool of his heavy uniform mixed with too much eau de cologne.

* * *

"She did what?" Rowland shouted at Joshua Gordon, nearly shaking the new rafters.

The footman's face turned four shades of red. "She and General Pymm were leaving Helston House in a phaeton when I arrived there with the message from you. The footman told me they were for Hyde Park. To the corner where the general's new great house is to be erected."

Rowland stared at Joshua, now his only footman as the other one had departed, having gone without pay for the last three quarters. "And why didn't you follow them?"

"I didn't know that you would want me to."

Death. Words of chaos and death. His blasted footman had no idea how his burble of words had formed a pit of black fury in Rowland's mind. Lord, what had Leland Pymm done or said to make her go about alone with the lecherous swine?

"Sir? Sir!"

Rowland looked down to find that he had gripped the edge of his plain, ancient desk with such force that the trim had come loose in his hand. A nail gouged his flesh, and blood streamed from the gash. The footman immediately took off his neck cloth to bind the wound as Rowland cursed a blue streak. Nothing was going as planned.

It wasn't as if he hadn't expected it. When it involved Elizabeth Ashburton, nothing ever went as planned.

The smallest smile teased his lips as he finally dismissed his footman. He realized it was the reason he felt the way he did about her. The woman actually seemed to relish disobeying men, and walking alone the tightrope of disaster.

She was a woman to save. A woman to cherish.

And he would do it whether she liked it or not. Tonight. After he spent the rest of the day contemplating what he had thought about for twenty-four hours of every bloody day—the dismantling of everything he had built the past decade. But then, was it not all built on pillars of sin? Dust to dust. Nothing was immune.

It was just a damned shame the whole affair had to entail the unpleasant task of entering Helston House with stealth eight hours later. There was no other way to avoid the phalanx of soldiers who appeared to forever troll Portman Square. He didn't want to give Pymm any more reason to suspect him later when he spirited Elizabeth away.

And so Rowland Manning, former bastard mudlarker, and quite possibly headed back to the same, employed his considerable skills at climbing and entering. At least the warm, summer night provided the key—Elizabeth's *open* window in the back of the townhouse, where a trellis provided the footing. He could only hope that she would not scream like a banshee if she awoke.

In the moonlight, he silently mashed dozens of full-blown roses on his ascent, and had the thorns in his breeches and gloves to prove it. He brushed away a small mountain of something on the sill. Seed. Of course, for the dowager duchess's bloody canary. And then he peered into the large chamber.

With furtiveness borne of years of evading danger, he slid his considerable frame into the room when a gust of wind rustled the leaves of the trees in the garden.

He crossed the room to stand over her, studying the woman who now tormented his every waking thought. Her lush fall of beautiful hair curled over her shoulder as she rested on her side, the bedclothes pushed aside in the warm night. Her hands were clasped beneath her face, like an innocent child's. Yet there was nothing childlike about the slope of her form, revealed by the thin night rail.

He hadn't been able to save Mary. Hadn't saved anyone of his family: his worthless half brother Howard, his mother lost to lung fever, and Mary . . . *bloody hell.* A numbness drifted through him as he thought of the night she had disappeared. She had sold herself to buy food for *his* damned belly and hers—despite her promises never to do such a thing. For years he had searched for her, never wanting to admit she had been vilely used and most likely tossed away like so many ruled by poverty. Well, he might have failed his sister, but he would save Elizabeth, if it was the very last thing he ever did.

He stared down at her for what seemed like forever and a day, his past washing over him, his future ever darkening. A restlessness now gripped her in sleep and she turned to her back. He leaned over her and kissed her brow.

She came awake within the blink of an eye and ready to do battle.

" 'Tis only I," he whispered, grabbing her hand as she prepared to strike at him.

She drew in a ragged breath and sat up, her eyes spearing him. "I thought you were . . ."

"I know," he said, his voice low. He reached for the extravagant beeswax candle on the heavy silver holder and scratched a flame.

"Why are you . . . Is everything all right?"

"You left without a word, Elizabeth." He stared into her lovely face.

She looked in her lap, where her fingers twisted. "I left because I knew you would not see reason."

"Reason? There's no reasoning to it. You're out of time. There are no solutions, so it's off to France with you." He couldn't stop the rasping in his voice.

"But I still do have a chance. I spoke to Leland today, and he—"

"So, it's *Leland* now, is it?" he growled.

"Now you're not going to be a fool about this, are you? You were always the one person I could count on to behave with a superior amount of rational thinking."

"Go on," he ground out.

"I've made some headway with him."

"Really," he said, his voice dripping with sarcasm.

Her eyes darted about the room, filling him with ill ease. "Yes, I have."

"What sort of headway?"

"I'm to dine with him tomorrow in his suite of rooms at the Pulteney Hotel. There will be chaperones from Helston House. I'm going to search his rooms for the letters."

He shook his head. "It will never work."

"You told me it could. Have you forgotten already?"

"That was before."

"Before when?"

"Before I realized . . ." His voice faded.

"What?"

"For Christ sakes, Elizabeth, I will not allow you to put yourself at such risk."

"Well, you've no choice, for I'm determined to do it and I won't go to France until I've exhausted every possible chance of staying here."

Hope flooded him. He had had the absurd notion that she would refuse to adhere to his brilliant plan. "So you agree you'll go to France, then?"

Her eyes were steady. Not a hint of falsehood showed. "You must give me until the day *after* the conferral at Carlton House. The wedding is planned for the next day and instead I would leave with you before dawn."

"I've an inclination to bundle you up right here, right now, and leave for France tonight," he said, furious that his ability to hide his every emotion was deserting him in his hour of need.

"But surely, I shall find the letters. Even if I cannot search for them tomorrow night, I'll have one other chance. You see, I will make pains to endear myself to his servants at the Pulteney tomorrow. And then I shall return with my affairs the very next day. He's asked me to have them transferred. I shall take pains to arrive after he's left for Carlton House. And I'll tell his servants I want to see our private chambers with my maid from Helston House. How can they refuse? It shall be a simple matter really."

He noted she was talking too quickly and adding far too many complicated details. She was unsure of herself, unsure of success. He highly doubted she had a prayer of a chance. "And then?"

"After I find the letters, I shall go to Carlton House and call a halt to the wedding."

He shook his head. "It would be far too dangerous for you to announce anything. If you are lucky enough to find the letters, I will confront Pymm along with Helston, Ellesmere, and my brother." He paused. "But it is far more likely you will not find the letters, Elizabeth."

"That won't happen. I know I'll—"

He cut her off. "Do you promise to leave for France if you do not find your father's letters?"

She nodded.

He reached to cup her heart-shaped face in his hand. "I would hear your answer out loud."

She paused, searching his face for what he did not know. "I promise not to let you down," she whispered.

He exhaled roughly. There was something odd in her voice—and he wondered not for the first time how far he would trust her to do as he bade. *Not far at all.*

"And will you promise to wait for me in this room then—two nights hence?"

"I said I would be here and I will."

She reached for his hand, so dark and brutish compared to her soft one. She pressed a kiss to his palm, scarred from years of labor. "You know, my father always promised me I would one day find a man better than he. A man strong enough to tame my unfortunate willful streak, he said." She smiled, a faraway look in her eyes. "And I would always correct him."

"What sort of man did you hope to find then,

Elizabeth?" He pulled her to within inches of his face.

"A man like you. A man capable of caring for me the way I would care for him."

"And what way would that be?"

"A love that never questioned, never doubted, never feared. A love without end."

He closed the gap and nibbled at her lush lower lip, and then moved his lips to her ear. "Well, then that just proves I'm not the man for you if you think for a moment I would never fear for you. And doubting . . . hmm, well, I think you know I was born with doubt instead of blood in my veins. So, you've misjudged the matter entirely. In fact, I'm of a mind to show you just how bad I am for you." His heart felt light in his chest and he chuckled. He would not think about the fact that in a few days, a week at most, she would be separated from him. She in France, and he facing ruin. But at least she would be saved from that hell named Pymm.

Elizabeth could barely speak for all the lies she'd dared utter. She wasn't sure how she had gotten this far. There was only one thing of which she was certain. She wasn't going to have to wait until death for her punishment. Oh, she would go to the Pulteney Hotel and search just as she had said she would. But she knew how carefully officers locked away papers of importance. And she had already set a course. So she had constructed her overly complicated story.

That utterly masculine scent of his drifted through her senses, and in one long, smooth movement he drew her closer so she could rest her head on his shoulder. "Rowland," she whispered into the silence that enveloped them. His fingers lightly skimmed the flesh of her arms.

"Mmmmm?"

"The last time I had to beg to . . ."

"Yes?"

"To give myself to you."

He smiled knowingly. "And?"

"I don't want to have to beg you to take anything I offer ever again."

He drew away from her and smiled in a fashion that made him appear so much younger than ever before. "You are a demanding wench," he whispered. "If I have the right of it, you don't want to have to beg, and at the same time there's to be no questioning, doubt, or fear."

"That's right." Honesty tasted so good on her tongue.

"You know, you never had to worry about the first one, *mhuirnin*. I'm essentially a selfish bastard, or haven't you heard?"

"You and I both know it's just a façade. A way to keep everyone at a distance. You're the least selfish man I know."

"Really?" he drawled wolfishly as he perused her form.

"Yes, really."

"Well then, you won't consider it a problem if I tell you that you have exactly five seconds to take that bloody night rail off before I tear it from you," he growled. "With my teeth."

She bit back a request.

He smiled. "You're not scared, are you? I thought there was to be no fear."

"Ummm, could you at least blow out the candle?"

He raised his eyebrows. "That sounds very like a question, Elizabeth. And no, I will not blow out the candle. Bloody hell, you're breaking every rule you just set for a man."

He had no idea how much he had the right of it. But at least she would make certain he would never doubt her love for him. Not after tonight. And certainly not after the remainder of this week played itself out on the rickety stage of her life.

She looked into his pale green eyes. She wondered if he knew how much she loved him. She wondered how she was going to live without seeing him ever again.

The first time they had lain together she had been determined to have a memory of him to hold close to her heart always. She had wanted to see the desire in her soul reflected back in his eyes. But now, armed with the knowledge of his past, of his sister and mother, she could only imagine how impossible it must have been for him to take her innocence.

But this time, this last time they would be together, she would leave him with the untainted happiness of a summer night to withstand all the winter days that would follow for all the seasons of their lives. She was determined to give *him* the memories he would need to see the depth of her love for him. Only then would he fully understand later why she had broken the promises she made to go away to France. For he was a man who deserved a surfeit of love after such solitary deprivation.

All thoughts of promises and doubts and fears were lost in a vortex of desire sparked by his hands as he pushed her back into her downy bed and removed every last article of clothes between them.

Chapter 15

It was as if he had never tasted her before. Rowland closed his eyes and breathed in the perfumed valley of her breasts. Such great whorls of longing unfurled within him. He no longer bothered to harness the feelings she evoked in his breast.

Yearning for a woman was something so little known to him. Until now, physical release had always been a momentary, empty sensation. Meaningless at the best of times, and something quite worse at other times.

But with Elizabeth? It was something sacred. Something not of this earthly plane. It was everything good. Without a doubt he knew why. It was because it was freely given. Always in the past there had been a price extracted from his soul. But this . . . this was a celebration of the very best life had to offer.

And he'd be damned if he didn't take every minute, every hour here to pour out his heart to her through his actions.

Rowland grasped her in his arms, protecting her in the way he wished he could do for the rest of his life. He kissed her forehead, her eyelids, her nose, and finally her beautiful smiling lips, tilted to meet his.

He kissed her until he was left drunk by the sweet passion of her. They kissed until one kiss blended into another and he was lost in her. All the while, he could feel the tips of her fingers weaving through his hair, down his neck, and his arms, tracing the raised veins on his forearms that gripped her to him.

When he tried to hold her still, she made little sounds of protest and refused to be put off. She prowled down his body as he had wished to do to her. She nibbled and nipped her way past his lips, his neck, chest and belly. He held his breath, his gut clenched in pain. In a rush, the exquisite sensation of the tip of her tongue ran along his arousal. And then he felt a swirl and he nearly passed out from the pleasure of it.

He grasped her shoulders and dragged her on top of him. His voice nearly broken, he stroked her gorgeous honey mane of hair, "Come here, my darling . . . my beautiful *mhuirnin*."

"What does that mean?" she whispered.

He could not tell her the truth of it. It would only make parting more difficult. "It means I want you." He rolled her to her side and proceeded to show her what he could not tell her. What he dared not tell her. She was his *beloved*.

He supposed, as he kissed her lovely shoulders and her breasts, he had somehow known a long time ago that she would steal his heart.

She was his counterpart. Never had there been created a woman so good, so trusting and guileless. Someone the very opposite of him.

He sighed and felt the softness of her against the roughness of his hands.

* * *

Elizabeth looked at him, into his enigmatic eyes, dark with passion. He eased her beneath him, and proceeded to tease to heightened awareness every last part of her.

Her hands found purchase on the molded contours of his back. The sinews and muscles of his body flexed beneath her fingers. The man did not possess a single spare ounce of flesh.

With a feverish look he whispered to her, staring at her, "Elizabeth, I should take more time to please you—ready you. But I want you too much. Stop me if—"

"I want you," she interrupted. "I always will."

His large hands gripped her hips then, and tilted her. Staring into her eyes, he rose onto his forearms and entered her slowly. The obvious effort he took to hold back caused tremors to race along his sides.

The sensation was unbearably pleasurable. There was no pain this time, just a long slide as his thickness tested her depths. He stopped and dropped his head, his longish dark hair brushing her breasts.

She pulled him closer.

"Impatient?" he whispered, looking back into her face.

"Yes," she admitted tremulously. "Impatient to know if it was all a dream the last time."

He bowed down and kissed her for long minutes. And yet he still didn't move.

She pushed her hips forward, and he groaned. He was so very careful with her as if she were fragile, breakable.

"Don't move," he whispered. "I want to draw this out—savor you. I don't want to forget it."

And without a single movement, Elizabeth felt herself begin to pulse against his length. Rowland surged fully within her and stopped again, taking away her breath and her reasoning, giving her all the pleasure he denied himself.

There was just this one starving man, determined to please her instead of himself. But she wanted the reverse. She would always want the reverse. She finally regained her breath and he waited silently, still deeply within her. For endless minutes they stared into each other's eyes. She stroked his hair back from his face, memorizing every line, every angle. She would never forget his eyes, so piercing, so mesmerizing.

"My *mhuirnin* . . . Oh God," his expression pained, he finally gave into his desire to move. He pushed even deeper inside of her, his thickness filling her completely. The unrelenting tempo, the desperate look in his face caused her to shatter into exquisitely sharp pieces. He held her there, his body trembling.

And yet he made no move to follow her. He merely stilled for a few moments, the first signs of his fatigue evident on his brow, and tremors again racing along his back and arms. One last time, he brought her to the pinnacle, and teased her by balancing there for long moments before pushing her over the edge with the gentlest of motions.

She could not stop the tumble of words that escaped from her hoarse throat when she felt sweat trickle along his spine. "Rowland, please. Please, you must be in pain. Find your ease now. With me."

He was at her breast again, her nipple almost sore from his ministrations. "Are you begging?" His voice was nearly gone. "I thought there was to be no begging." She could feel the hint of a smile on her breast as he pressed a soft kiss there.

She then clasped him ever so tightly with her legs and pulled him as close as she could. She clenched all of the muscles inside of her, savoring the feeling of him.

With a silent cry his head fell back. The next moment he tried to withdraw from her but her legs would not allow it. She felt a warm gush deep inside of her body.

"Oh, Elizabeth," he moaned. He sighed heavily and clasped her tightly to him.

God, it was the most exquisite sensation he'd ever experienced. She was so very warm and soft. He'd never, ever allowed himself to release his seed inside of any woman. He was a bastard. And he sure as hell didn't want to create more of the same on this earth. It might be the only sacred belief he had. No child should have to suffer—

"What are you thinking," she asked softly. "Just now?"

He rolled them both to their side, still clasped to her, hipbone to hipbone. "Why do you ask?"

"Because you look troubled. Have I done something to displease you? To—"

"Hush, Elizabeth. You are perfect. So perfect it is almost painful to be with you. It's just . . ." He closed his eyes.

"Yes?" Her voice was anxious.

"Well, now you might become with child."

She exhaled. "It's very unlikely. I overheard the wives of the men in my father's company speak of such things."

"Nonetheless, you will write to me. You will tell me. I would give the child legitimacy even if my name is not . . . But I would come to France to marry you even if I would not stay. I would send you money when I—"

"Of course you would," she interrupted, her voice still unnaturally low pitched. "And I would write to you. I promise. But I truly doubt I will have to go to France, you know. I will find those letters. And I won't find myself with child. I—"

Suddenly, a flash of yellow fluttered above them, and Rowland instinctively raised his arm to guard them against whatever it was.

Good God. It was the bloody canary. With a curse, Rowland reluctantly disengaged from her and struggled against the sea of tangled bedclothes to close the window. He collapsed back into Elizabeth's soft bed and they both laughed.

She pulled him into her warm embrace. "You are in for it now. Ata may very well try to marry you herself. She's been pining for her escaped bird for the last six months."

"Well, I'll trust you to tell her we found the damned thing in the mews instead of here. Otherwise there's a very good chance I'll face the wrong end of Helston's bloody pistol."

"Luc? But you have nothing to fear in that corner,

Rowland. He likes you. I learned a long time ago that the more he scowls at a person, the more he respects them. He's sort of like you that way."

He scowled.

Elizabeth smiled and he pulled her roughly to him and kissed her.

"Those bloody dimples of yours were planted by the devil himself to tempt all men to madness. It's no wonder Pymm is obsessed. It's—"

Elizabeth stopped him with her lips. She couldn't bear to have him pollute the air they breathed with that name.

He spent the next hour kissing and murmuring endearments to her in between an avalanche of instructions. He told her how to search the general's apartments at the Pulteney. He told her how to bribe the valet if she was unsuccessful. He even explained how to pick a lock, and provided the instrument. And then he extracted a final promise from her to feign a headache and to return to Helston House as soon as the Prince Regent conferred the duchy on Pymm.

If she had not secured the letters by then, they would leave a letter for Ata and disappear from Helston House that very night. He would arrange for several of his men to help them. And if she did find the letters, he would join her aristocratic friends—the duke, marquis, and Rowland's brother and they would go to Pymm to break the betrothal on the morning of the wedding. He would not hear of her trying to face down a crowd at Carlton House.

And she agreed to it all. Without a hint of hesitation.

Before the night threatened to deliver a new day, Rowland left her embrace. Pressing a last kiss to her brow, he disappeared out the window. Elizabeth sank back into the bed, hugging to her breast the pillow on which he had lain his head. A moment later she laughed despite her welling eyes as a particularly foul curse floated back to her from the trellis.

And then the tears fell in earnest as her fingers touched her abdomen. She dared not think of a child. *His* child. Of course, it was not so. She would not be . . . Her thoughts flew forward. She refused to consider what Leland Pymm would do if he ever detected a resemblance. But—she closed her eyes—if she did find herself with child, and had to endure hell on this earth with Pymm, at least Rowland's child would be her small piece of heaven.

The next morning Elizabeth tore herself away from the most recent phalanx of dressmakers Leland Pymm had sent to Helston House to drive her to silken distraction. She retreated behind the privacy screen in Ata's vast apartments to don the last of the gowns— the one she most dreaded.

It was the elaborate ensemble she was to wear to Carlton House for Leland Pymm's "crowning," as she thought of it now. *And for her wedding immediately following.* The color of the ostentatious, heavy gown matched the golden tones of her hair, and she thought she looked as stiff and colorless as a haystack while wearing it. The seed-pearl-encrusted bodice was dangerously tiny despite her pleas to the dressmaker to make it more modest. The woman had reminded her that she was following the general's instructions.

As the modiste and assistants fluttered about, cooing at the perfect fit of their creation, Elizabeth heard not a word. On a table nearby, Pip, too, flitted about in his cage, and Elizabeth suddenly felt very much like Ata's beloved canary.

Soon she would be living in a gilded cage of her own. Even now, these over-elegant clothes stifled her, and she chafed against all the new restrictions. She could not wander gardens or gallop in a park without a bevy of chaperones and a detachment of Pymm's men following discreetly in the background. The fashionable columns in the newspapers delighted in detailing her every movement. If only she could—

The door burst open sans notice and Ata flew in, her eyes wide and a smile diffusing the wrinkles on her face.

"Oh, Eliza, you will never guess!" Without waiting for an answer, she burst out, "Lord Wymith is below and he just requested a private audience with Sarah. Oh, I cannot stand the suspense." Her one good hand rested on her cheek.

Elizabeth had known this was in the offing. She also knew why her happiness was mixed with melancholy. "Oh, wait. Let me remove this gown. We were just finished, yes?" She ducked behind the screen with the dressmaker.

As she quickly redressed, she caught glimpses of Ata moving restlessly about the chamber, rearranging a bouquet of flowers, straightening a small stack of books.

Elizabeth could not stop the poignant memories of Sarah's husband, Colonel Pierce Winters. Admiration was not a strong enough word for how she re-

membered him. She had always considered him the
embodiment of everything true, good, faithful, and
courageous, as an Englishman and as a husband.

They had been an impossibly perfect couple—he
so handsome and so devoted, and Sarah so gentle and
loyal. Indeed, Elizabeth had yet to see their equal. And
the thought of Sarah giving her heart—for indeed, if
her friend married again she would do that—to another man seemed next to impossible.

She put on her best face when she dismissed the
dressmakers and rejoined Ata. "There is no doubt,
then? He will marry Sarah?"

Ata stood staring at Pip with a small smile. "Even
I could not have imagined a more brilliant match for
her. He is exactly as a gentleman should be—excellent
character, a fine fortune, handsome."

"And he loves Sarah," Elizabeth whispered. "He
sees all the goodness in her."

"Yes," Ata said softly. "He does."

"And he will take care of her."

"Yes."

"He will make her smile again."

Ata was silent.

"She used to smile all the time. Not like she smiles
now. She used to smile when her husband was alive,
and it would light up an entire room."

"I'm sure he will make her smile like that again,
Elizabeth," Ata murmured. "Actually, it is you whom
I am most worried about. Are you going to go through
with this marriage to General Pymm or not?"

Elizabeth nodded, unable to speak.

"I'm afraid we've all been cowards in broaching
the subject," Ata said quietly. "Indeed, I've never seen

Luc so on edge. You know it's not too late to cry off. It is never too late—even if General Pymm's attachment to you exceeds Lord Wymith's to Sarah."

She looked down to examine the hem of her green walking gown. She did not want to discuss it. It was going to be difficult enough to go through with it. And Ata had such piercing dark eyes.

She was so tired of lying to everyone. "Yes," she said quietly. "Of course, I'm going to marry him. I would not have allowed this insanity"—she indicated the elegant gowns now decorating the backs of every chair and chaise in Ata's chamber—"to continue unchecked if I had not decided."

Oh, she would make an attempt to recover the letters, but that was simply a gambit to try and remove the thing Pymm would hold over her head for the rest of her life. But her chance of success was next to nil. And she had taken her decision to marry Pymm the day Lefroy had told her the truth.

This was the only way to eliminate Pymm's threats to her and to ensure the financial security of Manning's stable. It was obvious she was the root cause of Pymm's animosity toward Rowland. And the race at Ascot had caused more harm than good, in the end.

Ata said something and Elizabeth was lifted from her reverie.

"Elizabeth?"

"I'm sorry."

"I asked about Mr. Manning."

"Yes?"

"You will not speak of him, then?" Ata was unable to keep the curiosity from her voice. "Well, I'm sorry for it, but I must ask you to help me choose a gift for the audacious man—for recovering my Pip. Will you not help me? What would he most delight in, I wonder?"

It was her inherent unhappiness that led to black humor. "Food. Delicacies of any kind. Especially gingerbread."

"Really?"

"Yes. That or *a lot of money*." She arched a brow.

Ata chortled. "Do you think if I give him enough, he might let me try one of his horses?"

Elizabeth's smile faded as she caught sight of the heavy, honey-colored gown the modiste had left on the chaise. "Ata, Luc would worry so if you . . . And Mr. Brown . . ."

"Oh, pish. Who cares about Mr. Brown? He wouldn't even take notice if I broke my neck now." All the good humor on the petite elderly lady's face fled.

Elizabeth felt a tug of guilt on her heartstrings. With her future in such a precarious state, she had not been the confidante to the dowager that she should have been. "Has the countess's house party broken up yet?"

Ata appeared miserable. "He's returned to Scotland. He did not even bother to take his leave of Luc. I've . . . I've even driven him away from all of our mutual friends."

"Oh, Ata . . . but surely he'll—"

"He even refused Quinn," Ata interrupted. "He actually declined Quinn's request to oversee affairs at Ellesmere House for just a week or so until Georgiana is safely delivered." Ata paused, and it became evident she desired to put an end to all discussion about Mr.

Brown. "None of us had wanted to tell you, Elizabeth, for you've so much to worry you, but Quinn is distraught. He's terrified Georgiana's accident of long ago will hamper the birth."

They had all of them been anxious since the day Georgiana had announced that she was with child. "I must go to her. Today," Elizabeth said firmly.

"No, you will not. You've far too much to contend with. Rosamunde and Grace are with her, distracting her every day. They try to keep Quinn from hovering."

Elizabeth studied the dowager duchess for a long moment. "Does it not feel like all of us are hanging on a precipice? Is this how life goes, then, Ata? Are there never moments of profound peace?"

"Rarely, my dear. There are peaks and valleys. But you've had a particularly difficult time—as has Georgiana. But you've managed so well despite the pressure of so many people following your every movement, and repeating your every word. And then there is that other distraction . . ."

Elizabeth darted a glance at her.

"Well, if last night is any indication . . ."

She could feel a blush mounting her cheeks. "Last night?"

"The head gardener informed me this morning that there is not a single bloom left on the climbing roses. The ones on the trellis outside your window."

"Ata . . ."

"No, you do not have to say a word. I realize you do not want to unburden your heart to me. Or, really, to anyone. And I recently decided I would stop pressing everyone to confide in me. In fact, I've decided to give up many things. 'Tis long past due."

Elizabeth rushed to comfort the dowager. "Oh, Ata. Do not say that. You've been my savior these last eighteen months. Like the mother or grandmother I never had. In so many ways you are very like a guardian angel to me. I think that is why I do not want to burden you. You have done so much for me already. For all of us."

"No, you misunderstand. This has nothing to do with you, dearest. You see, it has to do with me. The problem with old age is that one finally has no choice but to accept the sad truth." Ata glanced away. "Dreams of youth are not always granted, you see. Indeed, they are rarely fulfilled. Not everyone can find happiness in the end. And I suspect that you, of all of us, know that very well."

Elizabeth refused to pretend. "Perhaps. But one should never give up. To give up is to ensure defeat."

"Says the daughter of an army captain."

"No. Says the woman who lost that father," she said softly. "But, you are right. I would dishonor him by thinking anything else."

Ata closed the gap between them, hugging Elizabeth to her. "You know, all this time I was determined to impart my many years of wisdom and my considerable resources to teach and help all of you find the happiness you each deserved. And yet, you are the ones who taught me." She leaned back to rearrange Elizabeth's fichu. "And you, without a single doubt, have taught me the most of all."

"That cannot be so."

"No. Not one of us has your courage . . . your determination . . . indeed, your ability to persevere despite the discontent you hide so well from almost everyone. Oh, Elizabeth, promise me you will be happy. Promise me you're not making a grave mistake by marrying this general who is so besotted with you." Ata paused for a moment. "You know I will require a companion if all of you leave me. I cannot remain in my grandson's household forever. And I refuse to become the doddering old biddy who mumbles while eating her porridge. Would you not like to retire to Cornwall with me? Without Luc to spy on us we could ride the cliffs of Perran Sands every day."

Elizabeth smiled. "You do know how to tempt me. But you vastly overestimate my character, Ata. I'm not nearly as courageous—"

At the sound of the door opening, Ata and Elizabeth shifted their gazes to find Sarah, color high on her cheeks, rush through the door.

All three of them spoke at once. Sarah grasped their hands. "Oh. I—I've done something quite, quite impossible."

Ata tried to speak but Elizabeth's words resonated. "Lord Wymith offered for you?"

It was as if Sarah could not hear her. "He is so good. And I—I've caused him such pain. I never deserved his admiration, never—"

"You refused him?" Elizabeth whispered as she squeezed Sarah's hand.

Sarah met her gaze—her gray eyes lost and dull with pain. "It was as if someone else, not I, were speaking to him—answering his heartfelt plea . . . hurting him."

"But why, Sarah?" Ata's face was filled with amazement. "Why would you refuse him?"

"I-I don't know." She dropped their hands and walked to the window and gazed outside. The light reflected off her delicate, ethereal face. "Oh, I do know. I'm a pathetic wretch. I just cannot forget Pierce. I will never forget him."

"But no one is asking you to forget your husband," Ata said, now behind her.

Elizabeth joined them at the window. "Sarah, this is my fault. I should have encouraged you more. I've been selfish, living on memories of long ago—and wishing they were still with us. But Pierce would be disappointed in me for not telling you to go on with your life. He would want you to be happy with the earl."

Sarah turned around slowly. "No. It wouldn't be fair to Lord Wymith. And he agreed when I explained it to him."

"What did you say?" Ata handed her a handkerchief.

She buried her face in her hands. "When he pressed me, I finally admitted that I still dream of Pierce. He comes to me in my sleep, and he comforts me. Wraps me in his embrace, and there is such love and hope in his eyes. I would rather live the rest of my life with my memories—my dreams—than make another life with someone else. It would not be fair if I could not come to a man with my whole heart."

"Why did you not tell me, Sarah?" Elizabeth's eyes burned with emotion.

"Why have you not told me the real reason you've agreed to give yourself to a man who you dislike?"

Elizabeth held her gaze. "I thought you had changed your mind about the general. I thought you approved of him."

"I did not say that. I said that perhaps you were wrong to think he might be a murderer. I said it to suggest we stop running."

Ata touched her hand. "Are you hiding something from all of us, Elizabeth? Surely you can tell us if something is wrong."

Elizabeth shook her head. There was absolutely nothing they could do. And if she told them, they would only suffer from the knowledge. And so she took a breath and continued the lie. "You've misread everything. You must see that I've willingly chosen my future. You were right, Sarah. I was wrong before. And I've embraced my decision with my whole heart. I hope you will do me the honor of wishing me happy."

Sarah and Ata exchanged glances and then uttered the meaningless words. As soon as she could, she disengaged herself from her friends.

She had a letter to write. And a visit to make to the Pulteney Hotel.

After their brief meeting, Rowland escorted the Duke of Helston to the grand entryway of his enterprise. Gratitude reared its uncomfortable head. He had not had to deal with it very often. "I must thank you, Helston. I'd not expected . . ."

The duke waved his hand in that way all aristocrats knew instinctively from birth. "The mare was worth twice the price."

Rowland could not form a reply for they both

knew the duke was lying, and so he cleared his throat instead.

"I would ask that you come to Helston House on occasion to ride Vespers when my wife and I are at our seat in Cornwall," the duke said gruffly.

Something cold and hard knotted in his gut. This first step toward dismantling his kingdom was bound to be the worst. He thought about Elizabeth's beautiful face the last time he'd been with her and forced a smile to his lips. This money would help both of them begin new lives.

"As I said," Helston continued. "I'm determined to see the mare race at Ascot again next summer. You will oversee her training the four months prior. Agreed?"

Rowland looked down to see Helston's hand extended toward him. It was the first time any member of the peerage had ever offered the gesture.

He clasped the duke's hand. "Agreed. Vespers will be delivered to your mews within the week."

The duke did not release his hand. "Manning . . . what in hell is going on?"

Rowland tried to disengage his fingers, without success. "What do you mean?" he said offhandedly.

The duke stared at him, a myriad of thoughts coursing his expression. "I think you know very well what I'm asking."

"Uh. You may let go of my hand now."

The barest hint of a smile appeared at the corners of Helston's mouth. "Of course. Once you tell me what you're planning."

"I'm not telling you a bloody thing—even if you want to hold hands all night."

The duke raised his brows. It was to be a standoff.

"Bloody hell." For the first time in two decades, Rowland chose to trust someone other than himself. "If I'd known you felt this way, I'd have signed your dance card long ago. Well, since you're so determined to waltz, I have a favor to ask."

The duke released his hand. "Another favor?" Helston's eyelids lowered to half mast. "It's not going to cost as much as the mare, is it?"

Rowland bit back a smile. "No—but if you would like to buy another—"

"What do you want?" The duke's words were as guarded as his own.

"Immediately after Prinny bestows the duchy on Pymm at Carlton House, I would ask you to watch Elizabeth closely. She might be foolish enough to try and make an announcement—despite her promises to the contrary."

"Exactly what would be the nature of this possible announcement?"

He ignored the duke's question. "She would need at least one gentleman of good ton to stand by her if she speaks out. A *bastard* will not suffice. While she is not aware of it, I intend to be nearby—in the Music Room. But, I will not show myself. It would only compound speculation *later*." He could not fully explain to Helston without causing a thousand more infuriating questions. He could not risk an appearance, as further gossip would only tie him to Elizabeth when he meant to secrete her away in France.

Helston smiled, and scratched his jaw. "Well, I suppose I should be grateful you have enough sense not to try and stir up a royal fray again after that spectacle in St. George's. Very good. There is only this left then." The duke extracted a letter from his coat.

"What is it?"

"A letter from Elizabeth Ashburton, soon to be Elizabeth Pymm, the Duchess of Darlington *in case you have not been paying attention*. I promised that I would put this in your hands today."

Helston's eyes scrutinized him and Rowland returned the favor before sliding his thumb under the seal of the letter.

Chapter 16

The day played out exactly as Elizabeth had known it would. A sense of calm invaded her as she dismissed the two maids Ata had sent to attend to her. She had been sewn into the gown, just as securely as a Tudor bride. Only her husband would wield the scissors to extract her from this prison of jeweled silks tonight. But for some spectacularly odd reason, she did not fear it now.

She had so much for which to be grateful. She would avoid Newgate or worse, secure the future of the man she loved, release her friends from the worry and cost of supporting her for the rest of her life, gain a house and living for Sarah, and would, with any luck, have a child to love. A family, of sorts, again.

The cost was exorbitant, true.

She would have to spend the rest of her life with a pompous, awful man she neither liked nor trusted. And he might very well be far worse. But she tried desperately to remember that there were so many women who had experienced more gruesome fates.

She tried very hard to not think of Rowland and how he would react upon learning what she had done. She prayed he would understand in time. Her spirits depressed, she could not bear to have even Sarah or Ata with her these last moments.

Her efforts had failed—as she had known they would.

Pymm's servants at the Pulteney had been surprised by her appearance, but had granted her access to the apartments that would be hers. She had made use of the connecting door, and searched his apartments, her heart in her throat.

There had not been a single letter or locked chest in evidence, anywhere. And so she had had her maid hastily arrange a few personal effects in what was soon to become her temporary chambers at the famous hotel, and finally decamped to Helston House to be quickly sewn into her gown.

Of course there was still some small hope. She would have a lifetime to find the letters. It gave her something for which to strive.

Everyone needed something on which to pin one's hopes. She stared at the small looking glass, and almost did not recognize herself. She looked far older than her years—like a queen—in the overly ornate golden gown. A seductive queen, with a bodice cut far too provocatively. Pymm's gift of heavy emeralds— given to her last evening—nearly choked her neck.

She heard a commotion beyond her door and knew her time was up. The Prince Regent had insisted on sending two royal carriages to convey all of the Portman Square guests to Carlton House.

The short journey passed in a blur. For the life of her she would never remember what was said to her or what she replied. The only thing she would remember was the anxiety on her friends' faces.

All too soon they arrived at the Prince Regent's vast residence on the south side of Pall Mall. She glanced longingly toward St. James Park, now shadowy in the gloaming hour. As she entered the hexastyle portico of Corinthian columns, liveried royal footmen bowed in her wake as did the awed guests in attendance. It was ironic. For so long she had hoped to make her father proud by being accepted by the aristocracy, who had always ostracized her for her hoydenish ways. Now she would have given just about anything to be anywhere but here.

She entered the octagonal room flanked with Ionic columns of yellow marble; the elegant, courtly crowd parted. She turned slightly, only to find the Duke of Helston standing shoulder to shoulder with the Marquis of Ellesmere and the Earl of Wallace. None of their wives was present. Georgiana was still confined, and Rosamunde and Grace had agreed to Elizabeth's request that they not leave Georgiana's side. Only Ata and Sarah were to attend tonight.

The three great men behind her, the husbands of her dearest friends, all wore serious, purposeful expressions. There was not a hint of their usual relaxed demeanor. They looked like officers on a mission. And suddenly, she did not doubt for a moment that someone had drafted them. Or rather that someone— Rowland—had *impressed* them. It was actually quite convenient, for she had a task they would help her carry out—one that she dared not reveal until there was no further time for argument.

A tremor raced up her spine. Had he read her letter? Had he believed her?

She was escorted up the left branch of the grand

curving staircases. The second-story paintings of Atlas struggling to carry the world and one of the archangel Michael seemed to mock her ascent.

Her future beckoned beyond the open door in front of her. More hushed voices greeted her as she entered the royal chamber. She glanced past the court crowd only to see the man who would be her husband, standing before the empty throne on the slightly raised dais.

He smirked in that odd fashion of his and she made her way ever onward. A thousand eyes peered at her as she accepted the hand he offered. He nodded a silent greeting after her curtsy.

It was then that she noticed the two portmanteaus behind Pymm. *The guineas.* Pymm saw her glance and his sour countenance affirmed her guess. Atlas would be astonished by the weight that had just dropped from her shoulders at that moment. She stepped back to Luc, Michael, and Quinn for a last word.

"After the Prince Regent confers the duchy, the archbishop will come forward. When he does, I would ask you to discreetly transport those portmanteaus to Manning's. Under guard."

"Elizabeth—" Quinn began.

"We're pack mules? Not saviors, then?" The duke shook his head in disgust.

Under their probing eyes, she continued. "The wedding has been moved forward."

Michael intervened. "What have you done?" He was the only one whose expression gave her pause. There was something in Michael's face that would always remind her of Rowland.

She held his gaze. "It was my choice. Don't ever doubt it."

For once, luck was on her side. The entrance of His Royal Highness the Prince Regent saved her from continuing. She moved to join the general. With great royal pomp, the prince waddled forward, his jowls swaying.

It was as if a great invisible scythe parted the crowds before His Highness. As he passed, they all bowed and scraped. And finally Prinny was in front of Leland Pymm and Elizabeth, and they swept lower than anyone.

The prince smiled benevolently as he levered himself onto the magnificent throne and nodded his approval. The Duke of Wellington stood at the Prince Regent's elbow, dour and silent.

Upon the prince's command, a court speaker unfurled a scroll. His deep baritone informed the glittering crowd of Pymm's numerous victories and heroic efforts through the last decade and a half. He recited the string of Portuguese and Spanish battlefields that would always represent the nightmares of Elizabeth's past: Vimeiro, Corunna, Talavera, Busaco, Albuera, Ciudad Rodrigo. She nearly faltered at the mention of *Badajoz*.

These names were nothing more than faraway, romanticized battles to the people in front of her. Through sheer force of will she kept her tears in check. The recitation of the general's accomplishments droned on like a deafening army of insects on a summer afternoon.

And then it was over. With the sweep of his hand, the Prince Regent placed the invisible mantle of a duchy on Leland Pymm's dubious shoulders. He was now the Duke of Darlington, seventeenth in line to be king. The patent letters of nobility were transferred to the newest duke of the realm, who accepted the documents with a tremulous simper and haughty bow.

Pymm turned to her and nodded toward the Archbishop of Canterbury, who stood a few feet behind the throne.

"I would ask the court's indulgence," Pymm addressed the crowd with exaltation mingling with reverence. "The Prince Regent and the archbishop have graciously agreed to overlook the late hour. The latter has come to execute a surprise event this evening."

The words were fitting. Execute, indeed, thought Elizabeth unemotionally.

Murmurs of curiosity floated from the beau monde before them, and Elizabeth was forced to realize that everything she had planned was about to come to fruition. Her mouth was so dry she could barely swallow. The general's eyes roamed her face, his expression triumphant.

She would never understand why Leland Pymm wanted her, a woman who wanted no part of him. Ah, but such was the nature of an obsession, of course. There was no rhyme or reason to his fixation.

The Prince Regent chuckled. "Never has there been such an eager bridegroom as you, Darlington."

Pymm beamed at the prince's use of his new title.

Prinny grinned. "I am all amazement. Do tell the rest of the gentlemen here what powers of persuasion you used to encourage your modest fiancée to forego the pleasure of a wedding tomorrow in St. George's— every young lady's dream?"

"Why, Elizabeth did not want to inconvenience Your Majesty by begging your presence again tomorrow morning."

The prince chuckled and shook his head. "I see. She is impatient for her wedding night too."

Elizabeth felt the heat of a blush rise to her cheeks.

"No fool is she," the prince continued. "For she should secure you before another fair face steals away England's favorite son."

A few titters fluttered from the audience, but they were soon quieted by the archbishop, who had glided forward in his blue-and-silver vestments.

Out of the corner of her eye, Elizabeth spied the empty space where the two portmanteaus had rested in the shadows well beyond the throne. Her friends had accomplished her bidding. She could finally draw a breath, despite the long corset that constricted her.

Her feet leaden, she quickly glanced to where the trio had been, but could only find Quinn, supporting Ata, whose expression was deathly pale.

She swiveled her head toward Leland and encountered the same expression he had worn when he had informed her that her father was dead. The day he had insisted she must marry him. The day he had lied to her, insisting those were her beloved father's last wishes.

His pristine white gloved hand stretched out to her. Beckoning her. A sudden coldness enveloped her and she stepped forward to meet her fate. She slipped her hand into his.

She had been to so many weddings of late that when the familiar words began to roll off the archbishop's tongue, they meant nothing to her. She was chilled despite the heavy gown. Her feet were numb to the bone.

The archbishop asked if there was any man who knew of an impediment to the marriage. Her last hope was dashed when the chamber remained filled with the vast silence of ignorance.

"Leland Reginald Pymm, Duke of Darlington, wilt thou have this woman to thy wedded wife, to live together in God's ordinance in the holy estate of matrimony? Wilt thou love her, comfort her, honor, and keep her in sickness and in health; and, forsaking all other, keep thee unto her, so long as . . ." The Archbishop of Canterbury's voice trailed off.

It began with the smallest tapping sound echoing from somewhere. Growing louder within seconds, the noise became more distinct. Footsteps running . . .

A few murmurs drifted from the courtly guests. The Prince Regent flicked a glance toward the royal footmen, who rapped their golden staffs against the marble floor to silence the crowd.

A pounding at the secured doors threatened to interrupt all.

Leland ignored it, plowing forward quickly. His voice was almost inaudible, the ever-louder whispers echoing from the stone walls of the Gothic chamber. "I, Leland Reginald Pymm, the Duke of Darlington, take thee, Elizabeth Ashburton, to my wedded wife, to have and to hold from this day forward, for better, for worse, for—"

"It appears someone is late," the Prince Regent said, forcing Leland to stop his vows.

"Of course, we will ignore it. I *will* continue," the

general, now duke, demanded, his fury barely concealed. "For richer, for poorer, in sickness and in health, to love and to cherish . . ."

Like an ancient battering ram of centuries past, the pounding intensified.

"Guards," the Prince Regent waved his hand, his good humor unwavering. "Yes, yes, open the doors. Let us see who the madman is who would dare to interrupt my dear Darlington's wedding. And someone better have died, or soon will."

"Your Majesty," Leland whispered harshly, "I would prefer to continue. Elizabeth, your vows."

The prince sighed. "Yes, but *I* prefer to see who this fellow is. Then I shall decide if he is to be put in shackles or taken to my jester to become his apprentice."

The doors opened, and Elizabeth's vision tunneled to the man standing in the gap. *Oh God. No.*

The figure of the man she had not known if she would ever see again advanced. *Slovenly. Drunkenly.*

She had never seen him like this—his gait uneven, his hair disheveled, his neck cloth undone, his visage wild. He appeared every inch a gin-house reveler. Absolute blind dread consumed her.

In the course of the next few hellish moments she registered three things. First, the Prince Regent displayed a mixture of four parts astonishment to three parts curiosity. Second, unchecked rage overflowed Leland Pymm's face while he squeezed her hand, unrelentingly. And last, Rowland Manning appeared *ravenous* to eclipse every last scandal she had created this wedding season. *With a vengeance.*

Elizabeth stared at the tableau of humanity before her and knew without a single solitary drop of doubt that this was exactly how souls felt upon facing judgment at the end of their mortal stay. And there was no one to help her. Even Luc, and Michael, who had suddenly reappeared—now haggard yet resolute, stood lurking just inside the doorway, apparently unwilling to stop him.

She felt dredged in guilt. They were all there because of her. And she was about to dishonor them due to their association with her. She was certain her past sins and all her actions were about to be argued and dissected in her presence. And she was mute to stop it.

Pymm cursed softly under his breath and looked at her darkly.

"I swear I know not why he is come," she whispered. "I made a bargain with you and I intend to follow through with it. I—"

"Mr. Manning," the Prince Regent called out, with another chuckle. "I'm all amazement. Oh, perhaps I should not be—not after the spectacle in St. George's. Your manners shall ever and always be lacking, even if you are a damned fine horseman. Off with you, man. There's no place for you here in your condition—even if you were invited."

Rowland ignored the prince, daring to reel forward, crossing the expanse of gray marble flooring, only the sound of his uneven steps echoing in the vast chamber. As he passed, several guests grimaced in reaction to his apparent aroma.

A wild smile spread across his dark face as he

lurched to a stop in front of the entourage. "Ah, but Your Majesty will loikes what I 'ave to say." Rowland's slur of cockney betrayed him.

"Silence!" The prince's humor had vanished on a whim, as it was disposed to do.

Rowland swayed and scratched his head. "Can't figure why no one wants to talk wiv me 'bout it."

The prince nodded almost imperceptibly toward the guards, who immediately left the doorway to apprehend Rowland.

Elizabeth darted another glance toward Luc and Michael, who moved not a muscle to stop the insanity. A small smile formed on Pymm's lips.

And then the crowd parted and Ata tottered forward, her cane tapping those poor souls who did not make way for her. Sarah stood beside her.

"Majesty," she said in a gentle tone Elizabeth had never heard her use.

The prince raised his quizzing glass to his eye. "Who is that?"

"The Dowager Duchess of Helston." Her deep curtsy left her floundered on the floor. Elizabeth tried to rush to help her regain her footing, but Leland's hand stopped her.

"Ata?" The prince's smile returned and he crossed the distance himself to help her to her feet.

"I would beg your indulgence, Your Majesty. I am an old woman with few amusements left to me now." Her forlorn expression was so well done, Elizabeth's jaw dropped. "May we not hear what that man has to say? He has me curious." She had the extraordinary audacity to whisper something more into the royal ear.

Pymm blustered his objection but the prince chuckled. "You were always the queen mother's favorite." The prince sighed heavily. "Oh, all right. I suppose he must be given a few moments of leniency for winning the Gold Cup. If he chooses to use up any good will he gained in that endeavor by making a drunken fool of himself here and now, then that is his choice."

"My thoughts exactly, Your Majesty," Ata murmured with a tiny smile.

"Majesty," Rowland bowed with as little elegance and as much exaggeration as a drunken dockside laborer. Not once did he look at Elizabeth.

"Yes, yes, get on with it, Manning."

"A question fer the grand Duke of Pymmslydale."

Leland stepped forward, his chin jutting out. "That's *Darlington*. And if you had a particle of sense, you would know that men of your ilk are not wanted here." A sneer marred his cool performance.

Ata tapped her cane on the floor. "What is your question, Mr. Manning?"

Rowland straightened and pulled on the ends of his improperly buttoned waistcoat in a show of exaggerated bravado. "I should loikes to know why the general be marryin' a bloody traitor to the crown. An' doin' it *tonight* instead o' tomorrow loikes it was planned."

Rowland's furious eyes bore into Elizabeth's, and in that moment she knew he was as clearheaded as she. And he would never forgive her.

She felt lighter than the floating ash of the battlefields of her past.

Chapter 17

Leland Pymm gaped like a cod hauled onto the bow of a vessel. And Rowland Manning held the gaff. He could only hope the general was sufficiently stunned. Otherwise, there was no question as to who would be filleted and served to the royal entourage.

He dared not soften his heart to Elizabeth's deathly pale visage. The numerous gasps created a vacuum of silence. Every pair of eyes jerked to the new duke.

"I beg your pardon," Pymm said in haughty splendor. "First you dare come here in such a disgusting fashion, which shows your contempt for His Majesty, and then you interrupt my wedding. And now you dare to . . ." The general's words slowed and his brow furrowed.

Rowland would not give him a moment to decipher his actions. He pointed a shaky, accusatory finger at his beloved. "She be a traitor to every man, woman, and child in this kingdom. Drag 'er to the Tower, Majesty. And then 'ang her fer crimes against the crown."

Out of the corner of his eye, Rowland spied Helston's face, white as chalk, seconded only by the dowager duchess's stunned expression. Even his half brother appeared unnerved.

Rowland pressed forward, ever forward with his rambling charade. He was far too deep into the sucking mud to pull himself out. "Majesty, we canna blame the general. He be blinded wiv 'er beauty. She be a cunnin' liar."

Surely, nothing before had ever rendered the Prince Regent speechless.

It worked to Rowland's advantage, for he was not interrupted. "General, you'll join wiv me in condemning 'er, won't yer? Or 'as she duped you as she 'as so many other poor sods?"

Pymm's cold eyes glinted. "I told you already. I do not answer to bastards," he said harshly. "And I never will."

"One would hope you have some sort of proof, Mr. Manning," the prince said dryly, recovering his voice. "Otherwise, it is you who will be dragged to the Tower."

Rowland watched in horror as Elizabeth's lips parted of their own accord at the Prince Regent's words. "Your Majesty, Mr. Manning is—"

"*Not finished.*" Rowland's harsh words echoed in the chamber. If he failed in this he would never forgive himself.

The Prince Regent glanced first at one then the other of them. "By all means, Mr. Manning, do continue. How can I refuse a man so determined to make an utter fool of himself?"

He pointed again toward Elizabeth, praying no one would see through his camouflage. "Her mother be French. She told me 'erself. I wager there be more to it. Spyin' is wot she be doing." He added a nasal whine to his ridiculous words. "And she only fancies high-flown frog food. Upon my honor, 'tis true."

The teetering emotions on Pymm's countenance terrified Rowland like nothing else. The general's lips formed a grim line, and remained firmly closed.

And then, his half brother strode forth, to stand beside him. "Your Majesty," Michael began solicitously. "I do beg your pardon, but I fear I must intercede—explain, if you will. My poor brother is besotted with Miss Ashburton. I should not say it, but I must, to clear the air. It must be obvious to everyone here that he has formed an obsession with her—"

" 'ave not," Rowland said with a hiccough.

"He formed an obsession," Michael patiently began again, "when Miss Ashburton graciously agreed to ride Vespers during the Gold Cup, and—"

The chamber erupted in shocked sounds. The Prince Regent chuckled. "I knew you looked familiar, Miss Ashburton! I told you I never forget a face."

Michael cleared his throat loudly. "In any case, I'm afraid this is partly my fault, since *I* suggested she ride the horse when the jockey fell ill. I'm certain my brother will regret this unfortunate display in the morning."

"Will not," Rowland insisted unsteadily. "She be a frog lover. And the worst sort o' flirt. *On yer honor*, ain't she, General?"

Pymm grimaced, and yet his eyes took on a fevered intensity as he stared back into Elizabeth's unblinking, shocked expression.

The Prince Regent finally regained his voice. "This

is becoming tedious, Mr. Manning. General Pymm would never betroth himself to a traitor to England. Now, you've had your say. And you've proven you are once again not fit company. I'm appalled by your feeble attempt to malign this poor woman, whose only crime was to try and help a ne'er-do-well such as yourself. You should be ashamed, Manning. General, if anyone has ever earned the right to rebut or even . . . well, is there anything you would like to say to this man before I have him tossed out on his ear?"

It was the height of irony. If Leland Pymm behaved with any sort of honor toward the woman he obsessively loved—by defending her or even remaining silent in answer to these accusations, he would unknowingly condemn himself.

It was a gamble only a mudlark would take. A man used to risking his life, risking his love when others would not dare.

"He has the audacity to speak of honor," Pymm finally said through clenched teeth. "Don't you know, Manning, that no one cares about your lunatic ravings? You've done nothing with your life but groom horses at best. At worst, you are a petty criminal and now a slanderer. Any imbecile knows that most Englishmen possess French relations somewhere in their family tree. Get out of here before I demand reparation in so public a place."

Rowland watched the prince glance at his royal guards. He had but a moment. He took a smooth step closer. "And yet," he said with a quiet viciousness devoid of any cockney, "you have used this knowledge of her French relations to blackmail Elizabeth

Ashburton into marrying you. Do you deny it?"

A wave of shocked whispers erupted from the crowd.

The prince shook his head and sighed loudly. "Blackmail? Good God, Manning. You do like to tread the line of disaster. You now dare accuse our dear Pymm of such an atrocity?" But Rowland could see a hint of doubt blooming on the prince's face.

Pymm attempted to speak but Rowland continued, far louder, and without a trace of his former fabricated inebriation. "The general secretly holds letters . . . letters no one has ever seen, and he has suggested privately to Miss Ashburton that she and her father were traitors. He did it to force her to bend to his will—using blackmail. Well, Pymm, you cannot have it both ways. You cannot threaten her in secret, and now defend her in public. Or perhaps you can, since you have done so. But the one person you will answer to is me."

Still staring at Pymm, Rowland nodded to his brother and Helston, who brought forward the two portmanteaus.

Pymm's anger took control. "What have you there? Let me guess. Alleged blackmail money?"

The kill was sickeningly sweet. "Actually, I am curious to hear you explain why you have suddenly delivered seventy thousand pounds to me." He refused to give him a chance to speak. "Is it not the money you authorized from the royal treasury to silence me? To make me go away?"

Pymm's eyes widened as the full weight of Rowland's accusations rolled through his consciousness. He gritted his teeth in frustration and then smiled.

"You've lost your mind, Manning. You know very well that money is in payment for the eight hundred horses you were contracted to provide our country's cavalry." He sighed heavily, frustrated beyond endurance.

The prince scrunched his brows in confusion. "Why would you scrape my coffers to purchase horseflesh in this time of peace, Pymm?" He scratched his chin. "I am baffled. Displeased, actually. I loathe wastrels. Indeed, it almost makes me regret your elevation."

Manning would have chuckled if he had not been so terrified of failing his objective. The Prince Regent was not known for any remote form of personal parsimony. However, someone else dipping into the royal treasury was another matter altogether. Prinny clearly held blackmail a distant second in importance.

"Your Majesty," Pymm said stiffly, "the contract was drawn many, many months ago. Well before we had a notion we would drive Bonaparte so quickly through the Pyrenees."

Rowland Manning took the chance of a lifetime, swallowing back fear as he watched his beloved's desperate expression. "Majesty," Rowland said quietly, "I am returning this gold to you. It is not in payment for the horses your military *legally* contracted me to provide. A *very kind* Lieutenant Tremont—he is here tonight, in fact—informed me not two months ago that the contract was rendered null and void when peace was declared. These guineas are without doubt naught but blood money, brought to me tonight to keep me silent. I will not allow it to touch my hands. I beg you to take it—all of it."

The prince pursed his lips. "So you would refuse

seventy thousand pounds? And keep eight hundred horses unfit for anything but war?"

"Eight hundred *and twenty*, Your Majesty," he emphasized with expert reluctance. "But I do it for England. And I do it for her." He nodded toward Elizabeth. "I do it for the daughter of a noble British company commander, who is not here to protect his innocent daughter from the likes of that damned blackguard Leland Pymm."

The prince raised his hands to silence the shocked sounds from the guests and shook his head slowly. "Manning, you will ever and always be confounding. But I will admit that you amuse me like no other." His voice deepened. "And I shall have a full and thorough review of any and all of these charges. But first I must hear from Miss Ashburton."

Rowland had a crushing desire to leap onto the dais and wrest her away from Pymm, whose eyes were bouncing around, looking for escape and not finding any.

The prince continued, "I see but two choices before you, my dear. You must either refute Mr. Manning's allegations of blackmail and marry General Pymm, or you will implicate Pymm and take on the reformation of this horse trader before us. I fear you must choose if you want to keep a shred of reputation after today. So, which is it?" The Prince Regent, along with the hundreds of guests, leaned forward to hear her answer.

Pymm's countenance was wild now, and Rowland would have rushed to her side and pulled her into his arms—out of harm's reach—if six royal guards did not stand between them.

"Well?" the prince asked.

All this time, the archbishop had stood slack jawed during the exchange. "Miss Ashburton," he finally rasped, his sonorous voice quite gone, "you have nothing to fear. Tell all of us the truth." He offered her his aged hand and she took it, her hand fluttering.

"Your Majesty, since the day my father died at Badajoz, General Pymm has insisted he has letters from my mother's relatives that would compromise my father and me." She looked at her fingers, and Rowland's gut twisted. "I've never seen these letters, but I do have French relations. Indeed, the one in question is General du Quesne, although I have never met him or had any correspondence with him. And I have never for a moment doubted my father's loyalty to England. The general implied that my only recourse was to marry him, and that it was my father's dying wish, despite the fact that my father had refused General Pymm's offer for me not one week earlier."

The prince was, finally, shocked. "But why did you not come forward, if you are innocent?"

She laughed without any humor. "Because I doubted anyone would take my word over that of the most decorated war hero of the century."

"Well, I shall show you that you are wrong, my dear. Pymm, you will bring these purported letters to me personally in the next hour. My guards shall help you," he said sourly. "But you shall first tell everyone assembled if there is any indisputable proof that Elizabeth Ashburton or her father are guilty of crimes against the crown. And I warn you now that if you dare utter a single falsehood, I shall demand the return of every medal you possess."

Leland Pymm, third son of a minor baronet, directed his gaze to a distant corner and said not a single bloody word.

Just as Rowland had thought.

The Prince Regent reached forward and snatched the patent letters of nobility from Pymm's numb fingers. "You are hereby stripped of the duchy for behavior unbecoming. I shall see to the rest after I see the letters."

Pymm's countenance blazed. "And so this is how a grateful nation rewards its servants for single-handedly leading a nation to victory over its enemies?"

There was the smallest sound of someone clearing his throat and all eyes turned to Arthur Wellesley, the Duke of Wellington, who stared at Leland Pymm with a granitelike countenance.

The prince shook his head at Pymm. "You are a fool. I regret I did not see it before now. Guards, search his affairs and return this *man* to me along with every piece of correspondence you can find," the prince instructed. "You there, Mr. Manning. Come forward."

Rowland could have almost pitied the madman at the sight of his agonized expression if he had not wanted to horsewhip him even more. He crossed paths with Pymm and the latter sneered as if he could read his thoughts. Rowland saw nothing except Elizabeth, waiting for him, uncertainty on her fair features. Relief flooded him as he reached her side, yet he dared not touch her, dared not utter a whisper in her direction.

Prinny had no such qualms. "Now, Mr. Manning,

please keep in mind that I am fatigued by the folly of this day. But I recognize that no matter the reason why you have chosen to return this money that found its way into your possession—blackmail or otherwise—in the end you have done a noble deed. I like that."

Murmurs of approval erupted all around the chamber.

And then the unmistakable voice of the damned dowager duchess piped up. "Will you in your great wisdom reward him then, Your Majesty?"

Prinny lifted a diamond-encrusted quizzing glass to his eye and fixed it on Ata in a great show of annoyance. "Hmmm. Well, I suppose he has saved our nation a great deal by eliminating the need to reward a blackguard like Pymm, if he has the right of it. Might as well not waste what is left of the day. What shall I do for this man before us?"

"Well, Your Majesty," Ata inserted without hesitation, "bastardy is the very backbone of many of our great nation's bloodthirsty thirteenth-century dukes."

Rowland froze and then noticed Helston's horrified expression.

"Yes, well, I think we have enough dukes as it is, madam. I do believe your grandson would agree." A smile overspread the prince's flushed face. "But I have an excellent notion now that you mention it. There's a long-standing vacancy at St. James Palace. It is yours, Manning, if you should fancy it."

"Majesty?" he whispered with as much deference as he could muster, despite the rasp in his voice.

"Master of the Horse."

Something welled up inside of Rowland's throat. For the first time since he could remember, he couldn't speak.

"Well, say something, man. What? Is the Balreal viscountcy that comes part and parcel not sufficient? Or is it the income you find lacking?"

"Income?" his voice was nearly gone.

"Well, it might not be seventy thousand a year, but it is somewhat in the vicinity if I remember correctly. Of course, you would be required to oversee all of the royal household needs pertaining to carriages, horses, including the royal horse guards, and the like. Will it not suit?" The prince said it all with as much dry wit as the conferral of a windfall demanded.

Ata meekly began, "Is there not a residence that conveys with . . . Er, what of Pymm's property? Shall it—"

"Madam," the prince interrupted dryly, "there is no freestanding residence for the Master of the Horse. Royal apartments shall have to do. And, after all, the man does have a stable to run, apart from the aforementioned royal duties. The land I reserved for Pymm shall revert to the crown."

The prince offered the back of his hand to Rowland, who was too stunned to speak. A small, knowing smile appeared at the corners of the royal mouth.

Helston moved to within a few feet of him and whispered, "Kiss His Majesty's hand, you idiot."

Rowland managed a stiff approximation of the formality.

"Very good, Manning. I trust you shall do the viscountcy proud. Helston shall undertake to refine your manners, I daresay."

The duke's eyebrows nearly rose to his hairline, and Rowland could have sworn he heard Helston say something very like, "Not *another* bloody friend," under his breath before he bowed. "Of *course*, Your Majesty."

"Well then, I find I'm at the limits of my patience and munificence. I shall leave you all to make as merry as you choose, while I retire to pray for a return to some semblance of normalcy in the natural order of things—where generals behave with dignity and horse traders are the panderers we know and love."

The Prince Regent swept from the room in all his splendor, leaving the beau monde in attendance with enough scandalous gossip to entertain themselves for the next decade or three.

"And just where do you think you're going?" Ata's tone and the words were all too familiar to Elizabeth.

She had attempted to slip away from Carlton House a mere quarter of an hour after the Prince Regent's departure. Overwhelmed by the magnitude of events, Elizabeth could not keep the frozen smile on her face before the masses. Rowland had sensed her careening emotions, and without a word he had whisked her beyond the gilded screens in the Throne Room to the hidden exit and the fresh air she craved. They should have known better.

"Oh no, you don't." Ata blocked their entrance into Rowland's closed, dark blue Berline coach. "The guests are but a few moments behind you, and they would seize any new bit of tittle-tattle if you dared to leave together unescorted."

Elizabeth hazarded a glance at the face of the man who had saved her. She felt as if she was in a dream still, for he had not directed more than a few syllables toward her.

"Well, I'm leaving," Rowland said darkly. "Can't stomach another moment of that god-awful fawning."

"Yes," Ata said, "well, you should have thought about that before you put yourself up as London's newest hero."

"I shall go with him," Elizabeth murmured softly.

"Absolutely not," Ata insisted. "If you think your every step was commented on before, Eliza, you have no notion what it will be like after today."

Elizabeth could barely speak. "But, I don't care what they—"

"No." Ata was deep into diatribe. "He must court you properly. He may call upon you in a few days, or in a week, when the madness of this day wanes a bit, and then—"

Rowland leaned down and grasped Ata by her petite waist and hauled her into his carriage. The dowager was so shocked that aside from one very unladylike oath, she took a seat inside and fumed silently.

Rowland then looked at Elizabeth, that dearly familiar sultry half smile etched on his face. "Your turn." He swung her up into the darkened interior, his large hands gripping her waist. A moment later, he was beside her and closing the door smartly.

As the carriage jerked forward along the crowded roadway, Elizabeth checked the small window and saw a flood of guests leaking from Carlton House's magnificent entrance.

Ata was now muttering. "And by the by, young man, you are not to think about climbing the trellis again."

"Never fear, madam. I don't fancy more of those bloody thorns in my *arse* and—"

"Your elocution lessons"—Ata interrupted—"shall begin tomorrow. Luc's patience will be sorely tested, but—"

"Madam," Rowland growled, "I am not in the habit of enduring lectures. You shall remain silent now for I must speak to Elizabeth. I have something of great importance to—"

"*Oh . . .*" Ata interrupted and perked up with a knowing smile. "*I see.* Well, then, go ahead. You have my permission. I shall just help you over the rough spots—guide you in case—"

Rowland effectively cut off Ata by rapping on the ceiling of the carriage with his knuckles. The Berline swayed and drew to a stop. He sighed heavily and stared at the dowager, whose look bordered on petulant.

Elizabeth's heart raced, her voice stuck in her throat. Ata's dark, beady eyes glanced first at her and then at Rowland.

With greater kindness than Elizabeth thought him capable, he spoke to Ata. "I understand you have a fondness for driving, madam?"

Ata immediately brightened. "Why, indeed I do. But what has that to do with—"

"You shall join Lefroy on the bench outside. And he shall teach you everything you need to know about—"

"Impertinent pup. I don't need any driving lessons. I'll have you know that—"

"Do you want to drive the team or not?" he interrupted impatiently.

Elizabeth watched Ata stutter for the first time ever.

"Oh, very well. But don't think I don't know what this is all about. And if you muddle the proposal, it shall be your own fault, Mr. Manning. I could have helped you. None of the other roosters knew the smallest thing about how to go on. I'd hoped to save you the trouble."

He looked at her wolfishly. "Perhaps I'm not a rooster."

"Really?" Ata said with doubt.

"Perhaps I'm the fox."

Ata barked with laughter.

His hungry gaze swept over her, and Elizabeth suddenly felt very shy in the enclosed space.

"Perhaps, I don't stop until I get what I want," he continued. "Snatching things, whether I have a right to them or not, is my speciality, or haven't you heard?"

Ata's eyes widened. "Well, we shall just have to see how effective your unconventional methods are, Mr. Manning. Eliza, I shall come to your aid at the first squawk."

Elizabeth watched Rowland assist Ata to the outside driving bench with a surprising amount of gentleness. She heard his strict instructions to Lefroy.

And then he was alone with her. Across from her.

They gazed into each other's eyes for so long, her vision blurred.

"You've said naught but three words," he said in his gravelly low voice. "Are you all right?"

"Thank you," she whispered, afraid to let the torrent of gratitude and even stronger emotions past her defenses. Yet, she could not stop her eyes from welling.

"Tears?" He sighed. "Hell."

She blinked rapidly and turned partially away from him to swipe at her face with the back of her gloved hand.

"You'd better stop for I haven't a handkerchief," he murmured.

She laughed raggedly. "Neither do I."

There was such mystery in the shadows of his angular face. Yet, his hands gripped the seat as if he was hanging on for dear life.

"Is it to be kidnapping beneath the cover of darkness, then, Elizabeth?" he murmured.

"No, of course not." She felt unbearably reticent with him for some ridiculous reason—uncertain how to convey the tumult of her relief and bone-deep happiness.

He leaned toward her with all the slow certainty of a man who knows what he wants and isn't afraid to come after it. He gently gathered her in his arms and transferred her onto his lap.

She tucked her head into the hollow of his neck. "I love you," she whispered.

"I know," he replied gently. She felt the warmth of his hand stroking her head.

Her breathing was hitched. "I suppose you figured it out a long time ago."

"Actually, it was only when I read that ridiculous letter you wrote. The one suggesting you had changed your mind and were marrying Pymm. I didn't take it seriously, of course. Not for a moment. I was certain Pymm had made you write it. Just as I was certain you might not follow my instructions." He ran his hand through his dark hair. "But God, Elizabeth, I didn't think you'd go so far as to . . . Well, I lost ten years of my life—that I can ill afford—when Helston and Michael dragged all that blunt to Prinny's Music Room. Bloody hell . . . Elizabeth." His voice cracked.

"The Music Room? Is that where you were? Well then, you do not follow directions, either," she whispered. "I thought you were going to wait for me in my room at Helston House. And I lost *fifteen* years of my life when you appeared before His Majesty. Not that I'm complaining, you understand." She pulled away from him and stared at his shadowed expression. And then she began to laugh. And cry again. She laughed through her tears as only a woman inexplicably saved and in the arms of the man she had never thought to be with ever again. And yet, he had not said the words she most wanted to hear.

Perhaps he could not say them—would not ever say them. She had not a doubt he cared for her. He would not have given up seventy thousand pounds unless he did. The thought made her silently weep all the harder as he unwound his neck cloth and dried her tears with the end of it.

"So," he whispered into her hair in between kisses on the top of her head, "shall we risk a show again at St. George's? Or would you prefer something simpler?"

"Are you certain?" she whispered.

"Of what?"

"That we should marry? Is that what you really want, or are you doing this because you've been trapped into offering for me?"

"Elizabeth," he said, shaking his head. "Don't force me to play the rooster, cackling romantic nonsense. I want to marry you. Now, if you don't want to marry me, I understand. Actually, I'll only partially understand, since I do come with a title now. But in the end, I will bind and gag you, put you over my shoulder, and even suffer the indignity of thorns in my arse again, if necessary, and find some deaf-and-blind blacksmith in Gretna Green to do my bidding." He waited patiently for her answer.

"Yes, then. Something simple," she whispered, her mind still whirling by her outrageous good fortune. "But . . ."

"Anything," he whispered as he stroked the skin between the puffed edge of her short sleeve and the top of her glove.

"I should like it to be soon." She closed her eyes and drank in the masculine scent that was uniquely his. "As soon as humanly possible."

It was as if he could read her mind. "What are you thinking—worrying—about?"

She could not stop the words from spilling out. "That I will wake up and this will all be an impossible dream."

He tilted up her chin. "Elizabeth . . . I will not have you worrying. *Ever again*." He paused, his eyes searching her expression. When he appeared satisfied, he continued. "Then it shall be by Special License, if at all possible. I wager the archbishop will be delighted to help." He grinned and then dipped lower to brush an endless series of kisses on her forehead, her cheeks, her nose, and finally on her mouth.

Before she gave herself up to the cocoon of their happiness, an image formed in her mind at the same time that a smile formed on her lips.

There was one thing she would do—something *absolutely daring*—before she became the wife and very private chef of the man who had saved her—the man with whom she would spend the rest of her life.

And she knew just whom to ask for help in her quest. It certainly was *not* the archbishop.

Chapter 18

If someone had told him three months ago that he would face down a revered military hero and the Prince Regent, and do it all to protect and marry a woman this fateful summer, he would have laughed and then horsewhipped the man who had the temerity to suggest something so outrageous.

And yet, here he stood, impatiently waiting before the yawn of an intricately sculpted marble fireplace in the drawing room of one of Mayfair's grandest town-houses, flanked by his half brother and the Duke of Helston—two men who had taken it upon themselves this week to accomplish the impossible.

First, they had helped him secure the Special License. Second, they had *barred* him from seeing Elizabeth—this last at the insistence of that interfering dowager duchess, whom Rowland would have been tempted to strangle if she had not been so helpful the evening of the Carlton House debacle. All of them had tried to put a pretty face on their sodding reasons for keeping Elizabeth from him, but Rowland knew why they did it.

They'd been terrified he would muck it up—change his mind or say something to Elizabeth to make her reverse her promise. He smiled and cleared his throat. They knew nothing of it, the idiots.

Those long-standing members of the peerage might have respectable instincts toward their wives—all that self-sacrificing nonsense espoused by blue-blooded coves. But, Rowland was a mudlark and ever would be. When he found something precious, he didn't give it away or return it to its rightful owner. He guarded it like a wild dog with a bone. In this case, he was the starving mutt, and Elizabeth was—

"Well?" Helston was yammering again about some sort of trivial detail. It had gone thusly all week.

"Well, what?" Rowland muttered.

"Do you have it?"

"What?"

The duke sighed heavily. "The ring?"

He knew the duke had been marking off the days until this wedding. Helston could taste freedom—freedom from the responsibility of watching over his eccentric grandmother's flock of crows.

The Prince Regent had not withdrawn his generous gift to Sarah Winters despite the change in bridegrooms. With Elizabeth's marriage, the duke would be left with only one widow to coddle—although she was the most trying of them all. Ata.

"Well? Do you have a damned ring, or am I forced to retrieve one of my wife's baubles?" Helston asked impatiently.

Rowland just could not stop himself. "A ring? Hmmm . . . that might be a problem," he replied casually.

The duke turned to Michael. "One would think you would have at least accompanied your own brother to a jeweler. Helped him find a bloody—"

Michael sighed. "He has one, Helston. You haven't the smallest notion, do you?"

"Of what?" the duke asked darkly.

"That my brother has an odd fashion for showing gratitude."

"And what way is that?"

"By making you sweat before he does."

Rowland clapped his younger brother on the back and chuckled. "You have the right of it, Michael. But only partially."

"Which part?" Michael asked, his smile fading.

"The part about him sweating," Rowland replied. "But *I* have not a single reason to be anxious. Quite the opposite actually."

That set Helston to guffawing. Finally drawing a breath, he said, "We shall see, my dear fellow. We shall see. In fact, I predict we shall witness a shift in your cool attitude in nine months' time—if you use your time *wisely*. Ellesmere has been a prime example this summer."

"And of course, you were as cool as you please, Helston, when your wife—" Michael murmured.

"Do not say another word, Wallace." The duke glared at the both of them.

They were interrupted by the appearance of Ata, who darted a quick glance around the edge of the door and nodded to the archbishop and Lefroy, who stood at the opposite end of the chamber. It saved Rowland from trying to hide the sudden rush of fear in the vicinity of his heart. God, if she became with child. Birthing . . . The thought was enough to blur his vision. He just could not lose her. He swallowed back bile.

The ancient archbishop, dressed in far simpler vestments than those he'd worn in St. George's, strode toward them. "Shall we take our places, then, gentlemen?"

Rowland's loyal stable master hung back, lurking at the far window, uncertain.

"Lefroy?" With a small gesture, Rowland beckoned the man he had known longer than anyone else—a man who had started with him years ago and had been the only man who possessed the nerve to stand up to him.

"Master?" he took a step closer.

"Come over here," he murmured.

The older man made his way closer until he stood next to Michael.

"No," Rowland said. "Beside me."

Lefroy joined him and cracked a grin wide enough to make his ears dip.

"Hold this." He handed the stable master a slender, delicately braided gold ring that glittered with many tiny, exquisite diamonds.

The duke's eyes bugged out. "Where did you . . ."

He raised a brow. "I have sources."

"By everything holy," Helston muttered, "you've gone and bought *fenced* goods."

"Don't be ridiculous," he replied. "It's not filched. It's from *his* wife." He glanced at his brother. "On loan."

"On loan? As in you will return it?" Michael choked out.

"No. On loan as in you *might* get it back—if and when Elizabeth sees something she fancies more. But

I wouldn't hold your—" And then he heard a sound and all of them turned.

His eyes came to rest on a luminescent figure at the door. The backs of his eyes burned from the sight, and his throat closed. He would not for the life of him have been able to describe the white confection of lace and silk she wore. All he knew was that she looked like an angel flown down from heaven's perch to lead him to paradise.

As she floated toward him, he saw white flowers threading her magnificent locks amassed at the crown of her head. A few wisps curled on one shoulder to tempt him beyond endurance. But it was her eyes that arrested him, beckoned him. They were so true, and beguiling in their sweetness—so *green* against all that white finery.

She looked like a bride.

His bride.

He reached out his hand as she drew beside him. Without thinking, he brought her fingers to his lips and kissed the back of her gloved hand, lingering there. Her eyes told him she had missed him as he had missed her.

The archbishop cleared his throat, forcing him back to the moment. "Mr. Manning, if you please," the man said sternly. "May we go about this then in the correct order—*for once*? The vows first, and then . . . well, we shall see."

Rowland's eyes did not drift from hers. What had the man said?

A dazzling smile appeared on her face to enchant him further. He nearly reeled. And then she was turning to hand her small posy to Ata. Sarah Winters made a show of arranging the train of Elizabeth's gown.

He had never paid any attention to the words uttered during the scant number of weddings he'd been forced to endure. In the hushed atmosphere of the chamber, he absorbed every nuance of every phrase.

As he pled his troth to the woman who had saved him from himself, he let the vows wash over him, through him, until he felt an otherworldly sense of joy consume him. Never in his lifetime would he forget her heartrending promises in return.

". . . for better and for worse, for richer and for poorer, in sickness and in health, to love and to cherish, and to *obey*"—she lifted one winged eyebrow in amusement—"till death us do part, according to God's holy ordinance; and hereto I give thee my troth."

Rowland grasped the ring Lefroy held and then paused, uncertain, as he examined her long white gloved hand and arm. "Hmmmm . . ." He stuck the ring between his teeth and began to disengage her hand from her glove.

Helston cleared his throat. "Put it on over the glove."

"No. Once it's on she's never going to take it off," he said, softly staring into her laughing eyes and withdrawing the glove.

The archbishop shook his head but smiled. Surely this was the most unorthodox wedding he had witnessed.

"With this ring," Rowland began quietly, as he kissed it once and slid it onto her delicate finger, "I thee wed, with my body I thee worship, and with all my worldly goods I thee endow . . ."

They were pronounced man and wife, and Rowland released the longest-held breath of his life.

She was now safe. No one could take her from him.

Even if Pymm's future was still uncertain, the former favorite son of England had not a chance of touching her now. He was far too busy trying to hold on to some semblance of his battlefield laurels by building a sizable bulwark against incrimination using impressive, long-standing military connections.

Every last man in the room pounded him on his back—Helston the longest of all. "God bless you, Manning, for . . . well, you know very well what for." The duke laughed long and loud—the first time Rowland had heard him do so—and the rest of the members of the party chorused good wishes for their happiness.

A clattering from the hall interrupted the celebration, and Rowland's gut clenched. He'd known this was all too easily done.

The flushed face of his brother's countess, Grace, appeared. "Oh . . . I *am* interrupting."

"What is it?" Elizabeth said, her fingers still entwined with his own.

"I am so sorry. But, I thought all of you would want to know soonest. Georgiana is safely delivered. Of a son. Oh, this is awful of me. I didn't mean to interrupt." Michael went immediately to her side and cradled her in his arms.

Helston's wife, Rosamunde, entered behind Grace and hurried to her husband.

"What is it?" Helston asked.

Rowland's ears picked up the raven-haired lady's words. "Nothing, my love. It's just that Georgiana was so very weak. We didn't know . . . but the doctor assured us she will be perfectly fine. She needs simply to rest."

Helston smiled broadly as he clasped his wife closer—in a rare public display. "If I were to hazard a guess, it is Ellesmere who will require the most bolstering."

The dowager duchess clucked about new fathers and infants, and all manner of folderol. But it was Rowland who was perhaps the most delighted of all by the excellent news.

It provided the perfect rationale for an early escape from the elegant townhouse in Mayfair.

There was a reason Elizabeth had asked Rowland if they could marry at Helston House. If the fashionable columns had been rife with gossip about her whereabouts before, when she had been supposed to marry Leland Pymm, it was nothing compared to now, after the events at Carlton House. It would have been mad to marry at St. George's.

As she and Rowland stood just outside of Helston House's doors, she was overwhelmed by the sight of the masses crowding Portman Square. Her heart warmed at the outpouring of well wishes from the people, prosperous and poor alike, who had come to witness the commoner turned noble well and truly married to his scandalous bride.

A rich stew of cockney-laced words of congratula-

tions hailed from the crowd while a few white hand-
kerchiefs fluttered in the distance.

"Gives her a little kiss, then, Manning," a man
shouted in the distance. A chorus seconded him.

He looked down at her, his eyes glittering with
amusement. "Shall we?"

"I thought you disliked such public displays," she
murmured.

"Really? Since when have I ever refused the
chance?" His lips touched the end of her nose before
he swept her into an outrageous kiss designed to
impress.

The crowd cheered, and whooped and hollered
their delight. And for once, she didn't care that the
newspapers would be full of the vulgar antics. In
truth, this might just be the last time she would be
seen in public for a very long time. If she had her way,
they would not visit a ballroom for the next decade or
longer. She had only one desire, and that was to live a
very private, productive life with the man she loved.

Precisely one half hour later, Elizabeth found herself drifting in the world she had not dared to believe
would be her own.

The last week had dragged forever. Myriad doubts
and fears had crept in. Perhaps he did not, and would
never come to, care for her the way she cared for him.
His past had been so wretched that it was doubtful he
could trust anyone—even Elizabeth—enough to open
his heart and offer love unreservedly.

And so she had fretted—as only a young bride-to-
be can do.

After extracting themselves from the exuberant

well-wishers in Mayfair, they had, through the expert hand of Mr. Lefroy, inched toward Manning's stables, where his stable hands waited for them. Intent on celebrating the nuptials of their heretofore taciturn master and his new bride, they had arranged a simple but very heartfelt breakfast in the shade of the old oak tree.

Elizabeth became more and more anxious as the hour grew later and the revelry and toasts more scant. Twice, Rowland had come near and bent down to whisper the suggestion that they excuse themselves. And twice she had smiled, but allowed one of his men to distract her with yet another outrageous story of one of the auctions, or one of the horses, or of Rowland himself. It did not help that Rowland's face grew darker with each passing minute she dragged her feet.

And then without a word of warning, she was lifted in the air from behind. It did not take much effort to deduce it was her husband. She refused to struggle. It would be even more mortifying than it already was. A babble of men's laughter drifted all around them as Rowland turned her to face him and cradled her to his wide chest. "Come along, Mrs. Manning," he whispered in her ear. "Or have you already forgotten the promises you made?"

She could not meet his eyes. "Promises?"

"The ones about having, and holding. And the one about obeying. Although, I admit, I was fairly certain there might be some trouble with that last one." He kissed the top of her head and chuckled. "I just hadn't thought it would be so soon."

She still could not meet his eyes. He carried her

over the threshold to the main building and up the staircase. His long strides ate up the distance to his private chamber. It was the one room she had never dared to enter.

He somehow managed to open the door, and kicked it shut with the back of his boot. She dared a peek at him through her lashes only to find brooding eyes.

She glanced about the chamber with curiosity. One wall was covered from floor to ceiling with bookshelves, slightly swayed in the middle from the number of volumes. She swung her gaze back to his shuttered expression. On the opposite side, she found only four pieces of furniture: a washstand, a small desk, a chair, and . . . she swallowed.

White mosquito net draped from the ceiling, encircling a very large bed with plain white bed linens. There was something very spare yet very large about it—sort of like the man she had married.

No carpeting was in evidence. No paintings relieved the expanse of the white walls. It was the room of a scholar. The room of a hardworking man.

He swept aside one end of the netting and placed her in the middle of his bed, an intense expression carved onto his harsh face—like a man intent on having his way.

With her.

A mere five minutes later, she found herself still in the middle of Rowland's massive bed, on top of more pillows than she knew existed in London town, without a single stitch of clothing to hide her in the lengthening shadows of the late afternoon. He had said not a word as he had helped her undress. Tension engulfed them, like fog before a battle.

She watched him slowly tug at one end of his neck cloth as his eyes stared back at her. With his sure hands, he undressed in an economical manner just as he did everything else in his life, before he eased onto the bed beside her, and stretched out without touching her.

His body was like that of the marble statues at Windsor's gallery, with only his chest rising and falling to give away his vitality. He lay there quietly. Waiting.

"Elizabeth, what is wrong?"

She answered a little too quickly. "Nothing. Why would you—"

"You have that look about you," he said.

She picked at the bed linen and tried to cover herself, only to stop when he stilled her hand. "It's just . . . so much has happened so quickly. And I guess I'm just a bit anxious."

"About what?"

"Perhaps you lament . . ." she began. "Well, not regret, but, it wasn't as if you were given any sort of alternative to marrying me. Everyone assumed—"

His lips cut off her words and he kissed her intently, showing instead of telling her that he had no regret, no doubts about the day's work. His hands followed suit, touching every inch of her. Reverently. He looked down into her face, finally. "*Mhuirnin* . . . never doubt me. Ever. You, of all people, know I never do anything I don't want to do. You might have your work cut out for you trying to make a gentleman out of me, but I am not a quitter. And I never change my mind. You left your mark on me, and I will never let you go now."

She swallowed against the lump in her throat. "Come to me, then."

They stared into each other's eyes for a long moment, before she tugged at him to cover her. He deftly slid between her thighs, and she eased her knees wide. "Elizabeth, wait . . . I would—"

"I want you. I don't want to wait. I've been waiting forever."

Without further preliminaries, he grasped her hips, and suddenly, the large blunt end of him pulsed against the juncture of her.

The moments he waited, just outside of her for a final signal of her absolute desire for him, were of a poignancy unknown to her. She raised her head to brush her lips against the slight roughness of his hollow cheek, and he surged forward, his head thrown back.

She gasped at the force of his entry. It was as if he wanted to replace any of her remote fears with the strength of a lifetime promise of happiness.

There was something in his countenance that suggested he would not stop until all of her anxiety of the last weeks and months was obliterated by his intense desire for her. It would be something neither of them would ever forget.

And that was how the long afternoon and early evening went until it grew so dark he reached to light the sole candle in the room. Elizabeth was exhausted amid the rumpled bed linens. She had never been so happy, never felt so wanted, so protected and cherished in her entire life. Searching for a cool spot, she slowly turned onto her stomach, only to hear a surprised sound from him.

She turned her head on the pillow.

"What is that?" he whispered, shock reflected from his face. "What have you done?"

She was suddenly worried about her recklessness. Perhaps it would be a terrible reminder when she had meant it to be something else entirely. "I'm sorry," she said burying her face in the pillow. "It's just that I thought—"

"You haven't answered the question." His voice was cool, distant. She could feel him peering closer.

"The family crest," she whispered.

"The *what*?"

His large warm hand rested on the small of her back, holding her down so he could better inspect the tiny black *B* in a simple script she now had on her bottom.

"I require a name," he said hoarsely.

"A name?" Her voice was muffled even to her own ears.

"The name of the blackguard who put this on you."

She could not mistake the soft menace in his voice. Now she well and truly regretted her impetuous action. She squeezed her eyes closed, trying to ignore his lingering scent on the pillow. "A better question would be why I did it."

He waited for her answer.

"We are to be Lord and Lady *Balreal*, remember? And . . . I didn't want you to always feel so different. Different from . . ." She swallowed, "From me, and from the rest of humanity, as I think you do sometimes."

He said not a word but she could feel the tip of his finger smooth the still sensitive skin.

"You said that letter was placed on you so you would not forget who you are." She quickened her speech, "Now you are not alone. This is my own reminder of the name we will share. And I should also like it very much if it would also remind you how much I . . ."

Her voice stuttered to a stop as she felt his hot breath just above the tiny *B* etched on the sensitive skin of her bottom. "Yes?" he coaxed roughly.

"How much I never want to be parted from you . . ." She shuddered as his lips brushed against the tiny new mark. "Ever again."

"Do you have any idea . . ." His voice trailed off in suppressed emotion. ". . . how much I've missed you this last week? Of how much I've missed you every day of my godforsaken life?"

His words made her want to weep. She closed her eyes at the exquisite sensation of his strong, supple hands now stroking the length of her spine.

"Go to sleep," he said gently. "I've overtired you."

"I shall soon," she said exhausted. "But perhaps not just this moment." She did not want to tell him—worry him—about the nightmares. The one she had had several times this last week. It was always of Pymm at Carlton House. He would reach for her hand with his pristine glove, and a drop of blood would appear, growing ever larger until she would come awake, shaking. The dream was too vivid—too soon after her near miss with disaster.

As if he sensed her ill ease and exhaustion, he gathered her close in his arms. "Well then, I shall wait with you . . ." he whispered.

No argument. No teasing. Just simple reassurance.

He held her in silence, but she could tell by his breathing that he did not sleep. As she drifted, she reveled in the comfort of his sheltering arms. It had been so long since she had been allowed to rely on someone else to ease the burden of her life.

Memories such as these, she would keep close to herself in the dark hours, when a person had no choice but to tuck oneself into the privacy of their thoughts.

And their nightmares.

Chapter 19

He just could not stand having her out of his sight for very long. He felt like a bloody fool, a bloody helpless, mewling infant as he sat behind his old desk in the main building—alone for the first time in almost a week.

Even the knowledge of how idiotic he was being had not stopped him from seeking her out, or sending for her dozens of times each day.

At this rate he would be as fat as the Prince Regent, for he had not missed one meal—not even one bloody mid-afternoon cup of tea. And it was solely done to see her. His men delighted in every ridiculous change in him.

But he was a smart man. During that short period he had been forced to endure away from her, due to the machinations of that puerile dowager duchess, he had learned that he was going to have to surrender to the obvious—of being constantly terrified of losing her—of losing happiness after finally finding it thirty-eight years into his existence. Surely, he would stop playing the idiotic fool in time. Nothing was ever permanent in life. One had to guard against every eventuality.

Well, at least he had a host of new things vying for his attention, which worked fairly well as a distraction between rounds of succulent meals with his wife. His additional set of duties now as Master of the Horse made for an astonishingly overtaxed daily schedule. A phalanx of the Prince Regent's men reported to him each afternoon in the royal mews.

And now, after the extraordinary events at Carlton House, Rowland slowly came to the realization that he had managed the unthinkable. He had somehow exchanged places with General Pymm in the fickle London populace's opinions. Indeed, Manning's was suddenly considered the *only* place to see horses and be seen. Most importantly, it was considered the place to *buy* horses. Indeed, Lefroy had laughed long and loud when a gentleman's sporting journal had proclaimed him "Prince of the Equines" and had called on all patriotic Englishmen to buy his cavalry-trained horses.

Lost in thought, Rowland absently ran his hand over the end of his plain desk, his first possession. His mother's etched words of advice along the edge brought a flood of memories.

Forget not-want not.

And yet, he wanted to forget. There was no reason to remember his wretched beginnings.

He did not want for anything anymore. He never would, for he had everything now. And so he wished to forget.

And yet, his mind was like a magnet, drawing him to those words Maura Manning had carved. She had put them there to serve as a daily reminder of the importance of hunger and need, and how it could drive him to find a way out of poverty if he worked hard enough.

But unknown to his mother, it had also reminded him of Mary and how he'd been unable to save his beloved sister. Both his sister and mother had been taken from him because he had not been strong enough to protect them from the brutalities of poverty.

Suddenly, he grasped the knife from the breakfast tray Elizabeth had brought to him earlier and began to stab at the carved letters. He obliterated every trace of them in short order.

So intent was he, he didn't hear his wife enter the library until she was standing over him, looking at the havoc he had wrought.

She went behind him and wrapped her arms about his shoulders. "I never liked that desk either."

He bowed his head. "I just want you to know that I shall always protect you—take care of you. I don't want you to fear anything ever again."

"I know you will, Rowland," she said gently. "You already have saved me from a lifetime of unhappiness. You were the only one capable of it."

Brooding, he absently caressed her forearms.

"The landaulet awaits," she began. "The picnic goods are tucked inside. Shall we not go? The others are surely there already and—"

He drew her into his lap and pressed his lips against the soft column of her neck. He delighted in holding her—touching her when she least expected it. She was his wife . . . his life.

"I've seen to your favorite. Perhaps we should hurry, since the food might spoil in this heat unless—"

"Mmmm . . ." he interrupted. "Strawberry Fool?"

He was looking at the gathered edge of her bodice and remembering.

"No, gingerbread."

"I prefer Strawberry Fool," he murmured, and considered doing something unspeakably wicked with the tip of his tongue. It would make him forget all about the blasted words under the wreckage of his desk.

"I do too," she whispered. "But if we don't leave now, you shall have to endure the ribald comments of your brother and the duke all afternoon."

He groaned, his body disinclined to return to some semblance of decorum. "It would be worth it."

His wife cocked her head, and an impish smile complete with dimples overspread her beautiful face. She reached for the ends of his neck cloth and tugged; an impossibly innocent seductress at work. It was moments like these that were most painful to him. He was not meant for such happiness.

Elizabeth glanced about herself, and enjoyed the utter contentment of being among friends in the lazy haze of the park on a summer day. They were all there, the widows of the club—Ata, Rosamunde, Georgiana—looking pale and tired but radiant nonetheless, with her infant tucked in her arms. And of course, Grace and Sarah were in attendance. All the gentlemen who loved them were there too: Luc, Quinn, Michael, and Rowland, who lay sprawled beside Elizabeth on a length of cloth. They were gathered in a secluded corner of the Serpentine's western end, looking toward Kensington Gardens.

In the distance, Michael and Grace's two adopted children and Quinn's daughter, Fairleigh, tugged paper boats on strings along the water's edge, while Luc and Rosamunde's raven-haired twin cherubs napped in the shade. It had been far too long since they had all gathered together in one place.

She knew it was the nature of life—that fate brought people together for a time and then, seemingly on a whim, scattered them onto new paths. And so she treasured moments like these—celebrations of friendship.

In the late afternoon lassitude of abated hunger, plans were already being set in motion for separation.

"It is settled then, Sarah. I've informed the servants," Ata said, determined. "You and I are for Cornwall in a fortnight. Oh, how I long to feel the brine of sea air on my face, and savory pasties on my lips."

"I am looking forward to it too," Sarah murmured. "We spent so many happy days there. You are very kind to invite me to go with you."

Luc chuckled. "It is you we must thank. My grandmother is withholding from you the joy of discovering what the Prince Regent bestowed on you."

"Why do I suspect," Rowland interjected, "my wife is about to suggest a tour of Cornwall this winter?"

Georgiana sat beside Rowland, with Quinn behind her, supporting her back. She was clearly enjoying this chance to better know Elizabeth's new husband. Georgiana shifted her position and the infant opened his eyes and made known his discomfort in the heart-rending, bleating cries of a new-to-the-world babe. To everyone's shock, Georgiana leaned forward and held the infant in front of Rowland, who had no choice but to grasp the baby. "My arms are tired, Mr. Manning. Oh, Quinn? I think we need"—she lowered her voice—"new linen."

Elizabeth watched Rowland's startled expression as he gazed at the tiny infant he held at arm's length. Ever so slowly, he brought the child to his chest and cradled him. He smoothed his wrinkled brow with one finger and the baby stopped crying instantly.

She should not have been surprised. Had she not watched every last horse at the stable respond to his touch and his commands? But seeing Rowland here, with a tiny boy child in his arms . . .

As Quinn searched the baskets, Georgiana sent Elizabeth a secret smile. It was obvious she approved of Rowland. Very much. "Ata?"

"Yes, my dear Georgiana?"

"Quinn, Fairleigh, and I shall follow you in a month's time—as soon as the physicians advise it. My parents and brother long to see little John Matthew and I miss our own home in Cornwall more than I can say."

Elizabeth spied a trace of sadness in Ata's eyes, and so turned the conversation. "Rosamunde, I can't tell you how happy I am to have this afternoon with you, Grace, and Georgiana." Her gaze wandered to the latter. "I have missed you all so much. A fine friend I have been. I feel as if I haven't seen any of you this entire summer."

Rosamunde laughed and her black curls shined in the afternoon sun. "I think I speak for all three of us when I say that you are being entirely ridiculous. Darling infants and children are the ones to be blamed for interrupting perfectly good friendships. But," she cocked a slender brow, "I predict you shall find out all about it. Well, you won't be able to say you weren't warned. And I do think you went along perfectly well without us. Mr. Manning, I must personally thank you for saving our dear Elizabeth, as I've not had the chance."

Rowland relinquished Georgiana's child into the anxious arms of the father. "No need to thank me. But if you must, perhaps you would consider doing me the great favor of—"

"You are not to do him any favors, Rosamunde," Luc said darkly. "He is not fully reformed."

Rowland chuckled. "Still flummoxed by your grandmother's wedding gift, Helston?"

"Vespers was not a wedding gift," the duke insisted.

"Really? What was it then?" Rowland picked a piece of lint from his coat.

"*A loan.*"

Rowland nodded. "I see—like the wedding ring."

"*My* ring?" Elizabeth darted a glance at him.

"No," Luc said, put out. "Not at all like Grace's ring. That was a mere bauble. Vespers is—"

"Why is he saying my ring belongs to Grace?" Elizabeth interrupted.

"Don't listen to him, my darling," Rowland replied with a devilish smile. "This is a conversation between gentlemen about the joys of gift giving among nobs. No need to—"

"Well, if you're going to exclude ladies, we shall just have to see to ourselves. Rosamunde, I've been meaning to ask if you would like to have a very un-ladylike race 'round the lovely little track behind the—"

"I'm afraid she won't have time," Luc ground out.

"Really?" Rosamunde questioned, her eyes brimming with laughter. "And why is that, my love?"

"We are setting sail."

A half dozen voices babbled shocked questions at the suddenly heavy-lidded, mysterious duke. He held up his hand. "I promised my bride an extended sailing trip a very long time ago. Now that everyone is settled, and old Boney's on Elba, we're for—"

"Where?" Rosamunde's aquamarine eyes lit up as she interrupted her husband in excitement.

"Wherever your heart desires," he answered. "As long as there are no bloody widows within a hundred miles of any port where we dock."

"Paris!" Rosamunde shouted with glee. "And then the West Indies. And Vienna. Perhaps—"

Luc's head was in his hands. "I see a lesson in navigation, and plotting a straight course will be the first order of business."

Elizabeth's eyes drifted toward Ata again, and all of a sudden she realized why the dowager appeared ill at ease. Of course.

Mr. Brown.

He was in Scotland. And the dowager had given up all hope of his returning to her.

A boy's shout interrupted Elizabeth's thoughts, and she half turned to see Michael's son James from the orphanage hopping up and down on one foot, the two girls laughing behind him.

Sarah jumped up before Michael could disengage

his arms from around Grace. "No, stay where you are."

Michael chuckled. "All right, Sarah. You are the master paper boat maker after all, and I do believe James would be far happier to have your help than mine."

Sarah was already on her way to the children in the distance when Grace looked at Michael with such devotion in her eyes. "I shall ask Sarah to teach me before we return to Yorkshire, my love. James and Lara will surely sink a thousand ships in our pond, and then where will we be?"

So, it was as Elizabeth had suspected. They had all been waiting for her to find happiness before they departed.

They all loved her as she loved them. And she knew in that moment, that no matter how many miles separated them from one another, there would always be fellowship to tie them together. As she reached for Rowland's hand, she watched Sarah, the woman she loved more so than any of these perfect friends, drift far away into the late afternoon rays of sun.

Sarah ran lightly toward the band of laughing children in the distance. She was going to have to make another boat for the boy. She could already see that one of the three boats was half sunk.

She was actually grateful for the distraction. She did not want to go to Cornwall. She did not want to go to her empty, unknown property in the northern Lake District either. And yet, she did not want to stay in London. She was being ridiculous and she knew it.

She had done what she had set out to do. She had seen to Elizabeth's future when her own life had disintegrated two years ago. And now that was done, she had not a new goal. That was the problem. She had but to set her mind to something new.

She looked down into the smiling face of young James and saw all the promise of youth.

"Did I do it properly, Mrs. Winters? The ends won't come together the way you did it." He offered a fairly well-constructed boat.

She inspected it, moving to the shade of a nearby willow tree to kneel in the grass. He followed her, watching intently as she rearranged the ends.

"I see now. Thank you, ma'am." He ran off to join the two young girls at the water's edge, and she stared at the jovial trio.

She wished she'd had a child with Pierce. It had been impossible, of course. A string of battlefields was not the place to raise a child. And now there was no chance. She was too old, at thirty-four—and without any desire for someone to replace her husband in her heart.

She was so weary of pretense in front of her friends. And yet she was afraid to be alone, for then she would have no reason to wear the façade of someone who was content.

She plucked a tiny daisy from the grass, and tugged at the petals, watching them flutter in the wind to be lost to the dark water beyond. Like all her dreams.

She refocused her eyes beyond the water's opposite bank.

In the distance, something glinted. It was like a burst of sunlight reflected from a looking glass. Her eyes searched past the statuary and the ancient stone urns on pedestals. And suddenly . . .

She realized she had fallen asleep beneath the willow tree and was dreaming. For *he* was there, just as he always was in her dreams.

Pierce . . .

He was leaning against a pedestal below a verdigris angel, who pointed toward the heavens. And he was staring at her with all the love and longing she felt in her heart.

She was afraid to move. Afraid that if she did, she would wake up as she always did. But then he shifted away from the statue, and something was very wrong with the image.

His arm.

His right sleeve was pinned to his shoulder, and in his left hand there was a silver-handled cane that glinted again in the sunlight.

Her breath caught. In that moment, she knew. She was *not* dreaming.

Dear God . . . it was impossible. She was going mad—imagining him. Surely, it was someone who simply looked like Pierce. Oh, but she had to go to see . . . and she could not move quickly enough.

She could not make her body work properly at all. She tried to stand, but her legs tangled in her gown and she half fell. She couldn't see because of the tears. And she couldn't speak for it felt like someone had squeezed all the air from her chest.

She had to get to him before he disappeared. She frantically brushed at her eyes and regained her footing.

And finally she was running, and this apparition

had his one arm held wide for her, his cane now lying in the grass.

She was in his embrace. She could finally breathe. His scent reached the chambers of her mind, and she knew it was he. And suddenly, for the first time in two years, she felt whole. She hadn't even realized a part of her had been absent—until this moment.

"Sarah . . ." His beloved, deep voice caressed her. "My dove."

She nuzzled deeper against his shirt linen, her arms gripping his back. "Oh God. It *is* you. Tell me . . . oh, talk to me." Her voice sounded strangled to her own ears.

He gripped her more firmly to him. "I'm here."

She tried to speak properly, without any success. "You were . . . where were you—oh, you've been hurt."

She shivered as his hand rubbed the base of her neck. He kissed the top of her head. "Sarah," he whispered hoarsely, "it doesn't matter. There's just one thing. Have I lost you—lost your heart? You must tell me straightaway. You must tell me the truth of it."

"Lost my heart? I don't understand," she said, trying to decipher the pained, exhausted look in his eyes. "What are you saying? Oh, Pierce, don't be ri—" And then she burst into tears, unable to form another word. But she gripped him to her all the harder.

"Just nod," he begged, his voice almost gone, "if I'm not too late. If you still love—"

"Of course I love you—will always . . ." She stopped. She lifted her head and roughly brushed the tears from her eyes. "Why, I've the most constant, stubborn heart of anyone—"

His lips stopped the flow of words coming from her. He was kissing her the way he had always loved her—the way a man was supposed to kiss a woman. Oh, who was she to explain it? She'd only and ever had his lips on her own. Had only and ever wanted to be in *his* warm embrace.

He kissed her until her throat ached with emotion, and then he leaned his brow against hers. "I wouldn't have blamed you, you know. I know you thought me dead. And I very nearly was. But . . . I spied Lord Wymith with you—even after I arranged the letters to be delivered. "

She pulled away to stare at his exhausted expression. His face was thinner now, but more dear to her than ever before. "Letters? I don't understand. Why didn't you just come to me directly?"

"I paid handsomely to have notes secreted to you when I finally found you." There was such hope mixed with sadness in his voice.

She shook her head. "Pierce . . . there were *no* letters. What are you talking about?"

"I could not risk approaching Helston House. Too many of Pymm's men were on guard there. And I couldn't hazard telling you where I was, or why I could not come to you, lest one of the notes was intercepted. But I wanted you to know I was alive."

"I still don't understand. Why—"

"Because of Pymm, my darling." His darkly shadowed eyes searched hers, and he finally continued. "He murdered Elizabeth's father. I came upon him in the act—hidden behind the old castle in Badajoz—and then he tried to kill me when he turned and saw that I'd witnessed the act. He very nearly succeeded. But he made one mistake."

Sarah could barely speak. "Mistake?"

"He tossed me into the River Guadiana, thinking I was dead. I floated to the shore. I remember almost nothing of it. A Spanish goatherd and his wife were responsible for saving my life—if not my arm. And my leg . . . well, it is unfortunate that it was not well set."

She swallowed back bile. "Oh, Pierce . . . I shouldn't have left without looking for you. But I couldn't allow Elizabeth to leave all alone."

"No. You were right to go away. Pymm told me he would kill anyone who stood in his way. Said he would kill *you* . . . I just could not risk showing my face in town until I could form a plan that would not put you in harm's way."

She reached to touch his cheek, to reassure herself that he was truly standing there before her and would not suddenly disappear.

"I'm sorry it took me so long, my darling. I can't tell you how much I worried—was desperate to find you and Elizabeth. I'm so grateful you found protection and comfort with the dowager duchess and her friends. I learned you went to Cornwall and Yorkshire during the last year—before London?"

She nodded.

"Two weeks ago I was on the point of desperation. I secretly followed you to Windsor and prayed I would catch you alone. But you were always with your friends or with that man—Wymith." His face darkened. "I left another letter for you in the Helston carriage. Did you not re—"

"Pierce, I never received any . . . Oh my God," she stopped.

"What is it?"

"The note . . . notes. Elizabeth received many letters. We all assumed they were from Pymm. They had but a single initial—P. The handwriting—"

"Is nearly illegible using this hand, I'm sorry to say," he interrupted with a sigh. "But Sarah, what of Wymith? Are you engaged, as the columns hinted?"

She smiled slowly and shook her head. "No. Not at all. I refused him."

He closed his eyes and exhaled like a man who has won a reprieve from the gallows. He reopened his eyes.

"That is what happens when someone loves another so intractably, you see," she murmured, stroking his face. "But why did you not come to me after the events at Carlton House? Surely—"

"I was in Cambridge."

"*Cambridge*? Why on earth would you go there?"

"I was desperate—short on funds and hope. I'd gone to search out General Worth, who retired there. You remember, I served under him at the start of the war? His going to Portman Square would not have aroused suspicion. I asked him to warn you, put a stop to Elizabeth's marriage, and to form a plan to bring Pymm to justice. But as we were returning to London, we saw a newspaper relating the events at Carlton House, and so I rushed back—rode straight through last night to see you."

She suddenly felt dizzy.

"Where is Pymm now? The newspaper was many days old."

"I don't know," Sarah whispered. "I assume at the Pulteney still. I know he's been called to address the House of Lords. I don't know which day. The Prince Regent is put out with him, and several people—my new friends, the Duke of Helston and others—are calling for further investigation and punishment."

"Sarah, after I see you to a safe place and speak to your friends, I must go to the war office without delay. I will not rest until Pymm is held accountable for what he has done. I would have killed him myself if my sharpshooting skills were not so impaired now. I was on the point of it at Windsor, when I was so close to him in the flesh . . ."

Her beloved husband's gaze drifted over her shoulder and Sarah half twisted in his arms to see what had caught his attention. Elizabeth stood, wide-eyed in shock, not thirty feet away. A moment later, she crumpled to the ground.

A shout echoed, and Sarah spied her friends of the last grief-filled years coming toward them—some running, some walking. Even Georgiana, still weak from childbirth, was aided by her husband.

Rowland Manning was the first to reach Elizabeth, his usual nonchalant countenance wiped clean. Fear shone from him as he hurtled himself down alongside her.

Her eyes were already opening, and she struggled to speak.

"Stay still," Rowland insisted. "You hit your head."

"No," Elizabeth mumbled. "Where is he?"

"Who?"

"Colonel Winters," she said, disoriented. They followed her gaze, disbelief registering in every face.

Pierce knelt beside her and took up her hand. "Elizabeth . . ."

"You're not . . . what . . . My father? Is he here too?" Elizabeth's questions drifted to a stop.

Everyone understood the bleak expression on the face of the man who had been Elizabeth's father's closest friend. Sarah's heart broke as comprehension dawned on Elizabeth's face.

"I'm so sorry, my dear. I could not save him from Pymm's blade. I was too late . . ."

Chapter 20

Dawn had always been Elizabeth Ashburton's favorite time of day. It was the hour that held the most promise. By noon, half of the things she had meant to accomplish were usually still undone—*especially* now that she was married. Her eyes still shut, slumber wandered slowly out of her grasp, and she wondered why she did not want to open her eyes. And then with a blink, she remembered.

Her father was dead.

Not that she had ever doubted it. It was just that she had left Portugal with Sarah in such haste that she had not seen his body—had not given him the burial required for true peace of mind. Until now, she had not realized that she had held onto the slimmest thread of hope.

For a full half minute yesterday, that fondest wish had bloomed. And then been snipped from the vine. She refused to think about it. She could at least be forever grateful Colonel Winters had been spared.

And Sarah's heart returned. Her friend's eyes had not left her husband's for a moment all afternoon.

Elizabeth inhaled to harness her emotions. She had so much she was determined to do today. Nothing would stop her from seeing to the little details she had secretly planned. She refused to understand it was a reaction to yesterday's events. She would not grieve for her father today. She'd grieved for two years and she would make this day for Rowland alone.

Exhaling quietly, she eased to the edge of their immense, white-netted bed with the care of a feline. It was more difficult than she thought. Rowland seemed to sleep with one eye open at all times. Twice his breath caught, and he stiffened, and twice she became motionless, waiting for him to resume the slow, even breathing that was his signature in deep sleep.

Then, just as her toe touched the floor, she felt his hand grip her wrist. He pulled her on top of him.

"And just where do you think you're going?" he said, his voice gravelly.

She sighed. "Why am I forever being asked that?"

"Because you are never where you should be," he growled.

"Really? And where is that?"

"Come a little closer, my lamb, and I shall tell you precisely. And how I plan to keep you here."

"Well, perhaps I have plans of my own."

"Is that so?" He drawled his seductive words.

"Yes." She would not tell him. "But they are not your affair."

"Everything about you is my affair." There was something more than amusement in his voice. Something she could not pinpoint.

His hand was stroking the sensitive spot at the base of her back. The one that made her shiver.

"Come here," he said softly, sliding his fingers beyond her spine.

She smiled. It had been the way of it all night. He could not seem to get enough of her. And as she found it impossible to resist the unspoken promises in his caress, she did exactly as he asked. Once again her well-laid plans were going to wrack and ruin. And yet, when he held her like this, with his granitelike torso pinning her to the bed and his heavy sex pulsing against her hip, she didn't care. And when he whispered the sorts of things he would do to her, all her ordered ideas became nothing more than scattered good intentions—even if it was his birthday . . . and even if she had a celebration to arrange.

His hot breath fanned over her breast as he delivered the first of his many wicked promises. Like a match to tinder, their passion for each other ignited. She splayed her fingers over the hard planes of his immense shoulders and his body shifted over hers. As she reached down past the hard, rippled surface of his abdomen to caress his thick shaft, he groaned, and softly cursed his great need for her.

Each time they came together, she felt as though they were binding themselves ever closer, and yet, to Elizabeth, it also seemed as though Rowland always withheld a sliver of his soul.

His lovemaking now took on a desperate tenor in the darkness, and she wished she could see his face more clearly. He was relentless, drawing out her pleasure, again and again, with his fingers and his mouth, until she was faint with exhaustion. Then and only then did he guide the large blunt end of his erection against her intimate flesh.

"*Mhuirnin* . . . My *mhuirnin*." His low, husky voice repeated the words until they floated in the silken predawn air, lushly caressing her senses as he finally, finally thrust deeply, and allowed himself to find the pleasure that was his alone to take. Her body stretched tautly to accommodate him while he took extraordinary care to arouse her ever higher, ignoring her caresses. He was single-mindedly instigating every act in this interlude.

As he slowly buried himself deeper and deeper inside of her, Elizabeth began to notice his almost grim determination to bring her to a new level of happiness. Suddenly, intense pleasure blossomed within her loins, spreading like wildfire through her body.

His brow furrowed, his eyes closed, he drove into her one last time, filling her completely as he pulsed deep inside of her.

As he relaxed his grip and arranged her in the cradle of his arms, the luxurious pull of sleep followed soon after and she was unable to resist. It was only in her dreams that she was able to fully see the restlessness behind his fierce lovemaking.

He had always hated dawn. In the past, it had meant just another day of misery and unrelenting labor, of watching his mother and sister suffer in silence. His scoundrel of a half brother Howard and he had been far more capable of survival; both of them were cunning, and possessed a knack for skirting justice to bring a few meager bits to their dirty hovel in the rookery. For women, it was a different matter altogether. It was a terrible way of life. The torture had been watching the two females in his family suffer without being able to do a bloody thing about it.

But this morning, this dawn, was different. He was

capable of doing something, of correcting a wrong.

As he walked toward the stable, his soul felt light in his body—as light as his bones felt heavy, strangely enough. He thanked God Elizabeth had finally fallen back into slumber. Disentangling himself from her embrace had been one of the hardest things he had ever done.

He grasped the reins of the dark bay gelding from Lefroy. He had always avoided mortal danger until now. But he was an impatient man, with still no trust of others—especially lords or magistrates, all of whom usually had ulterior motives that could sway the winds of justice. And if there was anyone who could worm his way out of a noose, it was Pymm.

The others had agreed to meet him. He knew without doubt that they would play out all their myriad parts in this folly.

"I'll return in two hours or less. I won't miss a moment of her secret, bloody celebration. And by the by, if you nick a single grain on that new desk you've been hiding for her, I'll—"

"I knows," Lefroy said doggedly, "you'll dock me wages."

"Yes. And this time it actually might mean something, since I'll be a rich man soon enough."

He placed his boot in the stirrup and in one practiced motion swung onto his mount. The clatter of the horse's hooves as he wheeled the gelding about broke the silence in the stable. "Watch over her in the main building. Don't leave her alone for a second. And keep that gob of yours shut."

Lefroy opened his mouth and then thought the better of it.

"Very good. I knew there was a reason I employed you. Now go on." He nodded toward the main building and put his heels to the horse's sides.

Lefroy cleared his throat. "Master?"

"What is it?" He looked over his shoulder.

"I's proud o' you," Lefroy said so gruffly Rowland almost missed it. "We's all are. Thought you should know."

"Don't go down that path, old man. If you start blubbering," he said dryly, "I'll be forced to—"

"I knows." Lefroy made a pathetic attempt at a smile. "Good luck to you then."

It was a good thing he left at that moment, for a half minute later he might have had to bear witness to Mr. Lefroy's countenance, which crumpled altogether.

When Elizabeth woke again, she wasn't entirely certain of the hour. It was still more dark than light, but Rowland was already gone to the Prince Regent's mews as he had told her he would do that morning. Well, even if she was late getting started, her husband had dispelled much of her gloom about her father's cause of death. Even if Rowland could never say the words she longed to hear, he took such care to comfort her. And that was all that mattered.

She dressed quickly and ran down the stairs, hoping Mr. Lefroy had not forgotten her instructions.

For some odd reason the stable master was standing quietly at the base of the stair. Waiting for her. Without a word he followed her to Rowland's study.

"Oh, Mr. Lefroy," she said a little out of breath, barely glancing at the older man. "Is it not perfect here? Thank you so much." She ran her hands over the new burled walnut desk, which now rested in the same spot as Rowland's former desk.

He shook his head with a grimace. "Weighs fifty stone, it does. Took four o' me men to get it in here. And two o' them are now missing toes."

"I hope he likes it," she said.

"I would be willing to wager 'e will. Don't think 'e ever got a present." Mr. Lefroy's voice was devoid of emotion. "Then again, none o' us knew his birthday."

"Well, it was stated on the Special License. Oh, we must hurry before he returns. I'm determined to surprise him. But first, the two errands to—"

"I remembers, my lady."

"I think I preferred it when you used to call me lovey, Mr. Lefroy." She had thought her words would bring a smile to his face, but they did not. A fine case of the dismals appeared to be simmering below the surface of Mr. Lefroy's blank expression. But she had no time to tease him out of a sulk.

Threads of purple and mauve streaked the pink clouds of the eastern cityscape as they crossed the yards toward the stables. Elizabeth's thoughts darted among the things she had to do, while Mr. Lefroy checked the horses' traces and the carriage. They would go to the fishmonger to have first pick of the catch. She didn't mind the overly strong, briny scent of the docks. She would make Rowland's unacknowledged favorite—cod in red-pepper sauce. And flowers must be purchased and arranged, a dessert prepared, and they were still vastly understaffed. It would take her a few weeks to hire a full complement of servants.

All of her friends were to come that evening. It truly would be their last gathering with everyone present. She wondered if the Duke of Helston and Colonel Winters's dealings at the military headquarters regarding her father's murder would prevent them from . . . she glanced at Mr. Lefroy's impenetrable, grim profile as he helped her into the carriage.

"Wait," she said suddenly, refusing to let go of Mr. Lefroy's gloved hand.

He looked toward her, his face grave. She had only ever seen Mr. Lefroy smiling.

"Mr. Lefroy, by all that is holy, where is he? He usually goes to the royal mews in the afternoons—never at dawn. He is always here then. Where has he gone, truly?"

" 'e didn't say, ma'am."

"Oh no, you don't, old man. You will tell me this instant or I will feed you nothing but broth and stale bread for the rest of your existence." A terrible premonition churned her thoughts to clotted disaster.

But there was no need for Mr. Lefroy to answer, for the sound of a horse's hooves preceded the arrival of the one person who would not hesitate to tell her everything she would most not want to hear.

Colonel Pierce Winters grimaced as he carefully swung about his injured leg to dismount; his one hand pressed the pommel and gripped both reins. With all of the military precision for which he had been known, Colonel Winters stripped Lefroy of all information he did not already possess, and had the three of them hurtling helter-skelter in the carriage toward a destination that brought cascades of fear to her feverish mind.

Dear God, he could not. He would not.

But, in her heart, she knew very well that he could, and he would.

The ride through Regent's Park braced him. The dark bay's ears pricked up as a white-tailed rabbit darted across the path. He steadied his young horse with a gentle word and practiced hands.

Across the outer circle, and over Macclesfield Bridge, the sacred dueling ground of Primrose Hill loomed. It was the one part of London Rowland knew little about. It was reserved for idiot men of rank who had nothing better to do in the morning than shoot each other's bloody nobs off for perceived slights to their so-called honor.

Yes, well, he was very nearly one of those bloody idiots now, wasn't he? And here he was, playing the role to the letter already.

Several men lurked under an enormous hemlock tree ahead. On the approach, he recognized Ellesmere, Helston, and two other men, strangers both. Perhaps the surgeon and the starter?

Rowland dismounted and secured his horse with the other mounts.

"Where is he?"

"Impatient, are we?" Helston drawled his words. Only his dark eyes betrayed the duke's seriousness. "The guest of honor is due shortly."

"Care for a cheroot?" the marquis offered, as he puffed on his own.

"No," Rowland replied stiffly.

"Smart man. Filthy habit," Helston said, tendering a small silver flask.

"Absolutely, not."

Ellesmere chuckled.

"Hmmm, no whip?" The duke studied Rowland, his expression giving away nothing. "You're not going to bungle this, are you, Manning? My wife and I are to set sail no matter what happens."

"Of course you will, Helston," Ellesmere said in an exaggerated manner. "That's what we like most about you—all swagger and no follow-through."

Rowland sighed. "Look, since you're here as my seconds—and *thirds*, could you at least feign a little faith. Have a little more—"

The sound of four horses galloping over the bridge interrupted. Streaks of dawn finally broke through the cloud cover, and it was easy enough to discern their faces. His half brother Michael and Joshua Gordon flanked Leland Pymm and another man. Rowland nearly smiled when he finally recognized the choice of the general's second: the portly, fawning Lieutenant Tremont. Only now, the man's florid complexion was replaced with frozen-white fear.

Rowland felt like he was in some sort of ridiculous, cliché-riddled play on Drury Lane as he crossed the distance to Michael. He could only hope it was a comedy, all the while knowing a tragedy was much more in keeping with the tenor of his life.

"You're lucky we're here." His brother muttered an oath. "Damned near shot him myself for taking so long at his *toilette*." Michael's voice might have been relaxed, but his expression was not. "Are you still intent on this wretched idea of—"

"Michael, do join the other ladies in the hemlock gallery, won't you?" His request held all the cool insistence of a block of ice.

His brother grasped his shoulder and pulled him a few feet away. "Look, you don't have to do this. In fact, you should not do it. He's a dead man anyway."

It took all his willpower to allow his brother to speak. He did it as a favor, to ease the other's conscience.

"Prinny will have him executed, or at the very least transported for life. Colonel Winters will see to it—is seeing to the formal report this morning. In fact, the colonel will be furious that you've denied him his own chance for retribution. He has even more of a right to justice than—"

"Michael?" Rowland interrupted. "Get the hell out of my way."

"This will only hurt you. Your position, your title, has not even been . . ." Michael's voice slowed, and resigned, he finally released Rowland's shoulder.

Helston and Ellesmere now rejoined them, a pistol in the marquis's hands and a glum look on the duke's face. "Pymm chose pistols."

"Of course he chose pistols," muttered Michael, his ill ease returned.

"A fine lot all of you are," Rowland muttered. "I shall remember to call on Tremont next time. He may be useless, but at least he's silent."

"There won't be a next time, unless you tell us you've had a bit of target practice since the last time we witnessed your, ahem, *talents* with a pistol." Helston studied him under heavy-lidded eyes, no doubt recalling when Rowland had merely grazed Michael's arm while standing less than six feet away from him last spring.

The enemy approached.

"Change of heart?" General Pymm asked loftily, confidently. "We would all of us understand, Manning. These gentlemen and I never expected one such as you to go through with this. Why, it galls me to no end to think you have the audacity to ask me to meet on a *field of honor.*"

Rowland swept a glance at the entourage. "Perhaps you're right, General," he said softly.

Pymm visibly relaxed.

The man was such a coward. When Rowland had sent his brother to the Pulteney Hotel last eve to tender a challenge, he had not allowed Michael to tell the general about Colonel Pierce Winters's reappearance yesterday. Rowland had not wanted to chance Pymm slipping through the cracks of the huge hotel upon receiving such devastating news. But the time for such tidings drew near.

Rowland cleared his throat. "Actually, I think you misunderstand. I was having a change of heart about doing this honorably. Why waste powder and shot when I'd enjoy it all the more using my hands instead?"

Pymm stiffened. "Bluster all you like, mudlark. It is you who shall be warming your heels in hell today. That is where all mongrels such as you end up, is it not?"

If there was one thing for which he could be grateful to his past, it was his immunity to insult. "The day waxes, General. Shall we?" His fingers itched to shoot the man where he stood—honor be damned.

The starter motioned toward the slight rise a few steps away. "Gentlemen? It shall be ten paces upon my signal. You will then both turn to face each other. After I am assured you are each of you ready, you shall have until the count of three to fire."

"Did you understand that part, Manning?" Pymm sneered. "You are not to fire until *after* the signal."

"What was that, General?" Rowland raised the pistol and peered along its sight line in an awkward fashion, as if testing it. He directed it at the general's heart. "Sorry, I don't hear that well—must be the muck in my ears."

Pymm stumbled sideways, furious.

A moment later they were back to back. The general's body radiated heat against his own. Icy calm replaced every trace of foreboding in Rowland's body. "Oh, I almost forgot something of importance, Pymm," Rowland tossed softly over his shoulder.

The starter's brow wrinkled. This was apparently a first.

"What is it, you bastard?" Pymm sneered. "Postponing the inevitable yet again?"

"No. Just thought to inform that Colonel Winters has returned in time to give the eulogy. I wouldn't want you to think that a murdering, blackmailing lunatic such as yourself would not have a proper funeral and all—unlike the one for Elizabeth's father." He nodded to the starter. "Right then. Go ahead."

The man began the count. "One . . ."

"What? More trickery? You are a liar and a—" Pymm sputtered.

"Two."

Rowland continued pacing.

"Do you want a delay, General?" the starter's voice rang out.

Rowland stopped, yet refused to give in to the urge to look over his shoulder. Instead, he cocked his pistol.

Pymm's odd voice was low, yet traveled to his ears. "You're the fool, Manning. You don't understand today's game. The only reason I came is to make sure you never touch her again."

Rowland assumed the general nodded to the starter, for a moment later the latter resumed the count. "Three . . . Four . . . Five."

Rowland's breathing slowed as he paced.

"Six . . . seven—"

Rowland neared the stand of trees in front of him only to doubt his eyes. God, please let it be a mirage. Just an illusion of gargantuan disaster.

She was running *straight toward him* with two others behind her. "Stop!" Elizabeth's voice sliced through the cool morning air.

It was a goddamned sodding nightmare come to life. In that hair of an instant, he foresaw every last bleeding detail of the tragedy in the making.

Pymm would wheel about prematurely at the sound of her voice. He would see Elizabeth, and also Pierce Winters, the lone witness to Pymm's chilling crime. There would be no telling what the bloody general would do. The sole matter of importance was that his wife, his beloved, was in Pymm's line of fire.

And so, Rowland did the only thing he could do. He ran toward her, blocking her with his arms spread wide, his back still to Pymm.

Her horror-struck eyes told him his vision had been utterly correct. Her hand reached to cover her mouth in abject panic.

The sound came before the pain. A blast, and the almost sickening sound of flesh being pierced. He saw a cry leave her lips and his animal nature took hold fully to protect her. Turning, and with the precision borne of a desperate man, he took aim and fired.

Smoke filled the early morning gloom of the clearing. His head spinning, he saw Pymm falter and stagger back.

The reports of several other shots echoed, and Rowland was falling, falling. It felt as though he was slipping through clouds.

Fear set in. It did not hurt enough for it not to be mortal. His head fell back and her face was above him. A halo of smoke enveloped them both.

"Is he . . ." he rasped.

Her face was stark white. "Oh my God . . . don't close your eyes. Don't you dare *leave* me." She was struggling with his shirt linen, as several shouts rang out.

Hands were everywhere, grasping, ripping.

"He's saying something," she cried, leaning forward.

"Hold . . . my hand," he whispered.

Her fingers were so warm in his cold palm. His view spun wildly, careening toward darkness. Despair grabbed at him, trying to pin him down. He had to know. Had to know if he'd finally succeeded where in the past he'd failed. And had to tell her . . . tell her . . .

Chapter 21

Tumbling through clouds was a novel experience. He reached out to touch the illusion of spun sugar. Sparks of light darted past, and he longed to follow them. He glanced down past his feet, and noticed he was traveling fast. *Far too fast.* And then he remembered . . .

He was shot. But there was no pain.

He was dying . . .

He tried to care, but he did not. There was just such joy, such peace in the air, cradling his bruised and battered body.

But something nagged at him, irritating his tranquility.

Fighting the fog of serenity with such doggedness, images of a woman flickered in his mind.

Oh Lord, nooooo . . .

He fought the ever-growing lightness of being like a wildcat caught in an avalanche. *No.* He could not leave her. Would not leave her. He loved her. Loved her with an intensity too strong to extinguish.

He fought happiness. He didn't want peace. He . . . he wanted . . . *her.* He didn't want anything else. He wanted all the pain, all the sloppy, mucked-up misery and joy life had to offer.

And like the arc of an object thrown skyward, his ascent slowed; he hung motionless among the stars for what seemed an eternity.

Then, with the speed of a lightning strike, he hurtled backward. He was in the clouds again—now past them.

It was going to hurt when he crashed. He didn't care. Pain was good. He would endure it all to hold her in his arms again. He was not finished with life. He had left something terribly important undone.

At the last possible moment, as he glimpsed the verdant canopy of the treetops, his form slowed, like a feather wending its way earthward. A crowd was gathered over his corporeal body. Elizabeth was rocking and he looked too still, too pale.

In that instant, pain slammed into him. A cacophony of sound returned.

He forced back his lids only to find beauty before him, the pale glint of tears streaming down her dusty face.

"Elizabeth . . ." No sound came out of his throat.

"Rowland?" Her voice was but a whisper. "Rowland!? Oh my God! Oh please . . . don't move. Don't try to speak . . . Doctor?" There was such pleading in her voice, and he wanted to reassure her. But he could not make his mouth move properly, so he closed his eyes, trying to reclaim his strength.

"Stay still," a stranger's voice said, pressing against the blazing pain on his side. "You cannot afford to lose any more blood. The ball is out. I'll stitch it as soon as the bleeding slows."

Damnation. He had so much to ask—to say. He squeezed her fingers, only to feel a lock of her sweet-smelling hair fall onto his cheek.

"What is it, my love?" she whispered.

"Is he . . ." he rasped. "Are you . . ."

"Shhh . . . you mustn't struggle," she pleaded.

"I think he'd rest easier if you explained, lovey."

Ah . . . Lefroy was here. His eyes would not leave the sight of her face to confirm it.

"You killed him, Rowland," she whispered. "You took all of the blast, not me."

"Other shots . . ." He grunted with pain, but he had such certainty that he would pull through that he didn't care how much it hurt.

"His death will not be on your head," the colonel's voice informed gruffly. "I shan't have it. Yours will not be the only shot reported fired."

The murderous swine was dead. The heaviness on his chest lifted. Other voices hovered overhead.

"Your aim is improved, Manning," Helston said, respect tingeing his usual bland tone.

"Don't know what yer inferin', Yer Grace. Master's aim is always perfect-like," Lefroy muttered. His loyal stable master glanced at Michael's raised eyebrows. "If 'e had wanted to kill you last spring, 'e woulda put a ball through yer brains like that cove wot's in the bushes there."

God. He wished they'd all just go away—let him be alone with her. He closed his eyes again. He wanted to hear her voice. It was such a lovely, lilting slip of a thing. A voice meant for lullabies.

He wanted to assure her he would recover—that he and she would live long, fruitful lives filled with all the terrible, wonderful events that life had to offer. He knew it without a doubt for he had seen the angels laughing at him on his descent—as if they could see the many chapters of his life unfolding while he fell back to earth.

She wished he would open his eyes again. Each time he did, even in fever's grip, it had given her hope he would survive. He'd been so restless these last three days that it had been torture to nurse him. He refused to lie still and allow his body the chance to recover. But he'd finally quieted the last few hours and his brow was dry.

She'd taken to talking to him almost without pause. He seemed to be more at ease when he heard her voice. After telling him every last thing about her childhood that she could remember, she'd resorted to retelling the stories of when they had met earlier that summer.

"Darling," she whispered, "do you remember when I made dinner the first time? I tried so hard to please you. Meat pie, potatoes, carrots . . . and gingerbread. You appeared to loathe all of it. But I knew you liked it. You see, you have a particular way of wrinkling the space between your eyebrows when you like something—as if you're angry. I think I'm the only one who has figured out that it's really just a sign of deliberation. It's as if you don't want anyone to know how you truly feel about something. And—"

He came awake the same way he approached life— without hesitation. His eyes opened, pale and clear.

"Oh . . . you've come back," she said very softly.

He glanced at the glass of water nearby and she immediately retrieved it. Gently, she held his head and introduced the glass to his lips.

She said not a word as he swallowed long and deep. He pulled back and relaxed against the pillows as she replaced the glass on the table.

Elizabeth drank in the sight of him. "I thought you were"—she swallowed—"were gone to me—would never come back . . ."

His eyes followed her.

She traced a pattern in the white-on-white embroidery of the bed covers. "Rowland, you have to be far more careful in future. I cannot lose you. I've lost too much."

He raised a finger to her lips to stop her.

"No," she said, "I must have my say. I know why you did it—to save me and to avenge my father's death. But . . . it was not worth it. I would gladly live with that monster in this world, but I could not live without—"

"Elizabeth," he interrupted, his voice very rough around the edges.

"Yes?" She brushed a lock of his hair from his forehead. "You're still weak. Will you take some broth?"

He shook his head once, his eyes never straying from hers.

"What is it?" She gently straightened his pillow.

"Just sit . . . there."

She sensed he wanted something, and she would give it to him. "Maybe a wet cloth?"

"Shhh . . ." he murmured.

She gave up. And so she drowned in his eyes. She

had not seen his clear-eyed gaze in too long of a time.

Suddenly, the space between his brows crinkled.

Her heart expanded beneath her breast.

"I'm sorry to be so late," he rumbled.

"Late?"

"In telling you." He closed his eyes.

"Oh, you're exhausted. I shan't leave. I'll be here when you wake again and then I'll—"

"For so long," he whispered, opening his eyes, "I was entombed in a world black, devoid of naught but a millstone of time . . . grinding ever closer to eternal dust." He paused. "Until you."

Her throat tightened.

He struggled to continue. "I did not save you, Elizabeth. It is the reverse. You came along with your abundance of spirit and you made me aware of the cage of darkness I'd constructed in place of a heart."

She grasped his hand again and squeezed it gently, acknowledging with touch what she could not with words.

"And so it's decided," he said. "Henceforth, I choose to be happy, damn it. I will not go on as before."

"Rowland . . ." she whispered.

"I love you," he said simply.

She stared at him, aghast. "I never thought you'd . . ."

"What?"

"Tell me," she whispered.

"I know." He pulled her arms toward him until she was inches from his face. "Was it worth the wait, Mrs. Manning?"

"Yes." She brushed her lips on his. "Kind of like a soufflé."

"What? All air and no substance?"

"Not at all." She laughed. "And how do you know anything about soufflés?"

He cupped her face. "You've been reciting bloody recipes for the last two hours. I vastly preferred the stories from your childhood."

"I love you too, Mr. Manning," she murmured.

He pulled her into his arms despite the pain. "And thank God for that."

Epilogue

Three weeks later . . .

*Dear Mr. Manning (or is it Lord
Balreal—finally?)*

*I do hope you understand the singular honor
I am bestowing by sending this letter to you
before I write to my own grandson. You are
not to be your usual jaded self—thinking I only
write to you because Helston is likely halfway
to the East Indies.*

*When I bade all of you adieu two weeks ago,
I knew I was not for Cornwall. And by the
gleam in your eye, I had the distinct impression
that you alone knew it too. I suppose I owe you
a measure of gratitude now (since I would not
give it then) for your insistence that Mr. Lefroy,
personally, take the ribbons for my journey.*

*And so you have it. My gratitude, that is—
along with the return of your excellent stable
master.*

*But I daresay I owe you much more than
that, sir.*

*I must thank you for explaining to me as no one else has done—the true method for attaining one's dreams. I shall never forget your words—*I don't stop until I get what I want. *Yes, I engraved that in my memory all the way to Scotland.*

It might have taken me over fifty years to learn this lesson, but it is done and I now realize that is how fate wanted it—for if I hadn't married the Duke of Helston, I would not have my grandson now, and I would never have met the widows, the finest circle of friends a lady could ever wish for.

Rosamunde taught me that it is possible to find happiness after a dreadful first marriage; Georgiana taught me about the joys of kissing a man you've loved all your life; Grace taught me about giving away everything for love; Elizabeth taught me courage; and finally Sarah taught me that one should never give up hope.

And so in closing, Mr. Manning, I advise you (since my grandson is not presently available for any sort of satisfying lecture) that you would do well to find a group of widowers to learn a few life lessons yourself. You might learn a modicum of patience or at the very least restraint in your particularly colorful use of the English language. You are to stop laughing now. I admit that Elizabeth probably likes you well enough just the way you are.

If I have not lost your interest yet, which I suspect I have, I would request that you inform my friends that Mr. Brown and I have married—over the anvil—as we planned all those many years ago. And nothing sounds so very fine to these old ears as my new name.

We plan to travel to Cornwall for the winter, but shall spend a week with Sarah and Pierce at their lovely estate in the northern Lake District along the way.

I've reserved the most important part for last. When we come to town next spring, I expect you to present me with a wedding gift of your very finest pair of ponies—and a phaeton. It is only fair as I gifted you Vespers . . . and Elizabeth.

Yours, with affectionate gratitude,

Mrs. Brown

Rowland tapped the edge of Ata's letter against the escritoire in his chamber above stairs. He bit back a smile as he tried to stretch a bit despite the mounds of pillows surrounding him in his padded leather chair. He did not need a herd of bloody widowers to learn about patience. This last fortnight and a half, Elizabeth had seen to it inflexibly all by herself. He had been held captive by her in his bed—stretched out like a damned codfish on a platter. Until today.

"What does it say?" His beautiful wife placed a covered tray on the edge of the escritoire and drew up a second chair.

"She has a partiality for the name Mrs. Brown."

Elizabeth's emerald-green eyes filled with amusement. "Oh, I knew it!"

"What is this?" he cut in, eyeing the tray dubiously. "Did we not just have dinner?"

"Dessert," she replied with an innocent expression.

"Really? What sort?" he murmured, with resignation rather than hope.

She uncovered the immense silver platter to reveal an endless, boundless mountain of . . . *strawberries*. "I know how to keep a promise. I told you I would bring them when you were sufficiently recovered."

"I was sufficiently recovered three days after I shot Pymm," he said dryly.

She smiled. "No. You were delirious for three days. You are not sufficiently recovered now. But—"

He growled.

"*But*"—she smiled just enough to give evidence to the dimples he loved so much—"well . . ."

"What is it, *mhuirnin*?" He longed to pull her into his lap and nuzzle her, but could not quite manage the feat. He settled for taking up her hand in his and kissing the back of it.

"I have something to tell you—something to celebrate, actually."

"Hmmm?" He was too busy kissing her delicate, lovely wrist to listen.

"Remember how we agreed that we never wanted to see the inside of Carlton House again for the rest of our lives?"

Why did women prattle on about ballrooms, when there were perfectly good strawberries to—

"Well"—her voice took on that shy quality he adored—"we might just have to be a bit more flexible about that."

He drew his brows together.

"You see, if it's a daughter, she would have to be presented to . . ." She stopped. "Rowland? *Rowland* . . . darling, are you *all right*?"

"Daughter?" he rasped. Where had all the air in the room disappeared to?

"Or a son," she whispered, dropping to her knees beside him.

God, he wished he was back in that bed. Why had he wanted to leave it?

She was a mind reader, this perfect wife of his. "Come . . . let me help you."

He waved her away, determined to do it on his own. She joined him there, a smile on her lips, and such happiness shining from her eyes.

"I think you've forgotten something, Mrs. Manning," he whispered.

"Yes?" She leaned down to finally kiss him.

He clasped her to him, oblivious to any lingering pain. He would never, ever let her out of his sight now. "The strawberries . . ."

The sound of her laughter was of the same quality of those angels he had seen.

"You have to let me go if you want them," she whispered.

"Oh, I want them all right," he growled. "Then we shall see who plays the Fool."

AVON

978-0-06-170624-0

978-0-06-177127-9

978-0-06-112404-4

978-0-06-157826-7

978-0-06-185337-1

978-0-06-154781-2

*Unforgettable, enthralling love stories,
sparkling with passion and adventure
from Romance's bestselling authors*

At Avon Books, we know your passion for romance—once you finish one of our novels, you find yourself wanting more.

May we tempt you with . . .

- **Excerpts** from our upcoming releases.

- Entertaining **extras**, including authors' personal photo albums and book lists.

- Behind-the-scenes **scoop** on your favorite characters and series.

- **Sweepstakes** for the chance to win free books, romantic getaways, and other fun prizes.

- Writing **tips** from our authors and editors.

- **Blog** with our authors and find out why they love to write romance.

- **Exclusive content** that's not contained within the pages of our novels.

Join us at
www.avonbooks.com

Available order.

FTH 0708